The Fragile Breath

The Fragile Breath

A Novel

Sharon V. Agar

SHE WRITES PRESS

Published in 2026 by
She Writes Press, an imprint of The Stable Book Group

32 Court Street, Suite 2109
Brooklyn, NY 11201
https://shewritespress.com
Library of Congress Control Number: 2026902031
ISBN: 979-8-89636-302-6
eISBN: 979-8-89636-303-3

Interior Designer: Tabitha Lahr

Printed in the United States

This book is dedicated with utmost gratitude and respect to anyone who is prepared to donate an organ.

I also salute the medical workers, who often bear the brunt of suffering patients. They can make the difference between discomfort and misery.

Whoever saves one life, it is as though they have saved the whole world.

Part I

On the Waitlist

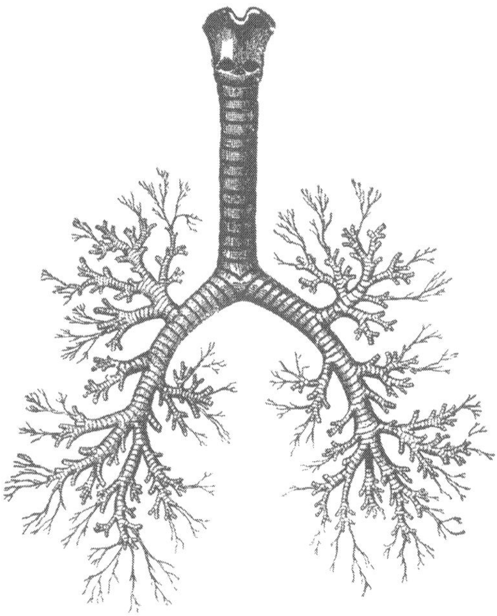

Chapter 1

December 2016, New York City

I'm standing at the window of the cozy kitchen of my apartment on West Ninety-Fifth Street feeling like the sick kid stuck at home, missing the party. Usually I'm happy here in this comfortable space: The apartment has tall ceilings, oak floors, and it's high enough to admit the wintry midmorning light. Dane and I painted over the gray walls with a pale yellow after our wedding; it was like bringing in sunshine after the storm. Today, though, everything feels dark and cramped. "It's not you," I tell the kitchen, "it's me."

Outside, the city is in full holiday mode. On the corner, Santa rings a brass bell while "Silent Night" plays on a tinny radio. Across the street, a pop-up stand is selling Christmas trees. Snatches of carols emerge from shops each time a door is opened. I miss all that *so much* (except the Frosty song). But I'm trapped here, constrained by my failing body and dependence on supplemental oxygen. The only activities for the next six months are: one, get my weight up; two, strengthen my muscles and aerobic capacity; three, don't get sick; and four, retain my sanity while hoping for a lung transplant. Good goals. So far I'm falling behind.

Trailing the long cable from my oxygen concentrator, I return to the kitchen table. It's not so bad to be eating bacon and coffee ice cream for breakfast. Not together, of course . . . though, come to think of it, why not? I crumble the bacon into the ice cream and eat before it gets soggy. The problem is that when you must choose between eating and breathing—when it's impossible to do both at once—breathing always takes precedence. I'm now thin, with great abs from all the panting. It's not as fun as it sounds.

What counts now is that my freedom only extends as far as my front door. The concentrator whooshes oxygen-rich air down a long, thin hose to the cannula in my nostrils. This gives me unrestricted mobility around the apartment, but not outside. For one thing, the concentrator is the size and weight of a large trunk; for another, it's plugged into an outlet. I am currently housebound. In my former life (aka healthy, real life) as an advisor to small businesses, we'd worry if a client routinely missed their key goals. I'm close to breaching the "keeping my sanity" goal, and the only fix for that is to get out of the damn apartment.

Then what if I did? Take the portable oxygen tank that we use when Dane takes me out in the wheelchair, and just go? It's risky—I haven't been out on my own in a month—but I can't spend what's left of my life shut in and dependent, hoping for a miracle. Because that's what the transplant game is. And the truth is that, while I won't admit it to my husband or friends, I don't believe this transplant will come through for me in time. I have to try, of course, because even tiny probabilities can happen, but I have no faith. Not with my particular condition, which can suddenly plummet at any moment, as my mother's did. So if this is my last Christmas, I don't want to miss it. Besides, going out hits the exercise goal.

The oxygen tank is by the front door. It comes with a roller base that I should be able to pull a few blocks. Hopefully. Cranking up my oxygen level, I begin the painstaking task of putting on the layers required to face a New York December. By the time I've pulled on my boots, I'm panting, but feeling the pull of adventure. I drop the tank in the roller, switch to its cannula, start the flow, and shut down the concentrator. Door keys in pocket, I head off.

The elevator groans downward until the doors open to the lobby. Jimmy, my favorite doorman, is at the door to West End Avenue. His eyes widen in surprise on seeing me. *Prison break*, I think, hoping he doesn't report me to Dane.

The cold air hits me with a blast, but once I start moving, my body adjusts. It's immediately clear that I'll need to walk slowly and carefully: New York City streets are uneven compared with oak floors. They're also unnervingly crowded to navigate without the wheelchair clearing space for me. I'm trying to stay alert and watch my footing, but the way is filled with wonderful distractions. The shops are alight with holiday decorations in every style and denomination. I shuffle past the grocery store . . . the coffee shop . . . the paper shop, drawing everything in, enjoying the brisk air on my cheeks and the sounds of cheery bustle mixed with traffic. At the drugstore I consider going in to buy candy canes, until the door opens and a synthetic "Ho, ho, ho!" roars out. A young child giggles and pushes the button again. Every part of me feels high on the thrill of being here, being *normal*. When I reach the bakery, I laugh out loud. The window is edged with fake snow and festooned with seasonal cakes and cookies. A toy train circles around them on a small track, tiny toy elves waving as it passes.

I'm stepping onward when a small dog runs in front of me, the leash stretching across my path. I try to stop, but the tank roller catches my ankle, and I go down hard. For a few seconds I gasp for air; I'm shocked and in pain, but most importantly I've lost the cannula and am breathing only cold street air. I search around frantically, then spot it. The dog's owner, a well-dressed older woman, is wresting it from the dog's mouth.

"I'm sorry," she says as she hands it to me, sounding annoyed, "but you shouldn't be walking on a busy sidewalk in your condition."

Several responses come to mind as she walks away, but I'm stopped cold when I see what's happened to the hose. It's chewed and torn, leaking out my precious oxygen in a steady hiss. I freeze, my mind whirring, then force myself to breathe slowly and stay calm. *Keep still, save your breath.* But it's not easy and doesn't solve the problem: How am I going to get home? The doctor was clear that I must be vigilant in avoiding germs. My body's too frail, and my lungs already too impaired, to withstand an infection. I don't think putting a cannula in my nose that's been dragged across a Manhattan sidewalk and chewed by a dog qualifies as vigilance.

A young woman kneels beside me and helps me sit up.

"Can you still use that tube thing?" she asks.

I shake my head, blinking back tears of dismay. How much oxygen am I getting on street air? Reaching in my pocket, I put on the finger oximeter and test: 84 percent saturation. That'll be okay for a bit if I don't move, but it's certainly not enough to walk home. Even staying calm is hard when people are walking all around, trying to get through. The woman and another bystander help me to the wall and the first one asks if she can call anyone for me.

I nod, pull out my phone, and call Dane.

"What's your name?" she asks, taking the phone.

"Fi," I breathe.

"Fee?"

I inhale deeply and reply, "Fiona."

New York from the sidewalk is a new experience. Pedestrians mostly ignore me. Some glance at me with distaste; one boy gives me a dollar. By the time Dane arrives from Midtown, my bruises are aching and I'm shivering. When the taxi pulls up and the tall blond figure emerges, I'm flooded with a mixture of relief and shame. Dane has too much on his plate already with a big work project for me to add unnecessary problems.

He crouches, holds my face briefly for reassurance, then reaches into his briefcase. Engineer that he is, he's come prepared with a small pack of disinfectant wipes and a pair of scissors marked "Abby's, DO NOT touch." Abby apparently guards her supplies. Or tries.

"I'm going to cut off the end of the hose and disinfect it," he tells me, then does so, cleaning the whole front section of tube and discarding the chewed-on remainder. When he gives me the clean section to suck, the first few breaths are dizzying. Like a sugar rush mixed with champagne. It takes a few minutes before I'm ready; then he lifts me and carries me to the waiting cab.

Inside, he holds me close until my shivers die down.

"I'm so sorry," I say between inhales. "I thought being . . . outside would help. Feel less claustrophobic. You shouldn't have to . . . steal office supplies."

I'm trying to lighten the mood, but Dane doesn't even react. He's seldom in a joking mindset these days, and anyway, joking isn't the coping mechanism for him that it is for me.

Back at our building he holds me upright in the elevator but looks muscle-weary. Once we're finally inside the apartment, with the concentrator turned on and its clean cannula in, I'm calmer. *Bless you, concentrator, my faithful friend. I promote you over the microwave.*

Dane goes to run me a hot bath, and when he returns he's wearing a clean suit, one without sidewalk dirt on it.

"I've added Epsom salts for the bruises," he says flatly. The fact that he hasn't commented or criticized makes me feel worse.

"I'm really sorry. I didn't think it would be such a problem."

He shakes his head. "I know that. And I wish there were some way to help you not feel so trapped here, but I don't know how."

He exhales, then finally looks at me. The Nordic blue eyes are veined with red.

"Fi, I'm running on fumes. It's been four years since you got sick. Stressful years. Trekking you to doctor after doctor, watching you get worse anyway. Terrified you might have your mother's disease, and fighting despair when we learned you *did* have it."

I wish he'd stop talking. IPF, interstitial pulmonary fibrosis, was the nightmare of my twenties. As it turned my mother's lungs into scars, it also ripped our family apart.

Dane's voice grows coarse. "When you decided to try for a lung transplant, there was hope again. Do you remember that feeling when you cleared the final testing hurdle and were accepted onto the transplant list? How we celebrated?"

I nod, blinking hard. It had been a conditional pardon from death by slow suffocation. For the first month I'd felt nothing but relief. But I hadn't realized how difficult it would be to wait, week after week for months, one ear always listening for the phone call that meant a lung match had been found.

"Honey," he continues, "I know it's hard for you. Sitting around being patient isn't your thing. But please, find a way. You know I can't quit work and be here with you."

My heart jumps. "Definitely not, we need the money and your insurance. Don't worry, no more stupid stunts. I promise, I'll be good until the transplant. Then afterwards I'll go back to work and everything will go back to the old days. I'll even start cooking terrible meals again if you want."

That scores a weak smile.

"Okay, let's get you in that bath, and if you're sure you can get out on your own I'll head back to the office."

He helps me into the tub and kisses me goodbye, turning up my oxygen level before leaving so that I have the extra breath to get out of the tub afterwards. I scan my body; the bruises aren't as bad as they might have been. Then I lean back into the blessed heat, thinking that hot water and a place to sit in it might be one of man's greatest non-essential gifts. Today wasn't the kind of adventure I'd been looking for. That said, does my promise to Dane mean I'll be stuck alone at home indefinitely? Waiting time for lung transplants in New York City is running to almost six months. That would be its own form of torture.

When I was working, my best ideas often came in the bath. If I were advising the client Fiona Copeland, I'd tell her to diversify her support network. Maybe get more friends. But that's hard to do when you're forty-two years old, have no kids, and are sick. Plus I was never a super-people-person to begin with. It's not that I dislike humans, but I've never managed the casual empathetic "Hi! *How are you?*" thing, and I can never remember which sports team they support. That was never an issue when I was working and had too much human interaction already. It's a big issue when everyone works but me.

Since no other ideas come to mind, and I've soaked myself wrinkly, I decide to call Bonnie. Bonita Alvarez whirled into my life in third grade, on a cloud of bushy brown hair, a sneaky smile, and a barrel of attitude. She packed a punch—as any boy who tried to sass her discovered. We are deeply woven through each other's lives. We've been friends long enough for her to have known my mother when she was healthy and vibrant. She mourned her beside me when the woman I adored for her ability to light up a life—especially *my* life—faded to black, leaving me with only a father I blamed for her death.

I haul myself out of the tub, wrap myself in a robe, and hit FaceTime. There's no worry about disturbing her at the office, because she doesn't have one. Bonnie has never kept a regular hour in her life.

"Hi, Fi-Fi," she answers in that rich contralto. She's the only person who could ever get away with echoing my nickname and turning me into a poodle.

Ordinarily I'd make a pointed comment about floofy dog names, but I'm distracted by her outfit. Bonnie composes music for kids' shows and frequently gets in the mood by dressing for the theme. Today she's wearing a long-sleeved khaki shirt and a necklace of giant orange seeds, and her hair is poking out from under a khaki hat with mosquito netting rolled on top. In Brooklyn.

"Africa?" I venture.

"Nope." She reaches forward and touches her console.

A lick with a Latin rhythm kicks in, overlaid with sounds of monkeys and parrots.

"Cuban rainforest," she explains, flicking the music back off. "It's an animated show called *Cuba-Dooba*, a cross between *Scooby-Doo* and *Go, Diego, Go!*—that's Dora's cousin, in case you're behind on your preschool TV."

"Wait, let me guess. The lead character solves mysteries in the rainforest?"

"Exacto." She finds this as funny as I do, and it takes a while for me to catch my breath.

"So what's up?" she asks. "Did you call to chat, or did something happen?"

"Something happened. And now I'm grounded."

Her eyes narrow as I tell her about my morning's excitement, my fall, and Dane's response. Not the reaction I'd hoped for.

"Fi, you know I think Dane's too serious for you, but in this case he has a point. You're at that stage where you're not sick enough to be content sitting around, but just strong enough to be a danger to yourself. We both know your condition isn't stable. What is it your doctor said?"

"That this disease doesn't proceed with gradual declines but unpredictable drops. There's no way to tell when the next big drop in my breathing will come, or how severe it will be. You know this, Bonnie, what's your point other than making me feel worse?"

"The point is that it's December. Flu season, cold season, everything season. The one thing you can't afford is to get sick before your transplant happens. Or to be lying on a cold sidewalk with a broken leg, unable to do your strengthening exercises."

"That's two things," I point out.

"Okay, wise guy, what are you going to do to keep busy enough not to get stupid? Weren't you trying hobbies or something?"

I roll my eyes. "Hobbies would be great if I didn't categorically suck at them. Needlepoint was fiddly and slow;

calligraphy was like preschool but messier. I'm so artistically uninclined that I'm practically vertical . . . or horizontal, whichever means I suck. My job was interesting, but I don't have the focus to do it right anymore. And the best part of free time was being outside, active. We see how that worked out."

"It's only a few months of waiting," Bonnie says affectionately. "Maybe you should learn meditation and practice Zen."

Sometimes I forget; she still believes I'll make it.

"Listen, Fi. Your mom's way of dealing with sickness was to retain some glamour . . ."

"Yeah, that won't work for me. I'm more 'wardrobe by Oscar the Grouch, hair by Bellatrix Lestrange.'"

"Exactly, so you'll do sickness in your own way. By analyzing what would make this period till transplant tolerable. Your strength is finding solutions. Go do that, and let me get back to my monkeys."

After we've hung up, I think how touching it is, her faith in me. But this isn't algebra, and I don't have the solution. What I have is a killer headache and a bunch of bruises, but that at least is fixable with painkillers and a nap. I down two Tylenol, then stumble to the bedroom. The curtains are still closed, and I stub my toe on Dane's grandfather's walnut bed before dropping into it and crashing out.

Chapter 2

My cell phone's ring drags me out of a heavy sleep. It's Dane.

"Hi, honey. Just checking in. I'll be back around eight, so eat something before then."

I mumble, "No problem," and flop back onto the bed.

I feel totally disoriented. I've dreamt occasionally, but this was unlike any dream I've ever had. So much so that part of me is still there, seeing every detail, still feeling the squelch.

It's nighttime, and I'm standing alone by the kitchen sink of my parents' house in the country. It must be summer; the air feels thick, and the window is open, letting in a riot of insect song. I'm searching for a flashlight, as I did as a kid, to see who's conducting the swells and falls of the music, when a figure runs across the yard right in front of the window. I pull back, adrenaline surging. In the moment that he passed through the light-spill, I saw him, a man straight out of film noir: trench coat, fedora, dark hair, and a grim face. A tough guy, out on bad business. My instincts yell run . . . but I can't move.

The sound of splintering glass comes from the back door, and I know instantly that he has come to kill me. Move! *I scrabble for the phone and dial.*

"911. What is your emergency?"

I try to answer but no words come out. I push the words harder until finally a sound emerges: a formless, guttural howl.

"Ma'am or sir, I can't understand you. What is your emergency?"

Something falls at the end of the corridor, and now there are sounds of a fight. He—whoever he is—is struggling with Dane, who is strong but no fighter. It can only be moments . . .

The voice on the phone is still talking when the scuffling stops. Grief slams me as I realize it is too late; no help can reach me in time. The phone is worthless now, so I drop it on the counter, and in that moment see a large chef's knife lying directly in front of me on the clean white surface. Where did it come from? It wasn't there before. Its blade is gleaming, the point weapon-sharp. Sharp enough to frighten, perhaps? Grabbing the handle, I spin around.

He is waiting for me just a few feet away. Handsome, in a dark, deadly way. I clench the knife tightly and he laughs. Not unkindly, but in amusement.

"Really? And what's a middle-aged broad with a knife going to do against an armed assassin with a gun?"

He raises his right arm, no hurry, and points the gun at my chest. I'm frozen, waiting for the impact, absorbing the truth of it: I will die now. But a germ of stubbornness creeps in. After all, I am holding a big knife, and what is there to lose? Squeezing the hilt and praying my grip is strong enough, I take a quick step forward and shove it hard, underhand, into his stomach. It makes an odd squelch and goes in deep.

The solidity of the sensation is shocking. I somehow imagined stabbing someone being softer, squishier. This was like cutting garlic holes into a thick slab of meat.

He stares at me in astonishment, then looks down to his stomach, to the two inches of blade and four of handle projecting from it. His expression reads: What the hell, lady? *The gun arm drops, his knees buckle, and he crumples to the floor like a marionette, morphing into a viscous puddle on the tiles. The last remaining feature is a disbelieving frown under a gray fedora.*

Replaying the dream in my head, it's just as weird as the first time. I knew with certainty that death was about to take me, but I tried anyway . . . and somehow stopped it. Stopped death. It feels ridiculous to be reading any reality into a dream, but throughout history people have believed in signs like this, and the fact is that I feel different. Maybe this is what faith feels like. I head unsteadily to the kitchen, find some yogurt and peanut butter, and sit. But even after eating I feel the same sense of portent. Maybe I can save my life after all, if I can find the right tool and use it.

The first step to finding a solution is accurately identifying the problem. The second is challenging your assumptions. The immediate problem is clear: how to survive for five or more months. There's not much to be done there. I have no control over the wait time, which is dictated by the availability of organs in this greater New York City region, relative to how many people need them. And suddenly, there it is—the blind spot I've missed.

My listing for transplant is at Empire General Hospital. The five-month wait time is based on their ratio of patients to available organs. But what if there's another center with different demographics that lead to a shorter expected wait to transplant? Somewhere with more lungs, or fewer patients?

Pushing back from the table, I drag the tubing along the corridor to the guest-room-cum-home-office. I don't like this room. The small window is bad enough, but Dane's choice of hunter-green wallpaper and dark-stained bookcase is worse. He thinks it's elegant. I think it's one moose head short of a hunting lodge. But I need the computer.

After not much searching, I find a chart listing average time on waiting lists for US lung transplant centers. There aren't that many of them, and the other ones around New York aren't any quicker than Empire . . . some noticeably longer. Others have very little experience with lung transplants, which is a tricky procedure; I flag them. But I find a couple of promising targets.

A couple of hours later, I've found a great option . . . with a significant downside. Regent Hospital is in a university town called Johnson's River, about six hundred miles southwest of New York, near the border of Virginia and Tennessee. It has a good track record for lung transplants and plenty of experience. It's also the only major transplant hospital in the area, so there's far less competition for donor lungs. Average time to transplant is about one month—a huge advantage over Empire's. Even better, it's officially deemed close enough to Empire that I could dual list at *both* centers, something I hadn't previously considered. If Regent accepts me, I can stay on Empire's list too, and get transplanted at whichever hospital offers me lungs first.

The big downside, however: Regent requires patients to live within an hour of their hospital during the whole process, from the first test until about a month after surgery. Possibly longer if there are problems. I'd have to move to Johnson's River. More than that, every patient must have a caregiver living with them who has no other commitments for the whole duration. No job, and no kids or aging parents needing their attention. And as if this wasn't difficult enough, the caregiver must be family or a close enough friend that they might as well be. Patients absolutely may not hire someone as their caregiver.

It feels like I was thrown a lifeline only to have it be snatched away. Dane's current work situation is too pivotal for him to take such a long leave. They'd replace him and phase him out, which we can't afford; we're reliant on his income and health insurance. But who else could do it? My only other living family member is my father, whom I haven't spoken to in years. I could never stand living with him for two months, even if he'd agree. Of course I have some friends, but they all lead busy lives, and most have small children. Even Bonnie takes care of her elderly father.

I stand up and pace to the degree possible in this small space. If the answer isn't with anyone I know, then—however implausible or unapproved—it will have to be someone else. But is it realistic to try to find a complete stranger for something like this? And would Dane treat it as a rejection if I suggest it?

This time, not wanting to interrupt Bonnie's major opus, I text.

Found a new angle. Significantly decreases transplant wait time but requires moving six hundred miles away—without Dane. Is that a good idea?

She calls back within two minutes.

"You're asking for relationship advice from a woman whose marriage exploded like a supernova?"

"Fair point. But it's a valid question. The shortened wait time could be the key factor in living long enough to get transplanted. But Dane has to stay here. Would it be crazy to hire someone else to come with me and be my caregiver? If all goes well, I'd have to live there for two or three months. But if I suggest it, would Dane feel insulted?"

She thinks about it, then says, "Maybe, but so what? You'll need a caregiver at some point if you stay home, so you might as well make it count. Dane can't handle everything already, and it won't help anyone if you die rather than upset him."

It's true, Dane's exhausted. If he has a couple of months free from taking care of me—especially since I'm only going to get worse—he can recover before helping me posttransplant.

"Agreed," I nod. "The second problem is Regent's other rule. They don't allow hired caregivers, only family and close friends. So we'll have to finesse that somehow."

She looks at me reproachfully. "With your outgoing personality and easygoing friendship, you can surely make some new besties in the next few weeks."

I stare at her for a moment, then we both crack up.

"You know I'd come with you if my father wasn't so bad," she says. "But he gets confused even when my brother visits now. I can't leave him."

"Of course not," I reassure her. "I wouldn't even consider it. I'll go on a caregiver website and interview some people, maybe even a trained nurse. That could be helpful."

She hesitates. "Tread lightly with that. It's a lot to expect a nurse to lie about your relationship. Besides, sometimes nurses read obviously as nurses. That lung place sounds like it might boom the alert for that and ding you."

"But how else will I find someone? I'm tired of everything being so difficult."

"Maybe there's a different way," she offers. "This could be a sweet gig for a creative type like me. We're used to a project style of working: When there's a job, you work as much as it takes, so you can save up for the dead periods. And musicians and actors are used to going where the gig is, which lots of people won't or can't do. Creatives almost always need money. If you offered the right price, I bet you'd have some takers. You might even enjoy being around that kind of energy for a change. Think about it."

When Dane returns home, dinner is waiting in the form of a hot chicken-and-wine stew from a local bistro. Steam is still rising as we transfer it onto real plates, the smell making me hungry for the tender meat and vegetables, which are easy for me to chew.

We eat in pleasant companionship, and when we're finished, Dane clears the table. While he's clanking at the sink, I prepare to tell him about my findings.

"Okay," he says when he returns. "Tell me whatever it is you have planned. You've got your presentation face on."

I'm thrown for a second. "I don't have a presentation face. Do I?"

He smiles gently. "Fi, in the past seven years I've seen that face many times, usually right before a big pitch, and I'm happy to see it again. What are you going to pitch me?"

It's good when the people you love know you so well.

"I've been talking to Bonnie . . . No, don't roll your eyes! She challenged me to come up with a creative solution for the long transplant wait, and today I might have found it."

He's fully attentive as I tell him the details of Regent's program: wait time till transplant, track record for both success during surgery and average lifespan afterwards. He knows the stats I'm currently facing at Empire, so he understands that Regent is a comparably good center but with a far shorter wait. Then I tell him the big catch.

"I've thought this through every which possible way, but the only solution I've found is for me to go there with someone else while you stay here."

He falls silent. I know how his mind operates: He's thinking this through. The odds if I stay at Empire versus the fact of being separated. How he would feel if I didn't go and died in New York waiting for lungs.

Finally he says, "You have to try it. I don't like the idea of us being apart, especially at this time, but it's the only thing that makes sense. People do live apart from their families if it brings their loved ones a better life. I'm hiring people now who are doing exactly that. If it increases your chances of survival, a few months is trivial. We'd keep in close touch via video and calls. But I'm concerned about finding the right caregiver. What kind of person would we look for?"

"Regent says their rule against hired caregivers is because it's such a difficult role. They don't believe anyone can be relied on to stick around unless they have a personal relationship with the patient. If it's that rough, we need someone mentally strong and resilient."

"Physically strong to a degree too," he adds. "You can't lift heavy things, and at some point you'll need physical assistance. Also, where you're going they'll have to be able to drive. They have to be plausible as a close friend, and they must be willing and able to leave New York for an uncertain amount of time. Most of all, it's a round-the-clock job: There's no such thing as off-shift or guaranteed personal time. Who will take a job like that?"

"I know, it's like looking for a buff Mary Poppins. But Bonnie had an idea."

I tell him about her suggestion to look for someone whose life is intrinsically irregular. I've no idea what he's thinking of me going away with someone so unlike most people we know. Does he think it's a flaky idea? That *they'll* be too flaky for the role? His face is blank.

Finally he says: "She's right, that's our best bet."

Then his expressions shifts into a small frown. I wait till he's ready to tell me.

"I can't believe I'm even suggesting this, and don't freak out, but what if this person was a man? The suspicion on your caregiver would be much less if they're your 'husband.' He's not expected to look like you. The medical people would listen to a husband in a different way than a girlfriend, and . . . I'm embarrassed to say it, but I'd worry less if someone strong would be with you. Would that be too weird?"

I'm surprised, but nothing more. "Fine by me. A roommate is a roommate."

"Good." He sounds relieved. "We'll just have to make the offer attractive enough that whoever we pick is invested in staying with you. And the worst thing that can happen is I come to you, or you come back home."

Before we go to bed, Dane and I draft an ad to place on the kind of sites our target audience might read. Pulling the covers over me, I feel a small ray of hope in my core. Finally there's a glimmer of real possibility.

Chapter 3

By Friday I've found four promising candidates: a novelist, a poet, a sculptor in clay, and an abstract painter. We schedule the interviews consecutively for Saturday afternoon at our apartment, setting out tea and butter cookies as though for a social event.

The painter is up first. I'd looked up his website and liked his work, so that might be interesting. He shows up in black jeans and a collarless, blindingly white shirt with teeth to match. Tall, sandy-haired, good-looking, and well aware of it. Dane's face sharpens instantly.

"Take a seat," Dane says, gesturing. His tone is almost hostile, but the guy doesn't catch it. "Tell us about your relevant experience."

"Sure. When I was twelve I helped take care of my sick father after school for three months. I volunteer for the local ambulance corps and I'm CPR certified."

He flashes me a brilliant smile, which judging from Dane's expression is the end of his candidacy. I can practically smell the testosterone from my chair.

We chat a few more minutes, then Dane says we'll let him know and shows him out.

"Sorry," he tells me, quivering. "This isn't as easy as it was in my head."

I'm laughing so hard that I need more oxygen.

"It's incredibly flattering that you think I'm still sexy enough for this to be an issue, but seriously, don't worry. There's only room for one Viking in my life."

"Thanks. But I hope the next one's butt-ugly."

The poet is next, but he's a no-show and my call goes to voicemail. *Two down already*, I think with dismay. *Please let the next two be good.*

The novelist arrives five minutes early. He's not ugly, just an ordinary guy. Average height or under, in blue jeans and a navy polo. Very dark eyes and hair, cut on the long side. Dane offers him a seat without hostility and asks about his experience.

"As I told Fiona . . ."—he nods to me, pleasantly but with no hint of flirtation—"I took care of my partner for two years through sudden-onset leukemia."

Dane's startled. "I'm so sorry. Did she pull through?"

"He died," the writer, Mason, replies simply. No comment on the gender assumption, no drama; the drama is there in the still-present fact of his loss.

"I was sole caregiver, just as this position calls for," he continues, "so I understand what I'd be taking on. The job is to do what's needed, when it's needed. No matter what. Also, I know how hospitals and doctors work. Insurance companies too. It's a steep learning curve if you have to start from scratch."

His voice is a calm, pleasant baritone. There's no sign of the pain he's been through, but there's an obvious question.

"Are you sure you can go through this again?" I ask cautiously.

He smiles lopsidedly, changing instantly from bookish to impish. "No offense, but it'll be a lot easier without the personal component. I'll be fine."

Dane and I share quick glances. So far, so good. "Why do you want this job?" he asks.

"Currently I'm a paralegal, which leaves me little time to work on my novel. I'm thirty-seven years old and tired of stealing odd hours to write when I can, spending half of them getting my head back in the story. This job would be perfect for me, and I'd take the responsibility seriously."

We talk about the move out of town, and then it's time to broach the tricky question.

"There's one other thing we haven't mentioned," I say, praying he won't balk. "The place we're going to has a strict rule against hired caregivers, so we'd have to present you as something else. As family. How would you feel about being, for those purposes, my husband?"

He leans back with a look of surprised pleasure.

"As a paralegal I probably shouldn't say this, but as someone who's had to fight dozens of rules that made sense on paper but not in reality, I'd have no problem at all. In my experience, the people who are loyal aren't always who you'd think. Being family is no guarantee."

There's a brief flash of anger, quickly gone.

"In my view," he continues, "it's about personal integrity, and I'd be happy to give you references on that. I keep my word."

Dane looks at me and nods almost imperceptibly.

"In that case," I say, "I think this could work very well. Subject to checking those references, we'd like to offer you the position."

We iron out the details, and when he's gone, Dane says, "He's perfect! I can't believe we found him. Paralegal, so he's competent and smart. Spot-on experience. And . . ."

"And he's gay, so you won't worry."

He blushes. "Well, there is that. Let's cancel the final candidate."

Chapter 4

Mason and I have been spending time together, preparing for the move to Johnson's River. He gave his law firm notice, found a sublet for his apartment, and will move his belongings to storage when we're ready to leave. He's also been studying up on lung transplants . . . and on me. He has both a sharp mind and a good memory, which means I'll have a backstop and won't have to absorb all the innumerable details on my own. That's an unexpected relief.

Our job now is to get knowledgeable and comfortable enough with each other to credibly pass as being married. I'd been nervous about this part, but he's easy to get along with, even-keeled and comfortable with silences. A good cook too; I'll probably eat much better once we're there. He's also, now that the interview's over, quite funny. It shows up in unexpected ways, a dry, quirky humor that I enjoy and suspect will make this process easier.

"Okay, muffin," he begins, sitting across from me at the dining table, "test time."

He has started calling me different endearments to get us used to the idea of acting close. Most days they make me giggle, especially since he's so deadpan about it. I wish I could think of something funny to call him.

"How can I be a muffin? I'm getting thinner every day."

"Your head stays the same size, but your body is smaller. Ergo, muffin."

"You know what, just start."

"Cupcake, Eugene here just asked about our first date. Do you remember?"

"How could I forget? You were drunk and kept ogling the girl at the next table."

He raises his eyebrows. I'm not supposed to ad-lib.

"Fine," I concede with a smirk.

"I was walking across Eighty-Eighth Street in a massive windstorm, umbrella in one hand, take-out dinner in the other. The wind gusted and I fell, dropping my take-out bag. You helped me up and took me to dinner at a restaurant nearby. Bodrum on Amsterdam, Mediterranean food. You proposed a year later, and we got married on May tenth at your family church in Alton, Illinois, because I don't have relatives and your church is beautiful."

"Remember to visualize it so you can tell it slightly differently each time and it sounds real. Stick to the truth wherever possible. Picture your actual wedding dress, and your father walking . . . Shit. Sorry. Your *friend* Yannis walking you up the aisle."

"Nice catch, Mata Hari. Let's move on."

"Your turn. Meeting my family."

"Your parents—engineer, accountant—were welcoming from the start, but your sisters were wary because I'm an East Coaster. Kristina came around pretty quickly after we all went hiking, and Annie always follows her lead."

"Angie, not Annie. Here, look at her photo again." He pulls it from a pile and slides it across the table. "Doesn't she look as if Mick Jagger would love her and leave her?"

"Isn't that most women? But yes, I'll remember it now."

"My turn. You're from Larchmont, New York. Father an entrepreneur, mother a teacher. You have a business degree from Michigan, and before you got sick you worked for a company that advises small businesses. You led a six-person team, so you're used to being in control and solving problems. Work was important to you, which is why we postponed having kids, and now we can't, but you're a doting aunt to my niece and nephews."

"Correct," I say. "Now transplant issues. You'd know that if you were my husband."

"Dane doesn't," he says matter-of-factly.

I'm jolted. Was that an insult?

"No offense intended. But seriously, I don't have to know all that before we arrive."

"Dane knows the basics." I'm a little defensive.

"Of course. Well, the biggest problem is getting viable organs. Half of Americans aren't registered donors. Then because of lungs' position in the chest, they're especially susceptible to damage from death-causing accidents . . . and even good lungs deteriorate fast after the donor's death. So there's a nontrivial chance of dying before you get one."

"Who decides who gets one?"

"Allocation is regulated by a government agency called UNOS, the United Network for Organ Sharing. UNOS's stated goal is to save the maximum number of lives, without regard to other factors. There's no attempt made to guess who might make best use of the lung by living longest, or who is more deserving. Those things aren't knowable anyway."

"Go on," I say. He twitches a little. We've been over this before and he always gets it right, but these details are what might trip us up.

"UNOS allocates lungs on a regional basis to the patient with the highest LAS score—lung allocation score—who is a physical match. First to patients within a 250-mile radius, then 575 miles, then anywhere in the United States. Match meaning the donor matches the patient's blood type and approximate height, height being a proxy for chest cavity size. The new lungs have to actually fit. All this provided the patient is deemed strong enough to survive the process."

That's what makes this the ultimate-stakes game of chance, I think. *Too healthy and you won't be given the transplant, too sick and you die first.*

"So there's no waitlist?"

"There is for kidneys, because people can survive on dialysis. But not for lungs."

"Good. Mr. Copeland, tell me why you chose Regent?"

"Very funny." But he's grinning.

"Sorry, Mr. *Wolfwood*, why did you choose Regent?"

"Actually, my smarty-pants wife chose it. As the only major transplant center in the area, Regent gets first shot at any lungs for miles around. Plus the population here trends younger and more likely to register as donors—which they can do by just signing their driver's license, since almost everyone has one."

"Exactly!" I blurt out, myself again. "Why doesn't everyone do that? What use do they have for their organs after they're dead? You know, in lots of countries you're assumed to be a donor unless you opt out. Nobody's taking away your choice, but 'not getting around to it' doesn't cost lives!"

He waits me out. He already knows.

"There's another reason for Regent," he adds. "But I'm not going to say that to anyone. Motorbiking is big there, which means more road deaths with transplant possibilities."

"That's pretty dark."

He shrugs. "At least they wear helmets, unlike where I'm from, where people regularly splatter themselves against trees unprotected."

"This is an awful conversation," I say, squirming at the image. "It's bad enough just knowing that in order for me to live, someone else has to die. I'm not going to be some ghoul looking at the bright side."

He turns pensive. "When my partner died, they couldn't accept his organs because of the cancer. I would have loved to know some part of him was living on. If someone's dead, that's the *only* upside."

I'm silent. There's no good response to that.

"Fi, by now I know enough about you and transplant for these purposes. And no one will be surprised if your memory's fuzzy: You're sick. Shall we call it done and set a departure date?"

I hesitate. There's something terrifying about actually pulling the trigger . . . leaving Dane and home, my friends. But the sooner we start, the greater my chances of success. There's no real reason to wait.

"Yes. Pack your gear and let's do this."

Chapter 5

February

I'm waiting in the lobby of my building as Dane and Mason finish loading the last of the gear into the station wagon. It's tricky trying to load a car anywhere in Manhattan, certainly on West End Avenue at Ninety-Fifth; the car's scrunched into the rightmost lane, cars honking as they curve around it. Sitting on the plush bench, I'm sheltered from the car fumes and wind, looking at the dark patches of sky and hoping it won't rain. The back of the wagon is packed beyond sight-line safety with the things two adults might need to start a new, if temporary, life.

I can't believe we're actually leaving. The last two weeks have been crammed with logistics. Getting on Regent's schedule to get tested (which luckily they will cram into two days); servicing the car; and figuring out what to pack for a long stay, so that if Regent accepts me, we can just remain there until it's all done.

Finally they're finished. Dane comes inside and walks me to the wagon. We hold each other for a long while, stocking up before the time apart. I grasp tightly . . . then let go. He helps me in, setting the travel-size concentrator between my feet, kisses me once, then steps back.

Mason slides the wheelchair into the final remaining sliver of trunk space and slams the tailgate shut. He leans against the car for a minute, then gets behind the wheel.

"That is one crap-load of stuff," he says, panting a little. "Thank God I'm good at Tetris. Evidently my youth wasn't misplaced after all."

"Thank you. Between the concentrators, oxygen tanks, medical records, and blah blah blah, it looks like everything there is mine."

"No, my stuff's there too—mostly books, sure, but a few clothes and maybe some deodorant somewhere." He turns to me. "We're doing this, okay? You'll get your new lungs, and I'll finally write my novel. It's a noble quest. Are you ready? Let's go then."

As we head south down West End and the building recedes behind us, I have a sudden heart-clutch. Is this a final goodbye? Will I ever see my home, my city, again? As each neighborhood rolls by, I catch the memories that attach, holding them tight. The run-down brownstone where I moved after college, throwing cramped but fun-filled parties with my roommates every February. Carefree days of skimpy skirts and enough energy to work a ten-hour day and still go out for a beer afterwards. "Goodbye, cockroach apartment," I mutter softly.

Further south is the diner where a group of us hung out on our first road trip sophomore year. We felt so cool with our knockoff purses, ordering celebrity-named sandwiches like the Elvis PBJ. Most of us are still close. "Goodbye, Hudson Diner. Stay greasy for me."

Lincoln Center. Passing the Metropolitan Opera House is a wrench: My mother took me there once when I was little, to see *The Magic Flute*. Why didn't I make time to go again when I lived here? "Goodbye, Queen of the Night; sing high and pretty while I'm gone." My voice catches.

"Is this some twisted version of *Goodnight Moon*?" Mason cuts in. "Because your breathing rate's shooting up. If you want queens and knights, we can watch *Camelot*."

"No—Mozart! *The Magic Flute*." Then I catch his expression and realize he's teasing. But I take out the oximeter: He's right, my pulse rate's too high.

He glances at me. "Look, this is hard, I get it. You've lived here a long time and you're heading into the complete unknown. It's natural to be scared. But it doesn't help to work yourself up and keep telling yourself it's goodbye. You'll be back. Let's just get you healthy. Right?"

I roll my shoulders out and nod. Look forward, not back. Or don't look at all.

We go into the Lincoln Tunnel and through into New Jersey, and just like that the anxiety is gone. A longtime response to heading out of town bubbles up a good kind of excitement. I'm on a road trip! To somewhere I've never been before, embarking on a quest to save my life.

"You know what?" I tell Mason. "Crazy as this seems, I feel happy. Whatever the outcome, after months of being cooped up at home this will be an adventure."

New Jersey passes by at sixty-five miles an hour. More memories, more pixelated than the Manhattan ones. I haven't spent much time here and have few memories worth storing.

"I still never think of this as New Jersey," I say. "It's supposed to be the Garden State, but this part is big industry—IKEA, Newark airport, Elizabeth's smokestacks. It doesn't smell like a garden either, unless the skunks got in. For me the state means lakes, fishing, bike trails. Kayaking and rafting on the Delaware River."

"Come on, this is iconic Jersey . . . well, this and shopping malls. I'm rather fond of where we are right now. The New Jersey Turnpike: Paul Simon and me, counting the cars and looking for America."

"You're joking. What's to love about *this*?"

"The rest stop names, for one. In what other context can you find Alexander Hamilton, Thomas Edison, and Joyce Kilmer together? Or Vince Lombardi just up the road from Walt Whitman? I like to imagine them strolling to each other's gift shops for a chat and some coffee."

I laugh. "Where do you come up with this stuff?"

But as we shoot past Molly Pitcher, I have an oddball thought of my own. "Mason, if I die, I'd like a rest stop named after me. They need someone like me mixed in with this riffraff."

His eyebrows rise. "Sort of like the tomb of the unknown common person."

"Well, no, I want my name on it. But I'd be representing the millions of people who die marginally bravely, but unmemorably, with nothing big and beautiful to mark their passing."

"Big and beautiful. Like a rest stop on the New Jersey Turnpike?"

"Exactly."

I lean back and close my eyes. This memory business is tiring, the initial adrenaline wearing off in the face of miles of automobile rear ends ahead. Miles and miles, I think drowsily, Paul Simon playing softly in my head.

Mason's hand jostles me awake.

"Time to get up. We've been on the road for three hours, and I'm starving. Plus I have to stretch my legs. I thought we'd stop here, in beautiful High Ridge, PA, for gas and food."

He wrestles the wheelchair and oxygen tank out of the back while I wrestle myself awake, and we stroll-roll along Main Street, USA. It feels so good to be outdoors and in motion that I look at everything: in windows, at buildings, at people, gawking like a toddler in a stroller with nothing to do but watch while someone pushes me around.

When we pass a small, dark shop crammed with old-style curios, I call for Mason to stop. In the window is a glass hummingbird, green with a speckled belly, about five inches tall. I couldn't feel less like a hummingbird (except for the frequent little sips of food), but I'm lovestruck. What better good luck totem for this endeavor than a symbol of life and energy?

Mason goes inside and buys it, emerging with a bubble-wrapped bundle that he lays gently into the purse hanging on the back of the wheelchair. We find a diner that smells of apple pie, where we order sandwiches and use the restroom, which thankfully is big enough to accommodate my wheelchair. Mason seats us at the checkered-tablecloth table that could have been in any diner in America, while I save mine for the car so as not to slow us down.

Soon we're back on the road, with nothing but trees, cars, and highway signs around us. Mason enjoys driving in quiet, so it's very peaceful. After so long in my apartment, the miles of green and open skies feel glorious; I could seriously consider hugging a tree. My cell phone interrupts the mood . . . I grab it quickly, then smile when I see the caller.

"Hi, Yannis."

"Hey, sweetie! How *are* you?"

"Pretty good, considering. What's doing with you?"

"I'm turning older, that's what. Birthday celebration at Niko's, with my favorite Greek food—well, *everybody's* favorite food, don't you think? Thursday night at seven. No presents, just be there."

"It sounds great, but I can't. For once your timing's bad."

"It wasn't my choice—they don't make date-changing apps for birth certificates. I looked. Where will you be, anyway?"

"In a university town you've never heard of called Johnson's River, about six hundred miles southwest of New York. Too far to turn back, even for your birthday."

I hear the sound of an executive chair snapping upright, and Yannis is instantly serious. "What's happening?"

So I tell him. My lung function has dropped, and I'm heading somewhere where the wait times are much shorter. Doesn't mean I'll get it, but it's worth trying.

He's uncharacteristically silent for a moment. "So that's it, then? You're gone, with no idea if . . . no, *when* . . . You know what I mean." His throat sounds tight.

Damn. This is why I didn't tell people I was leaving: Saying goodbye is bad for morale. Especially when they're afraid it might be permanent.

"*Until* I get transplanted, Yannis."

He coughs. "Well, I'm glad you're not just running from my party. What's this place like?"

"Johnson's River? I've never been there, but it's a college town, so there must be stuff to do. Plus three hours of mandatory physical exercise every day; I'll be too busy turning into G.I. Jane to check out the bar scene. But if I'm bored, I'll call so you can cheer me up."

"We'll video. Seriously, Fi, I will not forgive you if things start to get bad and you don't let me know. Just say the word and I'll find a car and come down there."

"I will . . . and thank you. This place has a good track record, so I'm pretty optimistic I'll be back home in a couple of months. Tell you what, plan a fantastic party for me when I get back."

"You got it. Be safe, honey; we'll talk again soon."

For once, this optimism isn't faked. For the first time since my diagnosis, I see a real possibility of future health. If all goes as planned, in a few months my diseased and scarred lungs will be gone, and in their place will be a new pair of healthy ones. Either that or I'll be past worrying.

By late evening we reach the Hotel Davide. Thankfully they haven't given away our connecting rooms, so I can call Mason if I need help. We're too tired to do anything but order room service and crash, which is fine, because on Monday morning I start another round of tests. I'll need to be well rested.

Chapter 6

Johnson's River

The next morning, the Davide's breakfast greeter welcomes us into what looks like a Tyrolean lodge. Pictures of mountain views are framed with red wooden shutters, below which sit green window boxes merry with geraniums. There's even a large cuckoo clock (which I suspect would be hell if you worked there). The festiveness matches my mood. As of now, everything is possible—I can be accepted into the program, have a quick and successful lung transplant, and return home healthy. By the end of the week this may not be true, so I intend to enjoy this suspended time.

Other guests' chatter, combined with clatter from the kitchen, enhances the winter feel. We order eggs Benedict, a cranberry scone, and cappuccinos—to all appearances an ordinary couple on a romantic weekend away.

When the young waiter arrives with more coffee, Mason asks what there is to do here on a Sunday. The waiter pauses. I can see him filtering his list of suggestions through the possibilities for a woman in a wheelchair and on oxygen.

"Well, there's the art museum. I've never been, but people like it. Or the botanical gardens. And of course the craft market . . . my girlfriend likes that."

A craft market sounds delightful, so we load an oxygen tank onto the wheelchair and head out into our first glimpse of Johnson's River. Outside, everything about the place feels lighter than New York City. The air is warmer, fresh and clean, as though it drifted across from an open meadow. There are no tall buildings in this part of town to block the daylight, and trees are already beginning to sprout spring leaves. This is a lovely place to be.

The craft market is in a nearby park, and it's hopping. Stalls with brightly colored awnings are arranged in an *L*, offering everything from home-baked pies to hand-dyed clothes, artisanal cheeses, wooden bowls, and quirky jewelry. The unmistakable aroma of funnel cake fills the air.

"This is great," I say. "But nothing like Manhattan craft markets."

"Of course not," Mason replies. "Real craft markets don't carry twenty-four-karat gold and merino. Look at this." He holds up a pair of wooden earrings shaped like watermelons with five tiny fruits dangling from them. "Do you already own a pair of these?"

I try not to laugh and fail. "Too bad I don't have an office to wear them to."

"Oh, then you need them. They're happy and colorful, and . . . fruitful."

I start to say no, then think, *Why not?* It's a new life, after all; that warrants some small changes. I put them on and shake my head to set the bananas jingling, then buy another pair for Bonnie. She and Mason would get along well.

On our way back to the hotel, we detour past the Regent Medical Center. From the road it looks huge: a large span of buildings running the length of two blocks, maybe seven stories high. It's set back from the road, so cars can drive around an elongated traffic circle to drop off or pick up patients, and it looks as though buildings on the adjacent blocks are Regent too. Everything looks modern—lots of glass and concrete block—especially compared with the stately brick buildings of Empire General back in New York. Even on a Sunday morning there's plenty of activity.

"This was a good idea," I tell Mason. "Now I have a visual to tie to."

All of which is trivial, of course. The real question is, what's the place like on the inside? And even more important, what will *they* find inside *me*?

Monday comes too soon, with a full schedule of tests. Thankfully Regent has accepted some of Empire's tests, so I don't have to do *everything* again. Anything that has an image that Regent's team can interpret for themselves is accepted. Those involving calibration need to be done again on Regent's own equipment. Numbers can differ from one machine to another, and the team needs results that track to their own frame of reference. It's aggravating to have to repeat them, but worth it in the long run. I just hope they clear me to proceed.

After we've parked and I'm in the wheelchair, I focus on staying calm. Worrying might impact my performance. Still, my stomach is prewarning me that it won't like the next few hours. The tests were physically and emotionally draining when taken individually; this time they're all compressed into two days. But at least it'll be over quickly. I can handle anything for two days . . . right?

As we reach the sliding doors, I square my shoulders and prepare to start. The atrium is tall and open, lined with huge tinted-glass windows. The two gray-outfitted men staffing the central booth remind me of Jimmy, my doorman at home, which is comforting. There are surprisingly few people milling around for a hospital this size, so it's not long before we receive our sticky ID tags and are directed upstairs. In the center of the atrium is a large escalator, with a long bank of elevators running along the back wall. *Good start*, I think.

In my lap is the printout of where to go and when, across a wide range of departments on multiple floors. I check in at the transplant center on the fourth floor and exchange my tank for a hospital issue. From then on I'm like a product in a factory—placed on a conveyor belt and stopping at each station for the next piece of the process. No one cares who Mason is; he's just delivering the package.

We go one floor down, and the testing begins.

First up are blood draws, both venous and arterial. It's astonishing how painful a needle in the artery is, and the needle stays in while the technician takes blood component measurements of oxygen, carbon dioxide, and pH. I press hard on the draw site as we roll to radiation.

Regent has accepted several scans from Empire (including colonoscopy, thank goodness), but they want another heart scan, to check a vein running unusually close to the heart. A team of three cardiologists is called in and a long discussion ensues, with members pointing at the screen, saying, "I'm worried about that," and "What if we . . ." The reality slams into me that my chances might be over immediately: If they deem the pathway to transplant impeded, I'm disqualified. I want to yell, *You know I can hear, right?* But I hold my peace and try not to shiver until finally I'm cleared to proceed.

The six-minute walk is easy by comparison. A serious-looking man hands me a headband with an embedded oximeter whose lead is plugged into a box slung over his shoulder. He clears the corridor of people and sets up two orange traffic cones, thirty feet apart. I stand at one, my hand clutching the handle of my oxygen tank roller, and when he says "Go," we walk together at my fastest speed, back and forth between the cones. After six minutes, he calls "Stop," and measures my distance walked. It's slightly less than at Empire, but still well within the acceptable range. Unfortunately, I'm now out of breath heading into the dreaded pulmonary function test.

My technician is a petite Asian woman with scarlet hair and a friendly smile. "I've got her," she tells Mason. She wheels me down the PFT corridor, past rooms with people yelling, "Blow! Come on, harder, harder, keep going," till we reach an empty room. It's almost identical to the one at Empire: a small white space with a faint odor of sterilizing alcohol. There's just room enough for her chair, the computer setup that reads the breathing results, and the PFT machine itself. This one is a self-contained booth with a built-in chair and a long movable arm. The technician attaches a snorkel-like mouthpiece to the tube on the end of the arm and hands me a nose clip to make sure all my exhalation goes into the machine.

"You know the drill, so just follow my instructions," she says cheerily. "Are you ready?"

Not at all, but I reply, "Sure."

She sets up her computer, then says, "Breathe normally for a bit. Good, now on the next breath, fill your lungs and . . . blow out as fast as you can! *Keep blowing, keep blowing!*"

I'm already pushing as hard as I can, but they want an accurate measurement of my lung capacity, so I keep going until finally she says, "Three, two, one . . . Now suck it in, all the way, and *blow*!" The inevitable retching coughing spree follows; when I've recovered, we start on round two. Of nine. Well past the time that my body is screaming at me to cut it out, you moron.

Afterwards, I'm beyond exhausted. Mason, seeing me as I'm rolled back into the waiting room, flashes a brief look of concern. Then he nods and wheels me to radiology.

Having noninvasive tests feels almost like a spa treatment after how my day has gone so far. The X-ray is quick and simple. MRIs are harder because I'm somewhat claustrophobic, but I'm learning how to detach myself; my body is required to be present, but I just have to be sufficiently aware to follow instructions. I can then step back inside my brain when it's over.

Inside the device, music is my best friend. There's an extensive library of songs in my head, going back to when I was a little girl, many with memories attached. The funny voice my mother put on when she sang me "Teddy Bears' Picnic"; line dancing at prom to "Achy Breaky Heart," which hilariously segued into "Play That Funky Music"; Dane humming off-key to "You're the One That I Want" at our wedding. As the scan starts, songs arrive intact, the lyrics following each other in a long crocodile even when I have no conscious knowledge of the playlist. If only my history classes had been put to song, I'd have fared far better. I'm almost reluctant to leave "Hey Jude" before the *na-na-na-na*'s end, but the scan is done.

Mason insists that before leaving the building we get hard copies of all of today's reports and tests; if possible, film of the scans too. He's been through this before. He says I'd be horrified at how many test results get lost or are so difficult to find in a hospital's computer system that the doctors just redo them. Maybe not at Regent, but why risk it?

The copying process will take a while, so we go to the cafeteria. Mason sets me at a table and joins the line. Within minutes I'm cold and shivering hard. It was rougher than I'd expected, going through all this again, and in such unfamiliar surroundings.

Mason returns with, to my delight, hot oatmeal with brown sugar and raisins.

"So far, so good," he says, looking pleased. "You've been through most of the medical tests and, as far as I can tell, you've cleared all the hurdles. Well done, I know it was difficult."

I swallow hard. It's surprisingly comforting to hear "congratulations, good job." Reassuring too, in this case: Mason's judgment is good and he's not a bullshitter. One day down, one to go.

Back at the Davide, I run a hot bath with a hint of the rosemary-eucalyptus salts I've brought and feel the day's knots unwind. Afterwards I slip on my softest fleece outfit (actually black pj's, but no one ever notices) and flop out on my bed while Mason takes his run.

Sometime later, he shakes me gently.

"Sorry to wake you," he says, looking completely unapologetic. "But you can't sleep now or you'll have trouble tonight. And tomorrow's another big day."

He hands me a light jacket, grabs a fresh tank, and we head out with the wheelchair for an evening stroll. It's incredibly calm here compared to what I'm used to, even beyond the obvious fact of fewer people and less noise. Folks aren't in a rush; they make eye contact or even say hello as we meander down River Avenue in the soft light of sunset.

As we pass a small restaurant, Mason stops. "Georgian!" he says, surprised. "The country, not the state. Shall we try it? Looks similar to Mediterranean."

We roll inside to a completely different atmosphere: burnt-orange walls hung with unfamiliar stringed instruments, and haunting male group vocals over the speakers. I'm charmed.

"This is the closest I've come to travel in years," I say happily as we're seated.

The menu is written in both English and Georgian, which is the most beautiful alphabet I've ever seen, and the food sounds incredible: dumplings, eggplant, cheese-stuffed bread, salads. We order a smorgasbord, then Mason wheels me toward the restroom.

But when we reach the sign, it's pointed down a long, steep staircase. There's no way I can make it down this.

"It's impossible," he agrees. "Even if you made it down, there's no way you'd get back up. There must be an elevator; I'll ask."

He returns in a minute, shaking his head. "No elevator. Can you last through the meal?"

"No." My voice trembles, all the good feeling gone.

"Let's have them pack it to go. It'll still taste good."

Twenty minutes later we're back on the street, hungry and mortified.

"I'm so sorry," Mason says. "It never even occurred to me to check."

"Not your fault . . . I didn't check either. The places I go to at home don't have stairs."

"Lucky us, I guess," he says, frowning. "That we've never needed to pay attention before."

The food is lukewarm by the time we get back to the hotel. It's tasty, but it's not the same. I resolve to check for stairs next time, and to be extra considerate of people in wheelchairs.

Chapter 7

Today's activity consists of meetings with key players on Regent's lung transplant team. I dress in nicer clothes than I've worn in a while, which means a cream button-down shirt with black elasticated pants. I've lost too much weight to wear my business pants.

Over breakfast, Mason asks how I'm feeling.

"Fine . . . no worse than usual, anyway."

"Good to hear. Just a reminder, today's meetings will be just as important as yesterday's tests—maybe more. The transplant team, especially the surgeon, have to decide whether or not to accept you, and it's not just about your test results. They won't matter if the doctors don't believe in you."

"Surely the tests would be paramount, though."

"You want to think that, but not every decision's quantifiable. These doctors have access to a limited number of rare and valuable items, whose placement affects lives *and* their own reputations. If you gave someone a rare orchid, you'd want to be sure they take care of it: protect it from contaminants, feed it well, give it exercise. Yeah, I know you don't exercise an orchid. But you have to convince them that you'll be responsible with those lungs—not just sometimes, but for the rest of your life. If nothing else, they want you to make them look good."

"I'm pretty sure I come across as extremely responsible, but point taken."

"The other thing is, you have to look strong. Even if you don't feel it, you have to act it. Later on it's another story, but if you're too weak now they might be afraid you'll fail and not accept you. So let your strength come through; get into presentation mode and unleash your inner warrior queen."

I nod, feigning resignation, but am actually glad for the advice. Mason is proving to be a strong advocate and an excellent coach. It's a comforting realization.

The transplant clinic feels very different from yesterday's stark, sterile testing labs. The walls are covered with outsized photographs of spectacular natural landscapes: mountains, lakes, tree-lined rivers. If they're intended to soothe, it's working.

A nurse swaps out my tank as before . . . We still have plenty back at the hotel, but I'm happy to save those. When my name's called, I leave the wheelchair behind to show I don't need it, then roll the tank into the room as quickly and confidently as I'm able. I take a seat, with Mason next to me. In contrast to the waiting area, this room is so bright it feels decorated by Colgate, and the chairs are a green molded plastic that's torture for someone without natural padding. But for these meetings I'll sit still and upright, projecting glowing health. Sure, there's that minor issue of failing lungs, but other than that I'm robust as heck. The perfect soil for your precious orchid.

No one else is here yet, so I shift into premeeting focus mode. It's impossible not to feel stressed. At Empire, I came recommended; here, I'm an unknown quantity. I remind myself that I've had difficult interviews before and I can handle this. *Except*, says the inner voice, *those other times you handled it by remembering it wasn't life-or-death.* I tell it to shut up. Be positive, confident. Most of all, be strong.

The doctor enters, white-lab-coated, folder in hand. She introduces herself as Dr. Stanton and sits in the much more comfortable-looking gray executive chair behind the computer. She's younger than I expected and almost glamorously blonde. Pulmonologist Barbie, in the flesh. I put on the most pleasant face currently accessible to me and wait.

"I have your chart here, and the results of your Empire General tests," she says, looking at the folder rather than at me. "We also have some of the results back from yesterday, which should help give us a clearer picture." She reads for a while, flips some pages, then places the folder on the desk. For the first time she looks at Mason, then back at me.

"So, you're from Manhattan. And a consultant." Something in the way she says this strikes me oddly. Is it Manhattanites she doesn't like, or consultants?

"Long hours at your desk, I'll bet."

Ah, sedentary lifestyle. "But I exercise and have done a lot of cardio therapy already."

"Good. Get on the examination table, please. Use the step."

She does the usual, listening to the crackling in my lungs—audible now even without a stethoscope—and checking the various orifices.

"Everything as expected. I'll look over your test results tomorrow and let you know if there are any others that need to be run. There is one more thing to discuss, and that's your antibody profile. I assume you understand the implications already, but I have to bring it up."

My *antibody* profile? I vaguely remember this being mentioned, but at the time too much was being thrown at me to grasp it all. "No, I'm sorry. I don't know anything about it."

"Oh." From her expression, she's not at all happy at having to explain the significance of my antibody count . . . or dealing with the many questions likely to follow.

"Well, as part of your blood workup we check whether you have significant levels of antibodies to different tissue types. You can't receive an organ whose tissues you have high levels of antibodies against; your body would fight the new organ and likely reject it. So we'd only perform a transplant with an organ that doesn't hit your antigen markers. Unfortunately your particular combination rules out a lot of potential organs. Around eighty-five percent."

I'm acutely aware of the doctor's pale pink lipstick as her mouth forms the words *eighty-five percent.* Wait—*85 percent?* My throat starts to close over; surely that's not right. My body's a match with only *15 percent* of the already-small pool I thought I had five minutes ago?

Dr. Stanton keeps talking, but my brain's occupied with wondering how firm that 85 percent is and trying to calculate my new expected wait time to transplant. I attempt a rough scale-up from Regent's average wait time and come out with about two hundred days. *Over six months! Do I have that long?* For a moment I consider turning around and heading straight back to New York . . . until I realize the antibody problem will affect my wait time there too. Empire's *average* time is almost six months; with this twist, I'd never make it.

She rises and shakes my hand before leaving.

Mason is leaning forward, staring at me. "Are you okay?" he asks. It reaches my ears as though through water. "Fi?

Fiona, please snap out of it." I force myself to stop and look at him. His cheeks are flushed.

"Look, that was a huge shock, but the surgeon will be here any moment, and he's the most important person in this whole process. You can deal with the antibody information later. Right now the *only* thing you can focus on is acing the next twenty minutes."

On automatic pilot, I get up to move around a little, but my foot catches on the trailing oxygen tube and I almost fall. Luckily, that gives me the adrenaline I need.

The surgeon walks in, looking exactly as scripted. Same crisp lab coat, tall, male, confident, dirty-blond hair, and good-looking to boot. Probably a varsity athlete and a big deal in his fraternity. He shakes my hand and Mason's, then sits in the boss's chair. I try not to squirm as my tailbone hits the back of mine.

"So you're a New York consultant." Again it feels like a criticism. "Let me tell you about the surgical procedure for a lung transplant."

Mason seems to know all about it already, but I'm fuzzy on the details . . . by design. I didn't want to visualize the surgery or the aftermath until it was too late to turn back.

When he's finished the recitation, the doctor turns fully to me. "You know this is a very difficult surgery to recover from, right? For it to work, you'll have to be as fit as possible going in and be prepared to push yourself hard afterwards. You may not have been an athlete in the past, but you'll need to become one, because the new lungs need exercise to inflate properly and stay functioning. That's why you have to complete the one-month physical rehab course first. If you can't meet the requirements, you'll be dropped from the program."

His eyes are an arctic blue, and I'm feeling judged as I haven't been since middle school.

"If we accept you, the next period of your life—especially the weeks after surgery—are going to suck. This is an endurance test, and the hard part doesn't even start until after the operation. So you need to be prepared and be tough. We have a saying that we took from the Navy SEALs: 'Embrace the suck.' That's our motto."

What? Suddenly I'm doubting everything about this process. I am definitely not an "embrace the suck" person. I know people who are, who prefer biking uphill to down, and whose workout only counts if most of their body aches afterwards. That's not me. In fact, that kind of pleasure makes me question their psychological makeup.

A nurse opens the door a crack and says, "Dr. Souther needs to talk."

He moves to the door. "Excuse me a moment."

This buys me time to get myself together, but all I can think of is how many push-ups he does at bedtime, and whether he does Ironmans or just marathons. And suddenly I'm angry. Who ordained that only one kind of person has the right to live? Some part of me knows this is unreasonable—he's just taking steps so the lungs aren't wasted on someone who won't survive the process—but I don't care. This motto business is ridiculous. I'll never be an elite soldier, but that doesn't mean I can't be tough. I won't embrace the suck, but I can *endure* the suck. I can and will persevere *despite* the suck. I deserve a chance at life and will fight for that chance.

By the time he's back in his seat, my game face is on.

"Don't worry about me being tough," I tell him. "I've faced difficult situations before, and I've never yet failed to come through."

His shift in body posture tells me he wasn't expecting the steel in my tone. He nods briefly, rises, and shakes my hand.

After the door closes, I turn to Mason. "That's the angriest I've ever gotten at any doctor in my life. He can stuff his motto, because I'm making my own. Mine is *beat* the suck. Being an educated woman from New York doesn't make me a wuss. Bring it."

Wordlessly, Mason hands me his phone. He's opened Urban Dictionary to "embrace the suck." *To consciously accept or appreciate something that is extremely unpleasant but unavoidable for forward progress.*

I calm down a little, and he retrieves the phone.

"Presumably we were supposed to know what that means from our Special Forces fanboy days. You're fine, Fi; don't get rattled. Just accept that it's going to be bad and move through it."

The final appointment is with the psychiatrist. It's clear now that they want to assess my mental toughness. They'll probably offer me support . . . maybe even medication if needed. Both Mason and I are ushered into the doctor's office, a cozy room with comfy furniture (*thank you!*) and a view of trees. The psychiatrist is in his early thirties, clean-cut, with trendy glasses, a casual jacket, and khakis. He looks kind and understanding; you could open up to a man like this.

He asks how the testing went and what my symptoms are, and he smiles at Mason. We chat for a bit, then he says, "This is a lot of pressure you're under. How are you holding up?"

My upbringing was, more or less, don't complain; no one likes a whiner. So my initial reaction is to say that I'm fine. But then I realize, this man's a medical professional and he wants to know how I'm *actually* doing. That's much more complicated. It's not just the fear of dying and the loss of my career; my whole identity has changed in the past year.

I'm about to say this when Mason takes my hand and squeezes it. It looks like a reassuring gesture, but the pressure's too hard, and while his mouth is smiling, his eyes carry a warning.

So instead I say, "Surprisingly well. I keep waiting to get depressed or fall apart, but it hasn't happened. Obviously I'm not happy about the situation, but I figure it's just another problem that I need to fix—and I hear you guys are good at fixing it."

"You're not on any antidepressant medication?"

"No. Never have been."

He sits back. "Good, because you can't be on them if you're in the program. We would have to wean you off and see how you do."

Though my poker face remains intact, I'm shocked. If someone needs meds, having to come *off* them now would be grim.

"Not an issue for me," I reply, putting on my optimist hat and hoping he won't see the holes in it. "For whatever reason, I'm not worried. This is going to work."

"Glad to hear it," he says, smiling; the student gave the correct answer. "Tell me, other than a general wish not to die so young, what specific reasons do you have for wanting to stay alive? What's keeping you here?"

I blink rapidly a few times. I'd never anticipated this question, and it requires a powerful answer. I'm applying for a rare prize, after all; I need to be worth his support. What specifically *am* I fighting for? It's dizzying to realize I have no ready response.

To his credit, he tries to help me out. "For example, are there any great events you're looking forward to attending, or a hobby or group that gives your life meaning?"

"Oh," I reply, thinking fast. It's unlikely that "getting back to my job" is what he's looking for. It comes to me suddenly that it's not what *I'm* looking for either.

"Of course," I say, making it up as I go along but sensing that it's true. "I've put off a lot of things for most of my adult life . . . chasing my career, mostly, because there'd always be time later for everything else. It took getting sick for me to realize how much I've missed." Specifics start to come to me. "I've always dreamed of going to the Olympics, actually *being* there and feeling the buzz. My college friends have a reunion trip every few years that I haven't yet made it to. And I want to learn to paint, even if I'm terrible at it."

Talking this much is hard, especially because it's emotional. I take some deeps breaths, signaling for more time, and then continue more slowly, pausing between phrases.

"Mostly, I want to stop building for the future and just *live*. And beyond that, to do something meaningful with the skills I've developed over the past twenty years. Once I'm better, my plan is to offer volunteer help to organizations that make a positive difference in people's lives."

Now I'm done. Have I just done something incredibly stupid? None of these things are concrete or proven—they're just dreams. Perhaps I should have invented a sister's wedding that I'm maid of honor for, or a half-written symphony I'm desperate to complete. But I've never been much good at presenting things that aren't true. With me it's pretty much what you see is what you get. Let's hope that what he saw is what he's looking for.

He nods thoughtfully, his expression unreadable. "Well, I wish you success. Thanks for coming in and good luck with the process."

As we leave the room, the impact of everything I've just said fully hits me. Apparently, the career I've been working at for two decades isn't especially important to me. Once, perhaps, but not now. On the other hand, making a difference and fulfilling my dreams seems crucial.

At the elevator bank, Mason leans against the wall and studies me contemplatively.

"That was quite a speech. Were you serious about volunteer consulting?"

"I think so. There are other women I know who aren't finding their work rewarding anymore. Maybe we could collaborate and use our knowledge to do good. Beyond the selfish bucket list things, I'd like to do something meaningful before I die."

"Wouldn't we all," he mutters.

"Was it the wrong thing to say? Did I just kill the deal?"

"No. You sounded passionate and sincere. It's better to be yourself, especially now; having a fake persona takes too much energy, and we're already pretending enough. Be yourself." He stands straighter and looks right at me. "Semper Fi." He pronounces it like my name. Always Fi.

Chapter 8

Now we have to wait. This next period will be a combination of high anxiety and stay of execution. I'm not sure whether it's better for the time to speed by so I can know the outcome or creep slowly so I can retain hope.

Mason thinks it will be easier to be doing something, so on our way back he takes me to an art supply store to begin one of my wish-list projects. He took some painting classes in high school, so he'll guide me. We emerge with a beginner's set of acrylics (I'd wanted oils, but apparently acrylics have less fumes and dry faster), a selection of paint boards and a pad, and some other supplies that I don't know the use of yet.

After lunch and a nap, we find a tucked-away outdoor table at the Davide and unpack our loot. I want to launch right in with painting, but Mason talks me through some basics, hands me a pencil, and pulls up a picture of a pear on his phone for me to copy.

After half an hour I'm totally frustrated. My very best pear looks like a fluffed-up beanbag . . . or a rear view of the person sitting on it. "This is absolute shit," I snap. "How come I can't even make a pencil sketch I don't loathe? I couldn't be any worse with a paintbrush."

Mason finds this hilarious. "Normally people start with weeks of drawing, learning how to compose a picture, create shape and depth, and so on. But *since*," he reminds me pointedly, "you're just doing it for the experience—for the *joy*—maybe don't trample that joy by imposing an unrealistic and unnecessary need for perfection."

I grump but accept his point . . . though it isn't easy. Maybe the doctors can transplant my personality while they're at it.

After another hour and some guidance, I have sketches with shading of a pear, an apple, and a banana. It's time for dinner and bed, and we've successfully occupied the first day.

The following day the sky is clear and warm enough for extended time outdoors. Mason rolls me to the hotel garden and parks the wheelchair in front of a flower bed in bloom, bordering a lawn. My extensive botanical knowledge tells me they're big orange somethings, with a small border of little frilly blue something-elses in front. He sets the easel at an angle so I can see both it and the flower bed, then pulls over a lawn chair and side table. I'd never realized the sheer quantity of things required for painting.

"Okay," he says. "What do you want to paint?"

"The flowers, obviously." Maybe that was a little snarkier than necessary; I'm still bothered by yesterday's failure.

"Which ones?" he asks calmly. "The whole bed? A section? Or maybe just one . . . your favorite one. Which is that? And do you want to include the dirt border, or even the grass behind it? How much sky should there be?"

In thirty seconds I've gone from irritated to blitzed.

"How on earth would I know?" I ask him.

"Because it's your art. You get to decide how it looks, what you want to focus on. It's not hard and it's not a big deal, because if you don't like how it comes out you just make another one." He looks at me with an encouraging expression. "Try it. No risk."

But I've no idea how to start and am reluctant to admit that I don't care how much dirt is in the picture—I just want the flowers to look like flowers.

Mason is annoyingly patient, but then he intervenes. "Here, give me the brush."

He lays down a watery streak of blue along the top of the board. Rapidly he squirts an array of colors onto the palette, mixes some together with some medium, and slaps down a psychedelic splash of spiky orange blooms—I assume they're meant to be blooms—two-thirds of the way up. He rinses the brush and adds a blue-violet smunch of little frilly things in the front. Rinses again and slides green (stalks and leaves?) below the blooms, finishing up with a long smear of brown on the bottom. Then he steps back and looks at me.

"What do you think?"

I'm at a loss. It's *awful.* This "painting" looks nothing like the flower bed. Although he does seem to have captured the colors quite accurately. "Um . . ." I begin, not knowing what's in the rest of the sentence.

"You hate it, don't you?" To my relief, he doesn't seem too upset. "Can you do better?"

Hell yes, I think. At least, I sure hope so.

He tapes his painting on the side of the easel and gestures for me to begin. I start sketching out, very faintly, the section of flower bed I like, realizing partway through that I'm using his version as a guide for proportion, flower direction, and so on. I like the colors he's made, and there's plenty of mixed paint left on the palette, so I just use it. Mason settles on the lawn chair, pulls out a ratty-looking book, and leaves me to my business.

An hour or so later I have only a rough version of what I'd wanted, but it doesn't suck so much for a newbie, and I'm actually quite pleased. I swish my brushes loudly against the water jar, see Mason grinning at me, and realize I've been played.

"You're a lot better painter than that, aren't you?" I say, tilting my chin at his original.

"Maybe," he replies. "Okay, yes. But so what? I've done this a lot more than you have. I'm sure I was terrible in the beginning."

"Were you really?" I ask, wanting to be mad but starting to laugh.

"Who cares? Aren't you happy with your painting, and wasn't it fun?"

I consider. "Yes. Objectively it's not good, but in a bizarre way I'm kind of proud of it. It's mine and I like it, for all its flaws."

He's pleased with that. "That's the nature of creating. Once you've poured some of yourself into something, you form a connection with it. The more you invest the more you care and can accept it for what it is. If God loves humans, I'm sure that's why."

"Make a good one," I tell him suddenly. "Paint something as you would really do it."

He doesn't want to. "Why? There's no point, and I'm hungry."

"Go on: I want to see what a real Mason Wolfwood looks like. I promise not to be intimidated. Take half an hour, do whatever you can in that time, then we'll eat."

He hesitates, looks at the flower bed again, then decides. He shifts the easel angle right. Rips off the palette paper and remixes the colors, the same as before but kicked up in intensity. Lays down some sky with a very diluted touch of blue in white, using a broad brush, not bothering to cover the whole canvas. Adds a swath of dirt and a base of spiky grass. Rinses the brush and waits. Then with just a few strokes, he creates the shape of one of the flowers—just one, enormous, silhouetted against the sky. He's focused completely on the painting now, adding a second, smaller flower and a smattering of blue blossoms peeking out along the bottom.

I watch, fascinated, from my chair a few feet to his right, watching the play of concentration on his face in profile as he works; the riffling of the dark, fine hair against his collar in the breeze; the close-trimmed beard; and the focus in his dark eyes conveying the sense of painter.

After a while he gets up, steps back about six feet, and looks, then returns and shifts the easel so the painting is out of my line of sight. Switches to a smaller brush and resumes. Ten minutes later he declares himself done and wheels me across to see it. By now I've already guessed he might be quite good, so the fact that it's stunning isn't what strikes me.

The painting is angled from just below the main blossom—the view of a worm or a cricket on the grass. From this perspective the sky is a million miles away, a soaring expanse of blue-white. The two blossoms fill the air with color, and we . . . humans, caterpillars, beetles . . . are tiny afterthoughts, insignificant in the grand scheme of things. The thought hits me that I've learned this truth recently about my own insignificance. This painting is nothing I would ever, in my literal way of seeing things, have even contemplated. But it's so much better than any accurate representation. This makes me want to shrink to beetle size, step into the shade of those flowers, and relinquish all my adult human worries to the skies.

"I like the first one better," I say, and he laughs.

"But I brought it in in under thirty minutes, so you owe me lunch," he retorts, packing up the supplies.

The next day I wake feeling optimistic. When we leave the hotel I notice, for the first time in my life, that trees aren't "light" or "dark" green, but a whole range of colors and textures. And there's a long wispy cloud trailing lightly across the sky that an artist would have real fun with. I'm pondering my heightened perception—this is the first hobby that has actually taught me something useful—when the smell of baking bread wipes out everything else. We head into the bakery, buy croissants, and sit outside on a bench to eat.

Today, maybe even now, the transplant team is meeting to discuss the patients evaluated this week. To decide our fate. *Please*, I find myself saying to the blue that changes marginally at the edges of the lone puff of cloud, *let me see more days like this. Let me have more time in this incredible world. I promise to appreciate it, to remember this moment. To be forever thankful.*

We're just leaving when my cell phone rings. Immediately my adrenaline spikes: It's the hospital's number.

"Is this Ms. Copeland?" A pleasant female voice. I say a quick prayer that she's about to tell me something good and miss the first few words.

". . . that the transplant team met and discussed your case this morning, and you have been accepted as a candidate into our lung transplant program. Congratulations."

The rest of the world hits pause as she continues. I turn away from Mason so he doesn't see my eyes well up.

"Do you need time to go back to New York and pack?" she continues.

I take a moment to get my voice under control (and sniff) before replying.

"No, we didn't want to waste time, so we brought everything we need with us, in hopes of being accepted. I'm ready."

"Great . . . we like optimism," she replies brightly. "The party responsible for the financial aspect needs to come in on Friday for about an hour. We'll go over the finances, have you sign some documents, and confirm your insurance. On Monday morning at eight a.m. there's an orientation session in our conference room, to go over transplant issues in more detail. Bring your caregiver and expect to be there around two hours.

"I must remind you that being in the program is not the same as being on the transplant list. First you'll do a month of cardio-pulmonary rehab, which we call boot camp, and attend all thirty transplant lectures. You'll have to maintain a weight level within the required range; we have dieticians who can help if you need to lose or gain weight. Your rehab sessions will start at nine a.m. on Tuesday at our center on Hill Street. Wear something comfortable that you can exercise in, and bring music if you like to listen while you work out. Do you have any questions?"

"No." I have nothing; she lost me at "accepted."

"I've put everything in an email, going out to you now. Welcome to Regent transplant."

I thank her, hang up, and turn. Mason takes one look at me and lets out a whoop. So much for my poker face.

I'm in. My face is tingling. Step One, the crucial admission into the race, is a go. The extent of my body's release tells me just how scared I've been. Which I *should* have been;

many times more people are rejected from these programs than accepted. Underlying health problems, psychological concerns—if it's something that jeopardizes the patient's ability to survive the process, the doctors won't risk it. I've no way of knowing if I was a clear "yes" or borderline, but all that matters is I'm in.

"Of course, it's only the very first piece," I begin, but Mason isn't having it.

"Stop!" He grasps my shoulders. "This is great news . . . a thousand miles, first step and all that. This is probably at least fifty of the hardest miles. It's cause for celebration."

I exhale deeply and smile. "I know. Let me call Dane and Rina."

Rina is one of my closest college friends. She's taken on the role of point person, updating people on my situation via the CaringBridge website and Facebook. I love my friends, but having to field all those anxious calls is more stress than I want—and certainly not what Mason needs. Plus, it gives Rina and me a reason to talk at least once a week.

"I'm in at Regent," I say, hearing the smile in my voice.

"*Hooray!* You just doubled your chances, kiddo. I'm so excited! I'll post that right away, but let me know when you have an address. Someone might want to send you something."

I laugh. "Don't need anything but lungs, but I will."

The call with Dane is brief. He just whispers, "Thank God. Go get 'em, honey."

Mason, looking pleased, asks, "Shall we check out boot camp? Since you're starting next week, maybe you should get a feel for the place beforehand."

He's right. Already my mind is jumping ahead to what boot camp is like and how I'll do there. Scoping it out will make me calmer.

It takes less than fifteen minutes to get to any of the hospital buildings from the park and hotel area. Regent's pulmonary rehab occupies the whole ground floor of a two-story building in a small commercial strip mall. Starbucks, a couple of restaurants, and a UPS store round out the block. Showing up in a wheelchair seems like a bad idea, so we drop the tank into its roller and walk in. The grandmotherly receptionist is kind and reassuring; she says it's fine to look around as long as I don't disturb anyone's workout.

The main space is large, high-ceilinged, painted light gray, and filled with an array of modern exercise equipment. It could be a high school gymnasium except that all the participants are pushing around oxygen tanks and in various stages of age and poor health. Pumped-in air keeps the room fresh, but even without the smell of sweat it feels like a real gym, with trainers and patients intent on their workouts.

On the right side is a small room containing oxygen tanks and walkers with attached baskets for the tanks to sit in. Patients are wearing cannulas long enough to reach the exercise equipment from the walker. Further along are restrooms, file cabinets, and a row of chairs, while directly ahead are two rows of exercise bikes, both upright and reclining. To the left is a collection of weight machines, weights, resistance bands, and other muscle-strengthening equipment.

At the front is an open space with chairs set out in a circle. It could be a group psychotherapy session, except for the mats on the floor in front of the chairs and the surreal vision of a circle of people lying on their backs doing leg lifts and bench-pressing hand weights while tethered to oxygen tanks.

Around the perimeter is an oval walking track, where people are walking laps, many wearing in-ear headphones.

It's clear that this is the kind of serious gym I've belonged to only for brief periods in my life. I've never liked that scene: too much adrenaline, sweat, and competitiveness—even if only with yourself. Being outdoors at my own pace always felt better.

One way or another, though, I'm going to have to get used to this. The prize at the end of the odyssey is that I'll be in much better shape, and the surgery and recovery will go much smoother. That's the plan . . . and I'm good at following plans. Besides, if Dr. SEAL accepted me into the program, even *he* thinks I can do it. Starting Tuesday I will learn to beat the suck.

Part II

New Yorker Looking to Transplant

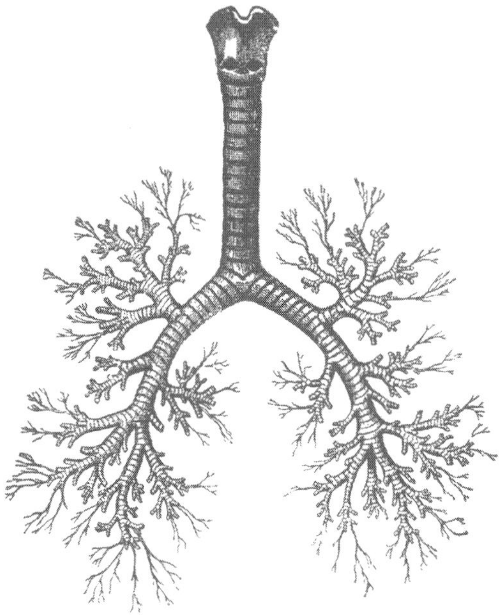

Chapter 9

March

On Friday Mason and I go to the financial office to do paperwork. The gist of the documents is that I acknowledge there are many costs associated with undergoing a transplant and agree to accept ultimate responsibility for all of them. I force myself to read as much as possible, but it's hard to focus and pointless anyway. What choice do I have? It's scary, though. The cost of a transplant and maintenance can run to over a million dollars. What if my insurance company goes out of business? What if I need additional care or tests that aren't covered? And what if my policy stops covering medications after a couple of years? After twenty years of work, I have savings set aside, but nothing on this scale.

It's a big relief when we're done: one more prerequisite checked off.

"Here's a crazy thought," Mason says. "What do you say we find somewhere to live?"

Somehow I'd forgotten this part of the process—my thought-horizon hadn't extended beyond being accepted.

"There's a list of short-term rentals in the neighborhood that I checked while you were signing documents. A couple of them look very close to rehab; let me make some calls."

I wait in the sun while he makes a call, then another, wandering away as he talks. I can't hear the conversation, but from the body language it's going well. He's saying goodbye as he returns, grinning the grin of the successful hunter.

"Okay. This one's a new apartment complex within half a mile of rehab. Lots of transplant patients live there because it's so close, and the minimum rental period is only three months, with monthly extensions. There's one ground-floor unit left, with a small patio. The manager says she'll hold it for us for an hour."

Of course she will, I think, *you're charming when you want to be. And she hasn't even met you yet.*

It's a five-minute drive. The complex is a series of three-story brick buildings, forming a large square and separated from each other by pathways. The center of the square is a large, grassy park, like a college quad, with a scattering of young trees dotted around. It's everything New York City isn't: spacious, peaceful, calming. Exactly what I need right now.

Mason ducks into the office and returns with the manager. The vacant unit has a reserved parking space directly outside and a small patio. The door opens into a living room/kitchen combination, kitchen on the right, living room to the left and stretching back. The left-hand wall has large windows overlooking the park and patio. All the floors are wood tile—which is important, because carpet fibers (and the things that live in them) are not friends to the lung-impaired. A corridor ahead leads to two bedrooms: medium-sized to the left, bathroom across the corridor; master suite dead ahead. The master bath even has a tub, perfect for soaking in after a long day of rehab. It's not palatial, but it's far better than I'd imagined we would find.

Our entire hunt has taken about half an hour. Can it really be this simple? It goes against the grain for me to pick a home with no comparison points, but I can't find anything wrong with this one.

"What do you think?" I ask Mason.

"Your call, but it looks fine to me." He's looking at the stretch of windows in the living room with longing; it's not hard to guess what he's thinking.

"You could set up a desk right underneath the window and do your writing there."

His face gleams. "Would you be okay with me cluttering up the living room?"

"Of course. If I get the bedroom with a tub, I'm happy."

I turn to the manager. "We'll take it."

I'm feeling completely energized now—we have a place to live! Not just that, but a nice one: two bedrooms, two baths, a lovely view and easy access to the car and the outdoors. And Mason will be protected from the loud industrial noise of my oxygen concentrator.

"Should we look for furnishings?" I ask him. "We can't move in until we have beds and a table and all that . . . Besides, I'm pumped now. Let's shop while I have the energy."

"Sure. There's a neighborhood with several restaurants nearby; we can make a shopping list while we eat. Let's go scope out our new favorite lunch spot."

We settle on an upscale burger place called Meat and Greet, where the aroma of the crispy fries grabs us from the street. I jot down items we'll need, underlining *comfy beds*.

List in hand, we drive to Courtly Rentals. It's the furthest we've been from the hospital, so we check out Johnson's River as we drive through. The town is a good size for us: Everything we need is within a half-hour drive, but still big enough for variety in food and activities . . . including a couple of museums. We might even enjoy it here.

The showroom is basically a huge warehouse. We take an order form and wander around to find what we want. Mason spots a modern-style couch with a wood frame, covered in white leather, and falls in love.

"Let's get this. It'll anchor the living room and match with everything."

"A *white couch*? Who in their right mind gets a white couch? I'll never dare use it."

"Come on. We wouldn't be the first people to spill on rented furniture, and besides, leather wipes down. Live a little."

Really? "Well then, can I get that funky blue chair by the entrance? With the dragon on it?"

"Absolutely. Seriously, don't get things to fit your bougie friends' taste. They aren't here, and their opinion doesn't matter anyway. Find things that make you happy."

From then on, this feels like a party. Shopping with Mason is utterly different from when Dane and I bought our furniture. Then, we took a holistic view, considering the whole room and how the parts would mesh. Dane had a strong leaning toward classic style and "good taste." Mason's philosophy is that if you buy things you love, then the whole will work. Especially if there's a big white couch in the middle.

In about an hour we've picked everything we need, including a full kitchen setup and TV. Amazingly, they have next-day delivery, so by tomorrow evening we will have a home. I'm excited in a way I haven't been for years. This is conjuring a sense of new beginnings—the way I felt shopping for college, setting off into something totally new and only half understood. Change can be good.

Chapter 10

On Saturday morning we load the car, check out of the Davide, and head to the apartment. I'm excited to be moving, even more so when we see the furniture truck. It takes shockingly little time for everything to be put in place. Granted, we have relatively little to move, but even so, it shifts my perspective. Pared down as this place is, it has everything we need . . . just much less of it. If I make it through this, I promise to do a giant purge at home. All those clothes, gadgets, and mementos I don't need can get tossed. Even thinking about it makes me feel lighter.

By the time we've finished unpacking the kitchen, the cable guy has come and gone, leaving us with TV, high-speed Wi-Fi, and a landline, because once I'm on the transplant list the hospital could call at any time with potential lungs. I can't afford the risk that cell service is poor or the electricity cuts out.

Mason assembles his new desk—a compact wood-and-glass piece with side shelves for his printer and supplies—and positions it directly under the window, looking out onto the quad.

He smiles at me happily. "Did you see the birds?"

I look again, and after a moment a bird flies into the small tree twenty feet ahead of us, pauses for a bit, then flies off again. Something occurs to me, and I look closer. Another bird is on the same branch, with something in its mouth.

"Are they building a nest?" I ask in amazement.

"Looks that way. They've been flying back and forth since we arrived. Great symbolism, yes? I can write, and you can work on healing, while the birds create new life outside the window."

My next breath feels deeper. I suddenly remember and retreat to the bedroom to fetch my glass hummingbird, which I perch on the top shelf of Mason's desk unit, facing out.

"Almost there," he says. "Now that this place is functional, we need to personalize it."

"What do you call this quirky furniture and my hummingbird?"

"We should get some of your photos printed up and framed, and some wall decorations that you find beautiful. Maybe even inspirational."

I roll my eyes. "Like what—leaping dolphins, saying I can leap high if I really try?"

"If you get anything like that, I'll make you recite the slogan every day before boot camp."

He sounds serious, so I consider his suggestion and realize it's valid.

"You're right, bare walls won't feel nurturing. I have a nice framed photo of Dane, and dozens of pictures on my phone of me with friends and on trips."

"Okay, pick a few special ones and put them on a memory stick. What are you most looking forward to doing once you're healthy? Something specific beyond simply not being dependent and sick. What images do you have in your head?"

I haven't thought about it quite this way, but there are many, many things I miss.

"Dancing with my friends to loud music, not worrying whether I look dumb, just moving. Kayaking, somewhere beautiful where the river is wide and calm, and you literally don't know what's around the next bend. Hiking up Bear Mountain in the autumn, looking down at the brilliant fall landscape that looks like Stephen Kincaid painted it."

Mason snorts. "You had me until 'Stephen Kincaid.' These are good. Anything less physical that you could do sooner?"

"Watch another Met Opera. Sing carols in Washington Square Park with a group of strangers. Browse the Christmas markets for gifts for the children's Santa drive . . ." Suddenly my throat clogs up.

"That's plenty," he says gently. "How about something aspirational? What if you could do anything you wanted?"

"I'd go to the Olympics. It's been my dream since I was a kid. But it's just that—a dream. No one actually sees the Olympics in person unless they're super well-connected or very rich."

"Who knows?" He shrugs. "The next one's not for two years. Is that too far-off to be inspiring now?"

I consider that and decide it's not. "No, I couldn't be in big crowds for a year after transplant anyway, because that first year is so risky. Two years would be enough time to make plans and put in ticket bids . . . but seriously, this is pure fiction."

"Fiction is my specialty. This is perfect: a concrete, realizable aim, with great visuals. We'll use the logo plus pictures of your favorite events and make a pastiche. So now that's your goal and your reward. You get through this, and in two years you'll go to the Olympics."

"Don't say that!" I'm surprisingly irked. "Tons of people try to get tickets, and hardly any of them succeed. Please don't promise things you can't deliver."

"First of all, I didn't promise," he replies, an angry edge to his voice. "Words are important to me, as you know. They have meaning—that's their purpose. A *person's* word should be even more meaningful, don't you think? If I promise something, that means I'm certain it's within my power to fulfill my word. That's different from *believing* something can happen. So here's the deal: You get better, and I believe I'll find a way to get tickets."

Strangely, something in me is responding to his suggestions. Focus on what could be mine if this transplant succeeds; fortify that with images I see every day. It's no less than a call to life—an insistence on keeping that desire for living right in front of me. Not only a reminder of good things in my past but an even more powerful call to *make new* good things. To imagine a future. Even at the edge of the precipice, to actively plan on passing through it to a new phase. And against all logic, when Mason says he'll find me tickets, somehow I believe him.

On Sunday evening a storm rolls in, bringing snow with it. I curl up on the couch under one of the new blankets and watch a detective show. Twenty minutes in, Mason joins me with hot cups of tea and lemon from his grocery run.

An announcement begins crawling across the bottom of the screen. Apparently the storm is expected to be bad enough that some schools are closing tomorrow. The crawl shows which children can sleep in on Monday morning and which parents will have to change their plans.

Having no kids, I've never paid much attention to school names, but rolling out in a list like this it's interesting how many are religious. Presumably they're private, since the public schools' announcement went out earlier. Some of the names seem pretty gory. Would I want to go to a school called Sacred Heart of Jesus? What would their mascot be?

"Hey, Mason. If you were naming a school, what would you call it?"

Immediately he replies, "Li'l Heathens Preschool."

I'm startled into a cough-laugh.

"Or Darwin Academy—fights at recess, survivors get A's."

"Camelot High," I add, scrambling. "No desks, just one big round table."

"School of Inquisition, where every day is torture."

I think hard. "Sherlock Holmes Elementary."

Mason puts on an evil face. "The College of Socratic Method. At year-end, the smartest kid has to drink a cup of hemlock . . . Well, just try not to be the valedictorian."

Eventually I'm laughing so hard it turns into a major coughing fit. He jumps up and increases my oxygen flow until I catch my breath.

"Sorry," he says. "That was dumb."

"Don't be sorry," I reassure him. "It feels so good to laugh again."

Chapter 11

Early Monday morning we join a dozen others in a windowless conference room on the first floor of the hospital. I spent much of my working life in rooms like this: at long tables with folders before each seat, with nubby-cushioned charcoal chairs and matching carpet, a whiteboard and screen at the far end, and a series of coffee pots that reek of breakfast meeting blend.

We arrive in matched pairs, one of each couple pulling an oxygen tank and wearing a tube in their nose, the other carrying a bag or briefcase. As if we're heading into the ark, looking for salvation from the impending flood.

As we wait, we subtly look one another over. The patients are a mixed bag of ages, races, genders, clothing styles. I don't know what the others are thinking, but I'm trying to assess their physical strength and mental toughness—not out of competition, but to gauge whether I'm in the ballpark. I'm reassured that some seem slower and frailer than me.

Right at eight o'clock a young woman with a confident stride and short brown hair walks in wearing scrubs.

"Hello, everyone. My name is Erin; I'm a transplant nurse here at Regent, and I'll be walking you through the process. Everyone should have a folder in front of them that contains all the information you need, so there's no need to take notes unless that helps you. Pens are right there." She has the perfect tone for this: direct and clear, but welcoming.

"Some of you have been wondering why we require you to stay close to the hospital at all times when other hospitals don't," she begins. "It's because an unusually high percentage of our patients aren't from around here. They come because Regent has the fastest average time to transplant in the country, and excellent posttransplant survival rates. Part of how we do that is by making sure our patients are in strong physical shape ahead of time and guarantee to be at hand when we receive lungs. Many of you might be tempted to sneak home for a special event or to see your families. If you do that, you need to let us know ahead of time, and understand that you forfeit your chance for any lungs that become available while you're away."

She does a slow scan of the room. Everyone is paying close attention. Someone coughs, maybe deciding not to leave campus after all.

"For obvious reasons," she continues, "we have a no-smoking policy. As of now, you cannot smoke, ever again. Anyone you live with must also sign a document stating they are and will remain smoke-free. Secondhand smoke is no joke for anyone's lungs, and you won't be allocated new lungs if you plan to damage them."

Two seats over from me, an older woman with a cannula casts pleading eyes at the young man next to her—likely her son, from the strong resemblance. He flushes crimson.

"Caregivers. You've read this in the early documents, but I'll repeat it. All caregivers must sign a contract saying that they will have *no other commitments* than the patient for the duration of their involvement in the program. No jobs, no children, or any others to take care of. The caregiver will stay with the patient until they are released to go home, however long that takes. This is a very serious commitment. Obviously there may be unexpected circumstances that make it impossible for the original caregiver to continue, so we need the name of a backup. Both those people *must* be relatives or close friends. This is an extremely tough job, and there needs to be a strong personal reason to stick it out. Occasionally there are caregivers, even spouses, who abandon the patient. So think hard now, because after today all of that must be behind you."

I'm trying hard not to look at Mason, but he reaches under the table and gently squeezes my knee. The middle-aged woman on my other side leans over and whispers, "Happened to my friend. She got cancer and her husband left her." My heart sinks.

Erin looks at each of the cannula-wearers. "Patients have obligations too, of course. One month, or as long as it takes, in our pretransplant rehab. Another month of rehab after transplant. You commit to remaining close to the hospital until the doctors have released you to go home. You further commit to doing whatever tests the doctors require and returning to Regent for checkups for the *rest of your life.* How often will depend on how well you're doing, but it's usually monthly to begin with, then every three months, then longer as time goes on."

As the information piles on, I'm increasingly glad of our info packet relieving me of the instinct to take notes. Mason scribbles periodically.

"After transplant you'll be on a restricted diet for three months: only cooked food, including fruits and vegetables. This is to minimize ingestion of bacteria, because your bodies will be weak and immune-suppressed, and unable to fight foodborne disease.

"Permanent restrictions. You'll never be able to eat raw or undercooked animal protein again. If you're a fan of sushi, ceviche, or rare red meat, you should eat it now. Also no grapefruit or pomegranate. And posttransplant, you are not to drink alcohol again. *Ever.*"

There's a collective murmur around the table. I'm guessing that for some people this will be the biggest hardship. It's less so for me: The coughing fits have largely weaned me off alcohol. But I will definitely miss the *ability* to drink. A salty margarita over a good Mexican meal with friends. Champagne for special occasions. Warm brandy on a cold night, or a fresh mint julep in the summer.

"I'll repeat," Erin says. "No more alcohol, sorry. It interferes with the effectiveness of your medication."

Mason slides over a note: *Probably interferes with people remembering to take their meds in the first place.*

"Pets. Hands up, who has cats? Dogs? Rabbits or other furry things? Birds? We all understand that pets are part of the family and it might be difficult to part with them, but furry pets can harbor allergens that could affect your ability to breathe even after transplant. Birds are a complete no-no because feathers are associated with some types of pulmonary fibrosis. And if you can find your pet a loving home, we encourage that."

"But I could never part with my cat!" says a plaid-suited woman indignantly. "She's my closest companion!"

The rumpled man sitting with her seems neither surprised nor bothered by this. "Well, I own a bird," he rasps. "What am I supposed to do with it?"

A wit at the other end of the room replies, "Feed it to the cat." Everyone laughs.

It's a much-needed release of tension. Mostly we are taut and focused. Relieved and excited to have come this far, but beginning to actually come to grips with how much our lives will change from now on.

"Okay, that's it," Erin says. "In the back of your folder are a couple of forms for you to fill out. Caregivers, please sign yours, then leave the room with me so the patients have privacy to make some decisions. Patients, take your time and come out when you're ready."

I'm puzzled and pull out the forms curiously. One form simply requires me to sign my commitment to abide by the rules of the program. So why the privacy? It becomes clear on the last form: a list of categories of donors whose lungs we can elect not to accept. Checking "No" in the first box means we won't be offered lungs from someone with a prior drug addiction. The next, someone who has served a prison sentence. The next, no lungs from someone who is gay. I sit up in astonishment and reread the notes: Yes, all lungs are checked for the presence of HIV and other STIs, and confirmed negative. This isn't about the donor transmitting disease, it's about such strong discomfort with certain groups of people that some patients would rather risk dying than live with those organs. Or maybe it's such extreme fear that no amount of testing could convince them the organs were safe.

I have goosebumps. If someone were generous enough to donate their organs—or worse, their loved one's organs—there's no way I'd say those organs are unacceptable because of who the donor was or something they did. I quickly fill out the form, saying yes to everything. Others remain, deliberating.

Now I just want to give Erin the forms and leave. But as I rise, I overhear a quiet conversation to my left.

"No, they tested him again, and there's still nicotine. Seems he can't quit."

"Or *won't* quit. So his wife's been turned away. Guess that's why they didn't show up."

My mouth turns dry. How would it feel if your spouse doomed you to death because of their cigarette habit? If Dane did that to me, would I leave him? The answer should be *of course*, but it's not that simple. It takes a lot to survive that kind of blow and keep fighting. And what if I didn't have the financial resources on my own? Or couldn't find another caregiver who fit the criteria—or was too sick and depressed even to look? Lately the world keeps throwing up disturbing questions. Unsettling things I've never had to consider before. I'm not sure I like these lessons.

Chapter 12

It's Tuesday and I don't want to go to boot camp. I want to return to Sunday, waking late to the smell of coffee and frying bacon, then shopping for fun and frivolous home goods. This room is totally mine now: Pictures of my friends are on the walls, and the Olympics display is the first thing I see each morning. Mason nudged me away from navy towels to coral and turquoise: insane but cheerful, like a beach house. He's promised to paint me a seaside sunset to go over the tub.

But lounging is no longer an option; it's time to kick my workout mojo into gear. I manage to get all my clothes on except the sneakers. That requires bending at the waist, which severely constricts my breathing. Mason has to tie the laces. It's yet another reminder of my dependence, but that doesn't grate as much as it used to. This is just the way things are.

He drives me to boot camp and again I feel like a small child, being dropped off for the first day of school. But "Grandma" at the front desk offers me candy, and the Mister Rogers look-alike at the oxygen tank station helps me put a fresh tank into the wheeler, and by the time I'm sitting with another newbie in front of the offices I'm more at ease. The room is busy with patients checking in and going about their exercise routines, but there's some friendly chatter too. The place doesn't feel as harsh as I'd expected.

A woman in a gray skirt with a lanyard around her neck hands us each a marked-up cardboard sheet attached to a clipboard. "Welcome to boot camp," she begins, sounding as though she's said this many, many times. "I'm Sheila, the head nurse."

I sit at attention.

"These are your personal charts, which you'll pick up from the filing cabinet each morning and return when you leave . . . in alphabetical order, please. Based on your height and general health we've given you starting levels for the exercises; we'll monitor your progress and make adjustments."

Suddenly I'm nervous. Please let them not have to adjust my estimates *down*.

"Every day you'll do a four-part circuit followed by a lecture. A strength and balance circuit, twenty minutes of stationary bike, twenty minutes of walking around the track, and group exercise class. The track times are monitored individually, so start in the far corner"—she points—"check in and wait for the trainer's signal. You'll get to pick a wrist bracelet with plastic beads on it—like a rosary, if you know what those are—and you click one bead forward each time you complete a lap. All exercises must be noted on your chart: every rep, weight, lap walked, everything. I review everyone's charts at the end of the week.

"Lectures are held in the glass conference room up front; each covers another aspect of transplant or posttransplant care. There are thirty lectures run in rotation, so by the time you leave you'll have seen them all, which is a requirement for listing. Caregivers are encouraged to attend. There's also a support group specifically for them, which I strongly recommend; they'll need a community too. Someone will help you at each location for the first week. Good luck."

I'm assigned to bike first. The therapist—most of them here are women—adjusts a reclining one for my size, speed, and resistance, and records the settings on my chart. The oxygen tank sits next to me in the walker, and she cranks the flow up two liters/second to allow for greater oxygen need. Too late, I remember about the headphones, but to my relief the exercise is no problem: I slip into a groove and zone out until the time is up.

Weight training is much more hands-on. There's a set list of exercises and reps for all the basic muscle groups, with a different therapist, smiling and friendly, watching this first time to make sure I'm doing them right. Some of these are surprisingly easy for me: I have decent arm strength. Others, like holding a squat against a wall for what seems like an entire episode of *The Kardashians*, are excruciating. On the plus side, maybe when I'm better I'll finally have skiers' thighs. Too bad I don't know how to ski.

The walking circuit comes next. An oval track has been marked on the wooden floor, looping around the exercise stations. Half a dozen patients are walking fairly fast around it, pushing their tank-laden wheelers ahead of them while two therapists monitor their times. Each walker is on their own time, but it still looks like a race, with faster patients overtaking the slower ones. This is the most stressful exercise, because by the end of the twenty minutes we must have completed at least twelve laps. Anyone who can't do that is deemed not fit enough for listing. I try to gauge their pace to see how I would compare, but a single figure stands out from the rest. A man with steel-gray shoulder-length hair is racing around the track. He looks so solid and invincible that, in my mind, I call him Mountain Man. In his basket, he is carrying not one but two oxygen tanks; evidently, it requires two tanks to complete his routine.

I head to the start of the track. Picking a peach-colored rosary in honor of my upcoming sunset painting, I set off at medium speed. Dr. SEAL's words provide good motivation. I manage sixteen laps in the allotted time, well above requirement, but already I know that as I get sicker this will become a scarier challenge to face every day.

Group class is led by a gruff male therapist who looks like a wrestling coach. I know that muscle strength and flexibility will be crucial post-surgery, but I barely have energy left, and lying on the floor doing resistance-band leg lifts reminds me of the old cartoon of aerobics classes in hell. Still, at least we're all suffering together.

We break for five minutes and the man next to me says, "Hi there." I'm startled. I've been so focused on today's tasks that I hadn't really registered the other moving objects in the room as people . . . more as things to be negotiated around. I say "hi" back just as class resumes.

Finally, the lecture. Today's is about potential complications following transplant. It's too soon for me to be hearing about the horrible things that might happen, so I try not to engage too closely until at last we're released. I collect my own tank and roller, file my chart, and leave.

On the way back I give Mason a brief rundown, then after a quick lunch head immediately to bed. Hygiene will have to wait for the time being; bathing is not a simple exercise these days and I'm out of juice. I lie on top of the sheets and am asleep in moments.

Chapter 13

This becomes my new pattern. Wake early, have breakfast, and go to boot camp. Return, have lunch, and go to sleep. Wake midafternoon and read an undemanding book. Have dinner, watch a low-gore detective show, shower, and go to bed. Lather, rinse, repeat, ad infinitum. My life is restricted to either exercising hard in an artificially lit room or recovering from that. The only respite comes on weekends, which I anticipate with weary longing.

By the end of the second week I know by face most of the other people in what I think of as my cohort: the twenty or so people who were here when I arrived or joined soon after. Many of us don't stop to chat, so I don't know everyone—or even their names—so I've started making up nicknames for people. We're a mixed bunch, that's for sure. Under normal circumstances, we would never have met, much less spent so much time together.

The man who joined the day I did is Joe, from New Jersey—which helps me remember: Jersey Joe. He's sixtyish and friends with everyone. Joe has no doubt that he'll quickly receive a perfect pair of lungs and return to his new grandson as though nothing had happened. Zuri, from Boston, looks about twenty but is actually a top environmental lawyer. She wears her sorority sweatshirt to boot camp, "Alpha Kappa Alpha" emblazoned across the front.

Drew, a pale man (despite being Floridian) in his thirties, looks focused and serious until he zaps you with his wicked humor. Drew has complications that mean he needs a kidney and two lungs all from the same donor; he'll likely be here a while. There's a Muslim woman who exercises in a full-length black robe and head covering, only the top half of her face showing. She never speaks except to her caregiver, who comes sometimes to interpret for the therapists, and wears heavy glasses under her face covering. Then Wanda, who was a missionary and has transferred her caring to the group of us here. She's well-loved and organizes weekly dinners for everyone here. Someday when I'm rested, I promise myself, I'll attend one.

I set off walking at a pace that should see me well past the minimum lap count. In the early days I would start out too fast—there's never been much sauntering in my life, and my body had trouble remembering its new speed. But I'm adjusting. I take a sneak peek to see how I compare with the other walkers.

Ahead of me are the three men here with cystic fibrosis. I think of them collectively as "The Youngsters," since they're all in their twenties and appear to be friends. They are the ones I feel for the most. They've spent much of their lives struggling to breathe through the gook that constantly floods their lungs; they cough a lot, especially when lying down for the floor work.

Recently I realized something surprising. There's no sense of competition here. This is a life-and-death situation with a limited supply of lungs; people die waiting for transplant all the time. It would be reasonable to view the other boot campers as potential competition for the lungs that might save us, but the reverse is true. Everyone is supportive of each other, wanting each of them to get the transplant call and succeed. It's as though every victory is collective, renewing the hope that one day it will be our name that's called.

It's time for group class. We start on our backs in a circle, feet toward the center, looking like a short-winded, landlocked team of synchronized swimmers.

To my left is the woman in the robe, which I think is a niqab. The only parts of her visible are her eyes and a strip of light chocolate skin between the hem and her shoes. The shoes fascinate me: pink sneakers, bright enough to colorize a black hole. They look expensive (not that I'd recognize high-fashion sneakers if they literally ran over me). The juxtaposition of those and the niqab is intriguing. Does she like being covered up, or resent it? Is there a secret stash of neon spandex in her closet? I dub her Kicks.

Today's presenter is a senior nurse from transplant ICU. She seems very earnest in her pale blue scrubs, like a Scout troop leader—except she's here to describe the first few days posttransplant. With some specific unpleasant examples, apparently.

"In many cases," she begins, "gas is trapped in the chest cavity during the surgery and can take several days to clear through the system. Like stomach gas, this can be very painful, but it's not likely to be damaging." . . . "You won't be allowed to eat or drink by mouth until you've passed a swallow test, which will be administered only after the medical team feels you are unlikely to aspirate the liquid."

Already my mouth feels dry. Someone asks whether we're allowed to have ice chips, and a deep growly voice behind me chuckles: a burly caregiver, in a red lumberjack shirt and big beard.

"I worked fixing commercial ice machines for fifteen years," he drawls, leaning back into his chair, grinning. "And I never eat ice unless I made it myself in ice trays in my own freezer. You can *not* imagine all the nasty things growing back there. Trust me, drink your soda warm."

Gross. How many millions of commercial ice cubes have I eaten in my life?

The list of tortures continues. "When you wake up you'll be groggy, in pain, and unable to move. Many people have hallucinations from the high initial doses of steroids. I've had patients tell me they feel fine, but why are there giraffes walking through the wards? Be prepared for a shock the first time you see yourself. You'll look like an octopus. There'll be tubes sticking out all over you: in your side to drain out fluids, in your neck to receive medications, and in your bladder to pee out of. As soon as possible, you'll need to get up and start moving around to get those lungs working, and you'll have to drag most of those tubes and poles with you."

She stops here and looks away from her notes, directly at us. "I want you all to visualize that now," she instructs, "so you can be prepared for it. You won't have much extra capacity to deal with shock when it happens, so close your eyes and visualize yourself in pain, with gas cramps, walking down the corridor wheeling an expanded IV rack with tubes hanging off it going into various parts of your body."

I do that and experience a moment of revulsion, followed by paralyzing fear. I hadn't considered the assault of so much bodily invasion. *Why is she doing this? She's making us afraid when we need to be brave.* Then I realize that's precisely the point. If we freak out just by imagining this, how will we react when it actually happens? The super-squeamish need to figure out how to cope . . . or pull out. With an effort, I get myself under control.

I check my watch. Ten to four; we're almost done.

"When your original lungs are removed," she continues, "lots of nerves are severed. The surgeon can reattach a few but can't do anything for most of them but wait and see if they grow back. Odd things can happen. Some patients can't tell that they have enough oxygen. I've seen patients gasping for air, convinced they couldn't breathe, while their oximeters were reading normal. One guy last week threw his oximeter clean across the room."

I'm getting dizzy. That would be my personal hell: still alive but feeling as if I were asphyxiating. How can humans exist like this? Why would they want to? I fight down panic and after the session ends, approach the nurse.

"It's not common," she says. "Or permanent. The body eventually figures it out."

Nevertheless as I leave I'm praying it doesn't happen to me. I'm feeling daunted. But when I reach the car, Mason is smiling, his eyes bright.

"I have something to show you when we get back."

He won't say what, but once we're home he leads me toward the window. We stop at his desk, a couple of feet from the glass.

"Don't move suddenly, but I think the first egg from the nest has hatched. I saw some motion out there while you were gone, and that looks like eggshell on the ground. Mama Bird is still there, nesting on the other two; probably they won't be far behind."

I hold as still as possible so as not to scare any of the birds, even though the tree isn't that close. We've been watching them every day since we moved in, tracking the finishing of the nest and Mama settling in for the duration. I can't actually see anything—the baby must be tiny—but simply knowing that something just got born right by my home fills me with incredible joy.

"I have the silliest feeling that we should congratulate them," I say.

"Yeah, me too, but I'm all out of cigars. Balloons maybe?"

Beneath the joke-cracking he has a sappy look on his face. Mason's soft side is coming out.

Chapter 14

April

It's just over three weeks since I started boot camp and I'm frantic with cabin fever. The first weekend I'd luxuriated in bed for an hour and a half, reveling in the bliss of not having to get up. My body and brain had been tired all week, so doing absolutely nothing felt wonderful. The second weekend was better, but I was still tired. By now things have shifted. My body is responding to the exercises, so breathing is somewhat easier. Now I'm craving doing something besides robotically following someone else's rigid protocol. Thinking about how many more weeks I might have of this makes me desperate to get outside and have some fun.

On Sunday I pull on stretch pants and wander to the living area. Mason isn't at the desk where he spends most of his free time, and his bedroom is empty. I draw a blank for a moment, wondering where he could be, then spot movement outside the window. He's on the tiny patio, wearing navy athletic shorts and a white T-shirt, doing squats and lunges with a weight in each hand. Because he's facing out at an angle toward the lawn, he can't see me, so I just watch for a bit. His form is perfect—it's like watching the therapists at rehab—and his arms and legs are tanned. He must spend time outside while I'm doing my own workout. He looks surprisingly powerful. Not big—he's a shade under average height for a man—but compact and efficiently put together.

He turns and sees me, then frees one hand to raise five fingers. I nod and move away. In a burst of energy, I think maybe for once I'll make *him* some breakfast.

The coffee has just finished brewing as he comes in.

"Hey," he says, cheerful and sweaty. "Were you there long? Sorry, I didn't see you. Give me a minute and I'll fix you breakfast."

"Coffee's already made," I reply, pouring it into the large "Angry Birds" mug we bought. There's a red Angry Bird on the front and a happy counterpart holding a steaming mug on the back. Mason can't function without coffee. I hand it over; he takes a gulp and sighs in pleasure.

"Thank God for good coffee. A little pampering every day for the price of a small machine. Let me enjoy this, then maybe omelets?"

"I thought I'd make *you* breakfast for once."

"That's a lovely offer, but not necessary: Coffee for an omelet sounds like a good trade."

I hesitate, so he adds, "You don't have to prove anything, Fi. You're working really hard, you're doing well, and no one's keeping score. Better you save your energy for something else. Unless you've suddenly discovered the joy of cooking. No? Then why don't you make yourself some coffee and I'll cook.

"How did you sleep?" he asks as he chops onions. "Restfully? Cheese in your omelet?"

"Um . . . fine thanks, very, and yes please." Without meaning to, I ask, "Would you be up for going somewhere today?"

He's surprised enough to drop the knife. "Sure. On the shelf behind you is a blue folder labeled 'Activities.' I picked things that appeal to me, assuming you'd be too tired, but if any strike your fancy we should do them together. It'll be good for you to get out of the apartment."

This feels strangely novel. Before I got sick, weekends were largely about running errands, getting some exercise, and squeezing in some fun before catching up on work ahead of Monday. Since I've been ill Dane's been too tired for fun, and here Mason does all the errands. In my current bubble, there *isn't* anything needing doing beyond workouts and waiting.

Inside the folder are flyers and printouts of upcoming art exhibits and shows.

"There's an afternoon concert today in the park," I tell Mason. "Looks like a Pops kind of deal. Is that too uncool for you? The weather's lovely and I'm dying to get outdoors."

He's surprised again. "I'd have thought that was too low-brow for *you*. It sounds great to me; I played trumpet in my high school band. I can relive my inglorious geek days."

We head out early. The concert is in a large park with a central trail that loops through areas of trees in blossom. There's a wide lawn where a family is picnicking and a group of teenagers are throwing Frisbees, wrapped up in youth and normalcy and spring. A stage has been erected in the middle of the lawn, a dozen long rows of fold-up chairs set in front of it. We find an empty seat on the edge of the sixth row. I kick free of my shoes and socks and feel the new grass on the soles of my feet, scrunching it between my toes with pleasure. Someone must have mowed it just today, because there are loose blades scattered everywhere, and the smell still lingers.

The band is a decent size. Lots of big brass, which I love; something about a tuba always makes me happy. My aunt used to comment on boys loving their "big yellow metal" and it was years until I realized she meant earthmoving equipment, not trombones. There's a spectrum of woodwinds, and best of all, a large percussion section, which always gets my blood pumping.

They play some classic marches, then switch to upbeat takes on popular songs. Mason looks happy and relaxed, his foot tapping occasionally to the beat. When the Isley Brothers' "Shout" starts up, people start dancing on the perimeter, fifty- and sixty-year-olds sinking on creaky knees to "a little bit softer now." They end with "The Stars and Stripes Forever," and I hum along to the piccolo part I know by heart, feeling young and carefree.

We roll back through a festive atmosphere of happy chatter, people picking up their wine and crackers and gathering their kids. For a few perfect hours, I became just an ordinary woman spending the afternoon in the park.

Chapter 15

It has been thirty days, and I'm finally graduating from boot camp. There's a whole ceremony involved: I'm handed a mortarboard and a certificate of completion, and my photo is taken as the trainers applaud. Cheesy as it seems, I appreciate the fuss and the acknowledgment of a milestone. I've made it through another stage. Only one person I know of hasn't progressed to this point: a local woman who's trying to lose enough weight to be eligible.

The most important and exciting part is that I'm now qualified to be put on the transplant list. There's still no telling how long it will take to find my lungs, but the preliminaries are over. The second-best part is that I can join the other graduates in the afternoon sessions. Most of the people I've become friendly with over the past weeks will be there.

But before that, I have graduation party goodies for everyone—not just the patients, but even more to thank the staff. They've worked hard to get us all into shape. Mason and I lay out coffee cake, cookies, and fruit, and tell everyone to help themselves. Right on the end of the table I place a giant box of lollipops, with a message in Sharpie: *Embrace the Suck*.

When we get back, Mason has an extra surprise. He leads me to the window and points. I'm not sure what he means until there's a movement just above the rim of the nest. I focus my eyes and suddenly realize I'm looking at the top of a tiny bird's head. I look again and detect a slight motion to the right of it. I stare in wonder. Mason's face reflects my own awe: Whole lives have been generated in the time we've been here. It feels somehow symbolic.

I want to share today's successes with Dane, so even though it's two o'clock his time, I call.

"Hi, honey," I say when he picks up. "I know it's work hours but today's been a good day. Do you have a minute?"

"About three, then I'm leading a conference. But I'd love to hear good news. What's up?"

"Today I graduated from boot camp, with a graduation ceremony and everything. That means my workouts will start at one p.m. instead of nine a.m. and be unsupervised. And I'll get home earlier, because I've completed all the lectures. On Monday I'm going to the clinic to update the tests that go into my lung allocation score—blood oxygen, PFT, six-minute walk—and then they'll list me. I'll be officially eligible for transplant!"

"That's wonderful. Congratulations. Don't try too hard at the tests, okay? You'll just end up further down the list. Okay, they're calling me to the conference room. Talk to you soon."

"You bet," I say, but he's gone.

Before I left we agreed to talk three times a week: Tuesday, Thursday, and "date night" Saturday, when we watch *Saturday Night Live* together on an open call and chat about it. It's a schedule Dane can work around and has kept us feeling connected—though in truth there's little new to talk about. But I'd hoped we could make an exception today. I didn't even get to tell him about the baby birds.

I call Bonnie, thinking she'll have time for me, but the call goes straight to voicemail. It's frustrating—I want to share my news. And then my cell rings: FaceTime from Yannis.

"Hi, sweetie. Can you chat?" He's perfectly groomed as ever, his dark hair curling above his ears, the maroon jacket a perfect fit. Yannis dresses better than any of my girlfriends.

"Definitely," I reply. Abruptly, I'm on the verge of tears. When did I get this fragile? "Your timing's perfect—how did you know?"

"It's always perfect." He smiles. "Actually your friend Mason called me."

I'm blank for a moment until I remember I gave Mason contact info for three friends: Yannis, Bonnie, and Rina.

I settle into my blue chair. "Two fun things happened today. One, there's a nest in front of our window, and today we got to see the babies: One poked his little fuzzy head out of the nest."

"Lovely! *The Circle of Life . . .*" he sings, holding up his arms. I laugh.

"And two, I'm now eligible to get on Regent's transplant list. I just have to take some tests to update my LAS score."

"Remind me what that is."

"Sorry. It's the number UNOS, the allocation agency, assigns to each patient to quantify how sick they are. Since donor lungs are allocated by urgency of need, a higher lung allocation score—LAS—puts you higher up the list. The patient with the highest LAS in the region who matches the lungs' profile will get offered those lungs first. Unless their body has too many antibodies to them, of course."

He frowns. "It's just so simplistic. What about the high antibodies you were telling me about? Shouldn't they bump you ahead, given that you can't accept every matching lung, even if you're not at the top of the list?"

I shrug. "What can we do? It'll take longer, but hopefully I'll get there eventually."

Yannis puffs out air. "Then good luck on those tests; you'd better not miss another of my birthday parties! I have to go, but please keep me updated. Or have Mason do it. And do you need a visitor?"

"Thanks for asking, but Dane's coming on Friday. I'm really excited to see him. I wanted to tell him about the baby birds, but he couldn't talk long."

"Sweetie, I don't think he would have been that excited, do you? Mr. Nature he's not. Let him take you out to a nice dinner, and some event—maybe a rodeo. Kidding . . . talk soon."

I'm smiling as we hang up, but beneath it I still wish Dane hadn't had to rush the call. Hearing that clear tenor (which speaks so beautifully but can't sing a lick) reminds me that I have another life than this. The fact is, I miss him. I'm often too tired by our evening calls to talk much, and video can't replace living human contact.

Mason comes over with a nutritional weight-gain drink. Usually those are for snacks, not lunch, but I'm currently too drained even to chew, so I pop open the can and stick in the straw. As always, it tastes like liquid chalk. Strawberry chalk or chocolate chalk, but chalk nonetheless. I draw a full breath and start to slurp.

Chapter 16

After rehab on Friday I speed through lunch, shower, and have a brief lie-down before my appointment at the hair salon. I'm getting it styled so I can look pretty for Dane's visit. After a month without him, I'm yearning to see him again—to be held, and kissed; to look into his eyes and know I'm loved. We'll have dinner, talk, maybe watch a movie . . . and I won't have to pretend anything, or worry about meeting any exercise targets. Two days of real life.

When my hair's fixed in a smooth, gentle wave, Mason nods approvingly.

"You look lovely. Dane will fall for you all over again."

As we return from the salon it strikes me belatedly that I never asked Mason if he was okay with being kicked out.

"Do you mind having to leave the apartment for a couple of days?"

"No, no," he laughs. "I'm totally good. As it happens I have plans of my own."

Now that he points it out, he *has* had an extra twinkle the past few days. I'd love to ask, but it isn't any of my business; presumably he'd have told me if he wanted to. *What is it, though?*

He grins. "I've rented a car and am staying at an inn about an hour away. I plan to have a wonderful weekend and come back refreshed on Sunday. On the off chance you get The Call, I can be back before it's a problem. If anyone asks, tell them Dane's your cousin."

Then he sets another protein shake in front of me and goes into his room to pack, whistling. Now I'm even more curious—is this a *romantic* getaway? But it's none of my business; it's probably inappropriate to ask. If he's found some happiness here, good for him.

Dane's flight is only a little late and he's at the apartment by seven. Mason lets him in, explains some mechanics about my needs, then takes his overnight bag and leaves. It's just Dane and me. My heartbeat quickens, but it's a little disorienting at first. Dane seems so *tall*. And he's wearing a suit and tie, which feels oddly inappropriate. I haven't seen either of those things in a while—in reality, only a month, but it feels like much longer. He comes to the couch, scooping me into a big hug, and a tingle starts in my chest, spreading down my arms. For weeks I've had no physical contact that wasn't clinical; I hadn't even realized how much my body needed this.

After a while we disengage and he holds me at arm's length, scanning.

"You're very thin," he says, a small frown on his face.

"But buff," I reply, flexing a bicep to hide my disappointment. I'd thought I looked really good. And he hasn't even noticed my perfect hair.

"You're still healthy though, right? Are you eating okay . . . Can the guy cook after all?"

"Yes, he's an excellent cook and he's taking very good care of me. Don't worry." I'm getting derailed from the joyful reunion by all these questions, and it bothers me to hear Mason referred to as "the guy" when he works so hard.

"Let's not talk about my health now," I say. "Maybe later if you want, though you're pretty well up to speed. Tell me about *your* things. What's happening at work with the expansion? Seems like you're always in meetings these days."

We sit back on the couch, holding hands, while he talks: about the extra face time he's getting with top management, the new plans, the quirks and shortcomings of his team members. I'm trying to follow it all, but he has over a dozen direct reports, and even though I've heard the names before, it's hard to keep everyone straight. I've never seen his new office or met any of them, so there's no image to attach to his words. Suddenly I realize that this is why he frequently seems to glaze over on our video calls: He knows nothing about my world either. The smell of the gym after rehab, the camaraderie I'm slowly building, or the shiny newness of Regent Hospital versus the quirky stateliness of one-hundred-year-old Empire General. No wonder he forgets.

Finally I have to stop him. "I'm sorry, love, but there wasn't time for a real nap today and I'm completely crashing. Mason left food in the fridge. Let's eat, and then . . . will you come to bed with me?" His expression softens.

We eat the reheated food, then he takes a shower to wash away any germs he may have picked up on the plane. I wait for him in bed. He emerges from the bathroom in just a towel, his short fine hair already beginning to dry.

"It's a bit 'loud' in there," he says. "Surprising you chose those colors. The sunset painting's really cool, though."

He looks around at the rest of my bedroom, noticing the photo wall and the Olympics compilation. For the first time I wonder what this place must look like to him. It's a far cry from our elegant, conservatively decorated home in Manhattan. Or come to that, any of the friends' and colleagues' homes we usually spend time in.

"It's cozy," he pronounces. "Definitely a change from our place, and the photo wall is a great idea. Why the Olympics thing?"

"It's motivational. If . . . *when* I get done with all this, I want to go to the Olympics."

Alarm jumps into his eyes, but he tamps it down. "Honey, that's not such a good idea. You'll be pumped full of immunosuppressants, and tens of thousands of people go to the Olympics, all pressed up against each other."

I take a breath. "Let's just let the pictures do their motivational thing for now. The Games are two years away; we can talk again closer to the date."

"Sure. So, Fi . . ." He's hesitant, which makes me nervous. "Am I in this room anywhere?"

"Oh, honey!" I'm flooded with affection. "Of course you are. Right next to my bed—look."

His shoulders relax as on the nightstand, next to my book and water bottle, he sees a photo of the two of us on our last real vacation: suntanned, happy, holding rum drinks, and wearing big straw hats at a beach party the summer before I went on oxygen.

"Come over here and get into bed," I say.

For the first time in months, we try making love . . . with mixed success. Dane is tentative in a way he never was, overly careful not to exert me. I find myself wondering whether he even still desires me, given my thinness and the apparatus.

"I'm worried I'll pull out the cannula," he says at one point. "Am I hurting you?"

"No!" I reply, ignoring the slight discomfort. "I need this."

More than anything, it's a reaffirmation of our relationship—the memory of his hands and many years of our bodies coming together. And while my damaged body has not felt sexual for some time, it's still a glimpse at a sensual world I'd more or less forgotten. But it feels more like completing a requirement than genuine satisfaction. Afterwards, we kiss gently and go to sleep.

A couple of hours later he wakes me and asks if I'd be hurt if he slept somewhere else.

"It's the oxygen machine. It's so damn noisy, and mostly that big thump wakes me up every time I nod off. But if you want me to stay, I will."

"No, I understand, you've grown used to peace. Go next door and use Mason's room. The couch is way too short for you and I'm sure Mason wouldn't mind."

Actually I've no idea whether he'd mind, but as long as we wash the bedding before he gets back it should be okay. While Dane looks for spare sheets, I peek in to make sure there's nothing personal Mason wouldn't want Dane to see. It's perfectly tidy. I kiss Dane goodnight and head back to bed.

It takes a while for me to fall back asleep. Now that Dane's reminded me of it, I'm acutely aware of the concentrator noise. Generally it's not so obtrusive anymore, just a genial robot that stays near me and keeps me alive—especially while I'm asleep, when oxygen saturation naturally drops. A dumber, cubic R2-D2, the Big Friendly Generator.

There's some relief at having the room be all mine again, which I don't like but is a fact. I've become used to not having to accommodate a partner. Dane is a big person and seemed to take up a lot of space in the bed. I'll miss his warmth, but I'll rest better alone.

How complicated everything has become. I wonder whether things will ever return to how they were. Having separate bedrooms seems the sort of thing that, once you get used to it, might be hard to come back from. I turn on the bedside lamp and pull out my book. Because I can.

On Saturday I decide to show Dane some of my new world. We start with brunch at my favorite organic café, which looks like a greenhouse, eating fluffy lemon-poppy pancakes and eggs Florentine. Dane nods appreciatively; against his expectations, it's delicious.

On the way out I suddenly spot two familiar figures in niqabs by the left-hand wall, staring at us. It would seem odd to ignore them, so I ask Dane to roll me there.

"Hello," I say to Kicks's (really Alima) caregiver. "What a nice surprise to see you here."

"Indeed. I thought we were the only transplant people who knew about this place." It's an accent I can't quite place, but American. I take great care with my next words.

"Mason—my husband—is good at scouting out special, off-the-path places. My name's Fiona, and this is my cousin Dane." Dane reaches out his hand and accidentally knocks over her water glass, then apologizes profusely and grabs napkins to mop the spill.

"It's quite all right. I'm Hazira, Alima's sister and caregiver."

"Nice to officially meet you," I say. "Enjoy your breakfast."

Dane waits till we're in the car to talk, his voice shaky.

"That was awkward. Quick thinking on your part to call me 'cousin.' Do you and Mason have to be careful all the time?"

"We should," I reply seriously. "Truthfully, I haven't been paying enough attention to that. We'd better step it up and start acting like a couple, just to be sure." He nods.

Afterwards we drive to the hospital, so Dane can see it. I want him to have a visual in his mind, but we're too unnerved to risk going inside. Then we spend a couple of hours at a park with a boat pond, watching the children sail their boats from a stone bench at the perimeter. "Isn't it lovely here?" I say, and he replies, "It's just good to see you happy."

By the time we've completed the whole loop at the park and reached the car again, Dane is rolling out his shoulders and stretching his back. It's hard work pushing a flimsy wheelchair designed to fold into a car—not to mention hoisting it in and out of the trunk all the time.

"Sorry, dear." I smile. "This is probably more exercise than you've had in a while, what with this new job, right?"

It was meant to be sympathetic, but he takes instant offense.

"When would I have time for exercise? I'm in the office at least ten hours a day, unless I'm on brutally long flights or staying in a crappy hotel. I'm well aware of losing strength, thanks."

I've hit a nerve. I'd forgotten how important it is to him to be fit and strong. He's desperate to get back to his gym, whereas I'd love nothing more than to be shot of mine.

As I climb in the car I hear, "Damn this fricking wheelchair . . ." He can't remember how it folds and caught his finger in the hinge. He sucks on the finger, slams the trunk, and comes in.

"Is everything okay?" I ask.

"Sorry, I shouldn't have snapped at you. My nerves are so ragged these days that anything can set them off. There's a crazy steep learning curve to this new job; it's unbelievably stressful. By the time I get home I'm exhausted, and there's never any me time at all."

I squeeze his hand and nod. Our situations are more similar than I'd thought.

When Mason returns late Sunday afternoon, Dane's carry-on is by the door and a car is due in twenty minutes to take him to the airport. The weekend was good in the end. We closed some of the gap that being apart had created; we're not yet fully grafted back together, but no longer two separate entities. We have a long hug and a sweet kiss before the honking outside pulls him away.

Mason looks at me and nods approvingly. I hadn't been paying attention earlier, but he looks windswept, sunburned, and extremely content. It looks good on him.

"Looks like you had a good weekend," I say.

"Excellent," he replies. "Fresh air, lots of exercise, a change of scenery, and great food that I didn't have to cook. I'm all set for another month. How about you?"

I open my mouth to reply—and unaccountably start to cry.

"Hey, I'm sorry." He looks dismayed. "I didn't mean to upset you—it looked as though the two of you had a lovely time."

I swipe at the tears. "We did. It's just . . . is it possible to miss someone like crazy and at the same time be relieved they're gone?"

He pauses, frowning in thought. "I'd guess yes. You've been apart a long time, so there was huge pressure to make this visit wonderful. Beyond that, you've been immersed in a very intensive experience that Dane's completely outside of. But now he's been here and seen the place. Don't worry, next time the adjustment should be much easier."

Chapter 17

Monday is my clinic day. I'm waiting for the dreaded lung function test, pondering what it even means to "do well" in this context. If all my hard work to increase my oxygen capacity has succeeded, that will slow my transplant time. On the other hand, I don't want my lungs to have deteriorated either.

When the PFT technician tells me to breathe out as fast and hard as I can, I do exactly that. I can't help myself. At the six-minute walk—the only other test with wiggle room—I again do my very best. Am I that competitive? Or so by the book that I can't fudge even to save my life? Dane would be annoyed. I just have to hope everyone else is being precise too.

Next my pulmonologist, who listens to my lungs, asks how I'm feeling and what level of oxygen I'm currently using at rest. Resting oxygen level, not exercise level, is what goes into my official lung allocation score. Then she studies a tan cardstock sheet that I realize is my log from rehab: She's checking my attendance and progress. A small worm gnaws at my insides. I can't skip a workout. Ever.

A different transplant surgeon comes this time, the new man on the team. (An actual man; there are very few female transplant surgeons.) He enters hurriedly and has only a couple of questions but seems to feel obligated to stay. So I ask *him* a question.

"Do you still feel a sense of awe when you do your work? Taking a disembodied lung and swapping it for the dying lung of a different human being. Does it still strike you as miraculous?"

He looks at me oddly, then shakes his head. "Not really; it's pretty standard by now. Like swapping out a carburetor. The old one goes bad, you remove it and connect up a new one."

I stare at him in amazement. Is this really how he sees it—this mundane?

When he's gone, Mason mutters, "Plumber. He's a fantastically skilled, exceptionally well-educated, and highly trained plumber. You fed him a line of poetry, and he responded by quoting the instruction manual."

Now that my rehab is after lunch, I can't use clinic as an excuse not to go—especially now that I know they're checking so carefully. But it's a slog.

I'm chatting with Drew before weights when Alima trips, catches her ankle on the metal weights rack, and goes down. A bruise is already forming, and she looks unsteady.

I step to her. "Alima, can I help you?"

She stares, seeming dazed, then to my surprise, turns away and ignores me.

I'm a little hurt, but Alima's a tough woman. With her fancy shoes, protected from even people's glances by her clothing, but determined. Good for her. Transplant is not for sissies.

Driving home, though, I'm uncomfortable. Something was off about Alima, if I can only think what . . . and then I realize. Her eyes. I turn to Mason.

"Alima fell down in rehab today, and when I went to help her, her eyes were wide open: mid-brown irises with flecks of gold, very distinctive. But this weekend Dane and I ran into the two women, and this one—same eyes—introduced herself as *Hazira*. Alima's sister. What are they up to?"

"Come on. You can't accuse someone of being 'up to' something because they have pretty eyes. They're sisters—maybe they have the same eyes."

"I've exercised with Alima for a month. I'd have noticed." But now I'm not sure. "Perhaps I'm just tired and jumping to crazy conclusions."

"It's been a very long day." He nods sympathetically. "Take it easy on yourself, okay?"

The following day I surreptitiously look at Alima's ankle. There's concealer on it, but through it the telltale indigo of a bruise. I feel like an idiot. Just my overactive imagination driven wild by the monotony.

But on the third day, Alima's ankle is pristine and smooth. And on the caregiver's ankle is a patch of makeup in the exact location of the bruise.

As soon as the car door closes I tell Mason. "There's no doubt; they're swapping places."

"Then how come nobody's noticed it before?" Then he turns pensive. "No, they probably wouldn't, would they? There isn't enough of her face visible, and people see what they expect to see. She's just a brown-skinned woman in a niqab."

"Mason, we have to report this. The obvious reason to swap is that Alima can't meet the physical requirements. You know how terrified I've been of failing the lap count—more so every day, and I'm not down to desperate levels yet."

"You saw the real Alima today. Was she having trouble?"

"No," I concede. "So does she just not feel like doing what the rest of us have to?"

"Are you jealous? No, don't get mad, I'm kidding. But there may be an explanation, and no one here will appreciate a fuss, trust me. Remember, you need them on your side."

"So what would you do?" My voice is rising. "Just let it go, to avoid a fuss?"

"Can you not be that way!" he says, forcefully enough to startle me. "I promised to do everything in my power to see you through this process safely. Reporting her might jeopardize that. Why don't you ask Dane's opinion?"

"Because . . ." It's hard to admit. "I know what he'd say. Keep your focus on the goal, and just get it done. But I can't do that. Please answer my question: What would *you* do?"

He sighs. "You're asking me to go against what your husband would want. Well, if you must do something, go and talk to her. Tell her what you saw and ask what's up."

So straightforward and direct that it hadn't occurred to me.

"But first, calm down and eat. I know where their apartment is. I'll go with you."

The women live one building over on the second floor, close enough to walk. Through the door I hear glass tinkling, and female voices, but when I knock, everything falls abruptly silent.

"Alima, it's Fiona from rehab. Please answer the door." I feel like a TV detective: *Open up! I know you're in there.* Complete silence. "Please let us in; I know about the swap."

There's rustling, and eventually the door opens. It's the woman with the lovely eyes. She steps back, looking wary. The room setup is identical to ours but tastefully furnished in gentle green fabrics. On the left wall is a large county map and a framed copy of the US Constitution. The other woman is nowhere in sight.

"Please, take a seat." She gestures to the couch and slides into an armchair opposite.

"You introduced yourself as Hazira, so I'll call you that. But a few days ago, when you fell, you were pretending to be Alima. Then today, Alima was back. How could that happen?"

She bristles, then sags. "It was the bruise, wasn't it? I was afraid someone would notice."

"Actually, it was your eyes. The only way to miss eyes like that would be behind glasses, but it's hard to work out in glasses, so Alima doesn't wear them. I'd like to talk to her directly, if you'll translate."

"I speak perfect English, thank you." An elegant brown-skinned woman, mid-forties, comes down the corridor, trailing a long cannula cord. She's dressed in black sweatpants and a neon pink T-shirt. At least now I know how she likes to dress.

She takes the other chair. "We're American. Hazira studied Arabic in college and spoke that here to convince people I had no English. We wanted to discourage them from befriending me. It worked. The niqabs are for disguise—I didn't think anyone would question who was under them. They seldom do back home in Boren's Mill, Indiana. Nor here, until now."

I stay silent, my stomach churning, waiting for an explanation. This had better be good.

"My town is experiencing an environmental crisis. Fertilizer runoff draining into our river has made algae growth so thick that it's clogging the water flow and killing the fish—totally toxic water. The river *is* the town. Tourism's our main industry, and boating's what we do. Or did. I got elected to the town council on a promise to find a solution.

I've been working two years to get a proposal that both fixes the problem and could pass a vote. You think big-city politics is hard? Try fighting with small-town neighbors over their livelihood. My bill comes up for vote next month. There's no way I can be gone for the lead-up and succeed: It needs bipartisan backing. So sometimes I go back for a few days, and when I do Hazira takes my place."

Everyone's looking at me. I pull out my phone and google Boren's Mill. Immediately a string of articles pop up from the *Boren's Mill Gazette*. "Fish Population Down," "Farmers Won't Change Fertilizer," and "Councilwoman Proposes Bill to Save Our River," with Alima's photo.

I look up. "What will you do if the hospital calls and you're not here?"

She shrugs. "Pray I can make it back before they give the lungs away."

It's a slap of a reality check. I've been all incensed about her moral standing, while she's risking her own well-being for a greater cause. There's no way I can justify causing her trouble.

"In that case, I wish you much luck—on both counts. I won't say anything."

"Thank you." She relaxes. "I know *you* understand the need for flexibility."

I'm puzzled, but Mason tenses. "What do you mean?" he asks.

She considers him astutely. "You two aren't really married, are you? Not to each other, anyway. The tall blond man I saw you with at breakfast, Fiona. He was wearing the matching wedding ring to yours. And Mason, you don't wear a ring, do you?"

Neither of us replies, but my heart is racing.

"Don't worry—I'm very sympathetic, I heard about your antibody situation. You needed a different plan from most people here. That's my point: Sometimes, when the situation warrants, you have to bend the rules."

After we leave, I'm trembling so hard Mason has to support me till we're home.

"We need to be a lot more careful," he says in a low voice, "and start acting more like a couple. Not lovey-dovey—not in these circumstances—but come across as more connected. I know you haven't done theater, but I have, and I'll help you. Are you okay with me being affectionate sometimes, if there's not much contact?"

"Absolutely." I exhale hard. It's not just that I agree with him. The truth is, I could use some affection. Even a little contact wouldn't go amiss.

Chapter 18

May

Graduation is a month behind me, with little to show for it. The unending relentlessness of boot camp is increasingly hard to bear; each day ticks past and leaves me a little bit weaker. Several of my cohort have received transplants and are beginning the recovery phase. I miss them. I'm so lucky to have Mason, who finds something for us to do outside the apartment each weekend, but even that's getting thin. There aren't so many activities available for someone in my condition, and there's a limit to how often you can visit the same small museum. The saving grace is that Mason is good company: interesting and insightful, with a real breadth of perspective. I'm coming to consider him less of a paid caregiver, and more of a friend.

At drop-off today, he kisses me on the forehead and smiles a goodbye. Since Alima's observation, we've been making a specific point to show affection in public. This is very strange for me; as a non-actor, I'm not used to separating reality from what I see. Sometimes when he's especially loving, I can feel myself blush and have to remind my body that it's all pretend.

The minute I enter rehab, I sense a strange vibe. Three of the long-timers are sitting together on a long bench, heads bent toward one another like a pregame huddle. They look angry and stay that way for the entire twenty minutes I'm on the bike. When they break away it's clear that Wanda has been crying.

I move on to weights, but the machines are all taken. Wanda is waiting right next to me, so, hoping I'm not being intrusive, I ask, "Is everything okay?" She shakes her head and tears form.

"I met with my doctor this morning. He said my window is closing."

We've been told about the transplant window. It opens when a patient becomes sick enough to be eligible for transplant and closes when the risk of surgery becomes too great to perform it. But I don't understand what Wanda's "window closing" translates to in real terms. Does it mean the doctors have to take drastic action while there's still time?

"What did he say about the next step?"

"Nothing," she replies somberly. "Just said my window's closing. I'm so scared it's hard to even function. I think it means that soon they won't be able to do anything and it's all over."

But I can't accept that interpretation. There must be a misunderstanding. "That can't be right," I tell her with certainty. "They won't just let you die without doing anything."

She wipes her eyes and says she hopes not, then gets up to start the weights. I feel a chill. Wanda doesn't look much different from how she did a month ago. But last week the rehab nurse made an unusual announcement: She said there were three people here she was worried about. Was Wanda one of them? And then I wonder . . . who are the other two?

When Mason picks me up, I'm still shaken enough to want to talk about it.

"Wanda's doctor told her that her window's closing . . . no other treatment plans. And the head nurse said there are three people she's worried about. Who are the others?"

He turns worried. "After I fix your lunch, I have to leave for a bit."

"Why? What's wrong?"

"Wanda's daughter Sara and I are friends. She's who I took the trip with, the weekend Dane was here. I want to go over there for support."

"Of course. Drop me off and go—I can reheat quiche on my own."

In the doorway, he turns. "I know you're worried, Fi. We'll talk later, I promise."

I push down as much quiche as I'm able, which isn't much. My weight is still creeping down despite Mason making me the highest-calorie food he could find: quiche with bacon, heavy cream, and high-fat cheese, adding different vegetables for variety. Today even looking at it makes me nauseous. *Will Wanda get transplanted in time? Who's next? Is it me?*

I'm in this nervous state when a surprise video call comes in from my former colleagues. My close friends have been in touch regularly, but this is a first from work. I'm still in the dirty T-shirt from rehab, my hair hasn't been washed in three days, and I'm not wearing makeup. But somehow I can't ignore the call. I hit accept and there they are, clustered around Laurel's screen: the three people I worked with most closely for over five years.

"Hey, Fi," Laurel says cheerily. "We all wanted to know how you were doing down there."

"Okay, more or less." *Better than Wanda, for instance.*

Seeing the group of them in their crisp shirts and blow-dried hair is like peering into a strange culture. I remember once being a part of this world, but it feels very distant.

"You look good," Amanda says. "Pretty buff . . . and you've lost a lot of weight."

"That's what happens when you work out for three hours a day," I respond, flexing for the camera. They don't know that losing weight isn't a good thing anymore.

"Seriously, though," John says. "How are you holding up? Are you close to transplant yet?"

"There's no way to know. I've been listed for over a month; it's a matter of waiting now—which is hard, you know me. But I'm having to learn patience. Tell me about you guys."

John updates me on "my favorite client," who was dismissive in our meetings but always took my advice afterwards, Laurel talks about new accounts and her rescue puppy, and Amanda discusses problems with the junior staff. I'm trying to care, but the only part that's interesting is the puppy. Before they hang up, they tell me I'm missed and wish me new lungs soon.

It's a relief when they're gone. I'm touched that they called, but there's a vast disconnect now between their world and mine—bigger than I'd even realized. How can they care so much about this stuff? How could *I* ever have cared *so much*, staying up all night to do the tenth iteration of a presentation for an unappreciative client? It's like meeting middle-school me, certain that failing a grammar test has ruined her life. I want to tell these bright, earnest people that it doesn't matter, none of it. Except it does, of course. If Dane and I hadn't had years of earnings, or had children to support, it would have been very difficult for me to be here.

When Mason returns two hours later, his whole body is drooping. He drops a bag on the table and goes to wash his hands. "Hope you don't mind, I got take-out barbecue. I'm not up to cooking tonight."

When he's clean, he joins me on the couch. "It's true about Wanda," he says in dead tones. "Sara's trying to stay positive, reminding her mother that the window is 'closing,' not 'shut,' and this will put her right at the top of the list. But inside, she's a mess."

"I'm so sorry," I say softly. And it's true. But as much as I want this to be all about Wanda, I'm scared for myself too. It's one thing to understand the probabilities of tragedy; it's quite another when the bad roll happens.

Mason understands my expression. "Susan told me Wanda's rehab numbers and PFT results. They're worse than yours; you're not at a critical point yet."

I try not to gasp from sheer relief, but I'm trembling. If only Dane were here . . . I need someone to hold me now. To my surprise, Mason reaches over and puts his arms around me, folding me gently to his chest. The tears break free. He doesn't rush me, stroking my back until everything has washed through and I'm calm. Then he hands me the tissue box.

"Thank you," I say, extricating myself. "I'm sorry—this must be so difficult for Sara . . ."

"Fi, come on, it's not just Sara. I'm concerned for *you*. I could pretend there's nothing to worry about, but you're too smart for that, and I won't lie to you. It's frightening. For both of us. And before you ask, no, not just because it's my job."

I study his face, but he's quite serious.

"You're surprised? We've spent a lot of time together over the last few months—more than I have with any other person in a long time, honestly. With everything going on, this has become my journey too. And despite everything, you still have a sense of humor and a kind spirit. Of *course* I care about you. Plus, of course, I hate to lose." The crooked grin returns.

"Thanks a lot," I reply sardonically. We're back on safe ground.

Chapter 19

Wanda still attends rehab but sticks to her closest friends, the older crew. I try to focus on my own routine, but it's hard to stay optimistic. I'm flagging . . . and if I can see it, so can the nurse.

One afternoon Mason approaches me with a recommendation from Sara. She's seeing a healer to deal with her stress and the back pains that started after Wanda's notification.

"Sara says this woman's amazing," he tells me. "She's a European-trained osteopath, but uses other techniques too. It's completely safe, and Sara says it's helped her energy level and mental well-being as well as her back. Why don't you try it?"

"I don't even know what a European osteopath is. And which 'other techniques' exactly?"

"She was vague—it's probably 'alternative' healing, but if it works, so what? You could use a boost of something, honestly. This isn't a game you can win if your heart isn't in it."

"Hate to say it, but you're right. Okay, sure, at the very least I'll get my spine realigned."

We have no problem getting an appointment. Monique's office is in a room of her house with a separate entrance off the street and a small vestibule. Mason sits and fills out forms while I roll the oxygen tank inside. Monique comes across as professional, not New Age: tan slacks and a white blouse, mid-thirties, brown hair in a ponytail. A desk with a computer huddles in the corner, but most of the room is taken up by a large massage table, prepped with a paper covering.

Monique offers me a chair, opens a manila folder with my name on it, and asks me a slew of questions: my medical situation, symptoms, health, and family history going back to my birth. I strip to my underwear, and she examines my posture from several angles before helping me onto the table. I sit, legs dangling, as she moves up my back and neck, applying pressure for a few seconds, then releasing sharply. She repeats the process on my right knee and ankle. After every release she makes a note in the folder.

"Okay, stand for me again, and rotate slowly." I do so, trying not to tangle in the cannula.

"Much better," she pronounces. "You're suppressing a lot of grief, and you're holding it in your body instead of letting it go. I've released some of it, but likely not all—it's been there a while. Be prepared for some odd body reactions over the next seventy-two hours; call me if that happens. Meanwhile I have homework for you. While I was working, there was a clear image of you spending time outside reading books. I'm getting a big rectangular park very close to your home: a few small trees, but mostly lawn. Do you know where that is?"

I nod, baffled.

"Good. Find some books on how to heal yourself—see what appeals to you and get it. Doesn't have to be about grief, just healing. Then go outside and immerse yourself."

She looks at me hard. "You need to do this soon. The message is that you only have three months."

I get a flash of dread. "Three months for what? What happens after that?"

But she won't be drawn in. "Get the books. Come back in two weeks but let me know if you have a strong reaction or if something changes before then. And by the way, look out for a globe with a bell in it. It looks shiny. If you see it, you should buy it."

Mason studies me curiously afterwards. As we roll away he asks, "So how was it?"

"Very strange. A bunch of pressure-point stimulation and release, but not in any obvious places."

"Do you feel any different? You're standing taller and moving better."

"I *do* feel better. But she said something worrying, if I believe it. She said I need to immerse myself in healing books, because I 'only have three months.'"

He looks alarmed. "Three months for *what*? Did she tell you?"

"No. So shall we get some books?" I strike a tone somewhere between "What a load of rubbish!" and "Where's the nearest Barnes and Noble?"

"Absolutely! I like books."

In the self-healing section we find several books with specific exercises inside, because I want something tangible. I pick three and leave with an invigorating sense of purpose. I've been given an important project with a deadline, familiar territory.

At home I start reading and am immersed until bedtime.

That night, I have a vivid dream of someone I haven't thought of in thirty years: Zillah, my best friend in fifth grade. We're in the playground and she's climbing on the monkey bars, showing off her agility. She jumps gracefully down, laughing, and drags me to the carousel, where we push to go faster and faster. I'm incredibly happy to be out playing together, but after a while, I start feeling uneasy. Then the memory hits. Zillah's dead: She broke her skull falling off the monkey bars. Worse, she doesn't know it yet, which means I'm going to have to tell her. But *I don't want to*. She'll be so sad, and I can't bear to bring that on. The sorrow hits so hard that it wakes me up, and no amount of effort can get me back to sleep.

At 8:00 a.m. I call Monique and ask if this was the sort of thing she meant by "a reaction."

"Exactly the sort of thing," she replies. "Now go outside and read."

I sit with this for a bit. Zillah's death was certainly traumatic at the time, but so many things have happened in my life since then that my conscious brain had forgotten it. Is it possible that the grieving was just buried in the process of growing up but still needs to be dealt with? I dress, pick up one of the books, and head to the living room.

Mason's already there, hunched over his computer. But there's a heavy frown on his face and his fingers aren't moving. I seldom see him writing lately; I've been getting up at nine and he's already fixing breakfast. He's quite good-looking, I realize, surprised he didn't strike me that way at first. I wonder if he feels isolated here. He doesn't have time to meet other men, and it's not exactly a gay-forward vibe. Mason isn't that gay-forward himself, for that matter—you wouldn't know unless you knew. But I'd miss his company if he started going out in the evenings, that's for sure.

About a month ago he stopped writing in the evenings, and since then we've taken turns picking the evening's TV. He has broad tastes. Depending on the day, he might choose a nature documentary, improv comedy, drama, or a sports show. It makes me wonder what his novel is like. I've never asked—it seemed very personal somehow—but maybe I should.

"Mason, what's your book about?"

He turns to me, looking both incredulous and irritated.

"*About?* It's not *about* anything. It's not a textbook, for God's sake!"

"Well no, I know that, but . . ." I falter to a stop. He's never this harsh. What did I say?

"Go on." He's glaring at me. "But what, exactly?"

He shakes his head, stands, rolls his shoulders, and stretches his back out, then motions me to the couch, wiping a tea spill with his hand before sitting.

"I'm sorry, Fi. There's nothing wrong with your question. The truth is I don't know what it's about anymore. The initial germ for the story was a young man leaving home in search of his Roma roots, who finds a situation more complicated than he'd realized. Prejudice, hate, and discrimination extending even to Romani music. But the story keeps wanting to go in a different direction: to become a love story, or a travelogue—something I'm completely unequipped to write. Most days I start out hopeful, then look at the previous day's output and it's just *bad*. Clunky and inelegant, like someone trying to steer a supermarket trolley that keeps veering into the canned soup."

He rubs his eyes, too hard. I've seen this symptom in every place I've ever worked.

"How late did you stay up last night?"

"Probably too late," he admits. "But when else do I have

time to write? Don't worry, I won't quit my day job, but yes, I'm probably cranky from lack of sleep. Plus I'm annoyed about missing the deadline for the tanks."

"Tanks? What's happening with the tanks?" That sounds bad.

His hands wave out. "Fi, your oxygen tanks don't just appear. There's a warehouse about half an hour away; I have to take the empty tanks there to swap them for refilled ones. The company will deliver, but it's an eight-hour window, which locks me into being here all day."

"But I thought you were here anyway, writing."

"Yes, when I can, but other things need to get done too. You've been great about eating quiche every lunch, but I have to mix it up at dinner or I'm afraid you'll lose interest in food. But the best store for easily chewable, calorie-dense food is in the opposite direction from the tanks."

I've never considered any of this. "What else do you worry about?"

He holds his arms out wide to indicate the magnitude. "Your rehab stats, for one thing. The reason I bug you for the lap count and reps and oxygen usage is that I graph them on a spreadsheet. It's the best way to spot any decline."

His insistence on me recording the data has felt like an unnecessary nuisance until now.

"Then there's the whole transport thing," he continues. "As your disease progresses, you're getting closer to a potential call from Empire, in which case we'd have to race back to New York. It's not as simple as doing a travel search on the spot. Some airlines require advance notification if you're traveling with an oxygen concentrator—which is impossible, since we'll never know in advance. And if you keep desaturating, the portable concentrator won't be enough for the flight. There are oxygen tanks that are designed for plane travel, but they're hard to get and I haven't yet figured out which airlines will let you use them.

"I have to deal with the insurance company: filing your claims and sometimes arguing with them, though that's more a nuisance than a worry. And Dane wants a written report each week."

He's sounding increasingly stressed the longer he talks. All of this is news to me. I've never thought about the transport issues—mostly because I've been assuming I'll be transplanted here—and the other parts were invisible to me. Mason writes to Dane every week? But Dane talks to *me* at least twice a week. Am I so fuzzy now that he doesn't trust what I tell him? Or does he not want to spend our phone time drilling into data? I'm not sure whether to be uneasy or not. Meanwhile Mason has been carrying all this weight privately.

"I'm so sorry," I tell him. "I had no idea. And you still have to cook and do all the other things to take care of me. How do you cope? How *are* you coping?"

He's getting calmer. "One step at a time . . . it's the only way that works. You get up in the morning with a sense of what has to get done in the day and keep going until it's done. The next day you get up and do the same. I imagine it's worse for soldiers and emergency medics: They don't even know what's coming until it gets there.

"The one absolute every day is going outside and getting exercise. I'd probably be batshit crazy otherwise. But that eats up another hour of that three-hour window while you're in rehab. Some days there's no time to write at all, but almost always the time is divided into small chunks. It takes me a while to slip back into the novel—I have to go back and reread the earlier parts before I'm in it again—and by then it's time to pick you up."

I'm silent. This is very different from the image I'd held of Mason having the luxury of three hours by himself every day to focus on his writing. If he's only working at the edges of the day, how much progress can he be making?

He's looking at me curiously. "Why are you asking this now? Not about my concerns, but about the book. We've been living together how long? You've never wanted to know before."

My face turns hot. He's right. This man has been taking care of my every need for over three months, and I've never once asked about the thing he cares about the most.

"At first I didn't want to pry; I thought you'd tell me if you wanted to. Then later, I stopped noticing. Working at your computer was just something you did . . . when you weren't taking care of me, of course. Pretty self-centered, right?"

He shakes his head. "That wasn't what I meant. Life's been hard on you for several years. I've never been surprised that you don't have energy or attention for problems outside yourself. But today you did. I'm wondering whether Monique's book is helping."

"It might really be," I reply, surprised. "I feel clearer. Not that it's anything I can imagine you reading. You probably have *War and Peace* by your bed, with a little Proust as backup for those long sleepless nights."

He rears back in mock horror. "*Proust!* God forbid. *In Search of Lost Time* is exactly how I felt after reading it. Plus, madeleines? They're the perfect storm of bland flavor, no texture, and hundreds of calories. Just munch a stick of butter and move on."

Now I do laugh. But of course I'm right in the broad sense. He has read it (or at least some of it), whereas it's never occurred to me to try. My caregiver is much better educated than I am.

Chapter 20

Dane has come for an unscheduled visit, piggybacking off an existing business trip. He's waiting when I return from rehab, already showered and in a clean polo shirt and slacks. I'm barely out of my sneakers when he holds out a small box, wrapped in silver paper. Inside is a jewelry box containing a pair of silver cuff earrings.

"Why thank you!" I exclaim, touched and surprised; he always remembers birthdays but seldom buys on a whim. "They're lovely. Let me change and I'll put them on."

Mason has bought me a nonslip mat and shower stool so I can wash without risking slipping; the door stays ajar to fit the cannula through. I put on the navy-blue dress I ordered online because it helps hide how skinny I've become. A quick dash of eyeliner and the earrings, and I walk into the living room feeling pretty.

"They're perfect," he says, and smiles. "Now you needn't wear those funny fruit things anymore."

I'm extremely fond of the jingly bananas, but there's no need to tell him. This is a very short visit—he has to be back tomorrow night—so we don't plan to do anything but hang out together. This is my favorite version of Dane.

Taking a day off midweek has given him the giddy energy of a schoolboy playing hooky.

"So talk to me," I say, flopping onto the couch next to him and snuggling in.

"Not much new to tell, thank God. I'm finally gaining some traction, especially with the Asian team; they're actually asking for my involvement now, which is a real improvement. Dennis and Amy are getting divorced. I was shocked initially, but Dennis seems happy."

This really is news. Dennis and Amy will be the first of our circle to split up.

"They aren't telling anyone the reason; maybe they're working out a settlement. Just told everyone they were divorcing via a jointly signed mass email, if you can believe that."

"God, that's ugly. Let's not do that, okay?"

"No," he agrees, pulling me close.

We spend the next couple of hours out in the sun, and then order in Japanese food: tempura for me, sushi for him. Afterwards we watch a movie about a baseball player whose girlfriend stands up when he's about to hit because she "didn't want to see him fail." I start to laugh.

"Why would her standing up have anything to do with whether or not he failed?"

I turn to Dane, expecting him to agree, but he looks pale and serious.

"You're missing the point. She's leaving the stadium because she can't bear to *watch* him fail."

Jesus. "Dane, I'm not going to fail. It's taking longer than I thought, that's all. I'm doing everything possible to succeed and I'll keep doing that until my lungs arrive. Tell you what, if things start to look really bad, I'll video you and you can stand up, okay? Wear a white suit."

He gives a little laugh and wipes his eyes with the back of his hand. "It's a deal."

But after that there's a sadness to the evening that we can't quite shake. Mason is staying in a hotel, so I'd expected there would be some form of sexual intimacy, but Dane just seems tired now, and I'm happy not to try. In theory sex should be safe, but even thinking about my heart rate isn't conducive to romance. Instead we just hold each other and relive good vacations, birthdays, and other happy times, then go to bed in our separate rooms.

The following morning over breakfast I mention my talk with Mason about how much is on his plate and how little time he has for himself.

"I'm worried that after all this, he won't make any progress on his novel."

"Maybe he won't." Dane shrugs and gets up for more coffee.

I find his dismissiveness irritating. "Don't you feel some sense of responsibility for that?"

"No. Mason's an adult. He chose to take this job, knowing as much about it as we did. Why is this your problem?"

"Because the arrangement was explicitly intended so he could develop his own work while he's here, and that apparently hasn't been happening."

"Fi, you're being ridiculous. Should I tell him he doesn't have to do everything your care requires, just the part that doesn't interfere with his writing? This is the way it is, Fiona—we're all struggling. Please just keep your focus on your own issues and let him do what he's paid to do. If you recall, this whole plan was yours to begin with."

I'm speechless. Dane never used to be like this—brisk, emotional, ungenerous. And this wasn't the way our special bonus time together was supposed to have gone.

"Fi, listen to me. You can't afford to make sacrifices for others right now. I understand this wasn't what Mason signed on for, but he made a considered decision and he hasn't complained about it. Not to me, anyway. And if he's complained to you then he's being unfair, because there's a very important difference in your situations. The worst that can happen to him is that he has six months of difficult work but earns decent money that he can use to fund himself for the next six months. The worst that can happen to *you*, if you compromise your needs for his, is that you could die. Please, keep it in perspective."

I stare at his creased face for a moment, then nod.

"Good. Then let's get you into that wheelchair so we can take a stroll around outside and have as much stress-free and enjoyable time together as possible before you have to get to rehab."

Even with the stroll and the lovely couple of hours before rehab, when Dane leaves for the airport, the visit leaves me distracted and out of sorts.

After a day of this, Mason calls me out.

"Okay, what happened with Dane to put you in this mood?"

I sigh. "Dane doesn't see a way to getting you more time to write."

He's surprised. "He's right. And I don't need—or want—you to be looking out for me. You asked what my days are like, what I worried about, so I told you. It wasn't a complaint. Listen, stop worrying about anybody else's needs . . . and that includes Dane's too. He's a capable man, and besides, it's not about him right now. Your sole job is to keep yourself as healthy and strong as possible. The rest of us will manage."

What a strange concept: just let go of responsibility for anything other than my immediate needs. I've never done that, from high school council to freshman advisor in college to team leader at work. Is it really as simple as just stopping?

"The first thing is, you need to get out of your head." He flashes a quick grin, adding, "Says the guy who's always up in his own. So how about this. Early blueberries have just come out, and there's a pick-your-own farm half an hour away. Have you ever picked blueberries?"

I shake my head. "No. Apples, but nothing else."

"Excellent. I'll bring the shower stool so you can sit while you pick, and we'll bring the small concentrator into the field. If we leave now, it may not be too crowded."

We pull in over a rutted track to A.J.'s Berry Farm. Mason strolls to the small wooden shack for instructions, while I gaze through the open car window at the acres of farmland: green crop-stalks in the foreground, a small grove in the distance. The air smells of fresh earth with a tinge of warm animal. My entire body relaxes.

He returns with two wood-handled berry boxes and a childlike smile.

"I can wheel you right up to it," he says, fetching the chair and laying the stool on my lap with the concentrator at my side. "The berries are down this path to the left."

There's little to compare with fruit harvesting for feeding the soul. The berries are so ripe that they roll off their stems into my palms; the basket is halfway full sooner than I'd like. The sun is bright but not too hot, and with my broad-brimmed hat casting shade as I pick, I feel a throwback to bucolic times, long ago, when stress hadn't yet been invented. Mason returns for another box, and we fill all three, leaving with dirt on our shoes and a recipe for blueberry muffins that Mason says he'll make for breakfast tomorrow.

"Nothing like blueberry therapy to cure the blues," he says with a sigh, and we return to the road.

Chapter 21

Mason and I are going to a dinner party! It wouldn't be a big deal in the outside world, but here it's incredibly exciting. Terry, one of "The Youngsters" with cystic fibrosis, has a younger brother in an a cappella singing group at Regent College. Lyle and his group are coming to sing, and Terry's parents are laying on pizza and drinks and have invited some of us to listen. I've no clue why I'm invited until we arrive and Mason hugs Terry's mother broadly. They must be friends through the caregiver network. Terry didn't invite me—his mom invited Mason.

The apartment is across the park on the other side of the complex. It's a three-bedroom, so it has a slightly different layout but the same wall color, same wood floors, same kitchen. It's striking how big a difference furnishings make. Everything here is traditional. The dark wood, brown fabric couches, and tan cushions must feel like home to them, but they make me realize how important my bright, fun environment is for me. I need all the uplift I can get.

"Okay, everyone," Terry's mother calls in a Midwest twang, her beaming smile filling the room. "The Caps will be here in half an hour, so please find a spot to sit near one of the tables, and caregivers, bring your folks some pizza and pop. There aren't enough chairs for everyone, so I'm hoping the young people can manage on the floor. I've laid out cushions."

I'd love to sit on the floor, but my diaphragm needs more room than that allows, so I take the couch, with Mason on the floor opposite. All the Youngsters are here, and Zuri, wearing a white version of the pink Alpha Kappa Alpha sweatshirt she wears to rehab. Terry and a young woman I don't recognize sit next to Mason and me, and I'm wondering whether she's Terry's girlfriend when he says, "This is my sister Beth. She should be in college at Clemson but wanted to be here with the rest of us while I'm going through this."

As Beth and Mason go for food, I say, "How lovely that you're all together. That must bring you a lot of comfort." At times like this I wish I had siblings.

"Yes." Then he frowns. "I hope I don't let them all down by not making it."

I'm searching for a response when Mason returns with an entire pizza box, Beth right behind him with sodas and cups.

Mason grins at Terry. "Your mom bought so much food I figured we'd better dig deep."

"Yeah, she does that." Terry laughs. "The Caps'll take the rest back to the dorms."

"Why are they called the Caps?" I ask.

"Short for Captains—the university mascot. Regent started out as a military school. Hey, everyone," he calls around the table, "Beth says eat fast or she'll finish the whole pie."

The pizza is good, and we're all chatting as we eat. The Youngsters are a lot more interesting and varied than I'd realized from the other side of the gym. One of them asks Zuri what Alpha Kappa Alpha stands for, and she replies, straight-faced, "Ass-Kicking Afros." His eyes widen momentarily, till Zuri cracks up laughing. "Gotcha!" she crows. "But if ever a situation called for some kick-ass, it's this one. Right?"

"Right!" we all confirm.

After a bit, Terry asks Beth how her new job is going. She deflates visibly.

"Hard to answer that. It's a nice church—very different from ours, but that's okay. The people are nice, and Pastor George is a true believer, but I think I'll have to leave."

"Why?" Terry is clearly surprised. "I thought you really liked the work."

"It's not the work that's the problem, it's the services, of all things. You know I love church, but their service is so formal, and some of the liturgy makes me uncomfortable."

"Can you give us an example?" Zuri asks.

"Okay, for one thing they haven't updated the pronouns. Everything is just in-your-face male. Obviously in the prayers it's always 'He' and 'Father' and 'Son,' but even the hymns only say 'he' and 'brothers' and 'men.' I feel completely shut out, like there's no place for me at all. After that I started noticing other stuff that sounds like *power*, not love. 'We bow before you, Lord, Master, King,' and so on. My God isn't like that. How can you think of Him as a father if you have to grovel to Him all the time, like ancient deities?"

"But Beth," one of the other Youngsters ventures, "that's just the language they used back then. And Jesus *was* a man—that's historical fact. If he wasn't, he'd never have studied the Bible, and no one would have listened to anything he said."

Just like that, the table is now discussing theology. It's all very amicable—an exchange of opinions among friends—but to me it's remarkable. My friends and I never discuss religion. God and the church are simply *there*. You attend or you don't, believe as much as you believe, and enjoy the community. But we don't *talk* about it. Maybe we should.

"Look," someone is saying, "the whole point of Jesus was to be human, right? A child of God but born into mankind. Wouldn't it have made more sense for him to be born normally, out of human parents? Why a union between a disembodied spirit and a virgin?"

A cheer goes up by the front door: The singers have arrived. Beth jumps up to hug her brother Lyle, and Terry follows more slowly with his tank. The singers are a dozen nice-looking young men of all shapes, sizes, and colors, wearing black baseball hats with orange lettering that reads "a CAP-ella." After hugs and a little chat, they remove their shoes and form a semicircle at the edge of the living room. Terry's family sits in the front on dining chairs, and Lyle steps forward, with a big grin and a bigger personality. The family resemblance is clear; I wonder if Terry would carry the same broad grin and swagger if he were healthy.

"Hey, everyone. We're the Caps, the Regent a cappella group most recommended by people in the audience here tonight. We're going to sing a bunch of songs for you, which hopefully will cheer you up . . ."—the singers raise jazz hands and stretch fake smiles—"not bring you down"—they frown and slump. It's corny, but charming.

"Seriously, though." Now he does look serious, and the atmosphere in the room becomes charged. "We're really honored to be able to sing for you tonight. What you're doing, everyone in this room, is inspirational. We salute the caregivers . . ." (*Yes!* I think, cheering along with the other transplant hopefuls) ". . . and we're rooting for everyone who needs a transplant to get one soon. And you, bro—next year you're going to come up and sing *with* us."

Tears prick my eyes as we applaud. Does that mean Terry is a singer, or would be if he had the breath? If so, maybe a transplant could give him that gift.

The Caps open with a rendition of "Uptown Funk" and continue with a wide range of songs that includes blues, jazz, and rock. It's such a treat to hear live music and watch their goofball moves. In this moment, I feel normal again: just a woman at a party with some friends who are just like her, having a fun night out.

When the set winds down, Lyle steps forward again. "Thanks, everyone, for coming to hear us tonight. It's been a really special evening." The kid is a natural. Even his speaking voice is mellifluous. I wish it weren't ending yet.

"This will be our last song," he continues. "I'm singing it for all of you . . . but especially for the best big brother anyone ever had." The group begins with some familiar notes that I can't quite place, and then Lyle sings—to his brother, to all of us.

Now I recognize the song, and it has never felt so powerful. So appropriate.

Lyle's voice and presence permeate the room as he challenges us, encourages us to do what can't be done—even though we all know it's *not* easy.

"*It's easy*," he counters.

Suddenly Mason leans forward, staring as though sensing something coming.

"*All you need is LUNG!*" Lyle belts, and my breath stops in my throat.

"*All together now . . .*"

The background singers clap in syncopation, and all around me people start joining in, singing with hope and joy, "*All you need is LUNG!*"

I want to join too but can't get beyond the first two words without choking up. Finally I surrender and cry like a child, glad to see that at least Terry's mother is sobbing as hard as I am.

After we make our goodbyes, Mason wheels me back across the green to our own apartment. It's a perfect night for contemplation: light-sweater weather, the half-moon only a few degrees above the tall lamps and casting the same gentle yellow light. Behind us we hear a sprinkle of laughter from other departing guests, and after that a peaceful quiet broken only by the night insects in the grass and the muted sound of my wheels on the path.

It has been a very long time since I had an evening like this. A sharing of views and experiences with people whose opinions I don't already know. Conversation that doesn't revolve around either work or illness. Thinking about new issues—important ones too, but less dire. Something in me is being poked, saying I don't have to be so isolated or so blinkered inside my transplant bubble. Life can go on even here.

Tonight I felt more attuned to the people around me than I used to . . . as though I could listen better, hear more clearly. Perhaps it's the absence of other mental preoccupation for the first time in my life. Or perhaps it's that despite barely knowing these people, I care about them. We are in this battle together. Individually and collectively, they are my comrades.

Chapter 22

Midmorning on Thursday, a call comes in on the landline. I'm sure it's a robocall, but it's not. A female voice says she's a transplant coordinator at Regent. I need to stop eating and drinking as of now and head straight to the hospital. They have lungs that might work.

I'm calm on the line, writing her instructions on the pad by the phone, but the second I hang up I feel dizzy. It's all I can do to stand upright as I walk to Mason.

His eyes widen as he sees me. "Are you okay?"

I nod, trying to breathe through the adrenaline and the constriction in my chest.

"Is it the hospital? Do they have lungs for you?"

I find my voice. "Let's go and find out. Just a few sips of water first."

What do I need to take with me? I've always been cool in a crisis, but right now my brain is full of dead air and static. Thankfully Mason is both focused and prepared. He reads the notes I've just made (which I'd already forgotten) and finds the checklist he prepared the day I got listed. I take three sips while he adds more items to the go-bag in my bedroom closet. It's the classic picture of a couple rushing to deliver their first child, except that I'm the baby.

Everything proceeds exactly as described in the classes. We check in, rushed and nervous, to find everyone else calm. I'm given a cubicle with a bed and asked to put on a gown.

It's my first time in the hospital part of Regent. The feel is very different from both the clinic and the testing labs. There's nothing extraneous: no paintings or photos on the walls, no chairs or side tables in the hallway. Here it's all business. This is where the medical work happens.

The nurse arrives with an IV cart. "Ms. Copeland? I'm Edgar. The lungs have just arrived. The surgical team will inspect them for viability, but it will likely take a few hours. Meanwhile, I'm inserting an IV so you're ready to go if we get the thumbs-up."

I hate IVs. They don't like me either and frequently express that by exploding a minor vein that they're supposed to slide into without a fuss. I'm really hoping I don't have to sit here for hours with a needle in me unless it actually leads to surgery.

I close my eyes and start breathing the way the self-healing books say: inhale through the nose for four beats, hold for four, exhale over four, and hold for four at the bottom. The slowest pace I can manage is fast, not nearly as slow as it's meant to be, but it's still box breathing. Apparently it's also a Navy SEALs technique, which struck me as pretty funny when I learned it.

When the needle's in, I call Dane and fill him in.

"Is it a go?" he asks frantically. "Should I come down?"

"Not yet. They haven't confirmed the lungs' viability yet, and lots of times it's just what they call a 'dry run.' Last week a man in my program waited for ten hours, prepped and ready to go, then was sent home. It was his seventh dry run, poor guy. I'll keep you posted."

"Okay. Call me when you know, whatever time it is. Fingers crossed, honey."

Three hours go by. Mason has gone out to find food—for himself, since I'm not allowed to eat. He returns with a packaged chicken sandwich and a cold Fresca, which I look at longingly. If the transplant happens I'll have missed my last chance at a grapefruit drink. Actually, if it happens I won't be able to drink at all for days. Just thinking of it makes my tongue dry up.

"Alima just came in," Mason says around the chicken, which looks as dry as my mouth.

A month ago I might have been upset by that, but now I'm not. She needs new lungs too. By now I just want something to happen—go or no go, just let me know.

Six hours after my admission, the nurse returns. "I'm sorry, Ms. Copeland, the lungs were not viable in the end. Hopefully you'll get another call soon; I'll remove the IV."

By now I'm so emotionally drained that the prospect of being home helps mitigate the disappointment. We stop on the way for a compensatory dinner: sushi platter, pomegranate, and two cans of Fresca. Everything that's not allowed posttransplant.

Alima, with no antibodies to worry about, is now in surgery. She's getting her new lungs.

The next day I'm back in rehab. It feels as though I failed a final exam and have to retake it, but at least I've had a call. That's encouraging.

Since Terry's party, I feel more integrated with the life here. The rehab itself is becoming more difficult, but at least I'm doing it with people I feel more connected to; Zuri in particular has become a friend. Her boyfriend, Robert, is working remotely to be here with her; sometimes the four of us get together on weekends. I've begun attending Wanda's group dinners and regret not doing so earlier. With few exceptions, we don't talk about our health, so it's a normal group dinner but with a very varied group of people, just chatting.

Today's dinner is special. Jersey Joe, who did exactly as he expected, completing the entire process—boot camp, transplant, recovery, post-op rehab—in two months, is back for his one-month checkup. And Mei-Lin, who is young, energetic, and very kind, will be leaving next week. She's sitting opposite me and I'm happy for the chance to talk.

"I can't wait to get back to DC," she says. Her long hair, always tied up during rehab, cascades over her shoulders like a victory flag. "It's been lovely spending so much time with my sister, and I'm truly grateful to her for caretaking me, but I'm so ready to get back to real life and my own apartment. I even miss my job!"

"You've earned it. I'm so happy for you. Do you feel physically ready for work?"

"I think so. I'm one of the lucky ones—no real complications with the surgery or afterwards, and I heal fast. The surgeon is very pleased." She pauses. "Fi, I know you haven't had any good hits yet, but something will come up. Hopefully you'll be recovering when I come back for my one-month. And DC's not too far from New York. Come and visit. I'll make you soup dumplings; they're my specialty."

"I'd love that. As soon as I'm well again."

A roar goes up further along the table. Joe has been complaining all evening that he can't drink beer with his dinner, and Drew, sitting across from him, has just ordered three glasses to taunt him with. I love these guys.

A few seats over, I see Mason telling a story to a rapt circle. I tune in.

". . . so my darling wife is arranging dinner place cards when her bridesmaid Bonnie rushes in, says, 'There's no cake!' and bursts into tears."

There are gasps, and someone looks across sympathetically, but I start giggling at the thought of Bonnie crying over a cake.

"'The . . . the bakery caught fire! And that tripped the sprinkler system,'" he wails, doing an absurd impersonation of Bonnie, whom he's never met. "'Should I have asked for a refund?' So Fiona says, 'No, the poor guy has enough problems. But we need another cake.' She thinks a bit, tells me to call my artist friends, and texts two of her business buddies. Ten minutes later, she group conferences them. 'Welcome to Team Cake. Business group, I need three delicious cakes: one chocolate, one fruit, and one you decide. Just no basic sponge and shaving-cream frosting. Art group, can you build an interesting display so people are focused on that? Fantastic. You have three hours till the ceremony.'"

The whole table's listening now—*ooh*'s and *no way*'s, and just plain laughter, me harder than anyone. What an imagination! He's a great storyteller too, even has my intonation down.

"Then . . ." He pauses for effect. "She finishes the dinner assignments and ignores the whole cake thing till after the wedding. Let me tell you, that was the most stunning cake imaginable: three round platforms at different heights, all connected with shiny silver rods—like a gorgeous chocolate, berry, and hazelnut spaceship."

I'm wiping tears of laughter, which just makes it seem more true.

"Do you have photos?" someone asks.

"No, but I can draw it." He flips over the paper place mat and draws a spectacular creation that now I really wish was my wedding cake. Everyone is impressed.

"And that's why I adore her," he concludes, beaming me a look so full of love and pride that after a moment I have to look away. Dane has never bragged about me like this, though he would have real stories to tell. Mason's an excellent actor, but beyond that, it says a lot that he thinks this way. I hope he finds true love; he'll make someone a wonderful partner.

Dinner ends with many hugs and promises to stay in touch, like family leaving after a big Thanksgiving dinner. Which, in a strange way, it is.

Chapter 23

A few mornings later I'm struggling for breath on the bike. It's the same exercise as always, but it feels like a mountain stage at the Tour de France. I check my oximeter (I bike with it on my finger now): saturation level eighty-eight. There's nothing to do but ratchet the supplemental oxygen up again, for the second time this month. It's the most obvious sign that the scarring in my lungs is progressing, leaving less functioning tissue.

At least here I'm seated; the walking loop is worse. Soon I'll be beyond the point where a regular nasal cannula will work—there's only so much gas that can be shot up a person's nose. When that happens I'll need a plastic mask that fits over my nose and mouth, creating an oxygen-filled space so that I can inhale through my mouth. One of the technicians tried it on me recently, and I became instantly claustrophobic. I'm putting that off as long as possible.

I'm pedaling away, entering mindless space as usual, but there's a buzz in the air that's breaking into my zone. When the time is up I look for Drew; he's usually in the loop.

"Hey, is something going on today? It feels odd." Even he looks oddly sad.

"Wanda died," he replies flatly. "Things took a bad turn and she went into the hospital on Saturday. Her family drove down to be with her yesterday, but it's not clear if she even knew they were there. She died this morning."

It takes a minute before I can reply, "Thanks for telling me." I'm in shock. Everyone knows that people die on the transplant list—of *course* they do, there's a chronic shortage of organs—but even so, I can't believe it has actually happened to one of us. Wanda was right here in rehab just a week ago. Wasting her last days doing worthless weight reps and dragging her failing body around the track instead of being with her family.

For the next few hours I'm in a zombie haze, waiting for rehab to be over. Does Mason know? He must, Sara must have told him. When he pulls up in the car, his grim face confirms it.

"How's Sara?" I ask.

"Exactly as well as you'd think. She called right after you left for rehab."

"You should be with her."

"That's where I've been since I heard; I just left to collect you." He's looking directly ahead, his hands white on the steering wheel.

"Mason, I'm so sorry. Drop me off at home and go back there. I'll be fine."

"I'll fix your lunch first, then . . ."

"I said I'll be fine. Go to her."

He unclenches a little, takes a breath. "Her family's all at the apartment, so I'll leave them to each other for a bit, and if you're okay, head back after lunch. If nothing else, maybe I can be useful helping Sara pack up the apartment."

"Oh." Of course, she'll be leaving. "You'll miss her."

"Very much. She's been my closest friend here."

His face clouds over, and an angry tic flickers at his right eye. "The thing that gets me the most is that Wanda worked so hard, left her home and her friends, and the story ends like *this*? Dying in a strange town without even getting to say goodbye? It just royally sucks!"

We get home and he warms me up some food, then heads out for a walk to clear his head. It's good; I need some alone time too. I sit on the couch looking out at the park, hoping the color and life outside will help fight the gray in my bones. Wanda died. I assured her that the medical team wouldn't let that happen, but that was stupidly naive. What did I think they could do?

I feel impotent, and furious that Wanda wasted her last few precious months for nothing. Suddenly I'm exceedingly frustrated with everybody who didn't volunteer to be an organ donor and might have saved her life if they had. And deep down I'm upset at myself for telling Wanda this wouldn't happen. In fact, right now I'm angry with pretty much everything in my immediate world.

Beyond that, though, I'm frightened in a way I haven't been until now. While death has always been an inescapable risk, the transplant program is, at heart, about working toward a new life. It became "*when* I'm transplanted," not "if." But that illusion has been punctured. This process is a crapshoot, and not everyone wins. Whatever my brain knew before, I now have a visceral dread that I may not make it after all.

The following morning I enter the living room to see Mason hunched over his keyboard, his head in his hands. He straightens, reaches for his coffee mug, and then halfway to his mouth slams it on the desk so hard the handle breaks.

I consider backtracking to my bedroom, but instead ask quietly, "Is everything okay?"

He jumps, spins, registers that it's me. When he speaks it's like acid.

"No, it's not! This is going *fucking nowhere*!"

Where is this coming from? Is he talking about his book?

"I keep thinking it's finding a direction, coming together into something I can finally grab hold of, and then it just *stops*! And I'm stuck again with no substance to mold."

He pushes back from the desk and goes for paper towels to mop up the spilled coffee.

"I'm sorry, Mason. I know nothing about writer's block."

"Of course you don't. I'll bet you've never had it, or the business equivalent of it. You're probably thinking what a sad little sack this guy is—thirty-seven years old and nothing to show for it. No money. A useless career. What's the point of him anyway?"

My heart is hammering. "No one thinks that."

"Bullshit. *Everyone*, with the possible exception of the Dalai Lama, measures people by success. Pecking order is innate even in chickens, certainly in humans."

"But . . ." What do I even say to this? I never saw this coming.

"Mason, you've set your sights on succeeding at something where *most* people fail. Unlike the rest of us, who took ordinary jobs, you took a risk. But if that's how you feel, do something else. You could be successful at many things."

He seems, if anything, even more annoyed.

"Perhaps that's true, but the fact is that I *haven't* been successful so far. The father who plays catch with his child is building memories. The hospital staff help patients or create a healthier environment. Wanda was an expert gardener. She owned a plot of land where she taught local children to grow vegetables and love the soil. In her will, she's leaving that land to the town. What's my contribution? My tiny apartment's barely big enough to hold a fern, and between working, writing, and paying off college loans, I have nothing left to give to others."

Now I understand. Wanda's death has brought this on. He looks sad and lost.

"I don't expect to change the world, Fi, but will I leave any legacy at all? And please don't say that merely finishing a book is a great accomplishment. To my mind an unread book is just smudges on a page—it doesn't become meaningful until people read it."

He turns away, raking his fingers through his hair before speaking again. Calmly now.

"Being here, where life can be gone at any time, I've become painfully aware of how much work and energy I've spent for how little result. Looking hard at myself, I'm not impressed."

There's a lump in my throat. I take a long, slow breath before replying.

"You're wrong," I say. "You're just wrong. I've seen some of your work online; it's excellent. And maybe this isn't quantifiable, but you're smart, and creative, and you make people feel good. More than that, you're steadfastly moral. That counts for a lot. Besides which, right now you're saving my life. I know I'm biased, but surely that counts for something."

He blinks a few times, unspeaking. I continue.

"I mean this without reservation: I could not do what you are doing. I don't have the temperament for it—most people don't. Whether or not you feel it right now, you are remarkable."

He wipes away tears that should not have needed to be there. He should know his value by now. Finally he gives a half smile, the left side of his mouth tilting up, and says, "Thank you."

That evening my glass hummingbird breaks. I was picking it up to feel the comfort of the cool surface when it slipped and caught the end of the table. It's not shattered, but the right wing snapped off. It looks lopsided and deformed, and given my current state, feels like a terrible omen. I move the wing and the body to my bedroom, where I can mourn in private.

Mason comes in and retrieves the parts, saying he can fix it—not back to its original shape, but at least to where it's a whole bird. I'm initially annoyed at what feels like idle talk but then remember that this is Mason: He wouldn't say it if he didn't believe it. He ducks out to the hardware store, returning with superglue, paint stirrers, and flexible wire.

"Hold the wing for a bit," he tells me. "We need to support it while the glue dries." He uses the wire to attach a paint-stirrer shelf for extra support, then wipes the excess glue.

After an hour it's exactly as promised. "You fixed it," I say in amazement. "The seam is visible, the bird isn't as beautiful as it was, but it's still here and I still love it. Thank you."

"You're welcome," he says, smiling. "After your transplant, the bird and you will be a matched *wabi-sabi* set: perfect in your imperfections."

For some reason this brings me great comfort. Perfection isn't a necessary condition for being loved.

Chapter 24

I am rededicating myself to reading the self-healing books and doing their exercises. During my second visit to Monique she did pressure points again—different ones this time—and afterwards I felt a weight lift, so I'm resolved to follow her advice for a while. In the mornings Mason brings a side table, yoga mat, and chair outside so I can sit with my tank in the fresh air. I'm becoming engrossed in the material, some of which is as much spirituality as medicine. I do at least one of the healing exercises, two if they're not very long, then lunch and rehab. In my forties I'm becoming a student athlete. To my surprise, what I'm reading both engages and calms me. I don't know if it's true, but it's interesting.

The books offer a wide range of styles, topics, and disciplines but share a common thread in their teaching that the world is interconnected far more than I'd ever considered. One contemplates cells as specialized members of the larger community that is the body—white blood cells as the warriors, hearing cells the early warning system, and so on. Another, almost poetic, delves into universal fundamentals that are replicated throughout the natural world. The golden ratio, phi, is derived from the Fibonacci sequence (1, 1, 2, 3, 5, 8 . . .) and runs throughout nature: the number of petals on a sunflower, spiral shells like the nautilus, tornados, and even spiral galaxies.

Energy is a recurring theme, in physics, new spirituality, and even the entertainment industry. Physicists posit that our world is not the three-dimensional entity we perceive . . . as do the *Matrix* movies. Healing modalities such as acupuncture view the body as an energetic organism to be treated through energy work. Is this what Monique is doing? Can she somehow tap into a field I'm not privy to?

This morning I try a color exercise. I lie face up on the mat, a wide sun hat balanced on my face to protect my skin and eyes. The grass hasn't been cut in a while; the blades are thick and sweet-smelling all around me and I relax for a couple of minutes, just breathing.

The exercise involves imagining a bright light shining through my body from the soles of my feet up, running in turn through each of the colors of the rainbow (also the chakra colors). I'm to note how the colors flow, and whether there's any place where a color gets stuck. I close my eyes and begin with red. It emerges darker than I'd planned, and thicker; it takes a while to work its way through and out of the top of my head. Orange is much easier, running smoothly all the way. The yellow is citrusy and bright, shooting through me almost immediately. This is fun. I move on to green, but my stomach starts hurting; the light doesn't go in. I have an odd relationship with green except in plants. I own no green clothes, and St. Patrick's Day parades make me queasy. But this is absurd: It's an imaginary exercise, and yet my body feels afraid. I take a breath, then "switch on" the green lights. All that emerges is a thick pond color, sliming slowly into my heels and up my shins. My body refuses to allow the green beyond my knees.

Finally I sit up and wave to Mason to help me get my gear back inside.

"That was quick!" he exclaims. "Exercise too easy? Or too hard?"

I explain what happened as he rolls the mat up and we head indoors, where I crash-land on the couch. He gets a thoughtful look and heads to his computer.

"Green corresponds to the heart chakra, which also governs—guess what? Lungs. In this system you have a blockage in your fourth chakra, which can lead to lung problems."

"Well shit, I didn't need a yogic exercise to tell me I have lung problems."

He swivels his chair to face me. "Can I ask you something? Do you believe in these healing things you're doing? The books, Monique? No judgment—I'm just curious."

"Honestly, I'm not sure. I've never been exposed to this sort of thing before. It's a new way of looking at things, and some of it is rooted in science, which is an easier jumping-off point for me. 'Believe' is too strong a word: That implies conviction, and I don't have that. But I don't *dis*believe . . . it might be true. I'm just absorbing the ideas and following the thoughts they set off, which are interesting. What if we really are interconnected components of a much larger entity?"

A grin creeps across his face. "Fiona Copeland, are you saying we're part of a continuum that leads to . . . God?"

"Oh, hell no!" I'm embarrassed. "But it's a good distraction from worrying about my laps."

"Speaking of which . . ." He heads to the kitchen for my quiche while I migrate to the table. While I'm eating (bacon and mushroom today), he watches me.

"You know, I'm not sure there's as big a schism between science and the spiritual as you think. Science begins with observation and the quest to explain what is observed. If you observe that Monique senses things she 'can't know about,' wouldn't it be scientifically reasonable that she *can* know those things? Maybe we just don't understand how this works yet."

I love this thought. I'm supposed to be dying, but some parts of my brain are more alive than they've been in years.

Monique says she sees some improvement at my next session. I tell her about some of the things I've been reading in the books, and she nods matter-of-factly. These are ideas she's taken for granted her entire adult life. Eventually I ask the question that's been bothering me.

"Many of these books assume reincarnation. The first time I thought it was because the author was Hindu, but it keeps showing up. What do you think about it?"

She's amused. "Do you believe in the soul? As a separate entity from the body?"

"Sure. They're connected, of course, but my soul is the essence of me, isn't it?"

"And do you believe in the physics principle called conservation of matter?"

"Absolutely. Matter doesn't simply disappear—it might change form, but it's still there."

"So why is it so strange to think of the soul as a form of spiritual matter that remains but changes into a different form over a series of presentations? Iron can be a magnet one day and a railway spike a year later. The development of a soul can be a long process, no? So doesn't it make sense that you'd have more than one chance to learn and improve? The alternative is much harder to accept, I think:

that each soul comes from nothing. That heaven began empty and keeps filling."

It's a strange thought, and appealing. When you're close to death, it's comforting to think you may get another turn at life. I'm about to leave when Monique stops me.

"Fiona—your mother just came in."

Damn. Just when I'm starting to think there might be some validity to her beliefs, she comes up with a seance message from my dead mother.

But for the first time, Monique seems uncertain. "Your mother says she feels your pain about the green bird. I've no idea what that means, but I'm hoping you do."

First I stare, then I try to figure out how she could have known. Could it be a lucky guess? Far too unlikely—what are the odds that I would actually be feeling pain about a green bird? I think about it all the way to the car but can't find an explanation.

"Cosmic Google," Mason says when I tell him.

I laugh . . . but nervously.

Chapter 25

June

One by one the people who were with me in boot camp have received their transplants. Only a few of us are left now: one of the Youngsters, Zuri, Drew (still waiting for his kidney-lung combo), and three of us with high antibodies. I should make new friends, but I'm out of sync with the newcomers, like a senior perpetually held back while class after class goes on to graduate. I'm not interested in even learning the names of more people who will soon leave.

Zuri has been in and out of the hospital for several weeks. Every time she's missing from rehab my stomach lurches: This is how it started with Wanda. The thought that she might not make it to transplant eats at me. We've been meeting after rehab, sitting in the quad with a cup of tea. Sometimes she talks about her work in the DA's office. She has helped put away some truly bad players. If Zuri died it would be a great loss to the world. And I'm not sure how I'd keep my own hopes up if that happened.

Since my one dry run there have been no further calls. I've been classified from the beginning as a double-lung patient, but at this point if a single matching lung is found the doctors will accept it. People can survive with only one lung, including, apparently, Pope Francis. I'd rather have two, of course, but my appetite for risk is diminishing by the week.

I may be clinically depressed by now but can't seem to do anything about it. I'm afraid to talk to the transplant psychiatrist, and while Mason has been trying his best to pull me out, I can't find any juice to respond with. Bonnie has called, Yannis too, but I have nothing new to tell them and talking wears me out. I'm having to stop more often to breathe, which makes my sentences choppy. It gives me pangs to hear myself speak to them like this.

The baby birds are long gone; I realized one day that the little heads weren't there. I never got to see them leave—abandoned without even a goodbye. I hope they survived.

Sara left shortly after Wanda died. Mason called a couple of times, but now that she's back with her friends she has all the support she needs. He's focusing more on his writing, which is still a struggle, and there's no sense of joy in the apartment at all.

Dane is back. I'd hoped he could break through my darkness, but instead I feel pressure to act happy, to shield him from some of this. Or maybe I'm afraid of scaring him away. He's visibly shocked every time at the change in my health. I suspect there's such a vast gap between the image he carries of me and the reality of how I am now that he can never adjust. Besides that, he's traveling a lot internationally now. We've had to drop our regular video calls, and it's even harder for him to get down here, so it takes longer to reacclimate each time.

On Saturday, Dane flips through Mason's folder of events and says, "What about a show? There's a Russian play at the Sonnet Theatre. You could just sit and be entertained."

"Dane, shows are difficult. I'd need an aisle seat, and it's a big time commitment. I'd rather be somewhere I can easily leave." I don't say, *I'm looking for uplift, not Russian plays.*

"Then what about the main art place—the Gideon Museum?"

"Sounds great." I've been many times with Mason, but that's fine; we'll enjoy it.

The Gideon is a two-story white stone building washed with pink in the late afternoon sun. Large flower beds flank the path to the entrance, and since my last visit yellow roses have come out in a torrent of color and scent. I let it wash over me as Dane wheels me up the ramp.

The first floor has rotating exhibits, so everything here is new to me. Since my painting day, I've been curious about how different effects are created, so I ask Dane to pause in front of a bold abstract with large spiky brush marks, as well as a landscape with imperceptible strokes and a reflective sheen on the lake. All very different takes on the Smoky Mountains.

"Isn't this great?" I ask Dane. "The curator's done an excellent job juxtaposing the pieces."

"I suppose so." He pauses. "It's just . . . they're not very *good*, are they?"

Disappointment and defensiveness hit me simultaneously. "Dane, this isn't New York. Think of it as a big gallery of undiscovered artists—we've been to plenty of those."

"Oh, okay. That does change things. In that context, they're much better."

We leave soon afterwards and find a café. "So," I say. "What's new with our friends?"

He frowns, and I notice that his creases have become deeper. Though he's still youthful looking, there's more gray hair too.

"Nothing you don't already know, honestly. You haven't actually been gone that long by most measures. Not much happens to ordinary people in three months," he adds wistfully.

I hadn't considered that. It feels like *ages* since I left. When people's lives can be so dramatically altered in the space of weeks, three months is a very long time.

As we eat, he watches me, and the frown reappears.

"Honey, I'm trying to eat more, okay? Please try to relax. I know it's scary to see me like this, but I'm getting closer and closer to the top of the list. Soon, God willing, I'll be transplanted and back home. Once we're part of each other's day-to-day lives again and I'm healthy, things will be so much better. We'll get back to how it used to be."

He smiles for the first time today, and I finish eating as Edith Piaf plays over the restaurant speakers, saying she regrets nothing.

When Dane leaves on Sunday, I'm sad to see him go, but wistful too. Home in New York seems very distant; it will take a while to reacclimate after all I've been through. If I ever get there. Mason returns from his hotel stay looking much less refreshed than when he went with Sara. Something has to break our way soon.

Shortly after two I get a text from Zuri:

Please call as soon as you can.

I'm anxious about what the urgency might mean and grab for the phone.

"Are you still in the hospital? Is everything okay?"

"Everything's fine. I'm calling because Robert and I are getting married this afternoon."

"*What?*" It comes out sharper than I intended. She laughs.

"You heard right. Things have been scary for a few weeks, but today I'm feeling good, and we decided to just do it. We should have been married ages ago, but we had this crazy notion of how the wedding should be, and getting my family's church and all, and then I ended up here. All that seems irrelevant now. We just want to be married, and we'd like for you two to be our witnesses. It'll be just the four of us. Will you come?"

I'm thrilled—and relieved—but mostly baffled.

"Of course. I'd be honored . . . but wouldn't you prefer someone else? A family member, or a close friend?"

"We can't wait till people free up and get here: I don't know how much time I have. Hopefully I get transplanted in the next few days, but however it comes out—whether I die now or twenty years from now—I want to go out as Robert's wife."

She sounds happy and certain. My heart fills with emotion: fear, love, respect.

"Tell me when and where," I say.

"There's a preacher who ministers at the hospital and has agreed to marry us. You don't need to do anything but wear something pretty and see if you can find Mason a real shirt. Robert's out now buying rings. We're aiming for four thirty, with a champagne toast afterwards. And about your earlier comment? I don't know what you were thinking, Fi, but you *are* a close friend."

I hurry to find Mason, who's outside with his weights.

"You'll never believe it: Zuri and Robert are getting married. In about three hours!"

His face lights up. "That's wonderful."

"Yes, but . . ." I have to express it to someone. "Don't you think it's a bit strange? Not for Zuri, but for Robert. He's marrying someone who might not survive long, in which case he'd be responsible for a host of issues he might not even know about . . . and be a widower too. I can't imagine doing something like that just to 'feel' you'd been married. Can you?"

He sets the weights down and studies me. "Of *course* I would. I can't believe you even asked. There's more to life than practicality, Fi. He *loves* her—even if she dies, he wants to honor that love in his life. Don't you dare bring any doubts into this ceremony. I mean that. This is the happiest thing that's happened around here for a long time."

Now I feel petty. "I won't, I promise. By the way, Zuri said you should wear a real shirt."

"A formal shirt, with a collar and buttons?" He grimaces. "I didn't think I'd need one here; they're back in New York. I'll run out now and get one. Text me if you need anything."

While he's gone I put on makeup, and on a whim, pull my hair into a ponytail and tuck the end loosely back down through the hair tie. It creates a sort of updo that looks fairly stylish . . . fit for a wedding even. Now I'm getting excited.

Mason returns after an hour, wearing new clothes and carrying a huge bag. He looks quite elegant: Navy pants and a crisp white shirt with thin navy stripes give him a very different vibe.

"Wow," I say.

"What? I have worn grown-up clothes before, you know." He's not upset, just amused. Inside the bag are a slew of artificial white lilies and three red roses, which he hands me.

"Here, help me make a bouquet. I figure roses for the three of us, and the rest to decorate the room. Weddings should be festive, don't you think?"

"What about a few of them twisted into a circle thingy for her head?" I suggest.

"Perfect. You do that, I'll make a garland and cut the roses. Wait, give me your wrist."

I hold my arm out and he places a rose on the back of my wrist, looping the wire all the way around and twisting it into a perfect corsage. I feel warm and fuzzy inside: The last time a man did that for me was at senior prom.

We arrive half an hour early. Zuri is already dressed, made-up, and sitting on the edge of the bed in a short white dress and pearl earrings. She looks radiant with joy. Robert looks, if anything, even happier, wiping his eyes occasionally as though he can't believe this is happening. Why did I ever doubt this wedding?

"Look at you two!" Zuri exclaims. "Boy, Mason, do you clean up pretty!"

"And you look stunning in white," he replies, smiling.

Her mouth opens in amazement when she sees the flowers. "Did you do this, Fi? You are the best bridesmaid ever."

My heart whooshes. "I didn't know I was a *bridesmaid*. I've never been one before."

"You're the maid of honor today, honey."

The garlands are hung and it's 4:20 when Robert says, "I just wish we had music."

To my surprise, Mason asks, "Would you like me to sing something?"

"Do a hymn," Robert says. "If you know a good one. It'll feel like we're in a church."

Mason knows one, the right one. "*Breathe on me, breath of God. Fill me with life anew . . .*"

He sings it from memory, three verses. One more thing I never knew about the man I live with: He has a gorgeous voice, rich and true, and he knows how to use it.

Robert joins in where he can, but I'm looking at Zuri, her eyes as wet as mine. This hymn is for us. If we had the power to call to God directly, he might hear and heal us. And maybe that's what is happening: Mason is doing it for us.

When we leave afterwards, the two of them are entwined, plain gold bands shining on their fingers. It was one of the most beautiful weddings I've ever seen.

"That was incredible," I say to Mason in the car. "Who knew you could sing like that?"

"I was a choirboy."

"Really? I hadn't pegged you as religious."

"I don't like religion without follow-through. People who'll pray for you but won't do anything else to help. Or who say things like, 'Don't worry, God will heal you.' Do you know how many times people said that to Wanda? What good did it do?"

"So then *are* you religious?"

"I'm pretty sure as my employer you're not allowed to ask me that."

"Oh, duh . . . I'm so sorry."

"That's okay, I don't see you firing me. The answer is that I do absolutely believe there's something out there much more powerful and important than me. No way am I the biggest, baddest cat in the universe. But my perception of that force isn't how most people think of God. Of the three parts of the Trinity, the one that truly resonates with me is the Holy Spirit. That's how I sense God: almost as an essence, like vanilla. Taste and smell and comfort and unlimited possibility all rolled together. But I have trouble tapping into that sense of awe unless I'm in nature. A fragrant breeze in a heat storm, or a flash of color in a forest. That's where I find God."

It sounds beautiful. And powerful. "Someday, if we can find a place with a wheelchair trail, I'd like to come with you to see your God. If that's okay."

He's surprised but pleased. "That's a wonderful idea. I'd like that very much."

I have a feeling I'll like it too.

Chapter 26

I'm awakened by the sound of Mason's voice in the other room. Do we have visitors? But who would be visiting us here? We know only a handful of people and hardly spend time even with them. I'm on the verge of slipping back asleep when I hear it again.

Rolling onto my left side, I leverage up to sitting, wait to make sure I'm not lightheaded, then pull on the fluffy robe that lives on the edge of the bed. I'm so thin now that sometimes I get night shivers.

Mason's on the couch, clasping his cell phone on his lap, his expression reminding me of a bad frog experiment.

"Everything okay?" I ask, feeling suddenly afraid.

His eyes turn my way, but I don't think he fully sees me.

"Mason? What is it?" He looks at the phone, as if to confirm that what he thought just happened did in fact happen.

"Petra just called." He sounds as if he's climbing through a long tube. I can't decipher his tone: sadness, surprise, certainly confusion. "She never calls without a reason, not since the divorce, so I knew it was something important. But I never expected this."

Divorce? I think. *What the hell? And who's Petra?*

He draws a shaky breath and continues, but it's not clear whether he's talking to me or to himself. "She wants me to take Michaela. She's offering me my daughter."

I feel a lurch. Apparently it shows, because his eyes jolt alert.

"Shit! Sorry, Fi . . . this is all news to you. Sit down, you don't look well."

"I'm *not* well, remember?" I snap, emotions I'm trying to suppress sloshing out all over the place. *He's married? To a* woman*?*

"You've never mentioned anything about this before," I say, the words taut.

"Excuse me?" he retorts. "Since when am I required to inform you of my past personal life? But okay. I've been divorced for four years and have seen my daughter once every couple of months since then, plus bonus time for her birthday. Not actually *on* her birthday, since Petra wouldn't want my presence shadowing her precious parties, but 'sometime around' her birthday. Has any of this *even once* impacted my ability to do my job?"

No, it hasn't, but that doesn't help. I'm angry, scared of what this development might mean, and don't know if he's been lying all along about taking care of his gay lover. Most of all, I'm hurt that he didn't share something as important as an ex-wife and child. It's surprisingly hurtful to learn that he doesn't consider me that close a friend.

"Sit down, Fi. Turn up your oxygen and breathe deeply. I'll bring your oximeter."

I sit on my beloved armchair opposite the couch, my mind awash with questions. *Offering him his daughter*—what does that even mean? It's like waiting for my first lung test results, hoping things weren't as bad as I feared but knowing inside that they were.

When he returns with the oximeter, my pulse rate shows 103. We both wait in tense silence until it reaches 85; it takes a while. Finally, I look at him in question, and he sighs.

"Petra and I met online." He looks at the phone again, turning it in his hands. "We got on well and enjoyed being together. When she unexpectedly became pregnant, we got married—I assumed forever—and named our daughter Michaela after Petra's father. Four years later she hit me with a divorce filing, asking for full custody. She insisted it would be better for Michaela not to be constantly shuttling between households, that she deserved a stable home where all her things were, not the stress of always worrying if she'd left her cuddle blanket or favorite dress at the other place."

I'm already anticipating the custody battle, though I can't imagine how he could have lost so badly. Surely Mason was a wonderful father.

"And I agreed," he finishes flatly.

I'm stunned. The Mason I know would never give up his child without a fight and just walk away. It's as though *I've* been betrayed. But maybe I've been wrong about who he is.

"So you didn't want custody of your daughter."

"Of course I did!" The sound of despair. "I loved Michaela beyond anything. That's why I stepped away. Because if I hadn't, the mud Petra would have thrown would have come back to land on my child." He sighs, rubs his eyes.

"Petra found out about an affair I'd had—not while we were together; it was over long before we even met. But Petra couldn't get over it."

"She divorced you over a relationship that happened before she even met you? Forgive me, but that seems hard to believe."

"Let me fix breakfast."

"I'm not hungry. Tell me what happened—please."

"Stop pushing me!" He stands and goes to the kitchen, muttering, "We both need to eat."

We're silent through the whole process: quiche, eggs, coffee. It might as well be slime. Eventually Mason pushes his plate away. I toy with the crumbs until I can face whatever he's going to say; when I look up, he's frowning, but calm.

"I didn't mean to be that hostile. It's been a very long time since I've thought of this, and I've only ever told a few people. It's painful. The affair I'd had was with a man named Jed, and the reason Petra was angry was that it was notorious in certain circles. I broke up what looked like a rare happy celebrity marriage." His mouth twists. "Marriage-buster Mason, that's me."

I'm trying to make sense of this but failing. If he *is* gay, why does he have an ex-wife and a child? Was he hiding his true self?

"Go on," he says, reading my face. "You may as well; everyone asks eventually. If I loved Jed—which I did, very much—then I'm gay. So why did I marry Petra? Right?"

"Well . . . yes. Was the marriage a sham?"

"No. It wasn't the way it had been with Jed, but Jed was gone, and I loved Petra honestly—enough to think we'd be happy together. The sex was good, if you care. I fully believe we'd still be together if she'd reacted differently."

"So you're . . . bisexual?"

He shrugs that off. "Whatever you want to call it; labels aren't really my thing. I consider myself simply a *person*. Someone who can be attracted to any other person with characteristics that resonate for me. Are they kind, intelligent, honest, funny? Do they have a sparkle, or talent? Is there a deeper connection? Sure, physical attraction is important, but sexual organs are about mechanics, not love.

You can have sex with a vibrator, or an inflatable doll, or a zucchini, if you're so inclined. I'm perfectly fine having sex without love, but a relationship? That requires something meaningful." He looks away, muttering, "Damn, I hate having to explain this."

I'm confused, but trying hard to sort out how I feel about this. It's unfamiliar territory.

He turns back and asks, "Have you always dated tall, blond engineers?"

I shake my head.

"Then you're open to different options too. You consider multiple factors. Think of it that my search field just has different criteria from yours. I don't begin by filtering for gender."

This is too hard. To shift the conversation, I say, "Tell me about Jed."

"No." It's definitive, almost angry. "Jed will always be a fundamental part of me, but I don't bring him out to play. Especially not for other people to play."

I feel chastened, though it wasn't meant to be intrusive.

"Anyway, that isn't the main issue today." He straightens up. "Petra called because there's been a major change in her situation. Her magazine has offered her a six-month stint writing articles in . . . one of the Stans, I forget which. Hopefully Kyrgyzstan—coolest country name of all, in our alphabet. The Scrabble score's probably thirty points."

"No way, it's a proper noun."

"True. Anyway, it's a fantastic opportunity professionally, but she's not comfortable bringing Mike . . . Michaela, our daughter. Petra wouldn't have time for her and is concerned about her safety, especially as Petra has no support network there. Her husband's a good stepdad but he's a jet-set type who can't be in New York full-time. Petra's own parents are dead and she hates her sister, so that leaves me. Which I suppose means she doesn't think I'm as unfit a parent as she once did . . . or as much as she told the judge, anyway. She wants Mike to live with me at least until school starts back up in the fall. Maybe for the full six months."

He stops there, his thoughts turning inward again. I don't know what to say. There's nothing *to* say. If my child were taken away from me and I was given another chance to be a real part of their life, it would feel like a miracle. And I know plenty about dreaming for miracles.

"I'm very happy for you," I say. And mean it. However, I am screwed.

Without Mason, I can't stay in the program. I can't take care of myself even now, much less after transplant. And since everyone here "knows" that Mason's my husband, I can't hire someone else. Though they wouldn't have to be my husband. They could be my brother . . . or my sister. But how can I find someone who's capable of doing all the things Mason does—and on such short notice? The obvious answer would be for Dane to leave work and come here after all; he could pretend to be my cousin again. But my gut tells me that's a terrible idea. Now that I know what caregiving involves, it's clear Dane isn't the right person for the job. He'd be continually stressed, and I'd end up worrying about *him*.

"I'll need your help," I tell Mason. "Finding a replacement won't be easy, and I can't advertise locally in case someone here recognizes them. Could you initiate a search further away and help me interview candidates?"

"What are you talking about?" He frowns.

"I'm happy for you, Mason, truly. But finding someone may take a while, and the transplant could come at any time. How long till you leave?"

"What are you talking about?" He looks astonished. "I'm not *leaving*. Mike's seven, not a baby. We could hire someone to help with the daily routine if necessary, but I won't just abandon you . . . What kind of person do you think I am? I wouldn't do that even to someone I didn't like, and believe it or not, I'm rather fond of you."

"Oh." And despite the gravity of the situation and the fact that this shouldn't even be in my top ten things to think about, Mason saying he's fond of me stops me in my tracks.

"Look, Fi, I've only just learned this myself. Right now I'm simply trying to absorb what's happened, but later I'd appreciate your input on next steps. You're good at this; we'll figure it out. If you're willing to be flexible about having Mike here, we can make it work."

Flexible? I think. Sure, I can be flexible, but how will the kid cope with being far away from home and friends, with her mother a continent away and her father taking care of a very sick woman?

I reply quickly, before I can change my mind. "I don't think so. It's too much for a kid to handle. You should just move into her home and give her that stability. I can manage."

He shakes his head before I've even finished speaking. "No, you can't, and you know it. Petra's leaving soon; there isn't time to find you another caregiver. And you know yourself Dane's not a good solution. You haven't even bothered to suggest it."

I can feel my embarrassed flush. Is it that obvious?

"Don't be too hard on him. Lots of people can't handle this constant stress and fear, especially when it's someone they love. You saw how terrified he looked last time, when he saw how much you'd declined. He used to want detailed reports on you; now it's just a brief summary. I'm your only option, Fi, and this is not negotiable. Kids have overcome much worse than this, trust me, and Michaela's an extraordinary kid. So I'm asking, could you handle having a seven-year-old girl in the apartment?"

A kid. *Here*. It's insane . . . but maybe this is the change I've been asking for. Seven seems old enough to do at least some things for themselves. They can talk and tell you if they're hungry or cold. A seven-year-old girl, *here*. Young life, fresh laughter, a beginning rather than an end? It is the very essence of optimism.

There's a hiccup, though: Dane would never agree to it. He'd be sure Mason couldn't handle both Michaela and me . . . and maybe he's right. I'd have to not tell him, and that feels like a betrayal. But now that the possibility is out there, I really want this. What's the worst that could happen? If it doesn't work, then I call Dane and ask him to come down.

"Okay, let's give it a try. Tell Petra yes."

Chapter 27

Since Petra's call we've made major changes to the apartment. We quickly concluded that Michaela should have her own room: She's always had a space to herself, and it seems wrong for her to share with Mason. Unfortunately this means he'll have to sleep in the living room, and I'm worried about him being stretched too far. Taking care of both his daughter and an increasingly weak me, while not getting good sleep, seems like a bad idea . . . but we haven't found a better alternative. We've bought another bed, a twin, which (barely) fits along the side of the dining table. As long as we don't spill our dinner on Mason's blankets it should be okay.

Petra is on her way from New York now with Michaela. She's not staying, just turning right around at the airport so she can get back to New York and catch her flight to Kazakhstan (not Kyrgyzstan). The plan is that once I'm transplanted, Mason and Michaela will move back to Petra's apartment till she returns.

Getting ready for a seven-year-old stranger to move into your home isn't an easy task, especially when you've never had kids. Despite being her father, Mason doesn't know much about children this age. We've each called some friends with kids and read up online, and we'll wing it from here. At least Michaela's too old to worry about sharp objects, and too young to worry about sex or alcohol, so I figure the most important part is taken care of.

Right now what we're shooting for is a fun, happy bedroom and some initial activities, since it's summer vacation. We'll expand from that once we know her interests better.

After a flurry of preparation and a nervous countdown, the day has arrived. It's Saturday, so I don't have rehab, but my stomach has been fluttery since morning. My head isn't fully around the concept that I'm about to be living with the partially estranged daughter of a man who's technically my employee but is also a friend and ally. I've no idea how Michaela will feel about any of this. She doesn't know a soul here, it's a small unfamiliar apartment, and I have no logical place in her life. I'm not dating her father, so she won't need to compete for her dad's affections, but I will take his time. Lots and lots of his time.

Mason left for the airport two hours ago, so there's nothing for me to do but fuss. I move around the living room, looking for something else to tidy . . . as if a seven-year-old girl could possibly care. *Oh thank you*, she'll say, *I thought I'd be miserable here, but now that I see your cushions are fluffed up, I'm sure I'll be happy.*

How truly terrifying it must be for an arranged bride-to-be, meeting her future husband for the first time. Knowing that so much of the rest of her life will be determined by whether he likes her, whether they're attracted to each other. Whether he's inherently a good guy or a total shit.

My phone pings. It's Mason texting: *Headed back now.*

I drop onto the couch, then jump up again. We need ice! She'll be thirsty after her flight and want something to drink. I trip over my oxygen tube on the way to the freezer, but catch the fall, and it turns out Mason has remembered to refill the ice trays. This is reassuring. In his usual competent way, Mason has prepared as well as anyone can for Michaela's arrival. Her room will be perfect, he'll have asked Petra what food her daughter likes, and it will already be in the fridge. I just need to not get in the way.

I sit down again, more gently this time, and meditate with box breathing. I'm pretty good at this now, Dr. SEAL, in case you're interested.

When the key turns, I jerk the cannula out of my nose; no need for Michaela's first impression to be this ugly. Perhaps I should go to my bedroom so she can get used to the place first? But it's too late—the door is opening and there they are, Mason and his daughter. She's fairer than I'd expected, given Mason's coloring, her blonde hair falling perfectly straight and long down her back. Her mother must be very fair. She's also quite beautiful and dressed impeccably in what look to be designer clothes: a lavender blouse with a creamy zip-up jacket that reaches halfway down the thigh of her—*are those tailored pants?* It's a disconcertingly mature look for a child. What must she think of my black stretch pants that barely stay up any longer?

"Hi," I say, having not figured out a more original introduction, "I'm Fiona."

"Yes," she replies. "I guessed that. But shouldn't you be wearing a tube in your nose? Daddy said it helps you get good oxygen for your breathing. He said if I asked you'd show me how it works."

And just like that I am charmed. The thing she's most focused on is the mechanics of my apparatus. Michaela has none of the diva affect her clothes imply, and a lovely speaking voice. Low for her age, and resonant. But mostly it's the girl herself. She doesn't seem put off by me or even scared by the new surroundings; she's just curious about my machine, which she's now peering at intently.

"Of course," I reply. "Do you want to see it now?"

"Maybe wash your hands first," Mason intervenes gently.

"Oh sure, because of the germs. Daddy told me about those too. I'll take my shoes off first—even Mommy makes me do that, especially when we've been somewhere dirty like an airport. My name's Michaela, by the way."

"I guessed that too," I add.

Mason takes her suitcase and backpack and leads her to her bedroom, which until today was his. I want to be there when she sees it . . . mostly because Mason was so anxious to get it right that he even asked *my* advice. As if I know what today's seven-year-olds are into. I never even knew that when *I* was seven. But he needn't have worried: The squeals Michaela makes as she spins slowly are all he needs to hear.

"I *love* it, Daddy! It's perfect. The comforter's so pretty, that corally pink, and I just love it with the orange cushions." She lowers her head a little but we can see she's grinning. "Mommy won't let me have anything pink with orange or red. She says the colors smash, or clash or something. But I think it's totally dope—it makes my eyes happy, like fireworks. And there's a bookcase! You got me the whole *Magic School Bus* series? And . . . what's *The Borrowers*?"

"It's about a family of very small people," Mason tells her, his voice clutching a little at the sight of his daughter enraptured by a shelf of books. "I thought you might like to try something new. If you have trouble I'm happy to read them to you till you get a little older."

"I can read them myself," she says, straightening taller. "But it might be nice to have you read to me anyway. I like the way you read: It sounds like real people. Thank you, Daddy. Wait. What's this little chair for?"

She looks up at Mason in puzzlement.

"That's for Lea," he replies. "In case she wants to sit near you while you're reading. Or being read to."

She lights up, runs to her backpack, and pulls out a pretty doll that looks expensive . . . and a lot like a rounder-faced Michaela.

"This is Lea Clark," Michaela pronounces to me, since Mason evidently already knows. "She's an American Girl Doll, but she's Brazilian and loves to search for adventures."

Suddenly she seems anxious and turns to Mason as if for reassurance.

"Like me, right? I love adventures too, like what I'm doing now, right, Daddy?"

Then I understand why she's so upbeat: This has been billed as an adventure.

"Daddy told me that this year's going to be a great experience for the two of us. We'll spend lots of time together, and meet new people, and he's going to take me to places I've never seen before and do cool stuff together. So even though I'll probably miss Mom sometimes, and Krystal—she's my babysitter—it will be very special. And when Mom gets back, I can tell her and Krystal about my adventures. Right, Daddy?"

"Right, sweetie."

She exhales deeply. Too deeply for my fragile emotions. I hope we aren't going to traumatize her with this strange, fraught world we're immersed in.

"By the way," Mason adds, "what name do you like to be called these days? Do your friends call you Michaela?"

"No. It's too long. Though the teachers still mostly call me that. My friends call me Kayla, and Mommy does too, mostly. Michaela if she's mad at me. And you call me Mike . . . but you knew that."

"Yes. Is it okay if I still call you Mike?"

"Sure, I like it."

"Should Fiona call you Mike too?"

She frowns and looks at me, then shakes her head and returns to Mason.

"No. That's our special name. Just for you and me."

"So what would you like me to call you?" I ask, hoping she doesn't say "Michaela."

"You can call me . . . Shmekoloop!" She cocks her head, delighted with herself, and giggles.

I blink, and say carefully, "Okay. Tell me how to spell it, so I don't get it wrong."

Her eyes widen and she turns to Mason, flustered. "Daddy? Can you help?"

"Sure. Say it one more time." He pulls a pen off the desk, yanks the luggage tag from the suitcase, and concentrates as she repeats it, exactly the same as the first time.

"I think this is it. Does it look right to you?" She looks and nods.

"You'll have it much easier, because if Fiona lets you use *her* nickname, 'Fi,' it only has two letters. You can write it in about five seconds."

"Three!" she announces firmly. Somehow I'm not surprised. Mason and I catch each other's eyes and try very hard not to laugh.

Once the original excitement wears off, she'll likely start to miss the familiar people and home. Hopefully we can make this a good experience for her despite that. One thing is certain, though: This is going to be an adventure all right.

Chapter 28

People often say that having a kid changes everything. I'm quickly learning that having someone else's kid changes a whole lot too.

Michaela dropped into my life like a miniature Mary Poppins and brought sacksful of sugar with her. Her innate curiosity and openness to trying anything have changed my days from "How do we get through this?" to "What can we enjoy today?" I don't step on Mason's time with her—I know how important that is—but adding the care of a seven-year-old to his plate is exhausting, so I spell him whenever it seems right. It's hardly a sacrifice. Being with her is a delight, and she has accepted me as part of her circle of adults who want to make her happy.

Mason is the happiest I've seen him; he soaks up time with his daughter like a man who's been dehydrated for years. They spend time talking about books, or inventing characters for new ones, and every afternoon they play catch in the grassy quadrangle. He's bought her a pint-sized mitt and several balls and is teaching her to throw hard and straight. From what I've seen, she's doing really well, throwing like a girl—an athletic, determined girl.

A week after her arrival, Michaela notices my painting supplies in the closet. Apparently her home schedule is too full with dance classes, music lessons, and playdates to do art—besides which, Petra thinks it's a waste of time, Michaela says. Spotting an opportunity for bonding, I ask if she wants to see the flower paintings Mason and I made when we first got to Johnson's River. All three hang in my bedroom out of everyone's sight but mine. Of course she says yes.

Mine is first, on the left. She looks at it carefully, pronounces it "interesting," then moves to Mason's fake splodgy mess and dissolves into an extended fit of giggles.

"Daddy did *that*?" she squeaks when she's recovered enough to talk.

"Yes. But he made it like that on purpose so I wouldn't be scared of messing up, because I'd never painted anything before. He's thoughtful that way."

"Oh," she says, nodding. "I get it."

"Here's his real one." I show her the single flower from the perspective of an ant and watch pleasure and pride flow across her face.

"I never knew he could paint," she says, then grows thoughtful. "Do you think he could teach me how?"

"Of course! I'm sure he'd love it. I'd love to learn more too; maybe you and I could practice together between his lessons."

"Like homework!"

Now that she's in my room, she looks around to see what's there. I get a nervous flutter again; I want her to like my taste—or at least not think I'm boring. She asks about the photos and the Olympics frame, and finally reaches the photo next to my bed.

"Who's that with you?" she asks, pointing.

"That's my husband. His name is Dane and he lives in New York."

"Oh yes, Mom told me about him. She said you two are Daddy's bosses."

It could be just my bias against Petra, but this feels mean-spirited, like a deliberate put-down of Mason to his daughter.

"Well that is true," I respond, "but your daddy's also my friend. A very good friend who's helping me with a difficult situation until I get better."

She sits on my bed. "Yes, and you're pretending to be married, because the hospital likes married people. Don't worry, I won't tell. But do you miss your real husband?"

"Yes," I reply, though the truth is I miss him far less since Michaela's been here.

"I miss my mom and dad," she says, and it's as though something gives way—she's wiping away tears, quickly, as if pretending they aren't there. Poor kid: She's trying so hard to be tough that I wonder whether this was a bad idea after all. But this was the only way her mother felt safe to leave, and it's an incredible gift for Mason.

Michaela sniffs, then turns to me in concern. "Does that make you feel bad? It's nice here, but I still miss them. Krystal too—that's my nanny."

"Not at all, it's totally natural. You used to be with them all the time, and now you're with different people who you don't know as well."

"I do know Daddy, though," she replies, more brightly. "And I love spending time with him—he's always so fun, and I don't see him much at home."

"Your daddy's really happy to be with you too. You know that, right? He's been wishing for more time with you since you were tiny."

She smiles slyly, her head tipped down. She totally knows that.

"Maybe you and I can do fun stuff," I venture. "Your daddy has lots to take care of, so if we're doing things, he can get his work done and have more time to play with you afterwards. Plus I'd like to spend time with you anyway. Maybe we can figure out things we both like, or even teach each other new ones."

She considers this. "Do you know how to make a friendship bracelet?"

"No. I know what they are, but I've never made one."

"I can teach you. My friends and me make them all the time. See?" She pulls up her sleeve to display the three colorful bands on her wrist. Bingo. We go to find Mason for a supply run to the craft store. I'm guessing this will come up again, but she seems in better spirits now that we have a plan.

A few days later there's a more serious break. It's midmorning and Mason has gone for a run. Now that Michaela's here he no longer has free time while I'm in rehab. The sleek pink cell phone that Petra sent with her daughter starts playing the tweeny-pop song that I recognize as its ringtone. Michaela jumps up and heads to her room. She prefers taking her calls there, especially when it's her mom. I'm guessing it's her because of the time: Kazakhstan is ten hours ahead of us, which limits the hours available for video chat. Petra has called several times, but not so often as to interfere with Michaela's adjustment to Mason.

When Michaela returns, she's clearly upset.

"Is something wrong?" I ask her gently.

She nods and sniffs. "Not bad wrong. It's just, I was talking to my mom and sometimes it makes me sad after. It doesn't mean I don't like you, Fi. I do. But sometimes I miss my real room, and my friends, and going shopping for pretty dresses with Mom . . . and even interrupting Dad when he's working and I'm not supposed to."

Poor kid. This was inevitable. But it seems as though there's something else.

"Is there anything in particular you're sad about?" I ask. She shoots me a slightly alarmed look, as though I've caught her out. I wait to see if she'll tell me.

"Yes," she admits after a bit. "I'm kind of scared, too, even though Mom told me not to be. She said I couldn't go with her to Kazakhstan because it might be dangerous. But doesn't that mean it's dangerous for her too? What if something happens there and she never comes back?"

She starts sobbing in earnest. There's no brushing this away, and I'm struck with the reality of my first real parenting test. What do I say? Do I promise Petra will be fine—which is the likeliest scenario—or do I hedge, which is more honest? What would Mason do? And then the answer's clear.

"Michaela, I would love to promise you that your mom will be okay. But I don't promise things I can't control, because I want you to always be able to trust and believe me. Promises are important. I can't promise you that a big wind won't blow her away to the land of the fairies . . . but I *can* tell you that it's really, really unlikely. And that's what I'm telling you now. Your mom loves you. She wouldn't do something that would risk not coming back to you. So I can understand why you're worried—I'd worry too—but I'm as sure as it's possible to be that everything will be fine. You'll miss her, and then she'll come home, and you won't miss her anymore."

She brushes her eyes and nods. "Maybe when I'm back with her I'll miss Daddy."

For his sake, I really hope so. "He'll be happy to see you any time you want, and he'll be in New York so it will be easy, if your mom says yes."

Finally, she smiles. Then, as an afterthought, she asks, "Will you be in New York too?"

"Yes indeed . . . and I'd be delighted to see you again there." Please God, let this not be a lie. I need to stay alive so I can see her after this is all over.

Chapter 29

One evening after Michaela's in bed, Mason and I crash onto the couch, which is a little less white and more scuffed-up now than when we arrived, and debrief.

"You know," he says, grinning, "for someone who says she's 'not a people person' and has never had kids, you're doing pretty damn well with Mike."

Since I've been thinking pretty much the same thing, I accept the comment graciously.

"It's possible I'm not as bad as I thought; I just needed to pay more attention."

"How are you feeling about this so far?" he asks, part curious, part apprehensive.

"She's wonderful." I can feel the grin stretch across my face. "Tiring, but I'm always tired anyway; may as well be happy too." I look at him. "How are you holding up?"

"Same as you. She's much easier than when she was a baby, but back then Petra wasn't working and my job wasn't so stressful. I'm just relieved the two of you are getting along so well."

"Certainly on my part. I don't know if she feels the same."

"That's just your insecurity talking. You don't need to replace her mother, you know—just be another person in her life who loves her."

"Is she like Petra, do you think?"

His eyebrows lift. "I haven't given it much thought. Children are their own selves, aren't they? But she seems more open than Petra, more considerate. Certainly more forgiving."

I nod, musing on genetics and heredity and sheer individuality. Then, not for the first time, I wonder about her coming into being . . . whether she was Mason's golden lining after Jed died.

"Out with it, Fi. That's a very pensive look."

Now I'm embarrassed. "I was just wondering whether becoming a father was in your plans before Jed got sick. I'm sorry—I know you don't want to talk about him."

He pauses. "Actually, he and I did discuss it briefly, but it was too soon for me then. Not for him: He'd wanted a child with Helen, but she'd been dead against it. We'd likely have got there eventually, found a surrogate and used my sperm, just to stick it to his father."

We sit in silence, each caught up in our own thoughts. Mine are about missed chances, and the parenthood Dane and I had thought we were indefinitely deferring but ended up losing. Like me, Jed never did get to experience it.

After a while, I sense something shift. Mason studies me, assessing something.

"Do you still want to know about Jed?"

I hadn't expected this. "Yes, if you're comfortable telling me."

"When you first asked, I wasn't. But it feels different now, watching you with Mike."

I'm surprised again, and moved. It feels like an important gesture of closeness.

"We met at a fundraising dinner for a charity his wife was involved in. Helen Magnussen, the TV money guru. I was working at an ad agency then and was sent to be the presence for the firm. Jed was at my table while Helen was working the room all night. I was obviously just a junior butt in a seat who no one wanted to talk to, so out of kindness, Jed did. To both our surprise, he found me interesting. He was a relationship manager at a bank, which is solo work. Helen was gone in the evenings, and anyway her only real interest was her career. He was lonely. He seldom had the chance to discuss things like art, or travel and foreign culture."

"Which I'm sure you were great at," I interject. He smiles sadly.

"At the end of the evening he gave me his card and asked if I'd like to meet again. He was only a few years older than me, and well traveled. I was happy to be his friend. We met at a café, then again in a bookstore, and by our third meeting I realized something else was happening. That's when he told me about his life. Jed's father, Buddy Dixon, was a prominent businessman and alderman in a small town in Missouri. Buddy's conservative circle makes a fetish of 'manly men,' and when Jed came out to his parents at twenty-one, Bud threw him out. Said Jed could never come near anyone in the family again if he didn't 'straighten up.' He wouldn't tolerate his son ruining his own reputation."

My God, some parents.

"Jed went along with that?"

"Not immediately. He went back to the house the next day to say goodbye to his mother and saw her being carried away on a gurney. She'd taken a massive dose of sleeping pills. Jed had been her life raft in a crushingly misogynistic world that she felt she couldn't fight alone—she didn't want to live if he was gone. She survived, but Jed wouldn't risk it again. He agreed to his father's demands and resigned himself to staying closeted for the rest of his life."

I'm appalled. "That's just horrible! So Helen didn't know he was gay."

"No, she knew—they were friends in high school. She was just fiercely ambitious and realized that having an attractive, well-connected husband could be an important asset. She liked Jed, and this was her opportunity to gain the cachet of his powerful and well-known family. While for Jed, marrying Helen appeased his father and meant he didn't have to live alone. They found sex partners infrequently and quietly: he with other closeted men, Helen with high-profile married men who would never tell. For all I know, she screwed Jed's father: It would be like him. But Jed was a loyal husband, and they played the happy couple well for the cameras when needed. The media loved them: attractive, successful, supportive . . . until I came along."

"Marriage-buster Mason," I whisper.

"One day Jed told me he was ready to leave his sham life and own who he was. If I was interested in a relationship that went beyond the coffee shops, he wanted to be with me, whatever the consequences. I thought about it a lot. My relationships to that point had been with women; I'd never envisioned becoming part of the LGBTQ world, with all that involves. But then Helen went away for a couple of days and Jed stayed with me. I woke up next to him in the morning and knew this was where I wanted to be every day. It felt inevitable, and so joyous that the rest was irrelevant. It wasn't that I woke up and realized I was gay; I simply loved *Jed*—for the kind, brilliant, thoughtful, and fascinating person he was. Anyone who would criticize or abandon me for that was free to leave my life."

Watching the certainty on his face, listening to him speak, this seems like the most natural thing in the world. Be with who you love, no matter their designation. Could it be that simple?

"What happened when Helen got back?"

"Jed told her he'd finally found love and was leaving. She was angry, but by then was a big enough name not to need him anymore. The press were told that someone had seduced and stolen her husband while she was so busy working; she wouldn't say who 'they' were. Helen never fussed about political correctness, so her use of 'they' started all kinds of speculation. I'm surprised you didn't hear about it."

"Sorry—I'm often clueless about this stuff."

He nods. "Probably a good thing. Jed got called in by his boss, who said none of his clients had complained, so just keep going. I wasn't so fortunate. We'd been seen by someone in my office. Unlike Jed, I wasn't senior enough to bother sticking up for, so they fired me with no references. I'd never planned to be in advertising forever anyway, but I was jobless with no money until I eventually became a paralegal."

"What a mess. Is that what split you and Jed up?"

"No. That was leukemia."

Abruptly he's sad: an old, resigned kind of sad, as though the pain settled into his bones a long time ago. This explains his ability to cope with my medical saga. He really has been through it before, with someone a lot more important to him than I am.

"It was relentless. Multiple rounds of chemo, weakness, bruising, terrible nausea. Endless pain. I wanted desperately to be a marrow donor for him, but we were hopelessly mismatched there. His father was already on the donor registry and would have been a great match, but he refused. Said it was God's punishment for Jed's sins. The bastard."

I'm stunned. God should punish *him*. "So you took care of Jed while he was sick?"

"Of course." A wry smile. "It's on my résumé, remember? Experience in critical illness caregiving. My only regret is that Jed didn't make it to the average survival rate—we had three good years before he got sick, and only two after. But they were good years."

There's a Mona Lisa expression on him now, of a secret and beautiful joy. Despite everything, I find myself thinking he was lucky. Maybe I'm not romantic enough, but I don't think my relationship with Dane has that sort of magic. Neither of us was looking for it.

Finally I ask, "How did Petra find out?"

"Ah. Well the thing about Petra, she's patient, clever, and *very* good with details. She noticed that every year around the same time I came home late with dirt on my shoes, wrecked. She made a note of the date, and the next year followed me from work to the cemetery, where I put flowers on a grave. If she'd asked me I'd have told her everything, and maybe things would have unfolded differently. Instead she waited for me to leave and then went to the grave. The name *James Edward Dixon* rang a bell. She looked it up and learned that James 'Jed' Dixon was the estranged husband of Helen Leger Dixon, cohost of *Your Money, My Problem*. And she remembered: Jed had left Helen for another man. It wasn't hard to guess who that was. She came straight home and told me she wanted a divorce. She was upset about my involvement in the scandal, but what she couldn't forgive was that I'd never told her about it. And that's on me. I just wasn't ready to be interrogated about Jed. But she was my wife; I should have told her."

Silently, I agree.

"To be clear, Petra knew I wasn't straight. But she was open-minded enough to understand that I was person-specific, not gender-specific. She knew that I would be true to her—which I was, always. When I'm committed, I'm committed. I never looked elsewhere."

I'm trying to imagine being Petra in that situation. Would I have believed him? Or would I wonder whether deep down he would always long to be with a man again?

"You're skeptical, aren't you?" He shakes his head. "People never seem to get beyond the labels. Gay people often want us to 'make up our minds' one way or the other. Maybe they think we shouldn't be under the same umbrella because we don't have to suffer discrimination if we don't want to. As if it works that way. I love who I love . . . and it doesn't come along very often."

"Anyway . . ." He sighs. "Petra wanted me to leave immediately. She wanted the apartment and felt she was entitled to keep it. If I agreed to let her have full custody of Michaela, she'd stay quiet. If not, she'd stir up the dirt over Jed again, including my name this time, and let public opinion do its worst."

"Would that have been so bad? Worse than losing your daughter?"

"I don't know," he admits. "I've never known. But other people I love would have been hurt. My parents live in a small, traditional community; people might have looked down on them afterwards. But mostly it was about Mike. No child needs bad publicity raked up about their father, and it could have been very ugly—Helen's fan base got much stronger after Jed left her. I've never forgiven Petra for being prepared to hurt our child to get what she wanted. Though she probably knew it would never come to that—that I wouldn't risk it. But it was an excellent bargaining chip. Aside from that, the dirt would have affected me too. I still wanted to have a normal life someday: a relationship, possibly even other kids. I didn't know whether anyone normal would want to be a partner to someone notorious this way."

I want to tell him that the right person wouldn't care, but I know it's not that simple. The uncertainties would mount up. If you were a woman, did he really want you? Were people snickering about you behind your back—or to your face?

"I'm sorry. About Petra and all of it."

"It's long done now." He smiles. "Get some rest; it'll be Mike time before you know it."

Chapter 30

August

If only I weren't so sick, this would be one of the happiest times of my life.

In just a month and a half, one small feisty girl has turned up the colors in my life and sunk herself deeply into my heart. My free time and thoughts are filled with activities I haven't done since childhood—like chemistry experiments and growing crystals—and others I've never done before, like toenail painting and hair braiding. However tired I am, there's always time and energy for that; that and my healing reading, which I do while Michaela and Mason throw and catch outside. Monique would be proud of me. She doesn't know how difficult it is sometimes not to just gaze at them through the window: the dark, protective man and his fair, ferocious daughter playing ball in the sunshine, Michaela's hair in a golden braid tucked under her baseball cap while she bites her lower lip in concentration. In its own way watching them feels like a spiritual activity too.

My special time with Michaela is mornings, before rehab, when I'm well rested. Now that I know her better it's easier to find activities to do together. My favorite is when we think of something she hasn't done before. I tell myself it's inherently good for her to try something new, but beneath that, it also provides new territory that doesn't raise thoughts of her mother and nanny. She hasn't talked about missing them in a long time. And selfishly (because there's always that) I'm hoping to build something she can remember me by. Our time together is limited, whether I survive or not. Part of me wants to imagine her years from now, maybe with her own children, smiling and thinking, *I used to do this with Fi.*

We've found a fantastic selection of science kits online. Twice a week we do experiments, frequently making an unbelievable mess, which Mason then cleans up. He makes a face and complains a lot, but we all know it's just for show.

Today we're doing art. Michaela is partial to air-dry sculpting clay, so over the past weeks we've made an entire ecosystem of animals. Some are real, while most are fictional or hybrid, like the zebraffe—a striped horse body with a very long neck, not limited to just black stripes and brown spots. Right now we're building a whimsical zoo, which we've set up on my bedroom floor because there's plenty of space here and none in the living area. This is a very progressive design for a zoo, with all the elements Michaela thinks she'd want if she were an animal living with her friends. There's a hair salon for the shaggier creatures (yak, lion, and orangutan), a running track for the antelopards, and a playground for the apes.

Michaela is busy making a flower bed to go next to the camelephant's swimming pool when her ringtone starts. She looks down at it, then up at me, and for the first time decides not to go to her room to take the call. It's her nanny this time, and they have the exact funny, loving conversation

I'd always imagined, only this time Michaela ends it sooner than usual.

"Fi," she says hesitantly, clearly not needing to go to the bathroom as she's just told Krystal. "Is it bad if I don't want to talk to Krystal so much anymore?"

Damn, I hate these curveballs. She'll need her nanny when she returns home; it's important that they stay close. But it's probably not good for her to feel split between two worlds while she's here either.

"It's fine, sweetie," I say in my best *Oh, pshaw!* tone. "It doesn't mean you love her any less, and Krystal knows that. It just means you're more comfortable here than you used to be. I'm sure nothing could make her happier than that. Plus, there's less to talk to her about, now that you're not in school. That will change when you get back home."

But she still looks anxious. "I just worry if I'm going to hurt her feelings, and then maybe she won't *want* me to come back."

I'm genuinely shocked. "*No way.* Are you kidding? Krystal knows how much she means to you, and right now she just wants what will make you happy. Believe me, she understands."

To my astonishment, Michaela comes over and hugs me tight, burying her face in my chest. It's so unexpected that I just let the feeling wash through my body like a field of warm sunlight. Her back is toward the doorway, so she doesn't see the shadow as Mason approaches, or the surprised look on his face as he sees us on the floor, hugging.

"Fi," she says, lifting her head. "Can I give you a new nickname, special for us? I want to call you Mee-Fee. It means 'My Fi,' like 'My Fiona,' but it rhymes: Mee, Fi."

"Of course you can. I would love that." I would lock-that-in-my-heart love that. The light shifts again and Mason is gone.

Later that evening, Michaela and I are playing cards on the couch when Mason bursts in with an iPad on his shoulder like an old boom box, blaring an opening lick that I recognize but can't place. He's wearing a black down vest over a white button-down shirt with the top two buttons undone, and a dark tie (where did he get *that*?) loose to the second button. Michaela looks as confused as I am. He prances for a bit, throwing smoldering glances at us as the music thumps, then puts the iPad down and sings along as the lyrics kick in.

> "*Ooh my little scrawny one, my scrawny one. Gotta keep those calories high, Fiona? Racing 'round the track, grab a snack. But don't you worry 'bout your time, Fiona!*"

As I already knew, the man can sing. And he's giving it the full works, gyrating his hips and putting on a pouty face, and Michaela—her eyes and mouth wide—is eating it up. He takes her by both hands and pulls her up to dance with him, the pair of them stomping around the room, tangoing, shaking, and wiggling to the music. As the famous lick approaches, he motions Michaela to listen up, then belts out, "*M-m-m-my Fiona!*" By the second time, she has it down, and they yell it to me together. They get progressively goofier and more out of breath, and by the time the song is over we are laughing uncontrollably in a big pile on the couch. The three of us. Together.

Chapter 31

Outside our cozy home, things are not going well. After a long period of slow decline, my health has begun deteriorating faster. The rehab nurse watches me more often and with a graver face; twice this week I've had major coughing spells and once had to fake needing the bathroom to get a break from the workout. It's very discouraging doing the same exercises as always but getting worse and worse at them. Every morning I've been measuring my basic pulmonary functions on a home PFT device. It's nowhere near as accurate as the hospital one but does give me a heads-up if things start to change substantially. Lately it has been drifting downward. The problem is that I don't know how much further it can fall before I stop functioning altogether.

Before leaving New York, I asked Dr. Hillier how low my lung capacity could go before I died and she just shrugged. "It varies from person to person. Humans are built with excess lung capacity: We can lose quite a bit without meaningful impact on our lives, except for those who have to perform at very high physical levels. After that, incremental loss lowers function—often not linearly.

Suddenly you realize you can't run anymore, then you can't walk much without resting, then it's no bending over, and so on. But at some point the body falls below survival level."

My big question is when the point will come when my next decline is my last.

I haven't discussed this with anyone because there's nothing to be done short of getting the transplant, and there's no way to accelerate that. So I continue to hope, but with decreasing faith. My days consist of joyful time with Michaela in the morning, forcing my way through rehab after lunch, and flopping at home with relief midafternoon. Evenings and weekends are my high points. That's when I can shed my sick, possibly dying persona and become simply a frail woman enjoying time with people she cares about.

Dane and I speak less often now. He's traveling a great deal, and conversation is constricted by my need to breathe after every few words. In my world here this is common; no one comments. Dane's face, though, vividly registers his pain at watching my deterioration. His panic becomes mine, which makes fighting that much harder. If my death were truly imminent, I'd either ask him to leave work and come here or I would return home. But what if I left and my lung match came in right afterwards? And Dane coming here permanently would feel like we've accepted the death sentence and are just performing a long goodbye. Probably wishing the axe would finally fall so it could all be over. As things are now, I still have a life.

We've hired a babysitter, three afternoons a week. Recently Drew said cheerfully, "I saw Mason with your daughter the other day. How long is she visiting for?"

I'm prepared. "Not long, unfortunately. Just until Mason's ex-wife returns from her business trip. We hired a sitter so Mason won't have to take care of both of us."

"Sounds great. Enjoy your time together."

We're hoping that having a sitter will address the program's issue of conflicting responsibilities, but she also buys Mason a little breathing space. He runs in the early morning, then while I'm with Michaela he does the chores: tanks, shopping, cooking, shuttling me, and so on. Any other free time he spends with Michaela. He's stopped even trying to write, saying there are more urgent matters and he can't find his creativity anyway. It's hardly what he'd planned on when taking this job, but there's no real likelihood of change. Michaela's an easy child but she's still a child, and the weaker I get the more I take out of the system rather than help. Mason makes a point of not complaining, saying time with his daughter is a gift, but I can only hope that he's not too depleted. Things are likely to get worse before they get better.

When Mason picks me up from rehab today he is alone. He seems solemn, so I'm not surprised when he says we need to talk. I've been wondering when things would come to a head: The constant pressure and lack of sleep are taking a huge toll on him. Sleeping in the living room proved to be a disaster. Summertime means that daylight starts early and lingers late into the evening. None of us can fall asleep early, and the flimsy living room shades don't block the sun much beyond dawn.

Yesterday I pushed him on it. "You're exhausted. Let me trade rooms with you, just for a few days so you can catch up."

"Fi, we've talked about this. Nothing's changed: The last thing you can afford is going without sleep. Anyway," he continues as the corner of his mouth curls up, "Mike took care of it."

"How? What did she do?"

"She overheard us talking and said she wants me to move my bed into her room. I was about to say no, but she gave me that look and said, 'Please, Daddy! Then you can read to me and go straight to sleep after and keep me safe all night. I don't snore, I promise.'"

It's impossible not to laugh. "I really hope that girl uses her powers for good."

"No kidding. Anyway, that's not what I wanted to talk about." He helps me into the apartment, hands me a strawberry-chalk protein drink, and sits across the table.

"You're getting worse. I know you've been avoiding talking about it, and I haven't wanted to force you, but we have to start making plans. Here's what I think. First, we need to talk to your doctors and get them to be straight with us. Since that one dry run you haven't had a single call. All the other patients have seen some action, but you haven't. Maybe there's a reason for that, and if so we need to hear it. If it turns out that Regent can't get you new lungs, there's no reason to stay here. I don't want what happened to Wanda happening to you."

My eyes well up. I desperately didn't want to have this conversation. All I wanted was to squeeze the remaining joy from what I have right now. Don't the teachings say to live in the moment? Now that it's been said I can't avoid it . . . it's time to plan the endgame.

"Next," he continues in a flat, businesslike manner, "we need to contact the doctors back at Empire. I want to know how many potential matches you're missing out on by being so far away. How many lungs have they not been able to offer you because their usable life is too short? At some point your chances will be better in New York."

I don't articulate what we both know. At least in New York I'll be with my husband and friends. When the time comes, I won't die alone.

"Did you ever discuss this with Dane?" he asks.

"No, the assumption was always that I'd get transplanted here first."

"You should talk it over with him." He frowns. "Come to think of it, he hasn't been here in a while. I want to take Mike to the water park lodge over his next visit. When's he coming?"

It's time to come clean. "There's no plan. Neither one of us has suggested it, and I've been avoiding it because he doesn't know about Michaela."

"*What?*" He's utterly shocked.

"You know how he is. Well, maybe you don't, but I do. If he visits, I'll have to tell him, and anyway he can hardly fail to notice that your room is now a little girl's bedroom. He'll be furious that you're splitting time between me—your promised first and only responsibility—and your daughter."

Mason slumps back against the chair, scraping his hair back with his fingers.

"And to cap it off," he says slowly, "he's still paying my full salary. He wouldn't be wrong; I just never looked at it that way. What if we got a full-time sitter for Mike? Would he still be angry?"

"Yes, because we should have consulted him before Michaela came. *I* should have; it was my responsibility, not yours. Truthfully, I wanted her here and was afraid he'd veto it. For the record, we pay your salary jointly. And he's been so uninvolved lately, why should he be dictating terms? If he'd visited, or even kept in better touch, I'd have told him."

"Jesus, Fi! Your marriage is even more screwed up than mine—and I'm divorced."

He sits forward again. "You have to tell him. I'll stay here if you want moral support, but you can't hide this. He's your *husband*."

At least he didn't say, "He's my boss."

I send Dane a text: *I need to talk to you in private, whenever you get the chance.* I'm half hoping he won't respond, but in a couple of minutes he video calls. He looks tense.

"What's up, Fi? Is there a problem?"

"Everything's fine. I just wanted to let you know that Mason's daughter is spending some time with us." Then I hold my breath.

"*No way!*" Dane's pale skin flushes deep red with anger. "In the first place, how does a gay guy have a daughter?" He turns to make sure his office door is closed. "Was that story about his dying lover just a lie so he could get hired?"

Across the table, Mason's hands curl into fists.

"No, it's true. But he was married once. Michaela's mother had to go out of town, so she came here. It's not a problem. We've hired a sitter, so . . ."

"It damn well *is* a problem! His job is taking care of *you*, not her. And what about the hospital rule that he's not allowed to have any other responsibilities but you? Does a sitter eliminate that requirement?"

"Actually, it does if Michaela becomes the sitter's responsibility. And it's temporary . . . we're allowed visitors. Dane, I like having her here. She's the only point of light in the place."

Now he looks disbelieving. "So the woman who wasn't eager for kids suddenly discovers she likes them after all?"

I take a long, slow breath, recognizing the inconsistency. He's right to be upset.

"Not kids generally, but this one, yes," I reply.

"How long has she been there? You arranged this without even telling me—what am I supposed to make of that?"

Only now does it sink in how much of a betrayal this was. "I'm really sorry, Dane. You're right, I should have asked you beforehand. I should have . . . but I was afraid you'd say no."

His eyes flare open. With a great effort, he says nothing until he's regained composure.

"Of course I'd have said no." Quiet but insistent. "Mason can't take care of both of you, and what if you get the transplant call? She can't stay there."

I feel pummeled, punched straight to the heart. What would this place be like without her?

Mason reaches over and rotates the iPad so Dane can see him too.

"Unfortunately, Dane, Michaela can't leave unless I leave too." His voice is cool. "So unless you can instantly find a new caregiver who's capable of handling this situation, you'll have to take an extended leave and do it yourself. I can fill you in on the long list of daily tasks, coach you on Fi's doctors, food needs, necessary tests, insurance problems, and so on. It's become complicated and sometimes painful to deal with."

Dane's face has lost all the red and fallen serious and still.

"Alternatively," Mason continues, "you can wait until we hear from Fiona's doctors what's causing the delay, and from Empire to learn how far up the list she is now. It might be time to consider returning to New York. Obviously we should all discuss that. And if she receives a call before then, we'll do what we always planned—call you and have you fly down. I have friends among the caregivers who have said they'll take care of Michaela if I'm tied up."

There's a long silence while Dane weighs his options.

"And you're right," Mason continues. "I was supposed to devote all my time to Fiona. It would be totally reasonable to reduce my pay."

"Oh, for Christ's sake." Dane shakes his head, but he's no longer angry. "It's not about the money. Okay, let's leave things as they are for now, but if it gets too much, you tell me right away. You have to take good care of her." His lip trembles.

Mason nods solemnly. "I will. I was always going to do that."

I hang up in a daze of joyous amazement. Michaela is staying!

"That was brilliant," I tell Mason. "You called his bluff."

"He's an intelligent man, Fi. He knows he's not the right person for this. He just needed a way not to feel guilty about it."

I ponder this. Poor Dane. It must be hard not being able to help someone you love.

"Now that's done," Mason says, "can I tell you what I wanted to discuss in the first place?"

Oh, right, I'd forgotten this was a tangent.

"Now that you're this advanced, there's a much greater likelihood of you getting a hit from Empire. If we do stay here, you'll remain on both lists, but we need to know how to get to New York very quickly. We should consider a private jet service."

I'm stunned. "You're kidding, right? Do you have any idea how much that costs?"

"Yes. From here to New York is about twenty-five thousand dollars for up to four passengers. I found an agency that matches up people who need a plane in a hurry with private planes available for hire. They can guarantee us a jet to take off within two hours of me calling. It's the only way to be sure you'd make it on time. I'm not even sure you'd be allowed onto a commercial airline now, given how sick you are."

"But I can't pay twenty-five thousand dollars for a plane flight!"

"*Yes you can!* I'm not talking about buying a Dior dress, for God's sake. This isn't a frivolous expense. Do you have twenty-five thousand in life savings? Then use them to *save your life*."

The response I was about to make dies on my tongue as his words replay in my head: *Use my life savings to save my life*. As I see the desperate concern on his face, the meaning sinks in. If I don't make it to the transplant theater, there's no point in having the money. This is the emergency it was intended for.

Something stirs inside me. Mason's not treating me as a lost cause—not yet. This isn't just a way to bring me home to die, it's a plan to give me my best possible shot at remaining in the present tense. We just have to work out the details and keep me alive until then. It's not normal to make decisions like this on the spot . . . but nothing about this process is normal.

"Let's do it," I declare, with more conviction than I've felt in a long time.

He breaks into a slow smile and a long exhalation. "Glad to have you back, Ms. Copeland. I've been waiting for your return. Semper Fi, Fiona. Semper Fi."

Chapter 32

Mason has taken Michaela for a morning out in nature, going to visit his God. We've done this as a trio several times since finding a wheelchair-friendly trail a half hour away. Thank goodness for children in strollers—I doubt the local parks department would lay a boardwalk through woodland just for the few wheelchair-bound visitors I've seen.

Today I'm taking a pass. I'm very tired, and I have an important letter to write.

After my mother died, my relationship with my father nose-dived. He'd always been a high-achieving, high-stress person, and when things were going badly he took it out on my mother. Not physically—he never hit her—but he'd yell about how everything he'd worked for his entire life was going to blow up and we'd be left with nothing. My mother was his release valve. His tirades released much of his pressure . . . and transferred it to her.

When her lungs failed I believed it was his fault. Not directly, but I was sure the constant stress had eroded her health. As her illness progressed he was an incredibly attentive caregiver—a type AA+ personality to the end—but it made no difference to me. You don't get credit for trying to fix a problem you created in the first place. Especially if you fail.

After my mother's funeral, I never wanted to see him again. Out of politeness I sent flowers to his wedding two years later, in London (he'd married his English sales rep, naturally). For several years I sent birthday greetings, receiving them in return from his wife, whom I'd never met. Eventually we all stopped bothering.

But now that it's increasingly likely that I don't have much time left in the world, this fractured history feels like an unnecessary burden. Whatever our relationship has been and become, it deserves a resolution. Maybe even a better ending. So today I'm sitting at Mason's desk, writing a letter that recalls the good parts—the ones I buried under anger and blame years ago.

First I state the simple facts: that I haven't been able to get a transplant despite months of waiting. While I haven't completely given up hope, there's a high probably they won't find matching lungs in time to save me. Then I thank him for the good memories of my childhood, which I painstakingly dig out and polish until they are beautiful.

Thank you, Dad, for the long bike rides along country paths we used to take together. They taught me a love of the outdoors that always brings me peace. I will always remember you telling me exciting and outrageous stories—with Mom in the background saying, "No, that's not how it was." Thanks for the countless silly jokes and the quirky sense of humor, which I loved then and now. For introducing me to science, and Erector sets, and most of all, for always treating me like a strong, capable person. I wouldn't have become who I am if not for that.

I take my time crafting the letter, honing it until it says what I need it to say. Many tears are required to cover the guilt and sorrow for what we have missed out on in the past twenty years. It seems unlikely that we'll meet again; this is my farewell.

When it's done, I recognize for the first time how different this reality is from the brave but fake face I wore before starting the transplant quest. The months I've spent facing death—both my own and others', sharing that experience together, has taught me a great deal about what is ultimately important. Reconnecting with my father is important. This feeling is genuine, and this letter genuinely reflects what I want us both to remember. The good things. Everything else is irrelevant. *Goodbye, Dad, and thank you.*

When Mason calls to say they're on their way back, I'm on the patio meditating. We bought a sunbed since it's too hard for me to get up from ground level, and I'm stretched out in a T-shirt and shorts, reveling in the feel of sunlight on my body and the sound of summer laughter across the park. My face is sunscreened, but nothing else. Skin cancer is too remote for me to worry about; if I live long enough for that to be an issue, I can regret it then.

I've finished all the healing books we bought and now just practice the lessons that work best for me whenever the time is right. The sunbed cover is cornflower blue, so I envision myself on an infinite ocean, floating with the current. The weight that lifted off me after writing this morning's letter is far in the distance, bobbing out to sea, and healing energy surrounds me as I travel to an unknown destination.

On days like this I can imagine myself truly being a part of the universe. It no longer bothers me to think what a tiny and insignificant part that is; I no longer feel the need to make my mark. Whether I'm remembered or not, I'll still have participated in this extraordinary endeavor that is life. And assuming the butterfly effect is true, it's almost certain that I *have* had an impact in some way. Maybe I gave someone advice years ago that changed their life for the better. Maybe I was kind to someone and they think of me on occasion with fondness. Perhaps I've made more of a difference than I realize.

I thank my organs in turn for all their work over forty-four years. They've done a remarkable job through all the hardships. My heart still beats without breaking, despite the losses of my mother, father, various loves, my career . . . and my own impending end. I thank my muscles and bones for dragging me around the rehab circuit day after day so I can stay in the game. And my lungs, sick and damaged as they are, for hanging in until they can be replaced. Then collectively, every cell in my body—all seventy trillion of them—for doing their part. We are a community, I tell them, the mayor addressing her people. I will do my best to keep us alive for as long as possible.

This is how Michaela finds me when she runs up, full of sunshine and trail detritus, to tell me about her morning.

"Mee-Fee, we saw a bunch of new birds, even some that Daddy didn't know the names of. And lots of squirrels and bunnies. And . . . oh, a *giant* turtle in the pond! It pulled itself up on the bank with this funny rolly walk." She proceeds to demonstrate.

Mason appears with a picnic lunch and a blanket for the grass, and the three of us eat and chatter. By the time we reenter the apartment my equilibrium is fully restored.

That night I head to bed early. I've just said good night to Michaela and am heading to my own room when I hear Mason exclaim, "Oh my God, guys!" From the end of the corridor I can see him at his screen, where a cluster of five people are crowded together, waving. They start chanting what sounds like "*Window!*" which then morphs into "Happy Birthday," everyone launching in on a different note as always. It sounds awful.

I kick myself again—it's never occurred to me in all the months I've known him to ask Mason when his birthday is. Thank goodness for these people, whoever they are, remembering to celebrate him. He's blushing but smiling broadly as he accepts their good wishes. I'm about to sneak away when he says, "It's so good to see all of you," and his voice cracks.

His friends' chatter dies as he covers his eyes, his shoulders trembling. They seem as distraught as I am to see him like this. One woman says, "Are you okay, Mace?" He nods but doesn't speak. Eventually he wipes his eyes and laughs shakily.

"Sorry about that. It's been a hard week. And month. And months before that too, honestly. It's just great to see your faces and not have to be so damn strong for a while."

One of the men asks something that I can't make out because Michaela is calling my name. I go to her room, and she says, "Daddy's being really loud! Is he having a birthday party?"

"Sort of, on the computer. Did you know it was his birthday?"

"Yes. I wished him happy birthday this morning and we had cake after our walk. Can you please make him be quieter?"

"Of course. He needs to talk to his friends for a bit, but maybe more softly."

I head back toward the living room but hesitate in the corridor; I'm not sure what I'm interrupting, and Mason sounds fraught.

"It's just so hard on every front. Physically hard, because she's too frail to do much for herself, so I have to do everything. Don't get me wrong, I don't resent it—but I'm just so tired all the time. And emotionally hard because I'm responsible for *her life*! I can't screw up or kick back, ever. I'm constantly worried there's something I haven't thought of that will turn out to have been important."

My throat tightens at his words, even more at the tone. What a burden I've placed on this man. Is what I'm asking of him even reasonable? The "family or friend" mandate is making more sense now. Before I can think it through, Michaela's voice comes insistently from the bedroom. "Fi! Please make them stop!"

Someone has said something funny and they're all laughing. Rather than yell, I walk up to tap Mason's shoulder. He doesn't notice me until my face appears behind him on the screen.

"Hey, is that Fiona?" one of the men asks. "Hi, Fiona!"

The others chime in too, which is embarrassing. Mason waves them down.

"Fi, here are my closest friends from college. Despite their occasional obnoxiousness, they're some of the best people I know."

"Which doesn't say much for your other friends!" the tall man in the back calls out. Mason nods a "Yeah, yeah" acknowledgment.

"The rowdy, shaggy-haired guy in the back is Lionel, like the soccer player—his hero, incidentally. Front left is Marin; she and I took creative writing together, and she's now a literature professor. The couple in the middle, looking like fashion plates, are Javier and Kerry; they were both in my dorm and are now married. To each other. And the intellectual-looking guy with the long face on the right is Simon. Don't let appearances fool you: He's got the mouth of a sailor on landlubber legs. Fiona, the gang. Gang, Fiona."

I'm supposed to say something but draw a blank. I'm tired, wrong-footed by knowing nothing about these people who clearly know about me, and feeling particularly unattractive with my faded robe, too-thin face, and cannula.

"Okay," I say, "I'd love to pull out a magnificent speech for the Mason Gang, but Michaela's asking everyone to be quiet so she can get to sleep."

Immediately there is a collective gasp of "Michaela!" and "Wait, is she there?" The gang hasn't seen her since she was three. They want to know what she looks like now, and what kind of person she's grown into after living with "that social climber" Petra and her "social-climbed-on" husband. I get an idea.

"Mason, why don't you bring your laptop to Michaela's door, tell everyone to keep it calm, and I'll open her door a crack. There'll be enough light from the corridor to see her, and she's probably still awake anyway. Then finish your call in my room; it'll be more private. You can even complain about me, I'll never know." I smile to show I'm joking . . . though I'm not.

He just looks at me, immobile, so I shoo him toward the bedroom. "Go on. It'll be good for you to share Michaela with your friends—God knows you've waited long enough. Take your time . . . and happy birthday."

I sit on the couch for a bit, then stretch out along it and cover myself with a fuzzy lavender-colored blanket that always relaxes me despite it having no lavender scent. Snuggling into the pile, I close my eyes. Today was emotional but rewarding. My father should have my email by now and, because email feels too impersonal, a handwritten shorter note by mail in a few days. It will be nice if he responds, but I don't need him to. It's enough that I've written it and sent it.

Mason's voice drifts gently down the corridor, mingled with subtle sounds from the iPad and occasional comments in Michaela's sleepy voice.

The last thing I remember before falling asleep is thinking how warm and close Mason's friends seem. It was lovely of them to gather so they could call him together. I've never had a gang of friends like that. Individual ones, of course—people I would walk through fire for—but not a bloc like this. There's a wonderful solidity to it, like a phalanx of Roman soldiers having each other's backs. *Good for you, Mason.*

I wake in the dark later with someone trying to scoop me off the couch.

"It's okay," I mumble. "I can stay here."

"No, you'll be woken at dawn. Let me get you to bed."

I let my muscles relax and enjoy being carried. Being *held*. He's strong and warm and smells good. Comforting. He lays me under the blanket and pulls off my slippers.

"Don't leave yet," I say, holding his arm.

He freezes. "Fi, that's not . . ."

"Please. Sit with me. I need to tell you how sorry I am for this terrible burden I've put you under."

"Oh, God." He sighs, sitting down and putting his arm around me. "You shouldn't have heard that. Understand that I don't regret doing this. I'm just scared and exhausted."

I nod and lean against him. It will have to do.

"What were your friends saying? It sounded like 'Window!'"

"Old inside joke," he replies with a sheepish grin. "Kerry always called me Mace. One evening we all went to an outdoor *Star Wars* marathon, you know, blankets and booze on the grass. Remember the Jedi Mace Windu? Every time Kerry said, 'Mace,' Simon yelled, 'Windu!' and eventually everyone was doing it. It stuck . . . all these years."

I try it out. "Mace. Winduuuuu!" I like it. As my eyes drift closed, I murmur, "If I ever fight the Sith, I want you at my side."

Chapter 33

An email from my father arrives.

> *My Dearest Fiona,*
>
> *I am so sorry not to have been in closer touch these past few years. Your original letter containing your diagnosis was quite a shock. It appears I have been refusing to believe that after taking your beloved mother in such a cruel way, this disease could also attack my equally beloved daughter. Your email has struck me with the inescapable truth that I can no longer indulge this fantasy.*
>
> *My response, you will not be surprised to hear, has been to take action. Over all these years I have kept in touch with Abbas-Arcasy Hospital, where your mother was treated. Yesterday I tracked down her old doctor, Dr. Sinha, who not only is still practicing but now heads their new thoracic transplant practice. Your mother, also not a surprise, was one of his favorite patients. It is rare for a dying patient to tell her doctor that she feels sad for* him. *That she thinks he has one of the most difficult jobs in the world, always getting to*

know people and then watching them die. Absolutely typical of your mother. Perhaps this is why Dr. Sinha has turned to transplants. At least now, most of his patients get to live.

The doctor responded that it would give him great joy to try to save the life of Ilana's daughter. He has promised to contact you to discuss whether and how he might be able to help you. Please be on the lookout for his phone call or email, and let me know the outcome.

With love and prayers for your well-being,
Your devoted and hopeful father

A whole cluster of reactions hit me simultaneously: A spark of hope that someone may have a different perspective or know something Regent doesn't. A huge aversion to even the thought of dragging myself to *yet another* transplant center for more rounds of invasive testing. And a potent reaction to my father being so upset by my news. It seems he loves me after all.

Returning from rehab, I check my phone. There's a voice message from Dr. Sinha, saying to call him as soon as possible. I quickly fill Mason in.

"It's amazing that he's willing to see me, but I'm torn. If we start down this road we'll have to go to his hospital, which is easily a thousand-mile round trip. He can't make an evaluation without meeting me and doing another round of testing. And I'd love to believe he has some miracle cure that only he knows about, but that seems incredibly unlikely, doesn't it?"

"Almost certainly," Mason agrees. "The transplant community makes a point of sharing information and best practices, worldwide. This would only be about adding a third center and getting triple-listed."

"Not even that. Sinha's hospital is even further from New York than we are now. I'd have to withdraw from Empire—without knowing anything about his program except that it wasn't there when my mother was dying."

"That seems risky, but I could look into it. Do you want to try?"

"No. Empire seems preferable, if only because it's back home. Plus, I hate to sound wimpy, but I'm not sure I can handle starting over again."

He turns to look at me, his expression confirming what I've suspected. It's not wimpiness, not at this stage. I really am reaching the end of the road.

"I should call and thank him for the offer but tell him I'm staying. Shouldn't I?"

"Damn it, I don't know. I hate to cut off any angles until we understand why you haven't been getting transplant calls. We're meeting with the Regent doctors next week; let's hear what they have to say and take it from there. Maybe you're sick enough now that you'll start getting hits. But I'm worried it's not simply a question of how high up the list you are. Lots of people who seemed healthier than you are have been transplanted already. Let's not blow this doctor off until we understand what's happening."

"That sounds smart." It feels cowardly not to respond, but I'm not confident enough to make such an important decision right now. I'll take a pass for a few more days.

When I stumble into the living room post-nap, Mason is hanging up the phone. "Bastards!" He sees me and explains. "Your insurance company has rescinded their approval of a test that they *previously authorized* and that was already performed, almost four months ago. Regent's billing department just told me that their ongoing account has been debited to cover the test, and you now owe Regent eleven thousand dollars."

I choke. "But they can't retroactively change their minds this far after the fact, can they?"

"Here's the best part. Their rep just told me the system only shows the most recent status of the claim—Denied. Someone must have gone into your record and overridden the initial authorization, which automatically wiped out everything that was there before. The electronic record now shows only that the claim is denied."

"They can't do that!"

"They just did. That's why I've been so completely anal about keeping records, not just your test results but every piece of correspondence. Somewhere I have both a scanned version and a hard copy of their original approval . . . they couldn't erase that. I'll have to challenge them."

"Please, this is one more fight you don't need. Pass it on to Dane and let him handle it."

"Fi, I'm a paralegal. I know how to write this kind of letter."

This time I'm not giving in. "You're also a caregiver for two people, and you're stretched too thin as it is. Dane can handle this perfectly well. Give me all the information and I'll pass it on."

He eventually nods but still looks angry. "It's the same issue again. What happens if you don't have paralegals and trained negotiators to handle problems like this? Most people don't have a spare eleven thousand dollars, or the emotional capacity for wild cards like this."

"We both know the answer to that. They are flat out of luck. It's awful. But you're running on fumes, and you can't save everyone. Please, put it aside and get some rest."

That evening, Michaela and I wait impatiently for Mason to go grocery shopping so we can open the secret package that arrived in today's mail: neon blue semi-permanent hair dye. Tonight we're getting matching blue streaks. Color and placement were settled days ago: a steely medium blue, and a two-inch-wide streak on the right side only. Our reasoning was that we like the color, we both have clothes that would (sort of) match it, and we don't want to make too strong a statement. Especially since we have no idea what that statement might be.

We use my bathroom and hurry to finish and dry before Mason returns. Remarkably, the only casualty is the towels, which now have a little extra pop of color. The streak looks great on her, and even on me it's not as dumb as I'd feared . . . not that I'd care if it made her happy.

Mason returns carrying two heavy bags and stops in his tracks when he sees us. Michaela can't contain herself.

"Look, Daddy, look! We got a blue streak!"

"So I see. What happened . . . did you talk too much?"

I snort, but Michaela's never heard of talking a blue streak, so she writes it off as grown-up nonsense and dances up to him, swishing her hair back and forth to show it off better. That girl is going to break hearts down the road.

We're experimenting with a streak-braid when Mason gets a call on his cell. He answers with a friendly "Hey there," then abruptly falls quiet and steps outside. I'm skittery these days, so I try not to worry while I finish putting the cereal and pasta on the shelf. Five minutes later he returns with a dazed look on his face . . . the good kind.

"Simon's found us a plane," he says, his eyes wide.

I've no idea what he's talking about.

"On the group call the other night I told everyone about the situation: how there's a chance we'll be coming back to New York but that we'd need a private jet. Simon apparently shook his bountiful tree of contacts and found a friend of a friend with a share in a four-seater jet half an hour from here. This guy, Roland, liked the idea of saving the life of a damsel in distress, and he's willing to take us to New York—or Abbas-Arcasy if that's the decision—for the cost of fuel and hangar fees plus an overnight hotel with a fancy dinner."

I'm stunned enough not to initially accept this at face value. "What if the plane's in use?"

"Then we rent a plane as originally planned. Fi, this can only be good news."

A thrill rushes up through me. He's right. Not only because of the money, though that's a big weight off, but because something important is swinging my way. Superstitions are less laughable when you're desperate.

Chapter 34

For several days, Drew (who's still waiting for his multiple-organ call) has been glancing at me, then looking away. I haven't asked why, because I already know things look bad. Today, though, he pulls me aside after rehab and asks if we can talk. In private. He looks serious and his eyelid twitches as he says Mason should be there too. We agree that he'll come to our apartment late this afternoon while Michaela is with the babysitter.

When he arrives, he has a small bottle of scotch with him and asks us to close the blinds. Now I'm really unnerved.

"Okay," he says softly as we huddle around the coffee table. "I have something important to tell you, but you have to promise you won't take any action that might compromise me."

"I promise," I say immediately. "Unless you're planning to hurt someone."

"The opposite," he replies shakily. "But it is a risk for myself."

"I promise," Mason says. "And I don't break promises."

Drew exhales and bumps his oxygen level up a notch.

"As you know, my situation's especially tricky because I need multiple organs from the same donor. I'm also very good with computers. Last month my parents were getting frantic about when I'd get transplanted, so . . . I hacked into the hospital's system to read my doctors' notes. It turns out everything's on track, it just takes time. But while I was there, I decided—God knows why—to check my friends' files too: the ones who have been here a long time and don't seem to be making progress."

Mason and I glance at each other.

"We've been wondering too," I tell Drew. "If you hacked my file, I'm happy."

His brow furrows. "Your big problem is that they've flagged you as 'local donors only.' You aren't being considered for any lungs that become available outside a narrow radius from their main testing lab. Which is where most of the lungs are."

I stare at him in incomprehension. The couch leather feels slick behind my neck and there's a low buzzing in my head. "They're blocking my access to the majority of the pool? Why?"

He pauses, looks away, then reluctantly pulls his attention back.

"My only guess—and it's just a guess—is that they don't trust anyone other than their own central lab to test the donor antibodies properly. For most patients, they can trust Regent satellite centers, or other hospitals, to do the blood screening. But in your case, there's a really narrow band of what lungs they're comfortable transplanting. The antibody numbers they've assigned you are really high. They're showing you as incompatible or highly sensitive to four different factors: Your lung match would have to not carry *any* of them, or there'd be a high risk of your antibodies rejecting it. If Regent's best testing equipment and experts are here, plus your stored blood, this may be the only way they feel comfortable to proceed."

We're all silent for a while. I'm trying hard to process all this: Drew's guesswork, and Regent's motives, all coming back to the cold fact that I'm severely restricted. My brain sticks; all I can take in are the incongruously cheerful sounds of people chatting and laughing in the park outside.

"Regent is scared," Mason says finally. "They won't risk transplanting you and having you reject the lungs. Especially now. There's a rumor that one of the other major lung transplant centers has been temporarily suspended because they've had too many deaths. Everyone in the network is nervous."

Drew agrees. "Regent does take on some high-risk cases—I'm a perfect example of that—but for all we know, they've already lost patients recently and can't afford to lose another."

My brain finally wakes up, and a torrent of outrage floods my body.

"But they didn't tell me that! Shouldn't they have let me know if my pool wasn't what I was expecting? I have a business background; I understand the issue. The hospital relies heavily on the transplant revenue—it would be a massive hit if the department was suspended. And they'd have specialized transplant surgeons and nurses, whole facilities geared to pulmonary care, sitting idle. But still!"

"What about the impact on patients?" Drew says softly.

I realize I've been shouting. "Yes," I continue at a lower volume. "Can you imagine getting almost to the finish line and then having the transplant unit close down?"

Saying it forces me to stop and think. Am I being unreasonable? If the risk of suspension is that high, would I even *want* them to risk an uncertain transplant on me? Knowing that others—including my friends—might die as a result? I think the answer's no.

Mason cuts into my thoughts, his voice tight with anger.

"That doesn't excuse them not telling you! We started the program with the understanding that your fraction of the pool was 85 percent smaller than Regent's normal. No one said anything about *the pool itself* being so much smaller. Even if there's a greater risk—and let's be clear, the risk is to *Regent*, not to you—deciding to limit your access to organs is one thing, but not telling you is another. You had the right to know. What if you had children at home, waiting for you? Did they want you to die like Wanda, far from family and home?"

The air is electric with his words and the fury of his delivery. No one speaks.

He's right, and the knowledge is corrosive. I was never even in the running for most of the lungs I was counting on. Even 15 percent of a normal pool isn't good odds; 15 percent of a small pool is minuscule. No wonder I haven't been getting calls. A donor matching my exact profile would have to drop dead at reception, donor card in hand.

My emotions kick in even harder. Has my pool been restricted from the very beginning? The whole time I've been here, was getting transplanted never a serious likelihood? After all the upheaval, I might just as well have stayed in New York. I feel betrayed.

"I'm really sorry, Fi," Drew says. "I should have told you sooner but didn't have the guts. Regent is my only hope; nowhere else would take me. I didn't want to risk getting kicked out for hacking their system. But the sicker you got, the guiltier I felt. What if I never got matched and we *both* died? At least now you can move on. Maybe you can find a center that specializes in high antibody transplants. Different hospitals have different risk profiles, you know."

"I *didn't* know."

"Oh. Well, the 'too high' designation for an antibody is a judgment call, determined by the hospital. Some centers may look at your levels and find them workable—or at least some of them. Your problem is that here there are too many factors being ruled as incompatible. If you were down to one or two, finding a match would be much easier."

"Thank you, Drew," I say earnestly. "You might have just saved my life. Or at the least let me die at home."

Mason rises and shakes Drew's hand. "Good luck with your own transplant."

Drew reaches his hand out to me, but I ignore it and hug him. "Let me know when you're transplanted and healed, okay? Maybe I'll come watch you in a comedy club sometime."

He leaves the scotch behind. Mason pours a large glass for himself and a few sips' worth for me. It's good and helps with the shock.

"So now what?" I muse out loud. "Does it even matter if Drew's guess is correct about why I'm restricted? If my pool's this small, there doesn't seem any reason to stay. We should leave Dr. SEAL and Pulmonologist Barbie behind and get out of here."

He frowns for a moment, puzzled, then figures out who I mean.

"Yeah, sounds like the pool they've left you is more like a bathtub. But if each center really has its own risk evaluation, you should call Dr. Sinha back and see if he'll work with you. I'll send him copies of all your tests and look for a local blood draw clinic that can ship blood samples. Hopefully he can do at least a preliminary evaluation based on those. If it's a nonstarter, we should just go straight to New York. Do you want to talk to Dr. Stanton first?"

My bile rises instantly. "No. I never want to see her or any of them again."

"Then let's start packing the apartment while we wait for Sinha to look at your results. If he'll take you, we go there; if not, we'll go to New York."

"The one person I do want to see is Zuri."

He nods. "Let's go now, while Mike's out. Then call Dane and fill him in. He'll be furious, but try to keep him from making waves, at least for now. If Sinha contacts Regent, I don't want him hearing you're a problem patient. Once we know our options, tell Dr. Stanton you've decided to leave the program. Meanwhile, leave a message at rehab saying you'll be out of town for a few days and they should suspend your listing. We'll play this by the book."

I swallow my own rage and agree; it's time to be smart.

This visit to Zuri is a world away from the last one. She's alone, the wedding garlands still round her bed, watching a Hallmark movie on low volume. We tell her only that we're leaving.

"You're not giving up, are you?" she asks, alarmed.

"Absolutely not. But I'm high enough on the list that Regent isn't an advantage anymore. I'd rather be home. You're not shaking me off, though: I'll be in touch. Tell Robert he needs to let me know as soon as you're transplanted, okay?"

"You bet." We hug long and hard. I pray it works out for us both.

Mason and I take the elevator down in silence. A couple of floors down, the car stops, and three med students step on, chatting away. This is a normal day for them. They pulled on their navy scrubs and comfy shoes this morning and set off to learn something without doing harm. How many of them have ever *been* a really sick patient, I wonder? How long until they have to give someone bad news and say they did all they could, but the patient died anyway?

"I don't want to see anyone else," I tell Mason once they're gone. "I'm so done with this place. Let's just get out of here as soon as we can."

My conversation with Dane doesn't go as predicted.

His entire response is, "So this whole thing was for nothing. Figures."

He doesn't even sound angry, more defeated. In the background there's a distant sound of clinking glass.

"Where are you?" I ask.

"We just closed a major deal, and I invited the team over for drinks. Everyone needed a break; it's been a tough few weeks."

I shouldn't care. It doesn't help me for him to be miserable. But something about him having people in our apartment, *celebrating*, feels so wrong that I can't even formulate a response. How can he tell me that *he's* had a tough few weeks?

"Are you upset about the party?" he says into the silence. "I didn't think you'd mind."

"No, it's fine. Congratulations on your deal. I'll let you know when we hear from the new doctor and decide if we're going there."

"Okay. I'll check out flights so I can visit you once you arrive."

"Sure. See you then."

I sit quietly for a long while. Have I become so edgy that I begrudge him even this simple release? So detached that I've forgotten that teams need to celebrate success? Or is *he* so detached from *me* that nothing in my world affects him anymore? Or worse, has he just had one stomach-dropping dive too many on this ridiculous roller-coaster ride? Maybe he's given up.

In bed later, an old phrase comes into my head. *Everything happens for a reason.* It always sounded like a platitude—a way to feel better when things are awful. But now I start thinking about positive things that wouldn't have happened if I'd never come to Regent.

The large rehab center and clustered housing are only possible because land is so easily available in Johnson's River. Easy access to daily workouts has greatly improved my physical condition, but just as important, living and exercising communally has given me friends with a common cause. These bonds could never have happened in a big-city program.

If I hadn't come here, I'd never have met Monique. I wouldn't have the different perspectives and new acceptance of my place in the universe that have made my life calmer and more meaningful.

Without this crisis, I'd probably never have contacted my father ever again, never released that anger or felt his love. We would have died estranged.

Most important of all, if I'd stayed in New York there would have been no reason to hire Mason. I'd have continued to spend most of my days alone, until eventually needing daytime companions who I would never have been so close with. It's hard to imagine never having met Mason and Michaela. And I wouldn't even have known how great a loss that was.

Chapter 35

Two days later the apartment is littered with packing boxes and bubble wrap.

Michaela is handling the disruption remarkably well—better than many adults I know. She's currently packing up her bookshelves and beloved items with impressive determination.

"What did you tell her?" I ask Mason quietly. "About why we're leaving."

"The truth. That we'd found someplace that might get you new lungs sooner. She asked how soon we could leave. She cares a great deal about you, in case you didn't know."

He pauses but doesn't say what I suspect he's thinking: that if I die, it will be hard on her. We didn't think this through enough. I hope this wasn't a mistake—not for me, but for Michaela.

Mason's in charge of logistics. He wants us to pack in order of importance. First, a small bag with items we want on us at all times: electronics, passports, Lea the doll, et cetera. Second, a suitcase of things we'll need in the first week if we go to Abbas-Arcasy: clothes, some books, medical records. A few things we need constantly, like the concentrator and wheelchair, stay out, while everything else goes into boxes. We'll ship those when we know where to send them.

Mason is very focused, but noticeably strained. His biggest fear is forgetting or mis-packing something critical—IDs or the plastic "keys" that open the valve on the oxygen tanks. He has a spreadsheet with categories of items, like clothes, electronics, personal items. One whole section details my oxygen-providing devices: stationary and portable concentrators, extra tubing, and a couple of special-order tanks that are airplane-safe. Hopefully they'll let us use them.

Simply making priorities and sorting items—plus naps—takes most of the day. We flop in front of the TV at 6:00 p.m. with take-out dinner. It felt strange not going to rehab on a weekday, but today has been every bit as physical.

At eight, a text comes in from Rina. I read it twice, because it makes no sense. This is nothing like her usual communication.

Getting a powerful lung vibration for you. Hopefully new lungs are on their way soon.

I check the sender, but yes, it's from Rina. The brilliant, ultra-logical scientist. The one who's so left-brained she can't even draw a cereal bowl without a protractor. I show it to Mason, but he's never met Rina, so he doesn't understand how bizarre this is.

I text back *great!*, wondering if she's been hacked.

She replies:

Fingers crossed . . . I want to see you at our next reunion.

Not hacked then. I'm still confused, but after dinner I go straight to bed. I want to sleep well . . . just in case.

The next morning I wake and realize it was just an ordinary night. The hospital didn't call; no lungs arrived. There's no logical reason for disappointment, so I try to shrug it off and shoot Rina a text saying at least I got lots of rest.

She responds immediately:

Good. I'm feeling it even stronger today.

Since there's nowhere to put this comment, I find Mason so we can laugh about it together. To my surprise, he doesn't laugh at all. Instead, after a moment's pause, he goes to the closet and pulls out two duffels.

"What are you doing?" I say to his back.

"I don't pretend to know everything about the universe," he replies, turning. His expression gives me goosebumps. "I'm not leaving anything to chance, and neither should you. The worst that happens is we unpack again tomorrow."

Ordinarily I'd think he was teasing, but it's clear he's not. So I head to my room, thinking how strange this is, and begin collecting the things I'd need if we had to make a sudden dash. From the next room I hear Mason tell Michaela the same thing. If a call came, it couldn't be from Abbas-Arcasy: They haven't even tested me yet. And if somehow Regent came through, we'd have everything here. The issue would be if Empire called. Luckily, New York is home for all of us—if we had to leave, we'd have plenty of clothes waiting for us there.

By lunchtime it's clear that our hopes were raised for nothing. Mason collects laundry, Michaela goes to her room to watch a video, and I take my lunch to the corner of Mason's desk. The view outside presents an extravagant display of life. Now at the peak of summer, the park is framed in color, vivid bushes flaunting their purples and reds like royal mantles.

I've just dropped my plate and fork into the sink when my cell phone rings. Hardly anyone calls these days, but it's a New York number so I pick up.

"Hello, is this Fiona Copeland?" a female voice asks.

"Yes," I reply, my heart suddenly lodged in my throat.

"This is Carol from the lung transplant program at Empire Hospital in New York. We have lungs that match your profile. The doctors are doing a final check now, but the preliminary inspection looks good. We need you to be in the hospital by six p.m. tonight for surgery directly afterwards. Can you get here by then?"

My entire body clenches, adrenaline pounding so hard I'm afraid I'll drop the phone. *Oh my God, it's finally happening.* But five hours! I'm hundreds of miles away; can we even make it that fast? I should say no. The right thing would be to let them give the lungs to someone who's right there and can use them. But for once I override the impulse. This is not the time for probability analysis—this is the time for hope.

"We'll be there," I tell her.

"Good. Come to the main hospital entrance and check in at Registration. I'll have all your documentation waiting for you. Safe travels."

I feel dizzy. The level on my concentrator is already at eight liters per minute, but I crank it up to ten and breathe deeply through the cannula until I'm clearheaded again. Holding onto chairs and walls as I go, careful not to trip over the trailing tube, I stumble to the corridor. Mason is dumping clothes into the washer but looks up as I approach. His expression changes sharply.

"Was that the hospital? *Do they have lungs?*"

My voice emerges eerily calm. "That was Empire. They have a match, but we have to be there no later than six tonight. Can we make it?"

He blinks a few times. "You remember there's a one-hour time difference, right?"

Everything turns cold. "I forgot."

"Call them back!" he says urgently. "Right now; tell them you need more time. An extra hour. It'll be close, but if we can get the plane airborne quickly, it's enough."

"Mason, there's no way . . . we can't make it by six." I'm trying to keep myself together. *So close. This was so close.* My knees go slack, and he has to catch me before I fall.

"Fiona Copeland, don't you *dare* wimp out on us now," he says, forcefully enough to shake me out of my fog. "This is the moment, Fi. We can do this . . . we *have* to do this."

And then I realize it's not just about me anymore. So many people have invested so much in my survival: Mason, Michaela, my friends, the medics. This may be my last chance; we'll simply have to push hard and pray that's enough.

I call Carol back, and to my amazement she gives me another hour. After that they'll have to give the lungs to the standby patient before they deteriorate.

"She agreed," I tell Mason, hardly believing it. Operation Last Chance is a go.

Mason springs into full-on action mode—Mace Windu raising his purple lightsaber—and everything shifts to hyper speed.

"I'll call for the plane," he says. "You finish packing. Cabin essentials in the red backpack, anything else you need between now and posttransplant in the blue duffel. Leave everything else; I'll come back for it later."

He grabs a few items from the washing machine, then finds Michaela. I hear her excited shriek of "New York! New York! We're going home!"

I go as fast as possible to my bedroom. *They have lungs for me!* Phone, wallet, Mom's ring, eye mask for the plane. *What else will I need in New York if the surgery happens?* Nothing comes to mind. *Wait!* If the transplant *doesn't* happen, I'll need the big concentrator.

Mason appears and hands me a printed checklist.

"We're bringing the big concentrator, right?" I ask urgently.

"Of course." His voice is taut; a lot is resting on him now. "Everything's here for both possibilities—surgery proceeding and not. Roland, our pilot, is filing the manifest now, then starting the plane check and filing the flight plan."

Page one of the checklist is labeled "Mason" and runs tightly down the whole sheet. Page two is labeled "Fiona." To my mental list he's added headphones and a finger oximeter. Being at altitude might affect my breathing; I'll need to read my oxygen level en route. *How had I forgotten that?*

"I've got this," he says, quiet but urgent. "Please trust me, I've been planning for weeks. Just take care of your list."

"It'll be fine," I mutter like a mantra, "it'll be fine." I grab the oximeter, then look around. This room has been my sanctuary for the past five months. Whatever happens, I won't be back. On sudden impulse, I take down Mason's painting—the deliberately bad one—wrap it in a sweater, and add it to the duffel before leaving.

Mason and Michaela are already at the front door. He switches me to my portable concentrator and starts wheeling the large one to the car, Michaela following with whatever she can carry. There's little physical help I can give, but I fill water bottles and scoop some granola bars into Mason's backpack.

Even knowing Mason is prepared, I mentally check off the items as they pass by: medical records box, backpacks, portable wheelchair, flight-approved oxygen tanks . . .

"Do you have the key for the oxygen tank?" I ask as he returns for the final batch.

"Shit! Top drawer right behind you—grab it and join us at the car."

So many things to think about, so little time, so many ways to screw up.

We're on the road in just over twenty minutes. While Mason drives, I run through logistics in my head. We'll have to leave the car at the airfield somewhere; check in (I pause to confirm that I have our IDs); load the plane (hopefully there'll be help); try to sleep (I pause to check that Michaela's game device has charge); then land at Teterboro, New Jersey's private jet airport.

It's my second adrenaline jolt of the day. Today is Friday! A Friday in August. We'll be landing in New Jersey and need to get across the George Washington Bridge into Manhattan . . . at peak summer rush hour. Hundreds of cars will be crowding that same small stretch to go home or north to the country for the weekend. With all the worry of finding a plane, we never considered rush hour traffic. *Don't panic, this is just logistics.*

I need a vehicle with bells and whistles to force traffic to move over. I call Empire's transplant center to ask for an ambulance. They say no: Ambulances are exclusively for emergency calls within New York City. *How is this not an emergency?* I try three private ambulance services and learn their business is prearranged pickups to bring immobile people to medical appointments. "Next time, call at least a week in advance," one says. I wish.

Mason is pale. "I'm so sorry . . . I forgot about summer traffic."

"Don't worry," I say as calmly as possible, "I'm dealing with it."

I regroup. Maybe Teterboro has helicopters. I call Empire back and ask if they have a helipad. They don't: City regulations prohibit helicopter flights near tall buildings. Now I'm pushing the fear back, but Mason's driving fast and we'll be at the airfield soon. In desperation, I call the Port Authority, which polices all NYC-area airports, and eventually reach someone senior and sympathetic enough to help. She'll have an officer meet me off the plane, but they can only take me a mile: That's the limit of their jurisdiction. I thank her gratefully. At this point I'll take whatever I can get.

We arrive at the airport, are cleared through the gates, and pull over at a small white stand-alone building. Inside is a waiting area and a single counter. Mason lets Michaela and me out to check in, then drives straight across the tarmac to the small plane bearing the tail markings Roland gave him, to drop off the luggage. Check-in takes minutes; we're the only ones there. I'm nervously hungry and reach toward a snack basket before remembering I can't. I'm in the run up to surgery now, which means no more food or drink until after it's done. *Long* after. I call Dane to update him, and when the call goes to voicemail, send a text. Then one to Rina: *You were right!*

Mason returns with the car, drives us to the plane, and then takes it to park. I've no idea when it'll get picked up, but that's not today's problem.

Roland is waiting for us in a bush hat; he sports a deep tan with a matching Australian accent.

"Good to meet ya, Fiona," he says. "I'll get ya there on time, no worries."

He offers Michaela his hand. "Good to meet you too, young lady. Have you ever watched *The Koala Brothers*?"

"Yes." She blinks. It's one of her favorite shows: two koalas flying a search-and-rescue plane in the Outback.

"Well, this'll be just like that, except I'm a person. C'mon, climb aboard."

Mason has just joined us, sweating madly. It's too hot for this kind of exertion. He takes my tank and grabs my waist, helping me move painstakingly up the steps to the plane.

Inside, the jet is steaming hot from sitting on the tarmac with the AC off. It feels sleek, a charcoal interior with two rows of two pearl-gray seats facing each other. It's not as cramped as I'd imagined. Mason sets me up in the back row, our in-flight bags buckled into the adjacent seat along with the oxygen tank. There's nowhere to plug in the big concentrator, and the portable one can only crank out three liters per minute, maximum. That's nowhere near enough for me now even at sea level; at elevation it's likely worse. I'll need both concentrator and tank.

Mason attaches a clean cannula to the concentrator and sets it to two liters per minute. With the armrest up, it fits snugly between me and the neighboring seat. I hold the second cannula between my teeth, and now I can turn the tank down a couple of liters, to prolong its use time.

Michaela is across from me, looking around the plane. Mason, sitting next to her, is focused only on me.

"I've ordered a car at Teterboro," he says. "Krystal will meet us at the hospital and take Mike home. Everything's set, so try to relax and conserve your strength."

I nod. "You have to take me to inpatient registry at the back of the lobby, then . . ." The thought hits me abruptly. "Mason. We're going to *Empire*!"

He looks puzzled for a split second, then his eyes widen as he realizes. At Empire, he has no authorization rights. We've planned everything assuming him being my legal proxy, but at Empire, Mason is not my husband. Dane is.

"Did you reach him?" Mason asks. "Does he even know we're coming?"

"I haven't heard back. For all I know, he's not even in the country!"

"Let's stay calm," Mason says, looking anything but. "There must be times when someone's proxy isn't immediately reachable; hopefully you can register yourself to get started and they'll have proxy forms to designate me if necessary."

"Okay," I reply but open my phone again anyway, my fingers trembling on the buttons. Before I can dial, a text comes in.

Incredible news! I'm in Connecticut—meet you at the hospital by 6:45. Safe travels.

Roland's voice comes across the speakers. "Buckle up, please. Weather's looking good all the way except for a patch of wind about an hour from now. Shooting for a 6:15 landing."

We start to taxi, the airport speeds by through the window, and we are wheels up.

Now that we're airborne, my plan is to rest as much as possible. My body is about to undergo extreme and prolonged shock; it will need all the strength it can get. Mason connects me to the flight-approved oxygen tank, then I put on eye shades and fuzzy socks and pull the oximeter out of my pocket: 92 percent saturation. Good enough. I leave it on so Mason can monitor it if I fall asleep. First, though, I reach for his and Michaela's hands.

"You guys are amazing." I feel a sudden rush of emotion. "I couldn't have got here without you—either of you. So now let's just use these few hours to rest and gather our strength. No worrying, Mason, please: I know that's hard, but we've done all we can for now. If there's one thing I've learned these past few months, it's that sometimes things are simply out of our hands. Michaela, if you can play quietly that would really help. And . . . would you both mind putting in a prayer for me—a powerful one that this works, and I get new lungs?"

Michaela nods at once. "What should I say?"

"Whatever you want, sweetheart."

She reaches for her father with her free hand and closes her eyes.

Mason is looking at me as though trying to fix me in his mind. He knows as well as I do that there's a 15 percent chance I don't make it through surgery. This trip may be the last time either of them sees me. He nods briefly, tightens his grip on my hand, and bows his head. I don't know who he's praying to, but it doesn't matter.

I close my eyes too and imagine myself floating among stars—enveloped by the universe, supported by love. Whatever is coming will be here soon. *Let it be good*, I pray. *Let it be worth all that has gone into it.* I pray for whoever has left their lungs for me to receive. *Go in peace, generous spirit.* I send solace to their family and friends, now grieving. If the operation is successful I promise to take wonderful care of these lungs. I'll nurture them and do whatever I can to make the most of this extraordinary gift. Let there be life out of death.

Chapter 36

I snap awake when Roland announces we'll be landing in twenty minutes and to please buckle up. The first thing I do is check my watch. *No! It's past 6:00 p.m. already.* How can we possibly get everything transferred from the plane to the car and reach the hospital before 7:00?

Mason looks like a warrior heading into battle. "We hit a headwind so we're running behind. Get all your things together now; it's going to be a race once we land. There's no time to unload the plane, just grab whatever you need and start moving. Roland will load everything else into his SUV and drop it off at your apartment. I gave him your keys—hope that's okay."

"Thank you, Roland!" I yell.

"No worries," he calls back. "Mason told me fancy steak dinner for two on you."

"Roland," Mason yells, "you are all the Koala Brothers rolled into one! Eat all the eucalyptus you can handle."

I stow everything fast, then watch through the window as Manhattan appears in the distance. *Home!* I'm returning home. My scalp tingles on seeing the skyline, and I'm suddenly more eager than frightened. I'd never realized how happy I would be to return to familiar ground. I'm ready to get my New York lungs—sarcastic or ambitious or cynical or however they come. I *lung* New York.

Once we're fully stopped, Mason grabs two of the extra tanks, plus the bulkiest backpacks, then races out. Michaela slings on her own heavy pack and helps me to the exit. From the plane door we see Mason across the tarmac, talking to our escort from the Port Authority Police. The officer shakes his head. But then he looks up to see Michaela and me struggling down the stairs with our burdens: the pretty blonde girl and the frail, failing woman. He stands stock-still for a moment, then says something to Mason and walks away.

Mason waves us to the hired car and returns to the plane for one more load. Everything gets dumped into the trunk except the oxygen tanks, which are wedged in the front seat where they can't roll. The humans are tight together in the back with Michaela in the middle. I'm glad for the solidarity. The officer raps on the front window and says to follow him. It's 6:35 p.m.

He pulls out of Teterboro with lights flashing, and we slide in behind him. The streets feel familiar to me: dense, noisy, gray, the small shops crowded together. We join the main road leading to Manhattan and within minutes hit solid traffic. I've no idea what will happen now but somehow I'm not afraid. Beginning with Rina's text, there seems to be a powerful force of grace on my side. I can only hope that since it has brought me safe thus far, it will bring me home.

The Port Authority car pulls into the opposing lane, siren blaring, and we pull right out after him, straight into oncoming traffic! Michaela lets out a shriek; Mason flings his arm across her at lightning speed. The cars heading at us in this newly reversed lane can see and hear us coming, so they pull over fast, but it feels surreal to be racing down the opposite side of a busy four-lane artery at forty miles per hour. Other cars try to horn in on the shortcut, so our driver closes the gap till we're right behind the Port Authority car. We're now way past a mile from the airport. Without daring to voice it, I wonder whether the officer has decided to go against his mandate and help us get there before my deadline runs out. *Thank you, thank you*, I think.

Signs appear for the George Washington Bridge. The officer ahead slows, lets us pull up beside him, and signs that we should all roll down our windows. "I have to stop now!" he yells. "Can't cross state lines. But the New York Police will take it from here."

We look ahead and sure enough, there are three NYPD cars waiting for us at the next block. We catch up and once again we're going fast, full siren and lights, heading toward the on-ramp and then onto the bridge itself. The bridge is busy but not completely jammed. This is my favorite view in all of New York: We are high above the Hudson River, looking across the wide expanse of water glittering in the August sun. From my seat I can't see much of Manhattan, but over the cars heading into New Jersey I can see north into greenery and what I know to be open spaces, lush with summer foliage. Freedom and fresh air feel so close now.

The megaphone in the lead police car kicks in and a tinny voice blares: "Driver of the white Toyota, pull over. Pull over!" The three cars ahead of us force their way into other lanes, and now we're traveling in a bubble, the NYPD cars and us, with traffic opening up ahead of us like the parting of the Red Sea. *No later than 7:00 p.m.!*

We're zipping past the other cars now, across the bridge toward Empire Hospital. *I'm in a high-speed car chase*, I think with amazement: Bruce Willis in a *Die Hard* movie, racing against time and heading into the emergency. The thought gives me power. I refuse to believe we would have been put through all this only to die in a car crash on the G.W. Bridge. Not three seconds later Mason mutters, "I can't believe we've been through so much, only to die in a car crash on the G.W. Bridge."

It's now 6:54 p.m.—six minutes till deadline. I call the transplant nurse and tell her we'll be there in a few minutes. My heart is beating faster as we exit into Manhattan and tear toward the hospital. The NYPD cars peel off, waving goodbye; they've brought us here in incredible time. As we screech to a stop at the main hospital building, I check my watch.

It is 6:58 p.m. I have to pause to acknowledge that fact.

Mason runs to grab a wheelchair from the array at the entrance.

"Thank you," I tell the driver. "Sorry about the craziness."

"You kiddin' me?" he laughs. "Fifteen years I been driving in this city, and I never had a ride this exciting. Good luck with whatever you got going, lady. Hope they fix you up right."

Mason helps me into the wheelchair and tosses my overnight bag on the back. Michaela is inside, hugging a young woman with olive skin and long dark hair, presumably Krystal. I blow a kiss as they head out to the car.

When I turn back, Dane is there. He's looking at me as though I were unfamiliar—which I suppose I am. Since he last saw me I've become even frailer.

"It's okay, love," I tell him gently. "I know it looks pretty dire. But if it didn't, they wouldn't have offered me new lungs and I wouldn't be here."

He exhales, leans over, and hugs me tight—too tight; I start to cough. He's startled, but I wave it off, then realize . . . he's *scared*. As if he's been unexpectedly called to a critical meeting but doesn't know the material. Which he doesn't. He hasn't been to any lectures or training, hasn't seen my recent medical tests, probably doesn't even know the details of the transplant procedure. Why would he? This was supposed to have happened hundreds of miles away with Mason in the role of my husband. Dane was meant to fly down while I was being prepped or already in surgery.

Then I catch Mason's expression, and it's worse. He looks betrayed—like someone just slammed a door in his face. I hadn't thought through this part at all. Mason's been preparing for this event for months: learning, coaching, working to exhaustion every day. And now that the moment is here he suddenly has no role. It's a terrible recompense for all he's done.

But I don't have time for this. "Dane, please wheel me to registration and sign anything you're asked to. Mason, can you come with us and field any questions? Let's move."

In the end it's as simple as any other surgical admission. We sign some papers—which Dane reads only the first paragraph of—then take the elevator to the surgery floor. It's immediately clear that this is nothing like my dry run at Regent. The medical team is already in high gear. I'm whisked into a cubicle, where I change into a hospital gown and nonslip socks. An IV nurse starts a line in my arm and begins running some fluids, then a third person shaves some of my body hair and puts a cap on my head.

As she bends over me, I hear a light tinkling, like a tiny wind chime. "What is that?" I ask. "That sound? It's an angel caller." She pulls up on the chain around her neck, and from under her uniform comes a silver globe with the continents enameled in dark blue. I hear Monique's voice in my head—*Look out for a globe with a bell*—and I shiver.

I ask where she got it, but she doesn't remember. Online somewhere. She looks at me and considers. "I bought two because I loved it so much. Do you want this one?"

"Yes please! My husband will give you the money."

"Don't worry about it. I'll give it to him to hold onto until after surgery. So now it's yours, and the angels are being called already. Okay, hold still."

I consciously relax, wondering again at the many things I don't understand. After the surgery I must remember to tell Monique about this. I suspect she won't be surprised.

The nurse outside the cubicle calls, "Who is Fiona Copeland's caregiver?" and then, "Well, which of you is it? No, don't worry, this happens all the time." *Really?* I think. I'll bet it doesn't.

It's Dane who enters, his face creased with worry and fear. Had there been more time, we'd probably have talked: said the things we wanted remembered, spoken the words we wanted to be sure were said in case there was never another chance. But maybe this way is better. My body's weak enough without more emotional drain. He kisses me, once on the forehead and again on the lips.

"I'll be here the whole time," he says, his voice cracking. "However long it takes."

"Should be around eight hours," I reply, then add, "Could you ask Mason to come in?"

He says, "Of course," but looks puzzled. Dane doesn't understand that Mason isn't just paid staff. Over the past months he has become possibly my closest friend. I can't imagine going into the operating theater without saying goodbye.

But when Mason comes in I discover there's nothing to say. He already knows everything: what I've been through, the hell-storm I'm about to enter, the risks and angles. He's been there through all of it. So maybe he can guess what I'm thinking right now.

"Thank you," I say.

He takes my non-IV hand. "You've got this. You know that, right?" He sounds determined. "You know what to do, you're thoroughly prepared, and you're a fighter. Get yourself peaceful now, and when the time comes keep fighting. See you on the other side." He gives a fierce nod.

"Sorry, chat time's over," a nurse announces as she barges into the room. "We're taking her in now."

This is it. Fast action and wheels up for the second time today.

I slide onto the mobile gurney that arrives at the cubicle, my tank somewhere behind me, and am wheeled down the corridor to the operating room. There's no time to worry or even think about what's going to happen; it's all systems go. I'm scrubbed down with disinfectant, all my lines are checked, and I'm asked one final time for the record if I understand and accept the risks behind the surgery; then the sedative is inserted into my IV. Countdown begins at twenty, but I don't make it to the end . . . thirteen, twelve, eleven, and I'm gone.

Part III

A Visit to Hell

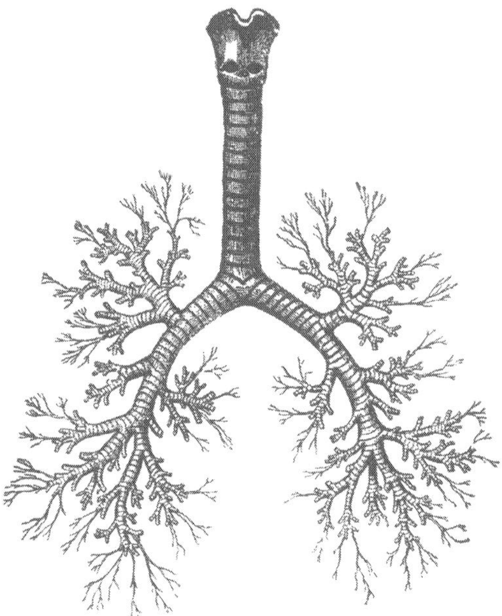

Chapter 37

August, New York City

Talking. And motion . . . not large motion, but general rustling. People in the room. More talking—to me this time. Someone's repeating my name, wanting me to pay attention. I do my best: I'm not completely under, just really fuzzy. And really invested in *not moving*—not at all, not even a little bit. Moving seems dangerous. Maybe not even possible. I think there are lots of things going into or sticking out of me, so I'll just lie here on my back staying as still as I can for as long as it takes.

It's medium bright in the room, but I can't tell much more than that. There's a cannula in my nose that is plugged into wall oxygen. There seems to be a big machine behind me, but I can't actually see it—more sense it—so maybe it's not really there. A figure appears at my right wearing a yellow paper-like robe over scrubs. Male, Asian, friendly. He leans in, asks to listen to my lungs, palpates my stomach. "Just thought you'd enjoy a belly rub," he says, and though I'm surprised by the comment, it almost makes me laugh. Almost.

"Okay," he says finally. "What I really need from you is to sleep. That's what will heal you the quickest. I know it's hard because you have so much steroid in you, but please try."

I do try, but my body won't let me. A deeply ingrained message from Regent's info sessions is that post-surgery I'll need to work really hard to reinflate my lungs or they may never work again. Part of my brain is keeping me awake, afraid that if I fall asleep I'll stop breathing and never wake up.

It's later now. I see that I'm alone in a hospital room, about regular size, with no other beds. The door is in front of me, beyond my left foot, and has a glass panel to the hallway.

Overhead, green curly vine tendrils hang down from the ceiling. As I watch, they slowly grow longer, spiraling down until they are several feet long. They're quite beautiful. I study them with pleasure, wondering if they're real. Something a nurse said in a Regent transplant lecture slips into my brain but is gone before I can catch it.

Much more important is the thing I know to be next door, in the room to my right. Closing my eyes, I glide through the connecting door. This room is smaller than mine, all white but with a large table in the middle. Resting there, on a white cloth, is the most powerful and awe-inspiring thing in existence: the Brain of the Universe. I become reverent, standing very still, mindful of what an honor it is to be here. The Brain is neon green, about ten feet long, and looks less like a human brain than a phosphorescent broccoli. I have no idea whether it registers my presence. Its power feels analytical and outwardly focused—as though its job is to direct what happens in the universe as a whole. Nevertheless I take great care not to disturb it as I return to my own room.

Everything hurts! A lot of air was trapped in my abdomen during the surgery, and the pain is excruciating. It's like the worst gas cramps possible, except that it never goes away. The nurses bring hot pads periodically, and eventually between those and the painkillers I get some relief. There's a tube coming out of the left side of my torso to drain off extra fluid buildup from surgery. It's not the physical discomfort that bothers me, but rather the idea of it feels disgusting; plus it makes me even more cautious of any side rotation. The thought of movement doesn't terrify me as much as it did initially, but even so I keep as still as possible.

The next few days all blend into one another. A nurse cleans the scars under my breasts regularly. From her movements I can tell that they run horizontally for most of the underside of my breasts. Whatever painkillers are in my drip are holding off the worst of it, but bizarrely, there's no sensation in my breasts at all. The nerves in that area must have been severed in order to get the old lungs out and the new in. I hope they'll eventually grow back but don't know for sure and I'm in no rush for sensation yet.

On my bedside table is an incentive spirometer, a closed plastic tube about eight inches long by two wide, with a breathing tube and mouthpiece attached. Every couple of hours I'm supposed to inhale slowly, as deeply as possible, and see how far up the tube I can suck the blue washer inside. It's extremely painful to inhale deeply so soon after surgery, and the necessary muscles are sore and weak. But it's the best way to open up the lungs, so I try to ignore the pain . . . I am literally embracing the suck. Expanding the lungs' capacity early on is a critical component of how well they'll work going forward.

I share my daytime nurse, Justyna, with only one other patient. Justyna knows everything about transplants generally, and my transplant specifically. She's strong, determined, and well respected by the doctors, who consult her regularly on my progress. Several times a day she turns me on my side and bangs on my back. The first time she explained, "Sorry if this is uncomfortable, but it helps release mucus from the lungs." Then she repeated the process on the other side. It's hard work and must be exhausting, but she seems cheerful about it.

My respect for nurses has grown exponentially since I got here. We should all appreciate them much, much more than we do. I hope Justyna gets pampered somehow after her shift.

For the first time in three days, I awake from a full sleep. A doctor by my bed tells me I need to get a port—a flexible tube inserted into a vein—put into my neck so that medications can be put into me in large volume, and immediately if necessary. I'm wheeled into a sterile room, where another doctor is waiting. I'm terrified. Animals are hardwired not to want anything messing with their jugular, and I'm no exception.

Inserting a port into the jugular is just as much fun as it sounds. There's a big infection risk, so the procedure is done under a draped cover, like the cones to prevent dogs picking at wounds. I'm so grateful that a senior doctor—German name, kind face—will perform the procedure until he asks, "Is it okay that my intern will do the procedure? It's a training hospital, you understand." I'm thinking *noooo!* but agree, because if no one let interns learn on them, we wouldn't have any doctors.

I close my eyes and mentally sing the first song that pops into my head. "Over at the Frankenstein Place". . . Nice one, subconscious. I am in fact a composite of multiple people's body parts, getting a device inserted in my neck. *Endure*, I think. That's all I have to do, just endure the suck until it's over. Unfortunately the intern has trouble getting the port inserted. The second attempt is a bust too, and I'm beginning to shake when mercifully the senior doctor takes over and finally we're done. *A small light in the darkness of my life.*

The light is dimmer now in my room. It's evening and I'm feeling unbearably sad. There has been a monumental screwup. An important procedure was required before they could proceed with the transplant, and it needed to happen within a tight time window. Justyna, whom I thought invincible, missed the window. Now, despite everything, I am going to die. It's impossible to process how awful this is; I'm lying here alone, waiting for it to happen, wondering what I will feel when it does. Outside in the corridor, Dane's brother and sister-in-law are furious at Justyna. Charlotte is screaming, "You had only one thing to do, but you screwed it up and now she's going to die!" Things are definitely bad if Charlotte is this angry. Something falls from my bed. It's a tube, and blood is flowing out of it, making an ever-spreading puddle. Is this it then? Is this how it ends? Alone in an antiseptic room, bleeding out on the floor?

Another wake-up. They're telling me about a procedure. Plasma something complicated. Plasmapheresis. They'll hook me up to a special machine and run all my blood through a machine that filters it before returning it to my body. I've moved from Frankenstein to Dracula. But I can hardly argue, so sure, go ahead. "It'll be cold," they say, "and noisy." Whatever, if it needs to be done, do it. As long as I don't have to watch.

The night nurse, a younger Taylor Swift with short hair, tells me the plasmapheresis tech will be here in an hour. No problem: I have no other engagements. He arrives late with a noticeable presence: big machinery, big personality, big Russian accent.

"Let me know *before* you get too cold," he says. "It's much harder to warm you up afterwards." But of course I don't. Everything seems fine till suddenly I'm shaking, and he has to layer me with thermal insulation to get my heat back. The loudness of the machine's thumping is bad enough, but the thought of my blood being sucked out of my body and flowing through a box in the corner is deeply disturbing. No wonder I got so cold: The room is far below body temperature, and that's where my blood is . . . outside me, in the room.

After two or three hours, it's finished. I'm desperately relieved. "See you next time," the tech says. "Two days from now, second session out of three."

It's nighttime again, and the ward is quieter. But nighttime is when horrible things happen—spiteful, terrifying things. The gentle and encouraging presence of the vines and The Brain are gone. My new reality is far more malevolent. Two of the nurses here believe that people over forty—especially those with increased chance of rejection due to antibodies—should not be receiving precious new lungs. The young, hurried man is sad about needing to make choices, but firm in his belief that given the organ shortage, new lungs should first go to young people who haven't yet had a real chance at life.

The female nurse has a mean streak; she's the one I'm afraid of. When no one is around, she pokes her head around my door. "Don't forget," she says, flicking her hair back, "those new lungs aren't yours. You're just keeping them alive for my patient until he's well enough for transplant. As soon as you reject them—which you will—they'll be his." She flashes a malicious grin and tapes a note in big bold letters on the window glass: "Lung incubator inside."

It's midmorning, and Dane has just arrived! I'm so happy to see him . . . someone who knows me from my old life, a face from the outside world. Finally, I can learn what happened after I went into the OR.

"This isn't easy to talk about, Fi," he says, looking haunted. "Shortly after the operation your body triggered a massive rejection. Your whole system crashed, and it seemed like you were dying. Or dead." He pauses and looks away briefly before resuming.

"They put you on ECMO for several days—a machine that takes over from your heart and lungs—and since then they've been working at fighting off organ rejection. You've been on sky-high levels of steroids: a thousand milligrams—about one hundred times an ongoing dose."

A thousand milligrams? That alone would explain my difficulty sleeping.

Dane strokes my arm and it's clear how big a toll this has taken on him. He looks utterly wrung out, his handsome face drawn and pale.

"You look worse than I do," I joke, my voice creaky from disuse and, presumably, the intubation. He manages a weak smile. He's going to hurt when I die—which can't be long now, given whatever that screwup was that Justyna made, and the blood loss I saw on the floor.

"I'm sorry, honey," I tell him, my heart aching. "I wish I could stick around to pick up our life together. Please know I really tried."

He looks surprised, and opens his mouth as if to reply, then closes it again without saying a word. What can he say, after all? I don't tell him, because it's too cruel, that sometimes I have daydreams—fantasies—that there's been a mistake and I'm not about to die after all. Returning from those dreams to reality is the worst part of being here.

I emerge from half sleep to the sound of a woman's voice, singing. It's so ethereal that for a moment I believe an angel has entered my room in a cloud of wavy brown hair. The song washes through me as she pushes a mop around the room, then the woman stops and smiles when she sees I'm fully awake.

"That was so beautiful," I tell her. "Please don't stop—I thought you might be an angel coming to take me away."

She eyes me curiously. "Do you think you're dying?"

"Yes," I tell her, grief pouring over me suddenly at how *painful* this knowledge is. She offers a hand, which I take gratefully, feeling the soft skin against my bony hands.

She looks hard at me. "Do you want to live?"

"Yes," I reply. If only that were possible.

She looks at me intently for a moment and says, "Then you will live."

I release her hand, but the energy of her words is active inside me, an electricity that lingers long after she's left. Tears slide from my eyes as I wonder whether whoever she is—whatever she is—she knows something I don't.

I've no idea what day it is or how long I've been here, but I've fully bonded with Justyna. She's told me about her daughters—one a dentist, the other studying to be a vet—and how she loves to run during her lunch break. By now I've been cared for by many other nurses too. Other than their profession, they're the most diverse group of people I've ever met—a rainbow United Nations. The first time a male nurse bathed me I was surprised, but I've become used to it. It's not as though my body means anything to them other than various parts that they need to ensure are functioning. Not only the carburetor this time, but the whole car.

The medical team comes through every morning and afternoon. I've met belly-rub doctor, who it turns out is my surgeon, several times. *He's the one*, I think as he enters now, looking at his youthful smiling face . . . and even more at his hands. Those hands on the stethoscope took out my old, stiffened, scar-riddled lungs and replaced them with new ones. Wondrous hands.

A slumber party's worth of medical students crowds in after him. "Do you mind if the students watch while I examine you?" he asks.

I find this hilarious. By now little registers as intrusive unless someone actually has their hands inside my chest cavity at the time. "By all means," I reply.

After maybe a week, when my prednisone has been reduced to a more reasonable level, I start tentatively walking. Initially it's enough just to get out of bed and try to balance—which I can't do unsupported—but gradually I build up to reaching the door of my room before returning exhausted to bed. That weekend, an unfamiliar doctor shows up for rounds. It's immediately clear from the size and erect posture of his student entourage that this is an important person. Tall and slender in his sixties, with deep brown skin and a white beard and gold wire-rimmed glasses. He looks so much the senior professor that I instinctively want to impress him.

He wants to see me walk, so I swing out of bed and try to walk as normally as possible along the corridor. It takes a couple of minutes before I notice the blood trail.

"Stop there," he pronounces in a deep professorial voice, his eyes piercing. "Pay careful attention now. A great deal of work has gone into giving you these lungs and performing an extremely complicated surgery. If you damage yourself because you aren't taking due caution, that's on you. Are we clear?"

"Yes," I nod, chastened but greatly relieved. My instincts aren't overly cautious; it's okay not to push harder than this.

I've woken and fallen back to sleep countless times over an unknown number of hours, but now something is pulling me fully awake.

"Fi? Fi . . . I'm sorry to wake you, but there's only a short time before the doctors come through for rounds."

I turn my head and in the chair to the left of the bed is Mason. *Mason!* My body floods with a heady mixture including joy, relief, safety, and more. Everything from the time since they rolled me to surgery suddenly comes pouring out, in wracking sobs that pull on my stitches and churn up the pain in my stomach. He strokes my forehead and gives me a minute to let it all out before saying, "It's okay. Just tell me."

So I do. I tell him about the fear and the pain, and being scared to sleep in case my lungs stopped. About Frankenstein and Dracula and the singing angel, and the brain of the world being in the room next door.

"Thank you for being here," I say between sobs. "I'm so happy to see you one last time before I die."

He shakes his head in astonishment. "What are you talking about? I don't know about the rest of it—the procedures and the pain sound real. But the rest of it isn't. You're not dying."

My heart wants to burst. "Mason, I know you don't want me to give up, but it's too late for that. I *know*. Once or twice there's been a brief flash of hope—like a small opening in the clouds—that says, 'What if reality were reversed: What if surviving were the reality and the imminent death is the dream?' But then the flash passes and the truth becomes clear again."

He leans in and takes my hand between both of his, clasping my forearm with his, all the way to the elbow. "Fiona, look at me. This is me talking. And I'm telling you, you're not dying."

I stare at him and gradually, very slowly, I realize what he is saying. This man doesn't sugarcoat to make things seem temporarily better. But if that's true . . .

"What about Charlotte screaming that Justyna screwed up the critical pre-op test?"

"There *was* no critical pre-op test. If there were, the transplant wouldn't have happened, and you wouldn't be in the

ICU with stitches and tubes everywhere. Think about it. Whoever Charlotte is, she hasn't been here. The only person who's been allowed in is Dane—that's why I haven't come before now."

None of this is computing. "But I *saw* it. I *heard* it." I think for a minute. "What about the nurses who want the lungs back? I think the evil nurse just wants Dane for herself."

"Come on, Fi, that makes no sense. They can't take the lungs back—nobody replants transplanted organs. And you've been around enough nurses to know that wouldn't happen. Clearly you were hallucinating. We were told that hallucinations were common; by the sound of it, you had them in IMAX and Technicolor."

He grows pensive. "Those 'nurses' were probably your own survivor guilt playing out. You've always secretly felt undeserving of getting new lungs while others might not. So get your head around this reality. You *do* deserve these lungs, as much as anyone. Your age and antibody problem were never a secret, but the transplant team still decided you were worth transplanting. Those lungs inside you are rightfully yours. Impressive imagination, though."

He grins. "Maybe *you* should be writing a book."

Could this be possible? The terrifying events mostly happen at night . . . the time of "sundowner's syndrome." Old or sick people often lose hold of reality come nightfall.

"Then what part of it *was* real?" I ask. "Did any of these conversations I've been having really happen? Justyna's daughters, the singing angel? Did I imagine the belly-rub doctor?"

"Jesus, I don't know." He draws a slow breath. "You've been through a lot, so it's not surprising that's taken a huge toll. Right after surgery, you crashed; it was touch and go for a while . . ." He looks away and regroups.

"But those dark visions you're having are false. The reality is that you're getting *better*, not worse. At this point there's no reason to doubt you're going to heal and get on with your life."

The kaleidoscope is slowly shifting. If there were curling vines dangling from my ceiling, couldn't the rest of it be imaginary too? But then why didn't Dane tell me this when he was here? Granted, I didn't unload on him the way I did on Mason, but he must surely have realized I'd been hallucinating? But now, thinking about it, the answer's not hard to guess. Dane hates giving difficult news. He wouldn't have wanted to upset me by making me doubt my own sanity. He didn't realize that instead he made me even crazier.

Chapter 38

September

Ten days after my transplant I'm released from the ICU to the step-down unit. My room is much the same as the ICU one—plain and strictly functional—but it has a bathroom, which is wonderful. By sheer bad luck I draw the only room that backs onto the janitor closet; there are no outside windows. I miss the bright colors and offbeat furnishings of the Johnson's River apartment.

This is a transplant-specific unit, so the medical staff have specialized knowledge in posttransplant care. Now that my condition is no longer deemed critical, I don't have round-the-clock supervision or a semiprivate nurse; instead I'm checked on regularly by a nurse assigned to several patients. The incessant beeps and nighttime wake-up calls stop, and without the constant need to test blood pressure and oxygen saturation, draw blood, and take pills, real sleep is possible. Best of all, my crazily high steroid level has been reduced, and the tormenting hallucinations have gone away. I still dread evenings for their half-lit space between life and death, but nothing like before.

In step-down, I'm allowed visitors. The ICU restrictions that required every visitor to put on a fresh paper gown, mask, and gloves aren't in place here, but anyone coming from outside the unit must still remove their shoes, disinfect their hands, and put any purses or bags somewhere they're unlikely to infect me.

The unit has its own nursing team, whom I'm gradually getting to know. Maybe it's the lack of other company, but I'm genuinely interested in their stories. A big departure from old Fi, who likely wouldn't have even considered their lives outside the hospital. I doubt they're curious about *me* beyond my patient history, but that's not important . . . unlike in the ICU, at least now the conversations are real.

Now I need to work on getting my strength back. My muscles have atrophied noticeably; apparently it takes three days to recover from every day of bed rest, so there's a lot of work ahead to get them operational again. Even more important, the new lungs need aerobic exercise. A physical therapist comes every afternoon. I'd half expected therapists might have their own color coding, in the way that doctors have white coats and nurses have scrubs in the hospital's colors, but they are mostly plain-clothed. The therapist gets me behind a walker for stability and escorts me around my new walking track. This consists of a loop around my section of the unit: from my room, past the nurses' station, then turning left at every corner until I'm back here.

Now that I'm heavily immune-suppressed, I wear a mask outside my room to protect against germs, and an oximeter on my finger to check that I'm getting enough oxygen while exercising. The therapist monitors all my stats, watches my gait, and encourages me when I falter. The first few times I had to stop for multiple rest breaks along the way, but I'm improving—not as fast as I'd like, but I'm learning patience late in life.

My favorite part of the loop is the atrium, a large open central space in the middle of the wing. At the top of the double-height ceiling are large skylights, and the centerpiece of the room is a gray marble table with a spectacular flower display of such height and vividness that it never fails to lift my spirits. The display is changed every few days and the prospect of seeing the new arrangement is a reliable way to lure me out of my room.

Four round tables are scattered around so patients and visitors can eat lunch, and comfortable cushiony seats line the edges. Every time I come through, I feel such gratitude at being here in a space that feels *normal.* I have dinner here with Dane every other day, and Mason and Michaela on the days between; I'm treasuring every visit before Michaela returns to school.

One day my admitting nurse comes in with a twinkle, saying she can move me to a much better room. Together we move my belongings, including a warm fleecy blanket—deep pink with white polka dots—which Michaela brought to decorate my bed and snuggle up with. "Those hospital blankets are icky," she'd whispered, her nose wrinkling.

My new room has a large window with a Hudson River view that encompasses a long stretch of river, including the George Washington Bridge and beyond. I'm so happy that I get emotional and vow never again to take sunlight and windows for granted. That evening the sun sets magnificently over the New Jersey Palisades, and I imagine I'm in a luxury hotel with an unparalleled view and room service for every meal.

My body continues its gradual healing. The terrible pain is gone, but the overall ache persists. The long row of taut stitches makes me feel like the cover of a football, stretched too tightly over a vulnerable interior and crudely sewn into place. I'm told it can take up to a year to feel fully myself again.

For a while now I've been completely off oxygen. It still sometimes surprises me to be functioning without a tube, unconnected to any machine, tank, or wall oxygen. My walks now reach to the long ends of the main corridor. One end has a seating area with tea and cookies, while the other goes past the family rooms where patients' relatives can stay overnight. A large family is there whose women all wear burkas; they make me wonder how Alima is doing.

After almost twenty years, I've started knitting again—the one craft I picked up as a child. A visitor I saw on one of my corridor walks last week was knitting a ball of fluffy blue yarn, and my hands began to twitch with muscle memory. Dane looked for my old yarn and needles but couldn't find them. When I mentioned it to Michaela her eyes lit up, and at the next visit she brought a gorgeous variegated yarn in fire colors—orange, scarlet, and yellow threaded with black—and two pairs of knitting needles so I could teach her how. It was a mess: Between the meds and the surgery, my fine motor activity is shot. But I love getting to do this with her, and she laughs like a Looney Tune every time I drop a stitch and have to unravel and go back.

Recently I've begun reaching out to friends, starting with the ones who live near enough to justify keeping the visits short. Each visit is another reminder that there is a world out there—a world I used to inhabit—that will welcome me back when I'm ready. I still feel a connection to some of my friends from Regent rehab. Getting married must have been good for Zuri because she got transplanted shortly after I left, and although it was rough going initially, she's being released soon. I hope Drew's next.

It has finally sunk in that I'm not dying. Along with that discovery come new questions. How much of my old life do I want to return to? On the one hand is the impulse to live as calmly and normally as possible from now on. On the other is a powerful feeling that in order to make all of this *mean* something, a grander gesture is required. That there's a duty, if not to change the world, then at least to change my own actions within it. Live somewhere else, learn something new, offer my time and skills for good purpose. Let go of relationships that exist mostly out of habit and develop more meaningful ones. These thoughts percolate in my head while my body works on healing physically.

Dane brings takeaway dinners from reputable restaurants, thoroughly cooked to reduce germ risk, and stories of work and friends. The fact that little has happened in our circle since I left town is both comforting and surreal—as though I've been living in an alien world where days have more time in them than on Earth. His work continues to go very well, which makes me happy. Every now and again I catch him looking at me oddly, but when I ask, he always says it's nothing.

Only now do I appreciate concretely how much my having a transplant has changed his world. He has a wife with a serious health condition who will be dependent on him to some degree for the rest of her life. I don't have the capacity to figure out yet what that will mean for us, but I'm sure we'll figure it out as we go along. We always have.

Mason has changed too, in just the few weeks since my transplant. He seems lighter, freer. It's not surprising: The outcome was successful, and responsibility for my survival no longer rests on him. With Krystal taking care of Michaela for a meaningful part of the day, he's been able to return to his writing. He and Michaela are now on their way to Johnson's River to pack up our old apartment. They'll pick up the station wagon and take their time driving back, an old-fashioned road trip with no set agenda. Mason plans for them to pick up local tourist leaflets at their hotel each night and plan no more than one day at a time. Finally they'll get to have the real father-daughter adventure they've both been dreaming of.

Chapter 39

Dane arrives later than usual today, seeming preoccupied.

"Hey," I begin. "Everything good at work?"

"Fine. Just busy."

"Well I'm sorry to add more to your plate, but there are several things I need you to buy. If all goes well I'll be released in a week!"

I'd expected him to be overjoyed—as I am—but he looks more scared than happy.

"It's not much," I say quickly. "Primarily a special electric bed with some of the features of a hospital bed. I'm still far from mobile, and breathing's much easier when I'm elevated. I figure there's just enough room to squeeze it into our bedroom, and hopefully I'll be well enough in a few months to join you in the big bed."

There's still something wrong, so I try to cheer him up.

"The first year is the hardest, as you know, but even after three months I'll be allowed to eat normal food again, and by the second year—if I'm doing well—we should be able to take a trip somewhere, as long as there's a transplant hospital within reach."

He looks away from me for a long time, so long that my chest tightens.

"What's the matter?" I ask. "Aren't you excited about us being together again?"

"*I can't!*" he yells abruptly. Then more softly: "I'm so sorry, Fi." There are creases on his forehead that were never there before, and deep lines between his eyebrows.

"I've tried so hard to want us together again, but I can't do this anymore. You've no idea how it felt to watch your bed light up with alarms and bells, and hear people shouting for the doctor on call. After everything we've been through over the past few years, I can't watch you being sick again; can't constantly worry whether today is the day the transplant fails."

"What do you mean?" I ask, my voice unsteady.

"I'll help you get back home—you can have the apartment, and I'll pay for whatever support you need—but I need my life back. I can't be your partner anymore."

My vision blurs and I'm suddenly dizzy, as everything falls into place. His increasing emotional distance, the long periods when he couldn't talk because of "travel." I'd known he had trouble coping with the painful phone conversations when my voice was almost too weak to hear, but I never realized it was this bad.

"Are you serious? We . . . we made *vows*," I stammer between gasps, struggling for comprehension. "For better and for worse—in *sickness* as in health."

I feel myself floating away, looking down at the memory of the two of us at the altar, making eternal vows with such assurance. How reckless we were back then. How sheltered from a true understanding of what "for worse" would be like. My body is trembling. Dane finds a cannula and plugs me into the oxygen wall, then wraps me in blankets and sits next to me, looking miserable.

"I wish I were stronger, Fi. Truly I do. But those years of taking care of you while you kept getting sicker and weaker were soul-sapping. When I finally accepted that you were going to die, I mourned you every day even though you were still alive. Advance payment on future grief, I guess, but it just about broke me. Transplant shook everything up again. I wanted *so much* for you to survive . . . but it's hard to be hopeful with so much fear. I'm ashamed to admit it, but being on my own, with only myself to worry about, was a massive reprieve. I thought things would be better when you returned, but now I see things will never feel safe. Life with you would mean having a sword continually over my head, and I just can't face it again."

As much as I feel like screaming at him, there's no counter to that. He's right: Transplant recipients lead precarious lives.

"Maybe if I'd been with you at Regent it would have been different." He shrugs. "But with the distance, and growing apart . . . I got to be me again. Can you understand that at all?"

I stare at him, not knowing how to respond. As furious and heartbroken as I am, I do understand that it's always harder to do something painful a second time . . . to pick up a hard burden after you've put it down. And beneath the resentment there's a small nugget of guilt for my own part in this. Since Michaela joined us, I have shut him out. Hid things. I was so focused on not losing her that I was actually relieved when he stopped visiting. *Meanwhile my marriage was slipping away.*

My mother's words from years ago come back to me: The most important thing in life is simply to *be there*. Relationships of all kinds can flounder in absence. Some can't even survive it. Those special events—birthdays, graduations, weddings. Health crises. You can hear the stories and watch the videos, but nothing is the same as being there when they happen. For an experience as intense and life-changing as the one I've been through, Dane not going through it with me has created a chasm. An unbridgeable one.

We sit silent for a long time, watching each other warily as the new reality sinks in. I focus all my energy on holding in the ugly, bitter words I know I won't be able to take back. But as my emotions churn, I become gradually aware that I'm not as devastated as I should be. Deeply wounded, yes, of course. Angry and let down. But not truly shocked. Rebuilding a relationship that has grown apart takes a lot of work, and neither of us has that sort of energy anymore. I need to focus on healing. And Dane hasn't truly felt like home for a long time.

For some reason I can't at first comprehend, I reach for his hand. This might be the last time I touch him. I look at that familiar face, those beautiful eyes and the dark circles under them, the streak of gray hair that wasn't there when I left home. It seems there are many casualties along the road to death. We still care deeply for each other, but things are not the same.

"I just . . ." His voice is shaky. "I just want calm and simplicity. To be with someone who I can be sure will still be alive when I come home."

"Oh, Dane. Have you not realized yet? No one can safely feel that."

"I know," he replies, and it's then that he starts to cry.

Chapter 40

Tonight as evening approaches, not nightmares but ghosts appear. The spirits of people I've loved who have left me gather to remind me of my losses. My longtime friend who moved to China. My first boyfriend, who joined the army and was killed on practice maneuvers. My mother. *Her* mother. The father who stepped out of my life. It's not clear whether they're here to keep me company or just to say, *See? It's not just us. People leave all the time.*

A few days later, Dane returns so we can sketch out a basic framework for separation. We've pooled our money since we first got married, so that will need to be sorted out, but at least there are no children to struggle or worry over.

"I don't want to consider division of assets until I've seen a lawyer," I tell him.

"You shouldn't," he agrees. "Look, I don't want to fight about this. On my new salary I'll have enough for my own needs—which aren't great—and still make sure you're financially taken care of for the rest of your life."

I believe him: Dane's not greedy about money, and the rest of my life might not be that long. He's probably more concerned about absolving himself from guilt.

His next question confirms my assumption. "Are you sure you don't want me to stay with you for a few months, till you're stronger?"

"I'm sure." My mind's in a weird floaty space where I'm focusing on small details rather than the big picture. Right now I'm stuck on the growing furrow between his eyes.

"Then I'll find a short-term rental until everything's resolved."

"Fine," I reply, barely listening. I should be a lot angrier and hurting, frightened for the future, but the truth is, I'm just numb. This is one more horrible thing to cope with in a year that has been full of them. My focus is instead on random issues: Do I ever want to move back to the master bedroom? What will the home Dane and I made after our honeymoon feel like when I'm alone? Most important, where will I find a good caregiver? Mason has his own life to live now.

Over the past few days, necessary next steps have popped into my head unexpectedly, like junk ads. Eventually I'll have to deal with them but not now. I'd love to ask Mason's help in thinking things through, but I can't—won't—disturb him on his trip with Michaela. And I'm not yet ready to tell my friends. This situation is humiliating enough without facing their shock and pity. But God do I feel alone.

That night the door opens, and the evening orderly enters. He's been here before, a quiet young man, olive-skinned with a small tidy beard and a limp in his right leg. He refills my water jug, throws out the wrappings from my dinner crackers, and is about to leave when I say my usual thank you, but he stops.

"I'm sorry I was late today." It's the first time he's spoken to me beyond asking if I need anything. "I had to move my mother to assisted living, and it was tougher than I'd thought."

"Oh." For the first time in hours, I think about something besides my own problems. "I'm sorry . . . is she okay?"

"Yeah, she's not sick or anything. It's just gotten too hard for me to take care of her properly. I'm worried something might happen to her some time when I'm not home. She says anyways it's time for me to have my own place and start living my own life. My friends say the same thing, so I guess that's right, but I'll miss her, you know? It's always been just her and me. I'm going to miss her, on my own in our home."

Tears spring to my eyes. *Oh yes, I understand better than you realize.* I blink them away fast; this isn't my story. But in an odd way, it feels like a shared moment. Maybe that's what life is all about, in the end. Finding people, loving them, losing them, and missing them.

"That must be really hard," I say, "having someone so important not be there anymore. My mother's been gone twenty years and it still hurts sometimes. Will you visit her?"

"Sure, I plan to go every day. But it still won't be the same."

"No," I agree. "Well, this is the start of a new era for you both. Your mother will have new friends around her, and you can visit whenever either of you needs, but you won't worry anymore about whether she's safe, and she won't feel guilty about holding you back."

He smiles and nods. "Yeah. It'll be okay once I get used to it. Hope you get healthy and back home soon, okay?" Then he's gone.

I lower the bed's back and turn out the lights, calmer now. It's good to know that somewhere, even if just in small pockets, people are still steadfast. As long as boys still love their mothers, there is hope for the world.

The following morning I don't feel good. No energy, and an overall sense that something is off. When the duty nurse takes my stats, my blood pressure is higher than usual. She humors me by paging the on-duty physician's assistant, and to my relief Meggie shows up. Meggie is a curly-haired dynamo who's both talented at medicine and good to talk to. We've had several late-night talks since I arrived; we've covered everything from careers to family to life philosophy.

"What's doing?" she asks as she breezes in.

I tell her about my symptoms, which don't seem so much when they're said out loud, not adding that the incessant weird, irritating clanking that started yesterday is driving me nuts.

"Let's do a blood test and see what comes back," she says. "If things get worse, have me paged again."

Breakfast arrives, but looking at it makes me nauseous, so I just drink the tea, chew some bagel, and lie down for a nap. Eyeshades are a girl's best friend.

Meggie wakes me some time later to say my electrolytes are crazily out of whack. A nurse follows with IV gear and a large drip bag. *Not another IV, please.* As the needle reaches my arm I flinch, for the first time in my life. Blood gushes everywhere, spooking us both. After as many sticks as I've had in my life, maybe this shouldn't faze me anymore, but the opposite is true. It gets harder every time.

"I don't know how you got this bad this fast," Meggie says. "How much water have you been drinking?"

"No idea."

"I'll check with your nurse. Anyway, we're going to keep you on the drip for quite a while, so settle in. The doctors will be around this afternoon, but I want blood draws every few hours so we can see how your levels are changing."

She looks at me more closely. "Is your friend coming today with his daughter?"

"No, they're on a trip. They'll be back in a week or two."

"How about your husband? Will he be in later?"

I pause. Should I tell her? But it's too raw even to tell Meggie.

"Probably not for a while," I reply.

"Then get some rest; I'll come back and check on you later."

After lunch she returns with the rounding team. My blood work has improved somewhat but is still abnormal. The IV has to stay in. Meggie sticks around after they've left and pulls something out of the deep pocket in her scrubs. It's a wedge of shortbread inside a paper towel.

"Sometimes patients' families bring us carb-y treats or chocolates," she says with a smile. "Usually a swarm of hungry nurses disappears them immediately, but I was first there today. Take it."

I take a nibble, then the sweet buttery taste takes over and I can't stop.

"Thank you!" This small, kind gesture makes me so emotional that I'm warmed through.

"You probably miss having visitors. Is there a relative or friend you want to call? It won't fix your electrolytes, but it might cheer you up."

"Yeah, I'll do that. Thanks."

When she's gone, I collect myself. My friends will have to learn eventually.

"Hey, Bonnie, do you have time . . ." I begin, and immediately burst into sobs.

"Whoa! Okay, cry it out, then tell me."

"Dane's leaving me. Left me. He can't watch me being sick anymore . . . he's had enough."

She's even angrier than I'd expected, and as always, she doesn't hold back.

"*He's* had enough? What the hell has he even *done* over the past months to 'have enough' of, the little shit?"

I start to chuckle. Bonnie does a great line in indignation. She rants on, saying things I won't say about Dane even now, but that feel so sweet to hear.

". . . sending you off with that caregiver guy—who's really cute by the way, I saw the photos—and *why are you laughing?*"

I'm laughing and crying, good cleansing tears, and Bonnie laughs with me.

"Okay," she says finally. "Welcome to the club. When it happened to me, I felt abandoned and scared and resentful. But that fades over time—even quicker if you encourage it—and then you're free to start over. You think of things you *didn't* get to do when you were married, and do them. Spending more time with your friends, watching shows and movies you skipped because your partner hated them . . . Have you discussed money and property yet?"

"No. It felt too exhausting."

"Good. I know exactly the right lawyer."

I balk. "Bonnie, you got hosed in your divorce."

"*Duh!* Obviously I'm recommending my *husband's* lawyer." She gets serious. "Your friends will be there for you, Fi, just as you've been there for us. I know self-reliance is practically a sacred law for you, but it's not always possible, and now's a good time to learn that. We can help support you until you're feeling strong again, so let us. You're not alone unless you choose to be."

Chapter 41

My electrolyte count is back up, but I feel even worse. The construction noise echoing throughout my room is driving me crazy, and I'm not sleeping well. On the second morning I drag myself out of bed and take the IV pole on a slow amble around the loop. Three doors down from me a sudden shout breaks out, loud enough to hear through the slightly open door. "You have to *eat*! Why aren't you even *trying*?" And a lower response: "Because I can't anymore. I love you, Dee, but I just can't anymore. We had a good . . ." before a nurse rushes in and closes the door pointedly behind her. It's a stunning new idea. Somehow it never occurred to me that you could just stop struggling.

Bonnie pays a flyby visit. "Do you know yet when you'll be released?" she asks.

"No one's mentioned it in a week. Which is fine: I'm in no rush to return to my home-that-won't-feel-like-home. Especially not till I've hired a caregiver. If you want to help, you can contact the divorce lawyer for me."

She frowns. "Are you sure you're well enough to be taking this on yet?"

"Probably not, but Dane's inside my brain in a toxic way, and I want him gone. Even an introductory call will feel like progress."

Having a video call scheduled in three weeks gives me a sense of purpose. The construction noise in my room has been joined by irritating weird music, so I start walking more; for some reason, it's quieter in the corridor. But I have to be careful because I'm not sure-footed anymore. I clutch the IV pole hard for stability.

The patient three rooms down is gone. The door is wide open, and there's laughter and chatting inside. I don't know whether they were discharged, went back to the ICU, or died . . . and I don't want to ask. It's hard enough pulling myself through each day. I do one loop, get back into bed, and suddenly feel droopy. The next thing I know, a nurse is leaning over me.

"You're back," he says, looking relieved.

"Back from where?" My words sound slurred.

"The person who brought your lunch asked where you wanted her to put it, and you just nodded and said 'okay.' She tried talking to you, but you just kept nodding, so she got me."

"When was that?" I ask, puzzled. I have no memory of this.

"About twenty minutes ago. I called a doctor and they've ordered you a brain scan. Someone will come by later and administer it here; I'll check on you frequently till then."

The thought that something might be wrong with my brain terrifies me as much as any news I've heard yet in this whole long ordeal. With a weak body and a malfunctioning mind, who am I? Not Fiona anymore, that's certain.

The scanner, a large white box on wheels, arrives that evening. The technician attaches a host of circular discs on wires to my head, fixing them in place with a form of glue that I suspect will be hell to remove when this is done.

"This'll stay on overnight; try not to move too much so the wires don't dislodge, okay?"

He rolls on to his next destination and I try to sleep, but the nodes on my head make it even harder than usual. I'm stuck here like a lump until morning—a bored lump. *That seems to be my life lately,* I think morosely.

Eventually I do slip into a dream. I'm in a shallow open grave a few feet below ground, my arms and legs pinned to my side. A team of Quakers arrives with ropes to rescue me, but they can't figure out how to attach the ropes and eventually leave. A shadowy figure appears with a large baking dish full of chocolate pudding. They crouch beside my grave, upend the dish over my face, and push down so that I'm smothering in goo. I wake in a panic. I've always hated chocolate pudding, and now it's a weapon! The adrenaline keeps me wired for over an hour—which is okay, because I'm scared to sleep.

Midmorning, the technician arrives, removes the wires and nodes, and rolls the machine away. "I'll be back in a few hours to clean off the glue."

But my head is itching like crazy. The glue is set solid, to parts of my scalp as well as my hair, and I'm desperate to have it gone. I hold out for almost two hours, then plead for help until eventually someone drops off a vial of solvent.

I apply it with my fingers, sighing with relief as much of the glue dissolves and I can scratch my head. To my horror, clumps of hair break away. I grab my hand mirror and scratch some more; thick clumps fall onto the bed. I look like a Halloween scarecrow, patches of hair of varying lengths around my head, bare scalp exposed between. I stare at myself in nauseated disbelief.

When the technician finally arrives an hour later, his horrified look makes me feel even worse. Apparently the solvent was supposed to be diluted. He cleans the remaining hair some more, then retreats. It's still only late morning. My breakfast has congealed into a goo that would probably be more useful on my hair than in my stomach, and it suddenly hits me that this is what my life is now. Brief bursts of health, always overshadowed by the fear of when the next problem will turn up. The idea of returning to work is pure fantasy; I can't commit to anything when I could be incapacitated at any moment.

What is there to look forward to, then? Occasional visits from friends, which will inevitably dry up over time; they have their own lives to live. Timid, fearful ventures outside, careful to protect myself from any germs, worried that at any moment I might have a blank spell? Or worse, wind up back in the hospital, where I *never* want to go back, ever again.

Do the rest of my Regent cohort feel this way, I wonder? Starting up my computer, I look up the Facebook website for Regent Hospital transplantees. Jersey Joe has posted a photo of himself with his wife and grandson, flying a kite as he'd always wanted. Terry is now enrolled in Regent summer school and will graduate next year alongside his brother. And Mountain Man, whose real name is Ernest, has died; the cause of death is not given. The image comes to me of that strong, determined body flying around the track. If *he* couldn't survive more than a year, what chance do I have? The lucky ones who are doing well live in a distant universe, an easier one than mine. It's Mountain Man I identify with.

And with that, everything collapses in on me. So much sadness and pain has been raining down on me for so long that they are all I can remember. Fear, pain, exhaustion, and betrayal. The realization enters my body fully formed that, like the patient down the hall . . . like Dane . . . I can't do this any longer. Can't go through another round of tests, not knowing what's wrong or whether it's fixable. Can't witness any more suffering—not mine, not someone else's—and won't spend any more weeks in a hospital. I don't want a life where even my mind doesn't work. This isn't a decision—for once, there's no analysis involved. It's a moment of clarity, of understanding. Nothing is keeping me here. No expectation of real health, or joy, or a life with meaning. At some point it's time to give up, and that time is now.

With great deliberation I walk to the atrium and sit in one of the dark stuffed chairs. Fixing my eyes on the patch of sky through the giant skylight, I think back on the highlights of my life. The friendships, triumphs, celebrations, loves. Forty-four years spool out in mental images that thankfully my mind still recalls. Beautiful places I've seen, wonderful people I've known. So many wonderful memories—more than I ever recall in the normal course of things. Seen this way, there's much good in my past . . . With the future looking so bleak, there's at least some comfort in that.

Now I'm getting itchy to take the step; too much has been out of my control lately as it is. I won't leave anyone lonely behind me: no husband or children, no colleagues. My friends will miss me, but they've been prepared for my death for a long time. My biggest regret is that someone else could have received these new lungs, but I can't change that now.

I return to my room and sit by the window to ponder the obvious practical issue. I've never thought about dying on purpose (lucky me, as Mason would say) and don't actually know how to go about it. I've no access to anything dangerous, and anyway I'd hate for anyone to know it was intentional. I'm ashamed enough as it is . . . for not being strong enough; for failing. For wasting these lungs. I'd like to just slip quietly away like an old jalopy out of fuel, rolling ever slower until I come to a complete halt.

Then it comes to me that maybe I can do exactly that. On this narrow walkway between life and death, it seems possible that all I'd have to do is stop fighting and my body would gradually shut itself down. From childhood it has been instilled in me never to give up, but maybe there's still time to learn a new life skill after all—the ability to let go.

But I want to ensure that no one tries to resuscitate me. I don't remember writing a living will—and can't ask for one now without raising suspicion. If I'm incapacitated, Dane would make decisions for me, and he'd feel too guilty to let me die if there were any possibility of keeping me alive—however horrible that life would be. Another wave of sorrow washes over me as I realize there's no family member, no partner I'm comfortable asking to do this instead. Mason probably still has my Regent power of attorney in his famous document box, and he knows better than anyone what I've been through; he'd understand that I'm terrified of breathing tubes and ventilators. But it would be completely unfair to ask him, after all he's done to keep me alive.

I ask the duty nurse for a sheet of paper and an envelope, and handwrite my instructions. No extraordinary measures. The only thing I want is not to suffer too much; slow suffocation seems the worst kind of torture. I've no idea whether this makeshift document will hold up, but it's the best I can come up with. It takes mere minutes to complete and sign, the hardest part being the fact of having to do it at all. It feels pitiful to be planning for my death alone.

There's one other thing left to do. When my mother died, I wasn't there. I didn't get the chance to say goodbye or hear any last words she might have had for me. I don't want to do that to my friends. They deserve some form of farewell—not individually, that's more than I can handle, but collectively at least. I go to my own Facebook page. "Change of status: New life condition" pretty well covers it. I've no idea who my friends list includes at this point, because Rina has my password and has been accepting friend requests for the past couple of months, but it's not important. If they read my page, that's friend enough.

I start by saying that it has been a long fight, but it seems I won't make it through. I thank them all for their presence in my life—for everything they've brought me over the years, and all the experiences and connections we have shared. It has been a wonderful journey. I close by wishing them much love, joy, and good memories. Then I hit *post* and shut down my computer, put on my eyeshades, and drift off to sleep.

My cell phone wakes me in the late afternoon. It's Rina, calling from a couple thousand miles away.

"Fi? *Thank God!* I was so afraid . . . What the hell is going on? I've been getting all these calls asking if you died!"

I try to focus and realize I've landed her in a mess. "I'm so sorry . . . I didn't think about what might—" She cuts me off.

"Have you seen your Facebook page? Just look at it, read it slowly, and call me back." She hangs up.

I log on to my page . . . and am stunned. Dozens of messages scroll down the page in response to what was meant to be my final communication. Friends telling me they don't want to let me go and they're praying for me to find renewed strength. Former colleagues saying how much they miss me and wished they had come to visit me. About ten posts down, someone recounts a kind act I did for them (which I'd long since forgotten), and after that, most of the posts also include a personal memory that they treasure. One near the end says they will always love me, whichever side of death I'm on. This is next to impossible for me to process. I haven't talked to some of these people in years.

After fifteen posts, I need an emotional rest. I call Rina back but don't know what to say.

"Shall I take that silence as surprise? You doofus," she says gently. "Did it really take you this long to figure out how much you're loved? Imagine if you'd died not knowing! You're almost certainly depressed, Fi, that's what's wrong, and after everything that's happened to you, you're entitled. But you're in absolutely no condition to draw any conclusions or make *any* decisions, much less big ones. Soak the love in. Sit with it for a while. Can you hold on for a few days—start with a few days—before thinking or doing anything important?"

There's an odd electricity running throughout my body, as though tangible energy is being plugged into my neural circuitry. The buzz spreads outward, energizing me. Something shifts; I feel a renewed strength to keep going. More than that—a *desire* to keep going.

"Yes, I think so," I tell her.

"Good. I can't leave for a couple of days, but I'll stay in touch and can fly directly to you if you need me. Meantime, promise not to do anything dumb until you've talked to me first, face-to-face, and met with a psychiatrist." Rina knows I don't break promises.

"I promise." And it feels right, because apparently I am loved. Parts of me reside in the memory banks of a lot of wonderful people; I would be missed. Who would have guessed? No, Rina my friend, I didn't know. Because the studious girl who listened more than she spoke, and became the serious professional who was all about her work, never realized that love can be generated in small acts, brief shared experiences, common spaces. That it mounts up over the years and with every new stage of life: schools, jobs, daily interactions in stores or on the street. Everything sows the seeds for how your impact will be measured, both good and bad.

Closing the computer, I pull on the wool hat I've been using since I lost my hair to keep my head warm and look less naked. Then I move to the chair by the window and gaze out again at the view that has brought me so much peace over the past weeks. Sunset is almost here, and from the look of the narrow clouds it's going to be glorious. Pink and orange streaks are already appearing over the New Jersey Palisades, and once the colors hit the underside of the clouds it will be magical. Something unexpected and beautiful happened here today. I sent out a genuine cry of despair, and the universe responded with unmistakable clarity. It's calling me back to life.

Chapter 42

Now that I want to survive, my ongoing problems are troubling again. The brain scan turned up nothing, but the occasional zombie states—I'm never unconscious, just blank—continue. No one seems to know why.

Saturday rolls around, which means I'm unlikely to hear anything for two days. Weekend rounds are covered by whichever doctor and PA happen to be on call, and absent an emergency they usually defer decisions for the patient's regular doctor. But when today's team walks in, I'm astonished to see Meggie and a doctor with a sprinkling of gray in his brown hair and a pleasant, friendly face. Dr. Sayer, head of the lung transplant program.

"It's nice to meet you," he says, smiling. His accent has a faint European smoothness.

"Likewise," I reply, thinking, *Who knew the head of transplant took his turn on rounds?*

"Meggie has told me about your situation. I've seen the results of your brain scan, but unfortunately they don't show anything useful. We still don't know what's causing the blank-out spells."

Dr. Sayer studies me thoughtfully. Then he asks, "How do you actually *feel*?"

I open my mouth to say the usual mild vagueness but instead blurt out, "Like I'm in Narnia!" Immediately, I'm mortified. Making such a ridiculous comment to the head of the unit? He'll never take me seriously now.

But to my surprise, he seems curious. "What do you mean by that?"

At this point, I might as well tell him. "Weird stuff happens all the time. Loud noises, eerie music, and now barking dogs. Why are there dogs wandering around the hospital? What are the open paint cans in the corner for? It's as if I've walked through the wardrobe into some bizarre fictitious place where nothing is real."

There's a lengthy pause, then Meggie says, "Can I ask you something? Do you feel like yourself?"

It's a strange question, but exactly the right one. "No. Not at all."

"I didn't think so. I have a pretty good sense of you, and you don't seem the usual you."

"Give us a minute," Dr. Sayer says, and they leave the room.

They return a few minutes later, looking decisive.

"We think you might be having an adverse reaction to one of your transplant drugs," the doctor says. "It's so rare that we seldom consider it, but tacrolimus can cause PRES, a syndrome whose symptoms can include blank spells and hallucinations. We don't like to take transplant patients off tacro because it's such an effective antirejection medication, but in your case we're going to try that and see what happens. We'll replace it with a different medication and check on you tomorrow. If that's the culprit, the symptoms should go away quite fast."

He leaves the room first; Meggie winks at me before following. For the first time in a while, I feel hopeful. Maybe I'm not irreversibly brain damaged after all.

The following morning, I'm eating breakfast when something moves in my peripheral vision. Through the bathroom door I spot a stout middle-aged woman in a long beige dress and puffy white cap. Next to her is a cartoon tiger: Frosted Flake Tony. Tony gives me a lopsided grin and sheepish look, then ducks behind the bathroom door.

That's odd, I think. Cartoon tigers don't move in real life, do they? And suddenly all the weird things I've been hearing and seeing become clear. He's a hallucination. He and everything else. The explanation for why they'd have dogs and ongoing construction in a lung transplant ward is that they *don't*! Tacrolimus starts to leave the body within twelve hours, and I've been off it for twenty. I'm coming down, and my brain is returning to normal.

For the next few hours I straddle the space between reality and fiction. Unlike the earlier nightmares, these visions are benign and occasionally funny. I'm impressed with the leatherbound lunch menu featuring caviar, lobster, and a selection of fine wines, until I think, *Hang on* . . . and the menu morphs into a sheet of paper listing boiled chicken and spaghetti. I'm almost there.

In the morning I wake clearheaded for the first time in a week and take myself on a tour of the floor. I'm just turning the final corner when something small and blonde comes tearing down the corridor at me, yelling, "Semper Fi! Semper *Fi-i-i-i-i*!" She stops abruptly when her dad calls, "Gently, Mike!" and gives me a careful hug that expands my heart a couple of sizes. Mason and Michaela are back.

I soak them in on the walk to my room. They're both so tan and healthy-looking. Mason has a half-healed cut on his cheek that is piratical and charming, while Michaela's shoulder is peeling where she missed on the sunscreen. I sit on the bed and the two of them pull up chairs.

"We took a long road trip and saw all kinds of cool stuff," Michaela gushes, though I already know that much. "We learned to kayak—well, Daddy already knew how, but I learned—and we picked two kinds of berries on farms, and oh! We stayed on an actual farm and milked *goats*. The milk was disgusting, especially since it was *warm*, but it was still fun."

When she's tapped out of her immediate cache of stories, Mason asks her to go and find some fun snacks for all of us.

"How are you?" he asks as soon as she's left. "Truthfully."

Thank goodness Mason isn't on Facebook. I tell him about the blank spells and hallucinations, and the discovery about tacro, then take off my hat to show him my hair. He takes it all in without interruption or comment.

"Sounds like you had more drama this past week than we did. I was wondering about the new hairdo. No offense, but it's a little cutting-edge for you."

"Very funny. Yes, it's hideous and will take forever to grow out, but I'm really glad they solved the problem while I was still here and not already home."

"Dane would have figured it out," he says, then frowns and stares. "What is it?"

Unpleasant as it is, I immediately admit the truth: "Dane's leaving me. Left me, actually. We're starting divorce proceedings and he's looking for his own place."

He frowns deeply, trying to comprehend, then sits next to me on the bed and envelops me in a tight embrace. I tense for just a moment, then release everything, even the humiliation and rejection—Mason can carry it for me for a bit, and then maybe it will be gone. My body unwinds . . . not so much relaxing as dissolving. It feels like coming home.

"Were you guys *kissing*?" comes a voice from the doorway. "You *were*, weren't you!" She sidles in carrying cookies, a huge "gotcha" grin on her face.

I'm mortified. Mason's trying so hard not to laugh out loud that the bed is shaking.

"Do you love each other?" she asks, sounding like a talk show host.

"Well, yes," I reply, "but like really good friends, not like Mommy and Daddy love."

"Better not be!" she counters immediately. "Mom and Daddy don't even *like* each other—though they try to pretend when I'm around." She gives Mason a top-notch stink eye. "I'm not *stupid*, you know."

Mason throws up his hands. "I could never think that."

She rounds on me. Please let me not be next: I'm just a little too fragile right now. But instead of telling me off, she studies me more closely, noticing my patches of hair and the tissues next to the bed. Her expression changes to concern.

"Are you okay, Mee-Fee?"

"I'm fine, honey. It's just been a really difficult week, and I'm tired of being in the hospital."

"I understand." She climbs up to hug me. "It's scary, I bet, and there's lots more fun places than a hospital. Like the giant barn off the road where it's Christmas all year. We'll take you there when you're better."

"Thank you, Michaela."

Her breath falls on my neck as she whispers, "You can call me Mike."

Chapter 43

October

The long-awaited day finally arrives: I'm being discharged. Mason has brought the wagon to take me and my hospital things to the apartment. Dane offered too, but I declined.

The caregiver problem has been solved. Michaela's beloved Krystal has a friend in need of work, and after a group of my friends interviewed Yuliana and approved her unanimously, she came to meet me. She seems lovely: competent and caring, and she even cooks. Yuliana will live with me until I'm well enough to take care of myself. It's an enormous relief, because posttransplant care is pretty onerous. I'll have to monitor my blood pressure, heart rate, oxygen saturation, temperature, and sugar levels—that means finger blood sticks every day, which I'm hoping will stop soon. And of course do lung exercises and walk as much as possible. Every week for at least a month, I'll have to return for pulmonology checkups and a blood draw.

For now, though, I'm focused on the immediate present. Once I receive and sign the discharge package of medicines, home care instructions, and documents, we can go. I'm more than ready not to be in a hospital anymore . . . but at the same time feel a bit unmoored. At least here I'm safe, taken care of. Who knows what's waiting for me outside this space? I'm still so frail, both physically and emotionally, that I'm yearning for the security of being with someone who knows me. Just for a little while longer.

"Mason," I begin tentatively, but he already knows. He always knows.

"No, Fi, I can't still be your support system. My caregiving days are over, hopefully forever. This year has been exhausting and wrenching on so many levels—not as hard for me as for you, of course, but still hard. I need to recover and focus on my own life again."

I hadn't really expected otherwise but still feel a wrench.

"Of course. Thank you for everything you've done. For taking this on in the first place, and for sticking around when it became so much more than we'd imagined."

He makes a slight frown of puzzlement and a tiny headshake. "Of *course* I stuck around. This was a long-drawn-out battle for your life. In any war people become deeply invested in the outcome—even the ones not directly on the front lines." He exhales a puff of air.

"Besides, this was personal. When Jed was sick I tried everything humanly possible to save him. He died anyway. I needed this win more than even I knew going in."

His relief is clear. I'm glad I could give him his win.

"And of course," he continues in an entirely different tone, "there was the bonus to consider."

"What?"

"The bonus Dane offered me if I brought you back alive."

I'm mute for a full three seconds before asking, "How big a bonus?"

"Not big enough."

He's kidding . . . I think. But I'm not quite sure. "You are kidding, aren't you?" No reply. "Mason, tell me straight up. Did my husband offer you a bonus if I survived?"

"Better than the other way around, don't you think?" Then he stops teasing. "Yes, Dane offered me a bonus. And my immediate reaction was *what a jerk*, assuming I'd need an extra bribe to see this through. Did he think I'd be half-assed otherwise? Then I realized that's probably just the world he lives in. 'However good the employees are, they'll work extra hard if there's a big shiny carrot dangling out there.' But it was totally wrong for this situation. I wouldn't slack off and let you die because the *bonus* wasn't big enough."

The question I'm holding back is desperate to come out, but I'm afraid to ask. It might be an irretrievable insult.

He starts to laugh. "You're dying to know if I took it, aren't you? I can practically see you biting your tongue. The answer's no. The money was tempting, but I couldn't get past how dirty I'd feel putting a price tag on your survival—which wasn't in my control anyway. I said that when we came back he could offer me a thank-you gift if he wanted, but he never mentioned it. And it was thirty thousand dollars, by the way. I guess he really wanted you back."

What a fiasco, I think. Well done, Dane: You offer a thirty-thousand-dollar bonus if I return alive, and when I do, you leave me. I wonder if it's too late for Mason to get his bonus.

Finally the nurse arrives with the signed paperwork and a bag full of my first two weeks of meds. I pull on the much prettier hat Michaela got me—the color of our Regent "blue streak"—sit in the hospital wheelchair, and set the bag on my lap. Mason takes my belongings and heads for the car, and an orderly wheels me out of the ward, into the elevator, and to the hospital exit.

At last . . . *at last* . . . I emerge into a glorious New York City fall. Blue sky, golden leaves, and warm dry air. I have been indoors, within an area of a few floors, for two months. In that time I have almost died several times, been on some crazy drug trips, and replaced an old and broken pair of lungs with a new set that I've yet to become familiar with. I've been discarded and ended my marriage. But I've made it through.

Leaning my head back, I take in the world outdoors. The complex aroma of street food competes with the odor of rancid garbage and an occasional waft of perfume. People clothed in every imaginable color, pattern, and style rub shoulders on the crowded sidewalk, circling deftly around the strollers and walkers. From the avenue, cars are honking and bicycle bells furiously ringing, while the halal vendors yell and a cluster of pigeons flap into the air. I soak everything in; it's all beautiful. It sounds, looks, and smells like freedom and living, a long battle over.

Mason pulls up, stows my belongings, and checks I can get into the car on my own. I can. As he drives to my building I look around, amazed that everything looks the same as when we left. My favorite doorman—the one who saw us off when we left for Johnson's River months ago—welcomes me home and says he's glad to see me looking so much better.

The elevator clanks more than I remember. It sounds like a horror movie, and as we walk down the hallway to the apartment, I feel a sudden panic. *I don't want to go in.* It's not just my changed circumstances: During the last few months of living here, my dominant sensations were fear and grief. The gut memory of terror and impending death is reaching for me.

Once inside, though, the apartment has a new look over a familiar face, like a childhood bedroom converted while the child was at college. Between them, Mason and Dane—my fake husband and my soon-to-be-ex-husband—have set up a habitation area for me that minimizes the amount of walking while allowing access to everything I need. I've decided to sleep in the office, close to the kitchen and living room. Dane has installed the hospital bed, and he had the walls painted a pretty, pale yellow. And someone, Mason at a guess, has hung his special flower painting over it. My most casual clothes hang in the closet—freshly washed by Yuliana—and the portable concentrator lies next to the bed in case I need it at night. Barring a major setback, the large one won't be needed. The room isn't large, but smaller is better because everything is within easy reach. This should work.

Mason introduces himself to Yuliana, hands her my dirty hospital clothes, and asks her to put Michaela's blanket on my bed once it's clean. Then he helps put the remaining items he brought back from Johnson's River where I want them. The hummingbird goes in the living room, the colorful towels into the bathroom. They feel more real to me than the expensive white ones from my previous life.

"Is there anything *you* want from Johnson's River?" I ask.

"No, I'm good, thanks. Unless . . . would you miss the flower painting you made?"

I'm touched. "Please take it! I'm going to hang your other one too."

That's it. There's nothing more for him to do.

"Will I see you soon? And Mike?"

"No, I don't think so," he replies, looking truly somber for the first time. "Let's sit down."

My body turns cold. I don't want to sit down . . . don't want to hear what he means by *no*.

He sits me on the couch and takes the chair opposite.

"Up until your transplant there were too many steps immediately ahead to even consider what would happen after you were through it. But now, that whole intense, terrifying phase is over. For both of us. Each of us needs to consider, independently, what our next phase looks like. For me it means focusing on the two most important things: Mike, and my writing. They're what I've dreamed of for as long as I can remember, and they've been shortchanged for way too long already."

"I know that's true," I acknowledge, "but . . ."

He's shaking his head.

"My time with Mike is on a short fuse. When Petra comes back, everything will change again, and I don't know what my position will be. This is my chance to be with her; it can't be postponed. As for my writing . . . if I can't make it work this time, I'll never find the strength to try again. We already know I can't create anything meaningful while I'm worrying about you, and if I'm in your life that will be inevitable. I need a completely clean break."

Nothing had prepared me for this. In my worst nightmares, I never dreamed Mason would leave my life altogether. As the knowledge that he means it sinks in, it's as though breath really has left me.

"But what about Mike?" I'm ugly crying now. "Mason, please! You can't take her away from me too."

He sighs deeply and looks away briefly. When he turns back, he looks directly into my eyes and slowly shakes his head.

"You know that wouldn't work. If you spend time together she'll want there to be more. She'll put pressure on me, and eventually I'd cave. That wouldn't be fair to her or me. Mike's just returned to her home and her friends, to life before Johnson's River; it's the natural time to make a break. I'd like to think you care enough about both of us to understand this."

The bottom drops out of my world, leaving me with an infinite distance to fall. But I know Mason is a thoughtful man. He wouldn't hurt me like this if he didn't believe to his core that it was necessary. He'll have considered all the angles and decided that this is how it must be. Nothing I say will change his mind now. And he's certainly earned my acceptance of his choice.

He waits until I have some small toehold of control.

"You'll be fine. Please trust me on that . . . more important, trust yourself. You're incredibly strong and resilient. But you need to find your way to whoever it is you want to be now, and I can't be a part of that journey. You're not the same person you were before—you couldn't be even if you wanted, because your previous life isn't available to you anymore. My advice is try not to view it as a loss but rather a clean slate. Find new options and see what calls to you. You'll figure it out."

The person who has been with me as support, partner, and friend throughout this whole ordeal is about to cut me loose in unknown waters. Already I feel as though I'm drowning, gasping for air. Mason fetches the portable concentrator, sets it on the floor near me, and returns to his chair. It's up to me to connect the tubing and turn it on. While I do, I wonder whether he's right—that I really will figure it out. Or even whether he genuinely believes it and isn't just mouthing platitudes. This last, at least, is easy to check.

I take several full breaths, then ask, "Do you promise I'm capable of doing this?"

"Yes," he replies solemnly. "I promise."

He lets this sink in, then leaves without looking back.

I am now truly, open-endedly on my own.

Part IV

A New Dawn

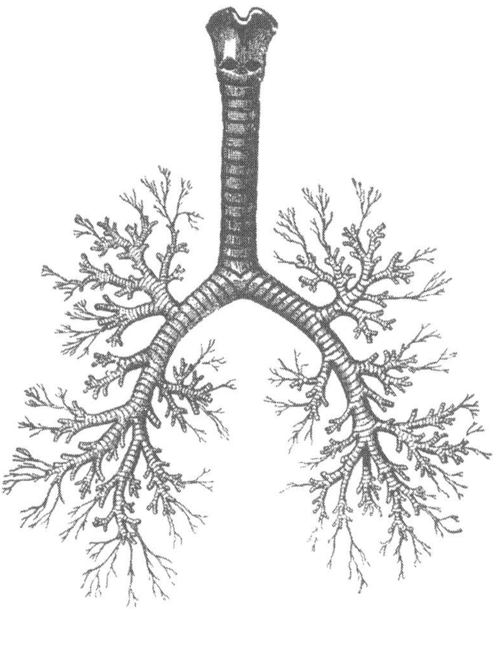

Chapter 44

The Following August, New York City

I stretch my legs, lean back into the cushiony chair by the large picture window, and take my first glorious sip of dark roast Hawaiian coffee. A foodie friend buys special blends from a roaster in Kona and adds a few pounds for me. It's one of several small luxuries I've added to my life in the almost-year since my transplant.

I open my laptop and see that I have received an email from my father.

My Dear Fiona,

I have long flagged this day as one for celebration. Congratulations on the first anniversary of your rebirth! I sincerely trust that there will be many more. Pippa and I so enjoyed meeting up with you in New York and seeing your charming flat. I had thought to get you a housewarming gift, but Pippa advised against it. She has selected a "rebirthday" gift, which will be arriving shortly.

Much love,

Dad and Pippa

The coming anniversary has made me reflective. This is a significant milestone: If you make it past the first year, you're through the riskiest stage, like the first trimester of any new life. It also means that I won't be a dreaded black mark on Empire's statistics, which pleases me: They came through when I needed them. Part of me wants to tell Regent that they needn't have written me off after all, but I won't. Why be petty when they were part of this process too? It all led here, to a new life filled with peace and contentment.

Undeniably, the first months home from the hospital were brutal. I hadn't fully absorbed how much the daily tasks of living were taken care of by the staff, food preparation team, cleaners, and so on. Back home even basic tasks were beyond my reach, so I was more dependent than ever. My body was weak from such a long period of disuse, but exercise was difficult because I was both in pain and afraid of opening up some seam inside. If I so much as dropped a spoon while eating, that became an issue.

Two days after returning I created a walking path. It began at the living room windows, ran the length of the room, then continued along the corridor to the bedrooms. My mandated goal was to walk twice daily, starting with five minutes and ramping up to twenty-five. The old workout playlist helped . . . especially played over a good speaker system and without an oxygen cart to push.

My immune system had always been strong, but now that it was deliberately suppressed to prevent it from fighting the new organs, healing was excruciatingly slow. The blood thinners meant that the smallest injury left a deep bruise. The biggest problem of all was the crushing sense of personal rejection. Being in my old home made it obvious that I didn't belong there.

But I didn't belong anywhere else either. Wonderful as my friends were, they had their own lives that eventually reasserted themselves. Yuliana became my biggest ally, living with me for three months, handling household needs and getting me to weekly physical therapy and checkups. Her sister relieved her when needed, and between them those two women provided the human contact and effort necessary to make it through. I'd already learned that nurses were underappreciated. Now I know caregivers deserve more recognition too.

Once I was strong enough I set about finding a new apartment with no ghosts. It took surprisingly little time to find my new home, several blocks south of Lincoln Center. Being here has healed my spirit as much as my body. It's not a ritzy address, but it's new and clean (no ancient mold or hundred-year-old dust to be allergic to) and perfectly suits the way I want to live now. The floor plan is open, with everything I need in the same orientation as the Johnson's River apartment: a living area plenty big enough for my minimal entertaining, a kitchen and peninsula with a small dining area, two bedrooms, and two baths. It's on the tenth floor, high enough to feel airy but low enough to make it down the stairs if necessary; I'll probably never feel safe without contingency plans. Best of all there's a terrace, which I go onto every day the weather permits.

Following Mason's philosophy, I furnished and decorated the place with things that make me happy. Color is everywhere, on cushions, walls, and paintings. A designer friend helped me find affordable and quirky items that make me smile: a blue-and-yellow-striped sundries cabinet like an egg on legs, and a wooden mirror carved into a bow. Less affordably, I treated myself to a couch I love, made of soft white leather.

Mason was on my mind a lot while I shopped. Losing both him and Michaela so abruptly felt like a double amputation on top of the transplant. Thankfully, Petra's neighborhood is on the Upper East Side, so it's easy for me to avoid. Even so, for many months my pulse raced whenever I saw a dark-haired man with a young blonde girl.

I pushed through by falling back on my transplant mantra. I *endured*. Like a recovering addict, I approached each day with the same goal: make it to the next one. After such a long dependence my self-confidence had atrophied like my muscles, but once I broke the inertia and got the apartment, progress came in a rush.

Dane bought me out of the old apartment at a generous price. Between that and my share of our joint account—much of which was my own money—I have a comfortable financial cushion that, since I don't spend much, should last a decade. That's likely enough.

There have been medical complications, as often happens. Just when it seemed I was finally clear, something else would happen—a sudden infection, electrolyte levels out of whack. In the winter I fell and landed squarely on my coccyx, putting me back in a wheelchair and in severe pain for many weeks. Each time I'd have to talk myself back into the right frame of mind to push forward and recover the progress I'd lost. Again. But the problems were balanced out by some oddly serendipitous events, like a vascular surgeon with cutting-edge experience transferring to Empire two weeks before I developed a massive blood clot in my leg.

Zuri and Robert paid a surprise visit that raised my spirits for weeks, taking them to my favorite haunts and talking, talking, talking. They are so in love, and so thrilled to be married. I believe her nearly dying bonded them for life. I've yet to get to Washington to visit Mei-Lin and cash in on the promised soup dumplings, but she wrote last month inviting me again. I'll get there someday.

The good surprises, often arriving right when needed, have been part of my altered relationship to the world. I feel supported by something inexplicable that no longer requires explanation or understanding. The earlier loneliness that felt like a dark, weighty burden has given way to a sense of singleness. I am a single atom, one of infinitillions, but I am not alone. We careen into each other at random moments during the day—"Hello, what a pretty dress," "Miss, your baby dropped a shoe"—and bounce off again to the next. Something in me must show this change, because for the first time, tourists stop me and ask for directions.

Going through the transplant experience has made me kinder and more empathetic. The bright line separating me from others has faded: I see myself in them, and them in me. Once, I subconsciously saw sick or disabled people across a divide—they were ill, I was healthy. Now I know there is no "them" and "us." Anyone can flip from one side to the other in a split second. Sometimes we even flip back.

Have I become a people person? That's a stretch, but I'm much more aware of those around me, more able to appreciate the small deliciousness of a neighbor offering a ripe plum, or the pleasure in being seen by a conscientious pharmacist.

I've lost some of my fear of an unknown crisis. Most things, I remind myself, are actually not a crisis even when they feel like one. And sometimes when I look up it feels as though something—maybe God, or my mother, or maybe the Brain of the Universe—is looking out for me and will see me through.

My phone alarm goes off, a reminder that it's time for my shot. I head to the fridge, where the syringes are stored behind the Irish butter. When my white blood cell count falls too low, I give myself a boosting med. Part of my new regimen, along with monitoring and logging my vital functions, is ensuring that my inventory of the eighteen different medications I'm on is current. A large pill case, divided into days and times of day, helps track that I've taken the meds—including antirejection, antiviral, antifungal, and antibacterial—at the right time, twice a day. It turns out I'm quite adaptable, which unfortunately meant that after some weeks I'd acclimated to my "take pills" alarm and would turn it off without registering that it had rung. Now I set backup alarms and vary the alert tones.

The upside of adaptability is that I've become very content in my changed circumstances. I've found new favorite places nearby: grocery, restaurants, a wonderful bakery, and a hair salon. My hair has finally grown out—though I wear it shorter now. I like its clean, no-nonsense look, and the fact that it's so easy to take care of; there are better ways to spend my time.

When my divorce came through in November, I felt untethered. Dane and I had been apart for almost nine months—a whole lifetime—but the official end was still profound. To my surprise, seeing the divorce decree in print opened me up to remembering the positive things about our relationship: the way we once were, before I got sick and presented Dane with a future he wasn't equipped to handle. There *had* been many good times. We'd experienced the New York scene with shows, concerts, and museums; had meals together and with friends; shared work stories; planned vacations; cuddled on the couch; made love.

I allowed myself to feel nostalgic for a while, and then it simply passed, leaving a comforting calm and release from regret. I hadn't been wrong about marrying Dane, hadn't spent those years foolishly. Life had just changed both of us in a way we couldn't have predicted or built into any plan.

The worst days were those that should have been celebrations. Thanksgiving, always a festive family reunion at Dane's parents' house, became a restaurant turkey meal with some single friends. Christmas was worse: Everyone was away. So I bought myself some presents and a small tree, and learned origami; at least the ornaments were special. Dane texted on Christmas Day saying he was engaged and his fiancée was pregnant; he hadn't wanted me to learn through friends. I cried, mourning the absence of children in my life, wondering what *our* children would have been like . . . then moved on. Dane will make a good father. I can't begrudge him that.

At midnight on New Year's Eve, I stepped out on the balcony to hear the honking cars, and on Valentine's Day I sent cards to people I care about who are also unpartnered. Endurance has shifted into acceptance. Each of these holidays only lasts a day (ignoring the advertising lead-up); I can work around them all. Maybe one day I will even reclaim some of them.

Doing things alone doesn't bother me now or even feel strange. There's too big a thrill simply from participating in the world again. Yannis kept his word and in April threw me a celebratory party with non-alcoholic sparkling wine, twenty friends, and my favorite music. I go out often, to inexpensive places: Lower East Side plays, niche museums, art house movies. My unbreakable rule is that I always wear a mask, only buy tickets on the aisle, and carry hand sanitizer everywhere.

My biggest moment came the night I finally went to the Metropolitan Opera. *Zauberflöte*. It was so exciting to be there again—in that grand auditorium with the giant sparkling chandeliers, amid the extravaganza of a full orchestra, elaborate costumes, and intricate multilayered sets. At intermission I went to the restroom, saw the line, and hurried back up the long, grand staircase to the second floor. As I reached the top, it struck me. The last time I'd thought about stairs to a bathroom was at the Georgian restaurant in Johnson's River. A small staircase then was completely unnavigable. Now, this long flight didn't even make me pause.

I looked around the atrium: sophisticates with champagne flutes alongside music students giddy with excitement. The soaring ceiling and magnificent Chagall backdrops; the fountain beyond the huge windows dancing its ballet in Lincoln Plaza. It was a magical realization: Fiona Copeland had her life back.

The next step now is figuring out what to do with the rest of my life . . . or even just the next phase. I'm still too fresh from counting my remaining time in weeks to make sense of a major commitment like a new job. I can't even picture what that would look like, especially as I still have so many doctor's visits to manage. At one point I looked for consulting projects but couldn't bring myself to reenter that high-stress world. Plus, I've lost the ability to promote effectively. What comes out of my mouth these days is the unadorned truth of what I'm feeling and thinking, and my lack of total commitment inevitably comes through.

Instead, I lend a hand to things I *can* believe in, like a water development project in Bangladesh my friend is running. And I'm thinking about a grassroots organ donor campaign, where hosts would throw fun "sign the line" parties, to raise awareness and bring in more potential donors. I'm hopeful that some people will embrace this idea of a personal way to make a difference that doesn't require money.

For now, though, there's no rush. The past few years have simplified my understanding of my place in the world. I no longer need a grand purpose in order to justify my existence—I'm here simply because there is a space for me. I have to trust that there is a way in which I am contributing, and that I am enough.

Chapter 45

Today I'm engaged in a very meaningful task. On August 21, it will be a year since my transplant, which means I'll be allowed to write to my donor's family. I've started working on a draft. Neither side knows anything about the other, so it's a cold introduction of a very personal kind. One way would be to tell these people how grateful I am for this life and assure them that I am making the most of this gift. But I'm concerned, too, about not making them angry that someone other than their child, partner, or parent is getting to do these things.

There's no certainty that they'll want to hear from me—or even that the screening readers will agree to pass the letter along. But maybe they will. Maybe they'll want to meet me, to watch me breathe and hear me speak, knowing that these are the same lungs that once spoke to them.

Knowing nothing about my donor opens a universe of possibilities. Sometimes I walk through my neighborhood and wonder whether my lungs came from someone who lived and died on these streets. Bikers tear by and I think: Is this how it happened? . . . A fatal crash and they're done? Is their energy in me now? . . . Maybe strong, or reckless, or angry at someone else's carelessness? People of all types pass by, and while I can never experience what it's like to walk in their bodies, part of me now identifies as every person. I could be part Black or Hispanic or Asian or Inuit; male or female or neither or both. I've learned the fascinating fact that there's almost certainly DNA from my donor free-floating around my body. Sometimes I imagine a cell in need of repair being fixed in accordance with my *donor's* DNA, not mine. I am no longer the old me, physically, mentally, or spiritually. And I'm growing quite fond of the new me.

Taking another sip of cappuccino, I reach for my laptop. The Angel Caller globe around my neck jingles; I wear it always, along with a medical alert pendant I've had engraved with the words *Lung Transplant* and the phone number of Empire's transplant department.

I'm still considering how much of myself to disclose in my letter when the doorbell rings. I wasn't expecting anyone, but friends do occasionally just drop in. It's another new and precious pleasure; spontaneity was rare in my previous life.

When I open the door it takes a minute to recognize him.

"Hello, Fiona."

He's clearly happy to see me, but his voice is uncertain. As it damn well should be. After almost a year of complete silence, did he think he could simply show up at my home and be welcome?

"Mason." I make an effort to be civil. "I didn't expect to see you here."

"Sorry—I should have called first, but I wanted to surprise you." He takes me in fully, from the puffy prednisone face and regrown hair to the increased muscle mass and hard-earned upright posture.

"You look different," he says, his mouth sliding into that quirky smile that means he's very pleased.

"As do you."

The beard and mustache are gone, and his hair, while still on the longer side, is a regular layered cut. It transforms him from a serious, bookish hipster to . . . what? I struggle to place it, then realize: He looks like an office professional. Classic dark pants, textured white button-down shirt that looks European, soft sweater in a pale teal. The man at my door is a very good-looking Upper West Side dad but isn't quite Mason. I'm not sure how I feel about the change.

"Can I come in?" Serious now, a real question.

I actually consider saying no. It has taken a long time to make peace with him walking away, even more with him keeping Michaela from me. But I've managed to let it go—or so I thought. Seeing him is churning it all up again: anger, hurt, abandonment. And, somewhere in the mix, worst of all, I'm remembering how much I've missed him.

In the end curiosity wins. I step back and let him inside.

He looks relieved. Kicking his shoes off first, he looks around the living area and nods.

"This place is very healing, very much you. Calm, happy colors with lots of pretty touches. I like it a lot. And you're wearing a green sweater—not what I'd have expected. Ah, there it is."

He's spotted the glass hummingbird, resting on a high shelf of the bookcase. He turns and hands me a tote bag. Inside are a bag of pastries and a wrap of cut flowers.

"I can't . . ." I begin, but he interrupts.

"I know—no cut flowers. Don't worry, they're silk."

"Right, you were there for the presentation. Well, thank you."

I place them uneasily on the kitchen counter. Why is he here? And why now? This place is my sanctuary. I don't allow people in it who aren't good for my well-being and having him here is making me itch. He'd better not want anything from me that I'm not prepared to give.

"You look so well," he says. "And strong. How's your new life going?"

"I'm doing fine," I assure him. "Is that why you came: to check up on me?"

"No, just asking. I'm here because I have news and wanted to share it with you."

It hits me with a *whump* so hard I have to suck in air. He's about to tell me that he's getting married . . . and I truly *do not* want to hear it. What if he wants to invite me to the wedding? I'm palpitating just thinking about it, and the fact that it's so upsetting is even more troubling. He deserves to be happy, I know that, but I am *so done* with hearing other people's joyful news. I wish he'd just sent me a text like Dane did, so I wouldn't have to pretend to rejoice with him.

He looks ridiculously cheerful as he goes to the kitchen and reaches toward an upper cabinet. I know what he's doing, but this isn't *our* place, it's *mine*.

"What are you looking for, Mason?"

He spins, startled at the edge in my voice. "I was looking for plates for the pastries. And maybe some tea to go with them?"

"I'll take care of it. Take a seat and I'll bring everything over."

I turn on the kettle and take down mugs, using the time to practice composing my face into an "I'm so happy for you" mask.

"Sorry about that," he says. "It's just old habit being around you. Clearly you don't need my help anymore."

When the tea has brewed I bring the mugs over and set them on the table. I'm about to get the pastries when it comes over me abruptly that I can't do this—can't just sit down and chat as though this is a normal social event. I'm too wound up for that, and I'm not a good actor.

"You know what, let's forget the pastries. Obviously you have good news; I'm pleased for you, but I'm not up for this right now. Just tell me what you came to say."

He frowns. "What's the matter, Fi? Why are you being like this?"

Seriously? That's the final insult. I sit down forcefully and lean forward, eye to eye.

"Are you *kidding*? After what you did—deserting me at the lowest and most fragile point in my entire life? You said your job was over and it was time to get back to your real priorities. Fine. But we're not friends, Mason. Did you really think you could just show up after a *whole year*—just bring me flowers and I'd be all smiles and sugar: 'Why hello, Mason, how nice of you to stop by'?"

His face pales. "I *deserted* you? Is that how you think of it?"

"How else *could* I think of it? You were quite clear. I can remind you if you've forgotten."

"No, I remember it perfectly." I'm not sure if it's shock or anger, but his voice is unsteady. "What I said was that we both needed time to get over the experience of those traumatic months. I needed to focus on Michaela and my writing, and just *rest*. For six months I was responsible for every aspect of your life: each mouthful you ate, every test you took, the oxygen you breathed. I needed a break. And I couldn't get one if I were still your main support.

Quite apart from which, you needed to figure out for yourself what kind of new life you wanted, and how to make that happen. Isn't that exactly what you've done? Isn't this better, more authentic, than where you were before? You're a strong woman, Fi. I knew you could do this on your own . . . could do it *better* on your own. Look at yourself—you don't need to lean on anyone."

As he speaks, something big slowly wells up in me that I never expected. Is it possible that I've mischaracterized his action this whole time? Filled myself with anger and resentment, when all along he simply had more faith in me than I did?

"Look, I don't want to be your caregiver. Never again. But I would very much like to be your friend, if you'll let me."

All I can think is that I mustn't cry—not in front of him, not now. I take the biggest inhale possible and exhale slowly. *Just play it cool, girl, real cool.*

"Then as my friend, could you toast those pastries and bring them here? The plates are . . . dammit, exactly where you thought they were."

He nods casually, but on his way finds a box of Kleenex and silently sets it in front of me. I never could hide anything from him.

By the time we've eaten and had some tea, I'm ready to hear it.

"So tell me your news."

His hands fall still. "My book has been picked up. We signed the contract a few hours ago; I'm now officially an author."

I jolt upright, so surprised I'm babbling. "Oh my God, that's your news? No, wait, I didn't mean '*that's* your *news*?' like 'big deal.' It's actually incredible. It's . . . I don't know . . . wow!"

His eyes have grown wide, and he suddenly dissolves into extended helpless laughter.

"Fiona Copeland," he says when he's finally caught his breath. "That was probably the most inarticulate garble you've ever made. Truly an A+ performance."

"Oh, fine . . . one lousy book deal and now you're a critic. Let me rephrase: I have no words." Which sets him off all over again.

Watching him laugh, the memory comes to me of Mason sitting at his glass-topped desk overlooking the quad, focused like a surgeon on his screen. It's followed by other images: the broken coffee mug, the long stretches of frustration, the eventual setting aside of his work to focus on Michaela's and my needs. It's so good to see him this joyous and stress free. Not every day can you watch someone's dream become reality.

"Congratulations. No one has earned this more than you have. And I bet it's brilliant. Can you tell me what it's about now?"

"No—I want you to read it for yourself. Feel free to revise your bet afterwards."

"You can count on it."

He turns serious. "Thank you, Fi. Not for the congratulations, but for the book."

"Thank me? What do you mean?"

"This wouldn't have happened without you. I needed to tell you that in person. Going through the fight for your life with you was the catalyst I needed to give my work depth. This book has the intensity that was missing in everything I'd written before. You asked me once what it was about, but I didn't really know then. It was only after your transplant was done and I had more brain space that the direction became clear. Please read it; it's not about you directly, but you flow throughout."

It's clear from his face that he means it, and now I feel like a fraud. He saved my life while I was needy and focused only on myself. How can *he* need to thank *me*?

"Don't look so doubtful," he says. "I've written a great deal in my life: short stories, essays, even a couple of novels. This, though? It's by far the best thing I've ever written. The publishers have given me a good advance and committed to throwing serious support behind it. If it's anywhere near as successful as they anticipate, they'll sign me up for my next book. Do you know what that means?"

I shake my head. He's like someone who prayed for the last spot on the Olympic team and inexplicably won gold.

"In the short term it means I can afford to do things that have been out of reach until now. Throw Mike a party and treat my friends to dinner for once. It means I can work only part-time and use the rest to write. But mostly it means I was right to believe in myself. I can stop feeling like a delusional idiot who traded in security and respect for a dream."

"Mason, you've never been delusional, and you're no idiot. But it was never enough for you just to write: You wanted to *be a writer*. And now you've been validated. Congratulations, author Mason Wolfwood."

He soaks it in, smiling. "So are you ready to celebrate with me? How mobile are you?"

"Thoroughly mobile, thank you very much . . . unless you're planning a steep uphill hike."

"I'm thinking a magnificent brunch, followed by maybe a trip to MOMA. But honestly, I'm up for anything fun and not too taxing. Are you in?"

He's on such a high that I'm reluctant to dent it even a little. But I can't. Even if I could pivot that fast, it doesn't feel right.

"I'm sorry, but no. There's been too much this morning for me to unpack and process yet, and I've been angry at you for a long time. Besides, this truly is a momentous event . . . I'm not the one you should celebrate it with. Maybe one day I can be that close a friend, but not today."

He studies my face, then nods. "Understood. I'm having a celebratory party on Sunday. The group you met on the video call that night at Regent will be there. They'd love to meet you in person."

"I'll think about it. If I do decide to come, is there a way to reach you? Or should I just wait by the phone for you to call?"

His back stiffens. "That wasn't necessary. My cell number's the same. You can text or call any time . . . or just show up. I'll text you the details."

After he's gone, I return to my chair rife with unwanted emotions. Was he telling the truth about why he left? I've never known him to lie. Maybe he's right about me needing to do this on my own; it's only in retrospect that I can see how much of my innate independence had been sapped by the illness. But if that's true, should I accept his friendship? My life is pared down to the basics now: good friends who don't care that I won't drink with them and can't keep up on hikes or go to crowded concerts. Only people who nourish me are allowed in.

Is there room for Mason in this picture? Seeing him again has set my body buzzing, and I'm not sure why. This might be a good time to talk to one of those friends. Like Bonnie.

"Hey, Fi. I'm on a quick break. Is it urgent?"

"Mason just showed up at my door. He wants to be friends."

"*What?* Did you punch him? Right hook, preferably—or maybe an uppercut."

"Neither. He explained his actions, and they actually made sense. He'd needed time for himself and felt we couldn't ever be friends without fundamentally changing the dynamic. But now he wants to be my friend and I'm wondering whether I should let him."

"Why do you need him? You have other friends—people who have stayed by you."

"Because . . ." Why indeed?

A host of farmyard noises come through the line. Bonnie swears and yells, "Felipe, you touch my equipment and you'll seriously regret it! Fi, hold on a second."

By the time she returns, I've figured it out.

"Sorry, my nephew's visiting and he hasn't learned consequences yet."

"It's fine. The reason I'm considering letting Mason in is that he's the only person who really knows what it was like for me. More than that, everyone else in my life sees me as so much *less* than I once was. Diminished. It's inevitable . . . and true. But Mason saw me this morning and registered me as strong and healthy. As *more*. It was empowering in a way I'd not foreseen."

She thinks about this. "You're telling me the upside first, but we both know the downside: You might get close to him only to have him push you off again. And what about Michaela? Look, this is a crazy time for me. Can we meet for a proper talk some other time?"

"Well, the immediate problem is that he's invited me to a party next week, with his really good friends who I met online about a year ago, and . . . Oh my God. It was exactly a year ago. Friday is his birthday! And I almost missed it again."

"Why would you need to remember? But a party's a terrific idea. You could use a little shake-up. When was the last time you socialized with more than two people at once? Maybe you'd even make some new friends to replace the ones you've dropped this year."

"I'll have to get him a present—if I decide to go."

"Don't kid yourself. You'd decided before you called me; you just needed someone to confirm your decision. Definitely go. If you hate it, leave early. Sorry, gotta run, bye."

I wash my face with cold water and munch on another pastry. It's good: sweet cheese and raspberry. What the hell present should I get for Mason? Even if we're not friends, I'd like for it to be a good one, something significant. But what? I rack my brain, searching my memories for a revelation, until finally it comes to me. On the bottom shelf of his nightstand he kept a book: James Joyce's *Ulysses*. Not to read—he said he couldn't read anyone else's work when he was writing. So maybe for inspiration. It was certainly beaten-up enough to have been reread many times.

I go online and look up "Joyce *Ulysses* First Edition." Lots of different printings, but *there*. In Robbins' Rare Books in Montclair, New Jersey. It's expensive: over two thousand dollars, which almost stops me. But how do you put a price on what Mason did for me? I call to confirm the book is still there, grab a water bottle, and head straight for the car before I can change my mind.

Getting to the store is an easy forty-minute drive. Robbins' has a faux-Victorian facade, complete with small-paned windows, and the minute I step in I'm surrounded by the faint aroma of old books and wood polish. The blond man shelving books is about my age, wearing hip red glasses and a black crew-neck top. He turns helpfully at the sound of the bell over the door.

"Can I help you find something, or are you browsing?"

"I called about the *Ulysses* first edition. Could I see it?"

"Of course." His immediate smile looks genuine. "It's a beautiful copy. I'm not a big Joyce fan, to be honest, but if I were, this is the book I'd want."

Taking a set of keys from his pocket, he goes through a door marked *Private*, and returns with a book the size of a standard hymnal. Immediately I know this is the right choice. It's bound in old black leather, cool to the touch, with just enough wear and small cracks to give it character. Even the font is beautiful: elegant but easy to read. I open a few random pages to check but find nothing wrong.

"I'll take it," I say, feeling daring and reckless. "Please wrap it for me. It's a special gift."

He wraps it in antique gold paper, then adds silver tape and a bow, and I leave feeling like a child with a happy secret.

Returning home is another story. My GPS routes me over some of the same path as Teterboro Airport to Empire Hospital. I haven't been here since the panicked race to surgery, and every marker ignites a detailed memory of that trip: the small shops, hurtling against the traffic, transferring to the NYPD escort. At first there's no obvious impact, but when I hit the on-ramp to the George Washington Bridge I begin trembling. I wait for the feeling to go away, but it only gets worse. Halfway across, my chest is clamped tight with a terrible pain, and the only way to release it is to *scream*, scream to myself in the car, my body shaking with the intensity of it. All the emotions I should have felt the first time—fear, hope, desperation—come flooding out, after a whole year, while I struggle to maintain control of the wheel and pull into the slow lane. It would be blackly ironic to die in a car crash *here, now*.

It's not until I approach the exit that I regain something approaching normalcy, and even then my entire body sags with relief when I've reached the New York side. There's a place to pull over not far from the hospital, so I wait there to become calm enough to drive home. I'm still trembling, my jaw chattering intermittently. It's a shock to realize that my body has been carrying this trauma for a year without me even knowing. What else is it holding on to that I'm unaware of, this battlefield inside me? Somewhere, deeply buried, there may still be land mines that I'll only discover when I trip them.

Chapter 46

On Sunday evening I head to the address Mason has given me. It's a high-floor apartment in a newish building near the Museum of Natural History. I've been careful to arrive twenty minutes late so I can blend in, but despite that I almost get back on the elevator and leave. What am I doing, going to a party full of Mason's friends? But I've come this far, and the slightly open apartment door is leaking enticing sounds of laughter, so I put on my mask and go in.

A small vestibule leads to a large living room backed by huge windows, with views of the museum and Central Park beyond. Around a dozen people are here, few enough that I can remove my mask and stow it in my purse. Most of the guests are relaxing, either in vast buttery sofas perpendicular to the windows or the plush chairs facing the view. This is an expensive apartment, decorated with nice furnishings and an excellent sense of style. Was that difficult for Mason, having such wealthy friends? I spot him sitting in one of the chairs, his back to me, and am tentatively walking over when my name booms out in Aussie twang.

"*Fiona!* Come on over here and let's get a look at you!" Roland leaves the couch and wraps me in a giant koala hug, then holds me at arm's length, appraising.

"You're a whole different woman. Amazing I even recognized you. Good on ya."

Mason's now standing next to him, radiating pleasure. Roland holds him back with one arm. "Wait your turn, you squirmy squirt. I'm the one who saved her life!" He hugs me again then grins at Mason. "Yeah, okay, you can have her now."

The others are laughing, looking welcoming, and Kerry goes to get me a drink. This must be her and Javi's place.

"Thank you for coming," Mason says, smiling into my eyes. "It means a lot." He puts an arm around my shoulders, points out the people I've seen before, and introduces the new ones.

Something strange is happening: Having Mason's arm on me is making me uncomfortable. The irony's not lost. This man has carried me when I couldn't walk and seen me naked—worse, he's seen the despairing, dark side of me unguarded and unfiltered. Yet now this small contact seems almost invasive. Maybe this is another sign of healing, that my physical boundaries are restored. I truly hope that's all it is.

I join the group, and occasionally the discussion, but mostly I listen and observe. There's old love here, the kind that comes from being young together and growing older in each other's circle. The conversation—the whole tone—is quite different from the dinner parties Dane and I went to, which revolved around work or, for those who had them, children. This group is linked by an appreciation of thought, of art, of funny anecdotes perfectly told. The words themselves flow differently—even from Roland, who's much more erudite than I realized. There's no pretension, simply an eagerness to share: a new book, a quirky show, an odd piece of news. An old, long-dormant part of my brain comes alert. Mason has good friends.

Javi announces that the food's ready, and Mason rises, a glass of red wine in his hand.

"Before we eat . . ." Everyone falls silent. "As most of you know, a few days ago I signed my first book deal. It's finally happening." He inhales deeply. "I'm being published."

The room fills with cheers as one by one they stand and raise their glasses.

"Congratulations," Kerry says. "We always knew it was in you. The question was just whether the right person would recognize it. You did it, Mace." Which is immediately followed by a swell of *Winduuuuuuu!*

"Well, I didn't do it alone. Without all of you behind me, I'd have given up long ago."

"Bullshit!" Simon yells, and everyone laughs, including Mason.

"Okay, even if I am too stubborn to give up, I'm really glad you were all there with me. Here's to my incredible friends."

We all drink, even me. This seems the night to cash in my occasional wine exemption.

"There's one more important toast," Mason says after we've drunk. "You don't know Fiona, so I'll tell you about her. Fiona is one of the bravest and strongest people I've ever met. I had no idea what I was signing up for when I agreed to be her caregiver. It could have been absolute hell in any number of ways—should have been, probably. But in spite of all the crap she went through, for such a long time, she never lost her humanity or consideration for others. She treated me like a friend, offered me the space and chance to write, and took my little girl into her heart. She demonstrated grit and purpose every day of this process . . . and without knowing it, she sparked something very special in my work. Here's to Fiona."

"To Fiona!" They call my name, raise their glasses, and drink, and then someone starts a round of foot-stomping applause. Amidst this wave of sound, I stand frozen like a startled deer. I've been toasted on my birthday, and thanked after a good presentation, but I've never felt anything like the wholehearted outpouring of appreciation and affection that's vibrating through me. I have no response . . . but none is needed, so I simply let it flow and absorb it.

Javi has covered the table in many different types of food, all delicious. We eat copiously, scattered around the room in small groups or seated by the window. I haven't yet talked to Mason one-on-one, but when I take a spot at the edge of the couch, he joins me.

"That was a beautiful thing to say," I tell him. "Thank you. I'm not sure it's true, though—I don't think I was braver than anyone else would be in the same circumstances."

"No, of course you don't," he replies, smiling. "Because you're you. That's the point."

"What do you mean?"

"Just as an example, when you confronted Alima about jumping the line, you put yourself at risk. Dane knew it, I knew it, you knew it. But you did it anyway, because you believed it was right. Not everyone's like that."

I'm not fully convinced, but it's clear Mason sees something in me that I never realized.

"I got you a present," I say. "I thought this was a birthday party."

He's surprised. "It is—the gifts are in the other room. But how did you know? Wait . . . did you remember from last year?

Holy shit, you did; that's impressive. Usually we don't open gifts at the party, but do you want me to open yours now?"

I nod, go for my bag . . . and immediately have second thoughts. Maybe I misjudged Joyce's significance to him, or perhaps the gift is way over the top and we'll both be embarrassed. But it's too late now, so I sit and hand it to him. He takes it with curiosity—it's clearly a book—and peels open the wrapping. It's not even fully unwrapped when he drops it in his lap as though it were on fire. After staring at it for a long time, he turns to me in shock.

"*Ulysses*," he says in a reverent tone. "First English edition, Egoist Press, 1922."

Picking it back up, he strokes the leather cover, then turns it to read the opening page. His hands are unsteady; I've got it exactly right.

"This was the book that made me want to be a writer," he says softly. "I saw this edition on a trip to London years ago, but it was way out of my price range. I can't believe you figured this out, but you couldn't have chosen anything better. I'm just not sure I should accept it."

"You turned down Dane's bonus, so I had to get creative. Now you can put something prettier on your nightstand."

"Ah," he replies, nodding. "That's how you knew. Thank you, Fi; it's perfect."

Marin appears at his shoulder, wanting to see what we're looking at. She's also a bibliophile, so he lets her hold it before wrapping it back up.

"And now," I say, rising, "it's time for me to leave. This was a wonderful evening, but I'm drained."

"I'll take you home," he says.

"No, stay and finish out the party. You're celebrating something you've dreamed of your whole life, with some truly wonderful friends. Enjoy every minute of it."

By the time I reach home I'm aching for a hot bath. I add eucalyptus salts and lie there soaking it all in: the evening, the camaraderie, Mason's reaction to my gift, his words to me. My mind drifts back, running through flashes of our time together. Starting our odyssey by learning about each other; setting up the apartment in Johnson's River; the long, high-stress waiting period; Michaela's arrival; the crazy trip back to New York; the two of them visiting me in the hospital long after his duty was over. I'm really glad it didn't all end with abandonment.

When the water gets cool I dry off, put on my comfy pj's, and brew some tea. I'm sitting with a book when the doorbell rings. Tempting as it is to ignore it, it might be urgent.

"Who is it?"

"Mason. Can I come in?"

Opening the door in astonishment, I see he's holding a bag with the *Ulysses*. Does he really want to return it? I wave him inside.

"It's sweet of you, but I don't want the book back. Your reaction was enough."

"No, that's not it." He removes his shoes and sanitizes his hands. Then he paces wordlessly for a minute and winds up leaning against the breakfront along the back wall. The light from my reading lamp catches the side of his face, highlighting the angular contours of his cheekbone and jaw that were obscured when his hair was longer and the beard a distraction.

"I don't know how to say this, Fi, and I'm a bit drunk, so I'll just come out with it. Otherwise who knows when you'll agree to see me again."

His voice is low and serious, and he takes a deep breath first. "I think it's time."

He's making me nervous. Is there bad news? "Time for what?"

"Time for us."

The words stop my thoughts in their tracks. *Us? What us? Us what?*

He gives me the straight-on look. The pay-attention look.

"We have a chance to be together now. Really together. All the bullshit's done with, you're single, we can do whatever we want. Do you want to give us a shot at a different type of relationship?"

Even after he's said it, my brain doesn't accept the words at face value. It's looking for the misinterpretation, for what he really means.

"Please don't tell me you've never thought about it. I can't have been that far off."

He doesn't seem embarrassed; he doesn't believe he's wrong. Which makes sense, because he *isn't*. I thought about it and forced it away countless times over those months when we were wrapped together like tangled yarn. Embarrassed by the fantasies of a desperately ill woman over a healthy, vibrant man as desirable as Mason. And when he left so abruptly, I shut it away with all the other parts of the "before" life. But I never imagined the feeling was mutual.

"You never said anything," I say at last. "In all that time we were together, you were always my champion, my guardian, my friend . . . but never this. Where's this coming from?"

"Of course I didn't say anything!" He looks at me as though I were insane. "In the first place, you were married; I've no desire to break any more marriages in my lifetime. Second, your husband was paying at least part of my salary. How inappropriate would that have been, taking his money and hitting on his wife? But most important by far, it would have been entirely unethical toward you. You were dependent on me for *everything*. Food, medicine, dealing with the doctors, getting all the test results, checking that no one screwed up. How could you have even known what your emotions meant? Maybe what you were feeling was really just gratitude. Maybe what I was feeling was an extended need to take care of you. And what if it didn't work out . . . how would you be able to reject me? It was a gross imbalance of power; no way was I going to abuse that. And then there was Mike. After being out of her life for so long, I couldn't add this to the mix. I owed that to all of us—you must see that."

He pauses, calming himself down.

"That's over now," he continues. "You're divorced, independent, and healthy. It's so good to see you like this, strong and at peace with yourself. For my part, I have some money—not much, but it's a start—and a path to the future. My relationship with my daughter is rock solid. So I'll say it again: It's time to give *us* a chance. Don't you want to see what can happen with nothing in the way—no caveats, no contracts, no . . . conjugal complications?"

"No cannulas."

"No cannulas," he agrees.

"No clothes," I say, and his eyes change. But still I don't move.

"What is it, Fi? What's holding you back?"

I'm not sure I can even explain it in a way that makes sense, but he's put himself so far out there that I have to try.

"For one thing, I don't think I can have sex anymore. Actually, it's more than that: I'm not sure I want to. I don't want the exposure—physical or emotional. It sounds ridiculous after so many people have seen me naked, like an old piece of equipment needing repair. It used to seem hilarious when doctors asked my permission for a student to observe. But enough time has gone by that my body is my own again, and it feels safer that way. Also . . .”

I draw a shaky breath, because the next part is difficult.

“Also, I’m not comfortable enough with the way my body looks or feels anymore to share it with anyone else. Not in that way. It’s strange, because I’d never thought of myself as vain. But now, while I love my body in every other way, I really hate looking in the mirror. I’m covered in scars, which I notice all the time. Not just the long surgery ones, but the place in my side where the drainage tube went, and especially the big scarred area on the front of my neck where the jugular ports were.

“My stomach is bruised all over from the injections I’m taking to raise my white blood cell count, and another where I hit a small vein and bled all night. My face is puffy and round because of the prednisone, as you can see. It’s a small price to pay for life, but seeing myself is a shock every time. That person doesn’t look like me. So the thought of being intimate makes me shut down. Especially with you.”

There. I’ve said it.

I push on. “You’re healthy and young and incredibly sexy. And you’re very important to me in spite of everything. I can’t bear the thought of you finding me ugly.”

Until now he’s been looking at me with empathy, even concern. But at my last words, his whole body releases.

“My proud, sensitive Fi . . . you should know me better by now. I’ve seen you at your worst and your best. When you’ve been bitchy and ungrateful even though I’m doing everything I possibly can. But also when you’ve braved through pain so a random med student can practice some nasty procedure on you. Or when you’ve seriously considered stepping aside so someone younger can take your new lungs. I've seen you scarily thin and hopelessly weak, I've bathed your wounds and cleaned your blood, and I'm here anyway asking for more of you. I'm not looking for young and blemishless, even if I could get it. We work, Fi. You make me feel proud, you laugh when I do, and I respect you more than you can imagine. I know who you are, and *that's* what I want. And if I can't make you feel beautiful, I'll never ask again. That's a promise."

I stay silent, trying to think. Resigning myself to being alone, for all its downsides, brings certain freedoms. I can choose what I want from my time, without being accountable or responsible for anyone else. Despite my friends' urging, I don't plan on ever diving back into the dating pool again. But this is different. *Mason* is different. Should I actually take this crazy leap?

Mason watches my indecision, then, to my horror, reaches to his collar and begins unbuttoning his shirt. I'm in disbelief but can't look away. He never went shirtless in all our time together, so I've never even seen his body. And I *want* to. Just to see . . . or maybe to touch. Just a little.

He reaches the bottom and pulls the shirt open, and that's when the real shock hits. Running down the left side of his rib cage is a long, violent red scar, the skin raised and puckered in patches. This is like no surgical scar I've ever seen. There are other scars too, but I'm focused on the one toward the middle of his abdomen: the smallest, but somehow the most frightening. This one makes me think of something sharp going straight in. This is what he wanted me to see.

"You showed me yours, I'll show you mine," he says, as though this were a casual thing.

I stare at his torso for a long time, trying to imagine what could have caused such violent-looking injuries and understanding now why he always kept them hidden.

"What the hell happened?" I whisper.

"After the press reports came out about Jed and me being together, lots of people were unhappy. Helen's fans. Jed's fans. Gay-haters of all kinds. Many of them blamed me for the breakup: Helen and Jed had been 'the perfect couple' for so long that clearly it was my warping influence at fault. We lay low at first but after Jed became sick it didn't seem to matter. A few months after his death, I was trudging home late from work and took my usual shortcut through a small side street when an innocuous-looking man approached and attacked me. I deflected the first stab, so it ended up on my rib cage, but wasn't so lucky with the second. That one went in deep, hitting some organs along the way. My life was touch and go for a long time . . . just like yours."

I'm stunned. Mason, the victim of a hate crime?

"Did they catch him?"

"Yes—not that it mattered. Just a madman who wasn't clear whether he wanted Jed for himself or was doing God's work by fighting homosexuality. God must be so sick of humans doing awful things in His name. Anyway, this man had somehow found out who I was and had been tracking me. My point is that, while I haven't been through what you have, I've been close enough to understand. Blood transfusions. Multiple surgeries, tubes, needles, weeks of IVs. The medications, fear. Despair."

I wrench my eyes away from the scars and ask, "Was somebody with you through that?" But what I really mean is, did you have a Mason?

"My friends—the ones you've met. They came every day to hold my hand and monitor my progress. Javi especially. He donated enough blood to truly be my blood brother.

"Obviously I made it through, but it left some very ugly scars. Scars that speak of hate and jealousy or bigotry.

That's *my* reminder in the mirror every day. Whereas you . . ." He gives me a small, beatific smile. "Your scars speak of love and kindness and hope. Of someone offering a piece of themselves to a stranger they'll never meet. Someone whose thanks they'll never hear. They speak of medical professionals who dedicate their careers to creating life where there would otherwise be death. And both our scars are testament to our incredible good fortune in being alive, and what it took for that to happen. They're not *flaws*, Fi. They're symbolic tattoos, reminders of events that helped shape us, and the fact that we survived them."

It's as though a warm, purifying wind is drifting through me, cleansing away my fears.

"Mason . . ."

"No," he says firmly. "No more words."

He comes to me and draws me in, pressing his mouth on mine until I can't breathe.

"Stop!" I say sharply. His hands fly off me and I grab some air. *It's okay*, I reassure myself. *He'll stop if I need him to.*

"Okay, I'm good now," I mumble, then move close again, feeling my way along his scars and around his waist as we kiss again, more gently. He pulls the pajama top over my head, lets it fall, and strokes my back from nape to waist. Those strong fingers follow every curve of my body; the touch of his hands on my skin leaves a firework trail.

In a state of giddy wonder, I lead him to the bedroom, where we shed our remaining clothes and I fall onto the bed, pulling him after me. Mason searches out my imperfections—my insecurities—and kisses them, one by one. Then he looks into my eyes and says softly, "For so long I've imagined touching you sensually. Like this. And this."

My breath turns ragged . . . I feel fuzzy around the edges.

How could I imagine I didn't want this? I think, pulling him to me, around me, in me, then free-falling into a wormhole.

Much later, I reemerge. Mason is awake next to me, propped up on one elbow, staring.

"Holy shit," he says in a scraped voice. "What just happened?"

My voice is still scattered in pieces around my body—I couldn't speak even if there was anything to say.

He sits up. "Seriously, Fi. That was . . ." He shakes his head. "Was that normal for you?"

"No. If you want a *serious* answer, I'd guess months of unacknowledged desire followed by a long dry spell. For me, anyway."

"Me too. It's a good argument for intermittent celibacy, but I'm not interested. I'd start again right now if that were even remotely possible."

I feel like a noodle. It's not remotely possible. We lie together comfortably for a while, until he turns pensive.

"I'm going to ask you something, and I need an honest answer. Does it bother you that I've slept with men? Mostly one man."

That was unexpected, but I tell him the truth.

"Before I knew you it would have bothered me a lot. But that changed in Johnson's River. You stopped being 'gay' or 'bi' or 'pan' or anything but Mason. Tonight all that was meaningless: I only wanted *you*."

"It's a real question," he continues. "Lots of women believe if a man's had sex with another man he'll never be fully content in a heterosexual relationship."

I sit up and face him. "I did wonder about that when you first told me. How Petra must have felt; how she probably thought your whole relationship had been dishonest. I'm no expert, but I suspect that's true for some people who are grappling with their sexuality. From everything I know about you it doesn't seem likely here. I believe you married her honestly and things just changed. I've been thinking about that a lot lately—that sometimes relationships just change.

"People have desires and temptations all the time. Their partner loses attraction, or they fall out of love, or they just want something new. Being with a straight man doesn't protect you from anything: There'll always be other desirable women out there. Just ask any woman whose husband has left her—including me. Dane had his reasons, but so does everyone. Believe me, I felt just as abandoned as I would have if he were gay . . . maybe more. In the end giving yourself comes down to one thing: Do you trust that one individual? And I trust you."

He sits with that for a while, then wraps his arm around me and kisses me.

When he leaves for the shower I remain still, with the peculiar immobility I learned after surgery: Don't shift until you've assessed the situation. Scanning myself, I find only joy—both physical and emotional. For the first time, I consider the possibility of finding love again.

Dane did me a favor when he left. I'm such a different person from the one he married: less focused on measurable success, more spiritual, less constricted, far more observant and empathetic. Dane would never have understood me not wearing makeup or fancy clothes, reading philosophy, meditating. And I would have struggled returning to the cocktail and dinner-party circuit, with its endless chatter about things I no longer care for. Perhaps after all it's not that I couldn't move on with another person . . . it just couldn't be someone like Dane.

Chapter 47

Mason is still here in the morning.

Our whole time at Regent he was always awake before me, so I've never seen him asleep before. He's remarkably peaceful . . . just the occasional rearrangement of limbs. I get up quietly, and am wondering whether to leave him sleeping when he mumbles, "Since you're up anyway, could you fix coffee?" His eyes are still dead closed, like a newborn puppy.

As I grind the beans, I can't help wondering what happens now. Did last night constitute some kind of agreement? Have I just committed to trying "us"? Or was it just something that needed to happen and did? But the coffee smells so distractingly delicious that I want to drink it directly as it drips, and this moment feels so perfect that I decide not to spoil it by thinking.

Mason stumbles in a few minutes later in his boxers and takes the mug while I'm still stirring it. I'm already deeply committed to his scars, so I run my fingers along them, feeling the ridges, touching the deep, healed wound that could lead me right inside his body. When he puts down the mug to kiss me I can taste the sweet coffee on him and we're right there again, except this time I'm aware of everything—every point of contact, every half-caught breath. We take a long time making it back to the bedroom. It's not as wild as last night, not as overwhelming, but just as intense. That's who Mason is; intensity comes with the package.

Afterwards I lend him my largest T-shirt, and we sit at the kitchen table drinking fresh cappuccinos.

He watches me affectionately, then stretches back in the chair like a contented Cheshire cat and says, "Let's get married."

I laugh . . . until I look closer. "You can't be serious."

"Why not? And don't even think of saying it's too soon. We've already lived together as husband and wife, and we got along very well. Plus it's safe to say the sex works."

"Because it's a ridiculous suggestion! It's one thing to enjoy each other for a while—even an extended while—but I could get sick again and die at any time. You've been through that once with Jed; I won't put you through it again."

He crosses his arms, his eyebrows raised sassily. He's enjoying this. "First, Fiona, you really have to put away that martyr complex once and for all. Second, isn't it a touch condescending to believe you know what I need better than I do? And third, it's precisely *because* of Jed that I know this is the right thing."

"Explain, please."

He sits up straight and turns serious. "After Jed died and I was attacked, in close succession, my friends were worried for me. Javi and Simon came over one night, and we talked for hours—about love and loss, fear and pain. What they could do to a person. Then Javi asked, if I'd known up front what would happen—that there would be only a few years of love followed by so much pain—would I still have done it? Become a pariah to so many people, almost died? It was a reasonable question, but the answer was 'absolutely yes.' If I hadn't loved Jed so much I wouldn't have made those sacrifices in the first place, so how could I regret that choice? The only thing that's ever made me question it came years later, when I lost Michaela. So the fact that you may not have much time is all the more reason not to waste it."

"You're saying life is short."

"No. I'm saying life is *unpredictable*. You're imagining dying and leaving me on my own. But I'm on my own now, and it's fine. You're not depriving me of the opportunity to meet someone who might be more long-lasting; if that's the way things turn out, I can look for someone after you're gone. But it's also possible that you have this upside down. I might be carrying some condition right now that will kill me before you. I could get hit by a bicycle messenger—not so unlikely, come to think of it—and then *you'd* have to take care of *me*. However much time we have—even if it's only a beautiful side loop off our main path, with flowers that bloom brilliantly for a day—isn't it worth taking?"

I'm quiet so long that eventually he says, "Well, maybe I shouldn't get married again. I've done this twice already. One more time and I'll either have to run for political office or become a televangelist."

I laugh in spite of myself, then ask, "But why do we have to get married? Couldn't we just be together without that?"

"Well first, because I want to: I'd like to have you as my wife. I'm a romantic, in case you hadn't noticed." The crooked smile I've grown so fond of emerges.

"But second, because of Mike. She'll love having us together, and you two would be close regardless. But if anything did happen to me and we weren't married, you'd have no rights with her at all. Petra's softened lately, but I don't see her letting Mike spend time with you if I wasn't around. If we'd married, I think she'd be more generous."

As usual, he's already thought this through carefully. Suddenly what he's suggesting makes sense—maybe the *most* sense.

"Still, that's not the main point, Fi. Even Mike isn't the point; she wouldn't always be with us. The real question is, do you want to open up your life to me? I don't want you to give up the way of being you've worked so hard for . . . I'm just asking if you want to share it with me."

"As simple as that?"

"Yes. Do you want me to go down on one knee or something?"

"Don't be silly. Wait—*yes!* Somehow I doubt that opportunity will return."

"Yeah, good luck," he retorts. "Kneeling isn't happening, especially now you've made a joke out of it. But I do have a ring for you. Five of them, in fact."

He finds his jacket where it fell last night, pulls a white envelope from the inside pocket, and lays it on the table in front of me. Inside is a stapled set of printouts confirming three specialty tour packages for July of next year, to the Summer Olympics. They include tickets to gymnastics, kayaking, and three days of track and field. It seems impossible that they're genuine, but I know they are.

"I brought them to the party last night, in case you didn't ever want to see me after that."

Is he for real? "If I'd done that, you'd have given them to me anyway?"

"Of course. I promised."

"All three sets?"

He shrugs. "You'd have found someone else to go with. On the assumption that if you turned me away, you'd hardly want to be sitting next to me at the events."

It's quintessential Mason: honorable to the core. And I'm remembering how important it is to feel this—to trust that the person you're with will do right by you and by others. All the counterarguments about preserving my independence and shielding against pain have come from the cautious, self-protective part of me that I don't want to follow anymore. There isn't time for that. If this doesn't work out, then I'll have to pick myself up afterwards and keep going. As I have before. As I know I can.

But I'm curious whether this is a sudden whim or an actual plan on Mason's part.

"When were you thinking this hypothetical wedding would happen?"

He can't stop the grin from dancing around his mouth. "Glad you asked. I thought September tenth. Ideally it would have been on your transplant anniversary—just so I don't have to remember two important dates, you understand—but it might be hard to get a venue the week before Labor Day."

He's teasing: If anyone would remember those dates, it's Mason. But his suggestion is nuts.

"You're talking about getting married in *three weeks?*"

"A little longer than that, but sure. Think of it as a work assignment. Don't tell me you couldn't plan a small conference in three weeks. You can even pick the venue—as long as it's not the same place you married Dane."

"Ugh . . . definitely not. Actually, it would be lovely to have it outdoors. If it doesn't rain, September's the best weather of the year . . . and I know that would be meaningful to you."

He's speechless for a moment, then says, "Thank you."

My brain is whirring. *How has this become a reality?* But I find myself saying, "It's offseason, so we should be able to find an inn somewhere with room for the gang and some of my friends. We just need someone to perform the ceremony."

"Marin's an ordained minister; I'm sure she'd love to do it. And I'm not in touch with my family anymore, but shall we invite your father? This time he can give you away."

My jaw hardens. "I don't want to be given away. I'm not a door prize, and I haven't had a man take responsibility for me for a long time."

Except you, I think. *Only you.*

"I'll come to you on my own. Walking on my own feet, breathing my own free air, coming to you as a single person to become a couple."

He's picturing it as I speak. "Let's invite him anyway. And his wife."

"Sure," I say, grinning. Who would ever have thought I would want to see my father at my wedding . . . much less my stepmother. I guess some things do change.

"He's still not giving me away, though," I add. "Just to be clear."

"There is one more thing," he says cautiously, "if you can handle more."

"Oh, Lord." My gut squirms. "Spill it."

"When Petra returned home, Mike talked a lot about how much she loved getting to spend time with me, and how sad it would be if we went back to the old routine. Apparently it had an impact, because Petra invited me to join the family for Christmas. It was . . . magical."

"I can imagine. That's wonderful."

"Yes." He pauses, remembering. "Anyway, Petra's pregnant again, so maybe she's hormonal, but she's offered to rethink the custody situation and have Mike spend regular time with me. Including staying over some weekends."

My heart thumps. If we're married, then she'd be with *me* too.

"Before you hyperventilate, we'd need to figure out where that would be. My current apartment is too small, so I'll have to move anyway. And this one, much as you love it, is far from Mike's friends, and not very child-oriented. Besides which, it's so clearly yours. I'm wondering whether we could hunt together for a home for three. Somewhere new that would be ours. Not either of our bachelor retreats, but *ours*. Could you give this place up?"

I look around. I'll miss it. This apartment has been an essential haven for me, and I love that it's my space to do with as I want, when I want, and as loudly as I want. But compared with finding *our home*? It's no decision at all.

"You have to help with the packing. And we have to find some new fun furnishings, things that bring both of us—all three of us—joy when we see them."

He looks utterly radiant. "One final thing."

"*Another?*"

"Just this. You haven't said 'yes' yet."

I start laughing. "*Yes!* Of course yes . . . as if you didn't know. Yes, Mason Wolfwood, I want to spend the rest of my life, however long that is, with you. Nothing in this world would make me happier."

"Oh, thank God."

"But I have one thing too. You've never told me that you love me."

He's startled. "I haven't?"

Rising and stepping around the table, he pulls me to my feet and folds me into a close embrace. His mouth is close to my ear as he says, softly, "Fiona Copeland, I have loved you since that night in Johnson's River when Mike and I sang to you and we laughed so hard we fell over. I've loved you first as a fellow fighter in the battle, then as a dear friend, and now at long last, as a lover. And . . ." His chest heaves; his emotion runs through me like an electric current.

"And I will love you," he continues, his voice catching slightly, "as my wife. That's a promise, my darling Fi. A promise."

I wipe my own tears, laughing. "As I have, and do, and will love you."

Though he's not really crying, I reach over and hand him the Kleenex.

"Just so you know," I add, "I'm asking Mike to be a bridesmaid. Long dress, flowers in her hair and everything."

He groans. "You know once you do she'll be intolerable."

"Good thing you only have to bear it for three weeks, then."

"Yes," he says, and grins. "It can't happen soon enough for me."

"Me neither."

"Then what do you say we go pick up Mike together and tell her the news?"

A rush of profound joy floods through me. One year ago I was far from home, preparing to die. Now I find myself planning a new life full of discovery and family, and the love I'd stopped believing in. If the essence of a story is in the ending, the story of Fiona Copeland is a happy one after all.

It's the new dawn of a new day in my new life.

And I'm feeling good.

Author Note

In 2023, a few years after the events in this story, the Organization Procurement and Transplantation Network (OPTN) changed the policy for matching lung transplant candidates with deceased donors. For more information on these changes and the new procedure, visit unos.org.

Acknowledgments

There are so many thanks due—for this novel as well as for my life—that it would take more words than I can spare. So I will mention, with enormous gratitude, some of the many, and leave you to imagine the invisible ranks behind.

I shall start with my family. They are the ultimate answer to the question: Why undergo a transplant?

Nick, your belief that I could write this novel (or any novel) encouraged me to meet that expectation. Matt, your advice and the example of your personal courage kept me on task. Huck, you supported me throughout, even when faced with yet another stupid tech question. (Is there any other kind?)

And, to my favorite husband, Rich Johnson, spouse without parallel. You have held me up, literally, stood by my side, nursed me, and loved me as though it were a privilege to do so. You have been my secret weapon in all my many battles. Thank you.

Right up there with family is my best friend, Dr. Rita Helfand, who kibitzed where necessary, kept everyone notified, and was always there when needed. She is the special sauce.

I would also like to thank all the medical personnel who have helped me through two separate lung transplants. The surgeons—Dr. Joshua R. Sonett at Columbia Presbyterian in New York and Dr. Abbas Ardehali at the UCLA Medical Center. The emergency room staffs both in New York City and Los Angeles. All the medical specialists who deal with the day-to-day challenges faced by lung transplant patients—Dr. Hilary Robbins, Dr. Selim Arçasoy, Monica, Maggie, Darrell, Flora, Leslie, Marina, and, of course, the incomparable Dr. David M. Sayah.

To The MMS Book Club for always supporting my work. And for their key help of various kinds: Jo and Yaell Agar, Gideon and Erin Agar, Kristen Bass, Elias Berezin, Monique Bureau, David Grady, Sam Hung, the Inbar and Bornstein families, Robert Jokel, Jeff Knishkowy, Lisle Leete, Bonnie Messing, the Mitrany family, Joe Teig, Anne Weintraub, Tavi Wolfwood, and Robin Clifford Wood.

Many thanks to all the folks at The Stable Book Group, particularly everyone at She Writes Press.

About the Author

Sharon Agar grew up in Hampshire, England, and later moved to the US to attend Yale. After business school, she worked in a variety of fields including both finance and not-for-profit. Her life took a major turn when she was diagnosed with a potentially fatal lung disease and, over the next two years, underwent two lung transplant operations. Her debut novel *Out of Options*, a business thriller, was published in April of 2014. A lifelong singer and a passionate advocate for organ donation, Agar has three sons and currently lives with her husband in Los Angeles.